VERY
OLD
MONEY

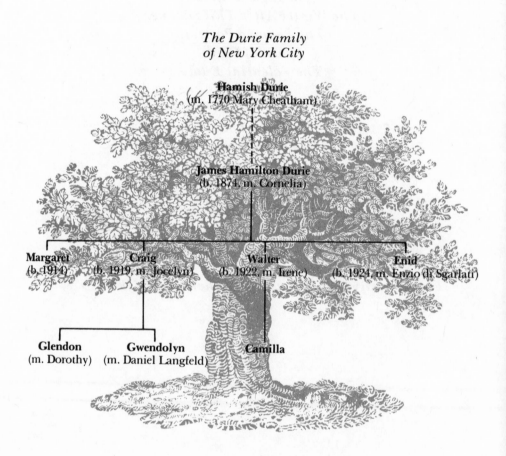

The Durie Family
of New York City

Hamish Durie
(m. 1770 Mary Cheatham)

James Hamilton Durie
(b. 1874, m. Cornelia)

Margaret   **Craig**   **Walter**   **Enid**
(b. 1914)   (b. 1919, m. Jocelyn)   (b. 1922, m. Irene)   (b. 1924, m. Enzio di Sgarlati)

Glendon   **Gwendolyn**   **Camilla**
(m. Dorothy)   (m. Daniel Langfeld)

VERY OLD MONEY

STANLEY ELLIN

ARBOR HOUSE
New York

Library of Congress Cataloging in Publication Data

Ellin, Stanley.
Very Old Money.

I.   Title.
PS3555.L56V4   1985   813'.54   84-42530
ISBN 0-87795-627-8

Manufactured in the United States of America

This book is printed on acid-free paper. The paper in this
book meets the guidelines for permanence and durability of the
Committee on Production Guidelines for Book Longevity of the
Council on Library Resources.

TO
OTTO PENZLER
WITH APPRECIATION AND ADMIRATION

PART ONE

Mrs. Lloyd and Lloyd

SEATED on a straight-backed chair behind her small desk, Mrs. Bernius was the picture of elegance. The half-glasses perched midway down her nose made her seem even more elegant. And cool, Mike thought. She exuded Upper East Side New York City cool. The closer you'd get, the lower the mercury. Which was probably what you'd meet when after shuffling off this mortal coil you abruptly found yourself seated in a small, charmingly decorated office in limbo while an elegant keeper of the gates, exuding a terribly ladylike cool, examined the dossier on your misspent life in order to designate heaven or hell as your next stop.

Come to think of it, what were he and spouse Amy doing here, placing themselves at the mercy of this particular keeper of the gates? Two adult, well-educated, middle-class American citizens — a proud people these Americans — kowtowing to la Bernius. After already, a week ago, having sufficiently kowtowed to the British lassie in the front office who, in that pseudo upper-crust British accent, had instructed them to produce their bona fides and fill out a ream of forms and documents.

Enough already. The comedy is finished. Amy, my love, we are leaving here. What we now do is buy a cut-rate Conestoga wagon and join a party in search of new lands beyond the wide Missouri.

Mike shifted in his chair, striving for a position that would in terms of body language indicate relaxed dignity. Amy, seated an arm's length away, gave him a quick little frown, and he stopped striving. Mrs. Bernius raised her eyes from the two folders open before her — the applications, the resumés, and Gawd help us, the test results — and looked from one to the other of them over the half-glasses, a falcon hovering up there thoughtfully taking notice of this pair of chickens that had wandered into its ken.

Mrs. Bernius said, "We will now be absolutely truthful with each other, you people. I'll start by remarking that with the minimum of advertisement, Domestique is a most successful agency, depending as it does on giving satisfaction. Of course, we have a seller's market these days. But it is known to the clientele that Domestique's recommendation guarantees the real article. That we are not merely adding to a household staff a personable young couple for the pretty picture it makes, but are providing a well-motivated, competent personal secretary" — she graciously dipped her head at Amy — "and an equally desirable chauffeur to a family that urgently requires their services. And" — the lilting voice took on a subtle emphasis — "who want my assurance that this couple is ready to settle down to the long haul. And will not be spending its salaried time thumbing through the Help Wanted pages for, as one might put it, more prestigious jobs. Are you following this closely?"

"Yes," Mike said. "Look, if you're getting around to telling us we're overqualified for these jobs — "

"Really, Michael." Mrs. Bernius was all gently smiling protest. "Now if you were an unemployed brain surgeon instead of an unemployed schoolteacher, I'd certainly be telling you that. But you're not, are you?"

Poisonous bitch, Mike thought, and Amy, who after three years of marriage could read his thought balloons in their ascent, gave him that warning little frown again. She said apologetically to Mrs. Bernius, "It's just that when Mike — Michael — submitted his resumé to some agencies the overqualification thing did come up. So there's — "

"Of course, dear," said Mrs. Bernius. "But I did warn that the painful truth must be part of this interview. And things are tough out there for some of us, aren't they? Unemployed schoolteachers all over the place. On the other hand, according to your applications it was an ex-schoolteacher friend of yours who recommended Domestique to you, wasn't it? Because whatever else that friend might be overqualified for, he was certainly well qualified to be chauffeur for an appreciative family on Long Island where he appears to be doing very well for himself."

"Yes," Amy said.

"Yes. And believe me, dear, according to my files he wasn't the first to change course in this direction. Painful truth to tell, we were all tilted just a bit off balance by those halcyon full-

4

employment years, weren't we? Now some of us must settle for a little less than professional glory. But"—Mrs. Bernius held up a flawlessly manicured forefinger—"but from Domestique's point of view the world still provides a large number of the well-to-do who'll pay a fair price for servants of quality. That might be a sticking point, you people. Servants. How does that word hit you?"

"Well," Amy said, "it doesn't really bother me."

"We did talk it over," Mike said, "at length and in depth."

"Good," said Mrs. Bernius. She glanced at the folders, then focused on Mike. "Your last employment was as cab driver. In response to my query, your company"—with distaste she held up a grimy sheet of paper by a corner—"attests that you were a valued employee. Why exactly did you resign from it?"

"Robbed once at knifepoint. I got over it. The second time it was at gunpoint. I didn't get over it."

"Life in the Big Apple," said Mrs. Bernius. "I suppose it was a passenger each time?"

"Yes."

"Which," said Mrs. Bernius, "is something you won't have to worry about if you get this job under discussion. Allowing for a fender-bender now and then, I imagine that chauffeuring a limousine for a genteel family is one of the safer vocations."

"Happy thought," Mike said.

"So it is." Mrs. Bernius returned briefly to the folders. "And before this you were, for almost ten years, a teacher at the Scoville-Lang Preparatory School. Literature and composition. As well as serving for two years as Dean of Students. Now what exactly would be the duties of Dean of Students?"

"Of its Upper School," Mike said. "I was supposed to have exceptional rapport with the teenagers there."

"Females included?"

"With decorum," Mike said.

At least, he thought, with *his* decorum. The fact was—no use shyly scuffing the toe into the ground about it—by luck of the genetic draw he had his father's sandy-haired, firm-jawed, slightly squint-eyed good looks. And despite a detestation of all physical exercise except skiing, the same compact, flat-bellied,

5

hard-muscled frame. Add it up, and what it had amounted to apparently was catnip to the more uninhibited female students in his ken.

"No hanky-panky in that department?" asked Mrs. Bernius.

"Never. What it came to was simply that some of the kids were getting into drugs, and this Dean of Students thing was created so that I'd have proper authority to deal with them."

"How?"

"A warning for the first offense, suspension for the second. Anyhow, I finally nailed four kids who were turning the place into pushers' paradise and gave them fair warning. A week later I caught them with the goods again, pill-peddling to some juniors. I suspended them for the rest of the term and wrote their parents to meet with me. I thought—"

"Ah, yes," said Mrs. Bernius. "But the parents thought otherwise."

"They raised hell. All that worried them was that the kids' college admission would be delayed. When I said sorry, but that's the way it is, they went to the headmaster."

"A George Oliphant."

"A George Oliphant. Who told me sorry, but he was lifting the suspensions. When I said this meant I'd have to resign he told me good-bye, you can pick up your final paycheck on the way out."

"Obviously very rich and influential parents," said Mrs. Bernius with amusement. She regarded Mike over her glasses. "I had a long talk with your Mr. Oliphant. He gave me a positively poisonous report on you. Does that come as any surprise?"

Mike's stomach turned over. "Yes," he said shortly. He found he couldn't let it go at that. "You must have told him I wasn't looking for a teaching job, just to drive a car for somebody."

"Oh, I did. And what he confided to me"—Mrs. Bernius peered at a folder—"was that as his employee you were insubordinate, emotional, couldn't adjust to the needs of the school community. School community," she mused. "He used the phrase repeatedly. Is that today's jargon for what I used to know as a school?"

"Professional language."

"I see. Well, it doesn't charm me. Nor did Mr. Oliphant. Too mellifluous. Too warmly concerned about your welfare while at the same time—if you'll forgive my language—giving you the vaselined finger."

What do you know, Mike thought in glad surprise. He glanced at Amy. She was staring open-mouthed at this elegant phenomenon before them.

"You see, " the phenomenon said to Mike, "what I did extract from him along the way was that despite your vices you were punctual, abstemious—at least on-site—and did get along with your colleagues. Considering his vindictiveness, this amounted to a dazzling tribute."

"So the job is mine?"

"Well, there's still some ground to cover. Amy, however, does seem to meet all specifications. No point making a mystery of that."

Amy looked troubled. She could read him like a book, Mike knew. He said, "But her job—secretary, companion, whatever—appears to be bigger than mine. Why the concentration on me?"

"Because a married couple-in-service has been requested here. Not only are accommodations available for it, but such couples have a reputation for providing very stable elements in household service. I sometimes wonder," Mrs. Bernius said reflectively, "if this isn't because whatever irritations the couple meets on the job can be confided to each other openly. Pillow talk, as the phrase goes. Get it out of the system that way." She considered this.

Mike considered the wallpaper. Alternating vertical narrow black and silver stripes. This whole scene had a dreamlike quality bordering on nightmare, and that wallpaper, the pattern rippling when he concentrated on it, made a perfect setting for a dream verging on nightmare. Close the eyes tight, open them, and with any luck he'd find himself waking up in home sweet home, third floor back on Thompson Street. No, not really that sweet anymore, the way the apartment had been denuded of almost all those furnishings, sold for what they could bring. And now two months behind on the rent. That, as this elegant lady had put it, was the nasty reality.

7

He cleared the throat to rouse the lady from her reverie, and she measured him over her glasses. "Adaptability," she said. "Amy measures up there. I'm not sure about you, Michael. And if you suddenly decide to walk out on the job, Amy will walk out with you. That would leave Domestique with two black marks on its books, do you see?"

"Suppose I guarantee I won't walk out? After all, I didn't walk out on the cabbie job. You could say I was persuaded out by a gun."

"True. But while you won't be facing any weaponry on this job you will have to deal with, oh, perhaps half a dozen people whose view of their hired help is authoritarian. In a genteel way, of course. But distinctly authoritarian. And each of them has a strongly defined temperament and in one case at least some marked eccentricities. And you'll not only be serving them, you will be living there with them. Think it over. Living in their home but—and I choose the word with care—invisibly."

"Invisibly?" Mike said.

Mrs. Bernius rose and went to the window behind her. She studied the vista of midtown Manhattan it offered, then turned and cocked her head at Mike. "Does the name Durie mean anything to you? Either of you?"

"No," Amy said.

"Vaguely," Mike lied.

"Vaguely at best," said Mrs. Bernius. "The family would be pleased by that. Low key, these people. Great self-respect. With an acute dislike of public notice. The house—mansion really—is in the upper Sixties between Madison and Fifth. And now observe my emphasis, you people: the Durie family is very old money."

"Goes back a long way," Mike said.

"To colonial times. And prosperous even then."

"And," Mike said, "this has something to do with our being invisible?"

"Speaking from long experience," said Mrs. Bernius, "yes. Hard to conceive perhaps, but to very old money even such as the Rockefellers are parvenus. Other kinds of moneyed people—Sun Belt, for instance—are not to be mentioned in polite company."

8

"Patrician company," said Mike.

"American style. But don't think I'm describing snobbishness. Very old money is not snobbish. It is simply"—Mrs. Bernius held up a hand, forefinger and thumb making a loop, and used the loop in delicate little gestures to emphasize each word—"wonderfully, totally unselfconscious. No glitter, no glamor."

It's showtime, folks, Mike thought, and she is really laying it on. He observed that Amy was taking in the show with fascination. Amy, at twenty-five, was sometimes asked for her ID when they entered a bar. When she wore this rapt look even her birth certificate was suspect.

It turned out that Mrs. Bernius was not too bad at reading his thought balloons herself.

She said wickedly, "All right, allow ten percent for exaggeration. But if you're as smart as you look, my friend, you'll understand me. What it comes down to is this. New money is always uneasy about its servants. It hasn't been brought up to deal with them so it deals with them uneasily. Too hard-boiled or too soft-boiled, it demonstrates insecurity one way or the other.

"None of this applies to very old money. Its servants aren't people, you see. They are invisible forces who somehow make life comfortable. They do not, for example, display any private feelings to the family because this is simply not done. On the other hand, the family may expose its private feelings before the servants. May hold almost embarrassingly personal conversations before the chambermaid or chauffeur, not because the chambermaid and chauffeur are assumed to be as discreet as the three wise monkeys—although they had damn well better be—but because they are invisible. The old-fashioned servant not only lived with this comfortably, he preferred it. He moved back and forth between the household world and his private world easily. But today—well, can a generation that's been so passionate about its personal freedom and its sensitivities and its enlarged ego do that? Can you, Michael? Be absolutely honest about it, so that a week after I've placed you in the job we're not all three of us regretting it."

"Absolutely honest?" Mike said. "All right, the picture you're

9

drawing seems to be of waxworks, not people. I'm not sure how valid it is."

"Enough. And, oh yes, those are people. You and Amy may not be people during your working hours. They most definitely are at all times. So where does that leave us? I mentioned the long haul, didn't I?"

"Yes."

"That must be taken into account, too. Several years at least. It's to your benefit to think in those terms. The good news is that the secretary-companion's job pays twenty thousand a year to start. The chauffeur's job pays fifteen thousand. A Christmas bonus, tax free, will add twenty percent to that. Not luxurious, but not bad at all. And most important, secretary and chauffeur make a live-in couple provided with a pleasant little apartment on the premises, complete medical benefits, and—do you own a car?"

"Not recently," said Mike.

"—and the use of one of the family cars when you're on your own time. A handsome package really. Rent, food, insurance, and transportation, all on the house. Which means that unless the couple is wildly improvident, the largest part of its income can go right into savings. Add up a few years of those savings, you people, and you'll find it comes to a surprising amount. Add up fifteen years of them"—Mrs. Bernius gracefully motioned at the wallpaper—"and you have this."

"Domestique," said Mike

"Domestique. My husband and I made it happen the hard way. He provided the inspiration, I managed the money. Unfortunately, he didn't live very long after we made it happen."

Amy said instantly and naturally, "Oh, I am sorry."

"Thank you. But that's how things turn out sometimes." Mrs. Bernius took aim at Mike. "Now that you know what the job entails—considering your background and disposition—do you feel you can handle it emotionally? That is the question."

"I'm more adaptable than I look," Mike said. "Especially when well motivated. Right now I am terribly well motivated."

Mrs. Bernius nodded acceptance of this. She turned to Amy. "How tall are you?"

10

Amy looked guilty. "Well—"

"Stand up, dear."

Amy stood up, drooping. By subtle drooping she had learned to keep her soaring six feet close to Mike's five-ten level.

"And don't slouch," said Mrs. Bernius crisply. "Straighten those shoulders. All the way, that's right, dear. Nothing to be worried about. I've been given to understand that height would be a distinct asset here. The member of the family you'll be secretary to is Miss Durie. Miss Margaret Durie. Age seventy, has her crotchets, and—you should be prepared for this—is unsighted."

"Blind?" Amy said with trepidation.

"Totally. Since a youthful accident. It seems to me that when this matter of height was brought up, Miss Durie was indicating she'd feel most secure in the company of someone tall."

"I've never dealt with anyone blind," Amy said.

"Few of us have," said Mrs. Bernius. "And I wouldn't let my imagination run away with me now, dear. I have a feeling you'll get along well with the lady. And that you'll find the family strongly supportive. And—I trust you'll take this in the right spirit—you do make a most pleasant appearance when you're not slouching in that awkward way. But that rather flamboyant red hair—"

"Auburn," said Amy. "And it's natural."

"Obviously, going by your complexion. What I'm suggesting is that you capitalize on your height and figure and work out a less—well—casual hairdo. Before you meet the housekeeper there. She's very much in charge and favors what might be called the sedate coiffure."

"Sedate?"

"Less flyaway. Keep in mind that the signals you get from the housekeeper—Mrs. McEye—are the signals she gets from the family. And where I have the power to hire—with her approval—she has the power to fire."

"But we are hired? Both of us?"

"Both of you." Mrs. Bernius reseated herself behind the desk—it was a demonstration, Mike saw, of how to seat yourself weightlessly—and scanned a folder. "Two years as kindergarten

11

teacher. Then a turn at various temporary office jobs. Receptionist and typist."

"Mostly receptionist," Amy confessed. "My typing isn't all that fast."

"But refreshingly accurate," said Mrs. Bernius. "You're the first one within memory, dear, who completed our tests without a single error. But—and this is only to satisfy my curiosity—did you give up that job at Scoville-Lang voluntarily or did your Mr. Oliphant—?"

"Oh, that. Well, after Mike left, Mr. Oliphant sort of encouraged me to quit at the end of the term. I would have done it anyhow."

"Of course." Mrs. Bernius looked almost fondly from one to the other of them. "Semper fidelis, isn't it? Well, then"—she closed the folders with an air of finality—"today is Wednesday. You'll start with introductions Sunday morning at eight. Sunday morning is when the family—or most of it—will be on hand. Your apartment is fully furnished, ready for occupancy. The one you'll report to—remember to use the service entrance, not the main entrance—is Mrs. McEye, the housekeeper. She'll give you your instructions in detail. Do not—I repeat, do not—try to improve on them." Mrs. Bernius held her hands wide. "And that's it, you people. The whole package."

"For the next five years," Mike said as he got to his feet. He felt simultaneously lightheaded with relief, heavyhearted with dark forebodings.

"At least the next five years," Mrs. Bernius said. "Wait. One little thing more." She regarded Amy over the glasses. "You're not pregnant by any chance?"

"No," Amy said, and looked down at her flatness in bewilderment.

"Oh, nothing shows," said Mrs. Bernius. "It's just that a little one on the way—well, it would be more than the family would care to cope with. Bear that in mind, won't you?"

"Both of us," said Mike.

*　*　*

12

MIKE jabbed the elevator button. "Unreal," he said.

Amy thrust her arm through his. "Want to walk all the way home from here?"

"Until reality sets in? Sure. By way of Sixth Avenue. The first bar we hit there is the bar for us."

"Your idea of reality," Amy said. She clutched his arm tight against her and managed to fit into the same section of the revolving door that bumped them out into Fifth Avenue. In the middle of the crowded sidewalk she stopped short. "Mike, it's just sinking in, that unreal part. Our money troubles are over. Completely. It makes me feel disoriented."

"Still," Mike said, "figuring in this and that—like overdue rent and my father's mite and the Silverstones' large charity —we're starting off at least a few thousand in the hole, baby."

"I know," said Amy. Which, as Mike was aware, understated it. One corner of her brain, he learned soon after they set up housekeeping, was a computer when it come to dollars and cents. She now had that computer look in her eye. "After you rent the van tomorrow so we can get the rest of the stuff up to the farm for storage—anyhow the TV and stereo and books—we'll owe just about thirty-three hundred. No sweat anymore, because we just arrange schedules of payment. So in two months—"

"Two months?"

"Mike darling, if we keep expenses down to basics, in two months we clear up everything we owe."

"Unreal," Mike said.

The first bar they hit on Sixth Avenue catered to a depressing lineup of threadbare geriatric cases. The warm blood still circulated however; every watery eye fixed on Amy with appreciation.

There were a few small tables available, none occupied, but there was a waiter indifferently flicking a towel over one of them. Mike led Amy to a table. "Name your poison," he said.

"Frozen daiquiri," she said predictably. She loathed all alcohol that wasn't camouflaged by cloying syrups. "Strawberry."

"In a joint like this?"

"It's a bar, isn't it?"

The waiter drifted over, and when Amy said, "A frozen strawberry daiquiri, please," he regarded her somberly. "You have to be kidding, lady."

Mike said, "The lady'll have a screwdriver, heavy on the orange juice. For me, Jack Daniels. A double. No rocks. Right?"

"Right," said the waiter and made his way off.

"Well?" Mike said to his wife.

"So I am no expert on bars. Or maybe just enough to know that a double anything on an empty stomach is extremely potent, isn't it?"

"I need it, dear. Between you and me, I still feel I'm under anesthesia."

The waiter set down their glasses. He watched Mike down a large belt. "Happy days," the waiter said approvingly as he departed.

"So it appears," Mike said. He said to Amy, "Man took me for an old gunslinger. He didn't know he was eyeballing Jeeves. And Mrs. Danvers."

"Mrs. Danvers? Oh, yes, *Rebecca.* Mike, honest to God, is that how you see it?"

"What I see, baby, is a stretch of role-playing for us. Something new in our lives. Two split personalities. Four altogether. Are we ready for that?"

"We'd better be. Because simple arithmetic—"

"No arithmetic is simple. If it was, I'd be a math or science teacher. I'd have school boards begging for my services. Hell, not even Bernius was begging for them. If she didn't want you to sign on—"

"She did want you," Amy said sharply. "And let us stick to the subject, Michael dear. Simple arithmetic. Which says that if we bank all we can, we'll wind up with about a hundred thousand dollars in the next five years."

"Come on. Not even fancy arithmetic—"

"It's true. If we keep personal expenses way down, that's what will happen."

"Possibly. But do you think we can put in five years of servitude stashing away Das Rheingold and then go back to

14

teaching just like that?" Mike downed the rest of his drink.
" 'Well now, Mr. Lloyd, we've considered your application, but
what with that blackball, and the best years of your life devoted
to chauffeuring the idle rich—' "

"No," said Amy, "you won't be putting in job applications
anywhere. Your job'll be writing, not teaching."

"Amy, darling, I've had one story published, and I have one
novel on hand nobody wants to publish. And your drink is getting warm."

She distastefully took a sip of the drink and said stubbornly,
"That novel is a good novel. And the one you're writing now
about the school is even better."

"Maybe."

"No maybe. So what you'll do while we're on this job is go back
to writing, the way you were doing before the cabbie job. At least
a couple of pages a day. And when we've got that big money put
away you'll write full time. And without having to go beg for
those grants nobody gets anyhow except people who don't need
them."

"I see," said Mike. "Our planned future."

"Part of it. For the rest—Mike, do you know how hopeless you
are about handling money?"

During the past three years there had been vague hints that
she might think this way, but it was the first time she had ever
come out with it. Now that she had, he found, it didn't hurt at
all. Had a certain flattering quality, in fact. Mike Lloyd, easy
spender, ready lender, generous host, a man for all seasons.

He said lightly, "Hopelessness with money runs in my family,
baby. You can't blame me for it when it's in the genes, can you?"

"Yes, I can. So—"

"So?"

Amy took a deep breath. "I want to handle all our money.
Paychecks, budget and all."

Mike contemplated this through a faint haze of bourbon.

"Suppose," he said craftily, "I told you this kind of arrangement could psychically demolish me?"

"Fat chance."

"You know all the answers, don't you, kid? All right"—he made a broad erasing gesture in the air with his fist—"the misspent past is wiped out. Now for the implausible future."

NOT that the recent past itself, commencing with the entrance of this woman into his life, had been all that plausible.

The entrance had been made on an Orientation Day, traditionally the day before the school year opened, when the faculty gathered in the auditorium for some positive thinking from headmaster George Oliphant, pilot of the good craft Scoville-Lang—like it or not, it did live on Dalton and Brearley rejects—and for sketchy introductions to the newly signed-on members of the crew.

A stupefying occasion usually, but this time brightened for Mike by the view, a few empty rows ahead, of an unfamiliar crown of blazing red hair sunk to the level of the seat top and apparently unattached to any body, though second glance revealed that there was a pair of blue-jeaned knees also visible at seat-top level.

When her name was called—Amy Belknap—and she awkwardly rose to her full surprising height and came to the platform to murmur that she was instructor of Kindergarten-B, it turned out that aside from those fiery tresses this was no big deal. The tresses had hinted at, if not a Miss America, at least a Miss New York State. The reality came off as an ordinary-looking kid, obviously fresh out of college and awed by this, her first honest-to-god paying job as sandbox supervisor. Rose DelVecchio, head of the Lower School, which included the kindergartens, had once confided to him in her cups that what she looked for in a kindergarten teacher were steely nerves and immunization

16

against all childhood diseases. So much for Amy Belknap.

Over the next month he occasionally saw her from a distance, but since he was an Upper School heavyweight—now Dean of Students, George Oliphant's idea of a high-toned title for a combination English teacher and grade adviser—and since the Upper, Middle, and Lower Schools lived academic lives apart from each other, there was no reason to pass the time of day with her. Besides, females who had the edge on him in height were a distinct turn-off.

The first time he did talk to her was on his own turf, the closet-size office awarded him as Dean of Students. Corned beef sandwich in one hand, pen in the other, he was at his desk having lunch and grading essay papers when there was this barely audible knock on the office door. "Come in," said he, and there she was. Triumphantly, he found her name leaping instantly to mind. "Miss Belknap. Amy Belknap."

She looked startled at this recognition. "Yes. I'm supposed to talk to you. About a problem."

"A kindergarten problem? I have a feeling that you're at the wrong address."

"Oh, no. I mean, it's rather a personal problem. I told Mrs. DelVecchio about it and she sent me to Mr. Oliphant." She remained standing there in the doorway, and in those jeans and that Scoville-Lang T-shirt, Mike observed, she could have been one of his senior writing class. She cleared her throat. "Anyhow, when I talked to Mr. Oliphant he said you might know what to do about it."

"Did he?" said Mike. So George, the old smoothie, had set him not only to nursemaid troubled adolescents but also troubled faculty. This he'd have to settle with George. Meanwhile, let good manners prevail. "In that case," said Mike, "come in, close the door, sit down."

She did, and where any visitor made for a tight fit here, this one's lanky frame made it even tighter. When he pivoted his swivel chair toward her their knees almost touched. It struck him that her face seen this close—sherry-colored eyes, high cheekbones, short straight nose, wide mouth—was not an altogether uninteresting face.

17

"And the problem?" he said.

"Well, it's one of your Upper School boys. Gerald Mortenson. He's been making himself offensive to me."

"How?"

"He aims remarks at me in public. Sexually oriented, not quite sotto voce. In front of his cronies."

"Cronies," Mike said. An almost forgotten magic work in this context, right out of all those magic boys' books read beneath the blanket by flashlight beam.

"Yes," said Amy Belknap. " 'Hey, Miss Belknap, you're *my* kind of teacher.' 'Hey, Miss Belknap, want to share an experience?' I find it offensive in the extreme. I'm not sure Mr. Oliphant does. I can only hope you do."

"But definitely," Mike said. The Mortenson kid. Big, smart, going on eighteen. Parents divorced, father a wheel in TV production. And—this would explain George's evasive style here—Mortenson senior was the school board member who handled Scoville-Lang's fund raising for free. "Did you," Mike asked the plaintiff, "try to straighten out Gerald?"

She shook her head. "Hard to see how, considering his total arrogance. I know he wants me to engage him in a slanging match in front of his audience, so I won't. The best I could do last time was give him a really scathing look." She took in Mike's expression. "Is that so surprising?"

"No, no. It's just the way you put it." He couldn't hold back a smile, and to his pleased surprise, instead of showing resentment she returned the smile. "By the way," he said, "do I detect a touch of Boston in your voice?"

"It's my hometown. And I graduated from Boston U."

"What do you know," Mike said, "so did I. But the hometown's Spruce Pond up Middlesex way. I doubt if you've ever heard of it."

"Not really."

"Nice place," Mike said. "Old New England. Or what's left of it." He suddenly realized he was openly reading her face, feature by feature, and that her cheeks were coloring. Blushing, for God's sake. Here on Central Park West at the close of the twentieth century. He abruptly pulled himself together. "Anyhow,"

18

he said briskly, "I'm glad you brought the problem to me. You can now forget about Gerald Mortenson. I'll attend to him first thing."

He did so, restrainedly for openers, but when the kid responded with a man-to-man leer Mike cut loose with an anger he vaguely realized stemmed from the picture of Amy Belknap appealing to him, Sir Galahad, for help against this snotty, teenage dragon. Overreacting, of course, but he certainly did take all the fire out of the dragon.

Simple.

What wasn't simple was the way he then seemed to have this Amy Belknap on his mind. Certainly, he assured himself, when you took into account that awkward height, the almost fey naivete, those ready blushes right out of crinoline times, he wasn't being driven to pursue the fair maiden. So what it had to be was just curiosity about an entertaining and unusual specimen. In that case, Rose DelVecchio, Belknap's immediate superior, was the one to pump for information. Rose was an old acquaintance, hard-bitten, straight-talking, and as a matter of fact, now going through a miserable divorce, hence always ready to share a drink with a sympathetic listener at Dicey's Saloon over on Broadway.

During the first round of drinks she brought him up to date on the divorce proceedings, still a mess. With the second round, when she said, "Enough of this. How about a cheerier subject like, say, the incidence of cholera in Third World countries?" Mike said "Sure," and described his resolution of Amy Belknap's problem.

"Figures," said Rose. "I should have sent her to you right off instead of George."

"No big deal," Mike said. "But what got me was this Belknap kid herself. The kind of weird helplessness that she —"

"Helplessness?" Rose's eyebrows went up. "Mister, obviously you don't know you're talking about the second coming of Mary Poppins, toughest nanny of them all."

"Go on. That baby-faced flagpole?"

Rose's spirits had been bleak up to now. Now they appeared to brighten. "That flagpole came out of college into a one-year in-

19

ternship in a problem school in Boston. They sent me a one-line recommendation of her. Highly motivated, creative, well organized. And that's what she turned out to be."

"Our Amy Belknap?"

"None other. Shy, a little bit oddball, but a darling kid. Catches you off-balance sometimes. The first time I complimented her on the way she handled her class do you know what she said to me with an absolutely straight face? She said, 'Well, isn't it true that a stern but loving preceptor is the answer to most pedagogical problems?' Just left me standing there with my mouth open, if you know what I mean."

"I know," Mike said. "I've caught her act."

"No act. The genuine Belknap. The fact is she lights up my life."

"Obviously. And anybody else's? One of our faculty studs smitten by the view of Pippa passing?"

Rose shook her head. "I doubt it. She's boarding cut-rate with some old couple in the neighborhood here. Grim team, from what she let drop. And from what our faculty eligibles let drop, well, I have a feeling that she may be just a shade too different from what they're used to." Rose finished her drink, then took her time lighting a cigarette. "Michael dear, are you between affairs of the heart right now? Is that what this little tête-à-tête is really all about?"

Mike weighed this. "So it would seem, wouldn't it? You're a wise bird, Rosie."

"Oh, yeah, Just slow on the uptake, that's all. Still I can't feel too dumb about it, considering that this Amy person — we'll discount those big brown eyes — is a long way from the usual Michael Lloyd cuddly little kitten type."

"Hey, don't rush me. I haven't even dated her yet."

"I have an idea it isn't long coming," said Rose.

It came next afternoon. Classes had been dismissed when he went upstairs to Kindergarten-B; the room looked as if a cyclone had hit it, and teacher was clearing up the wreckage. When with a minimum of preliminary he proposed a friendly chat over drinks at Dicey's she said, "That would be nice," and so after they put the room back into shape there were drinks at

20

Dicey's — Coke on the rocks for her — and a long talk, both holding their own, starting with the shared experience of Gerald Mortenson, and then they adjourned to the deli down the block for sandwiches and more talk, and finally there was a directionless ramble, which somehow wound up at the door of her apartment. Where, disconcertingly, she suddenly went inarticulate, barely managing to get out a murmured good-night and thank you before closing the door behind her.

Halfway down the staircase Mike stopped to think it over. Then he reversed course and went back up to knock at the door. When she opened it he said, "You didn't give me any chance to sign off properly. I just want you know how much I enjoyed the evening. And if there's nothing special on your calendar, how about a repeat tomorrow?"

She looked doubtful. "Do you mean that? Really?"

"Amy, you heard me say it. Why wouldn't I mean it?"

"Oh, God," she said woefully, "because I talked so much. I never do that. I don't know what got into me. And you were so quiet after we came into the building I knew I must have bored you to death."

"Not for an instant. Matter of fact, I thought I was coming on a little too intense."

"Responding. That's different."

"It is not," Mike said. "Besides, what led to my silence when we came in was contemplation of an age-old question. Do you kiss the girl on the first date?"

That was the comic truth. He couldn't recall having given thought to that innocent question since he first laid razor to some barely perceptible fuzz on his chin, but as he had followed her up that staircase the question had popped right up out of fuzzy-chinned adolescence. Kind of a time machine, this girl. Make contact, and next thing you're back there getting ready for the junior prom.

From her expression he couldn't judge whether she was contemplating him or the age-old question. Finally she said, "Were you really wondering about that? And me?"

"Yes. Yearning but insecure."

"Don't be," she said, and leaned forward to rather bumpily

21

press her lips to his. Her kiss was at first tentative, then enthusiastic, and ultimately—by now they were tightly locked
together with arms around each other—abandoned. Even ex-
ploratory, as were Mike's hands, although carefully kept in
bounds between those bony shoulderblades and that slim, hard-
muscled waist.

When they broke it up they kept their arms around each
other. Amy drew back her face to focus on him. "Now I can tell
you," she whispered. "If you hadn't come back, I would have
had a dreadful night."

"So would I."

"Mine would have been worse."

"Look, darling, if you want to be competitive about it—"

"No, truly. I have kind of a deep self-esteem. That makes it all
the more painful when you think you've made a fool of yourself.
But I didn't, did I?"

"Far from it. Meet me at Dicey's tomorrow after school, and
I'll reveal just how far."

So it was at Dicey's, lately geared to Upper West Side chic,
that she had her first daiquiri. And her second, when Mike,
having ordered a follow-up bourbon for himself, pointed out to
her that he had found solitary drinking, especially in company,
made him instantly melancholy.

Then with joints well oiled they settled down in a Chinese
restaurant where they alternated between gluttony and fond
argumentation and, at unpredictable intervals, spells of moon-
struck silence. During one of those spells it struck Mike that this
whole thing was wildly improbable. Wildly. Consider that he
had shared this stranger's company for about ten hours of his entire life. And consider his hitherto rich contentment with his
lot—a nice job, a gem of an apartment in the Village, a couple
of devoted friends, attractive females to move in on occasion and
provide all necessary gratification and sometimes even light
housekeeping, the dandy little BMW he had virtually rebuilt
with his own hands, a story published and a novel in the making—because contentment was the word for it. But now fixed on
that happily flushed and slightly glassy-eyed face across the
table, feeling the pressure of those long, bony, stockinged feet

22

resting on his shoes, he knew that the contentment, however rich, had been watery stuff compared to its intoxicating replacement.

Blissfulness, for God's sake. An unnerving, gut-twisting blissfulness. For the first time in his adult life.

But then, there had to be a first time for everything, no?

Oh, yes. In fact a whole series of first times.

They spent that weekend in his apartment on Thompson Street — three neat little rooms including eat-in kitchen and backyard view — and here he was given the evidence that she had indeed spoken the truth when she had earlier confided that she had never before been to bed with a man.

Mike managed to take this without blinking.

"Aren't you even a little surprised?" Amy asked.

"Why? I imagine there's a considerable number of women who refuse to settle for whatever casual roll in the hay they're offered."

"That is so true." Amy regarded him meltingly. "But how many men know it? Not that I regard my virginity — or any other woman's — as sacred, that kind of nonsense. Funny thing in college, any time I did get an offer, even if the boy and I had gotten along so well previously, I suddenly found myself judging him very harshly. Seeing how callow he was, for all his fine airs. College boy self-assurance is very hollow really. Harvard and MIT self-assurance especially."

"Good thinking," Mike said.

As it turned out, when she settled down in bed it all went very much like that initial kiss in the hallway — a tentative warm-up, then enthusiasm, finally abandonment — although both days of the weekend were needed to obtain the desired results.

Sunday at midafternoon — clearly satiation time — he raised himself on an elbow, brushing aside a couple of copper-colored hairpins to get elbow room, and studied her as she lay there, eyes closed, hair in disorder over her breasts. After a little of this pleasure he yielded to temptation. "One question," he said.

"Mmm?"

"Was it good for you, too?"

Her expression became all wide-eyed wonderment, an obvious

23

put-on. "How can I tell," she asked plaintively, "when I have no basis for comparison at all?"

"Touché," said Mike. "One more question. No fooling this time. How do you feel about giving up the nunnery and moving in here?"

"Fine."

"Just like that? No doubts? No fears?"

"None. No, wait. I'm paying rent in advance, and I've still got two weeks to go this month. I doubt very much they'll—"

"I'll stand treat," said Mike.

She moved in next evening, and one month later —Thanksgiving Day—they were married. Afterward, they found that neither could clearly recall which one had first broached that idea. They finally agreed that since either might have been the prime mover, it was obviously an idea whose time had come. Maybe ESP. Whatever.

The wedding took place in the home of Amy's widowed mother—the longtime family home—in not quite Back Bay Boston. As the time had approached, Mike found that if he was supposed to feel pangs at the surrender of a free and easy past, well, he was sure as hell marching to a different drummer. The fact was that he had so far thoroughly enjoyed keeping house with this woman who made these now close quarters just the right size. What did sometimes make him uneasy was the flickering concern that living this way was a little too much like living with their front door always open wide and her belongings stacked beside it, ready for instant pickup.

That uneasiness was most acute after their occasional flare-ups. Of course, as they acknowledged each time peace was made, these battles were always brought on by the damndest, silliest kind of nonsense. They acknowledged it, made resolutions, clung together all the more closely now that good sense had prevailed. But, thought Mike, there was really nothing to keep her, during one of those bouts, from simply walking out of his life. True, she might agonize about it afterward, but that would be afterward. So never mind all those tales of woe told by divorced acquaintances, a marriage license did make a difference. Might not lock that front door but would at least push it shut and store the female luggage away in a harder-to-reach place.

He saw the paradox in this, too. Not only did he, once the laid-back loner, cherish her because, like someone going off a ten-meter board without even a test bounce, she had confidently delivered herself to him, as the song goes, body and soul. Had provided him with what turned out to be the sweetest ego trip of them all. Thus he loved her all the more because she loved him, and she loved him all the more because he loved her and so on and so on, and that took care of all the classical versifying about unrequited love. Mark it unrequited self-pity and shove it.

Therefore, Mike asked himself, why this worry about her breaking up the menage, that unlikeliest of events the way things were going? Well, call it a case of semantics, but maybe it was that word *menage*. It had an unpleasantly temporary sound to it.

When it came out that she shared this line of thought that settled it, though neither was ever clear about who first came up with the word *marriage*. But of course that was the word.

They drove to Boston that Thanksgiving morning with Rose DelVecchio as guest and passenger, and an hour before the ceremony first met each other's parents. They had talked endlessly about their parentage and childhoods, so Mike was not surprised to find Mrs. Belknap barely camouflaging an innate biliousness of spirit with a too-sweet manner and at least as wary of him as he was of her. The two older brothers also lived down to advance notice, prosperous, unimaginative, and condescending clods, both yet unmarried, both with a fund of merry tales about the kid sister's infinite gaucheries.

Still, there was no mystery about how anything like Amy had come to flower in this arid soil. She had early provided the answer to it by her worshipful descriptions of her father, now six years in the grave. A merchant mariner—a ship's captain, no less—a towering redhead, chillingly sullen and uncommunicative in the company of a verjuiced wife and loutish sons, he had given himself only to his daughter, his one tall, redhead progeny. Home for a few weeks at a time between voyages, he'd silently apply himself to home repairs, waiting each day for Amy to return from school, and would then become doting father, best friend, Olympian deity.

"Books," said Amy. "He was mad about them. Evenings, starting when I was about seven or eight, he'd come up to my room and read to me. Oh, God, that beautiful deep voice. And no baby books either. *Moby Dick* was the very first one."

"You couldn't have understood much of it at that age," Mike commented. Foolish of him, he knew, to be jealous of the late Captain Eli Belknap, but willy-nilly he was.

"I understood enough," Amy said. "At the very least I got the music. And then when I was like about ten or eleven he turned me on to Dickens and Thackeray and —"

"Thackeray? Even at eleven, sweetheart, even at a terribly mature eleven —"

"*Vanity Fair.* I loved it. I went around being Becky Sharpe for months. My role model."

"Oh, boy, did you miss the mark," Mike said.

Anyhow, there it was. His Amy had been molded for him by a father who not only cherished her but respected her and let her know it. Just the father. Once you met the mother and brothers, there was no question about that.

And for the first time Amy met his folks and, after sizing them up, decided there would be no problem here. In turn, his folks, no doubt fearing that what their Greenwich Village son would offer them was a vampire in black leotard and with opium pipe in hand, were patently relieved to find that the reality was this lanky, nicely mannered schoolgirl.

Thomas Lloyd got his son aside to give him the consensus. "Mom and I think you're a lucky man, Mike."

"That I am."

"How old is she anyhow? She can't be as young as she looks, can she?"

"Almost twenty-two."

"Oh. Nice age. Just about right. This was all pretty sudden, wasn't it? You know, Mom wishes you'd keep in touch more."

Meaning that both wished it, but Dad, as usual, was laying it on Mom. And the reason for their only child not getting in touch more—it was the same reason for this kind of talk making that child so uncomfortable—was, Mike knew, his own sense of guilt.

Unnecessary guilt at that.

In his youth Thomas Lloyd had inherited the dairy farm outside the town of Spruce Pond. Eight hundred acres free and clear, three dozen high-production Holsteins, a few thousand high-production Leghorn hens, a going concern. What was left of it in Mike's youth were eighty mortgaged acres, a dozen Holsteins, a few hundred hens, a losing proposition all the way.

So Mike had cut out and headed for college in Boston and a career in New York, feeling a lump of guilt in the Adam's apple whenever he was moved to drop a line to the folks or phone them, or, most acutely, when he was in their presence. Crazy to feel the guilt when, after all, the folks had backed his decision all the way, but there seemed no antidote to it.

None. Not even the realization that they now stood in awe of him. When his story had been published in *Harper's*—it was about a farm boy who in sorrow knows he must remove himself from a dying yesterday to a promising tomorrow—when the story was published, so his mother confided, Dad had ordered two dozen copies of the magazine to hand out to their circle. Didn't just hand it out either; insisted it be read to the last word, it was that good.

Heartwarming, touching, whatever, it made the guilt even worse.

Now he looked at his father knowing that the shadow of the old farm hung over them both. Six generations in the family, and that would be the end of it. Continuity fractured, the past wiped out. He tried to see his father and mother nested in some shiny, superefficient little Florida apartment, and it made a depressing picture. He said, "Solve the hired-man problem yet?" because that problem unsolved certainly put Florida right up front in the picture.

"Solve it how?" his father asked. "With them useless high school dropouts? You saw it coming, Mike. Small farm's got to be either a rich man's hobby or a bad joke. Anyhow, the house is kept up nice, so I've been wondering—"

"Yes?"

27

"You're off Christmas week. Any chance of you and Amy coming up for that week?"

"We'll be there," Mike said. It had been two years since his last visit to the old homestead. "Amy'll like it."

"Looks like the kind of girl who might," said his father.

There was a wedding lunch and Thanksgiving dinner combined, and immediately after it, stopping only to see a teary Rose DelVecchio onto the New York shuttle at Logan Airport, the bride and groom drove up to the Laurentians for a honeymoon weekend of skiing where, it turned out, the bride proved more adept on the slopes than the groom. What portended a bright future for the marriage, as the groom pointed out, was that, unlike every other male on the premises, he didn't in the least resent her superior talent, and so convincing did he make this that he almost believed it himself.

And they did go up to Spruce Pond for Christmas week, and Amy did like it, including the Christmas morning service at the old Congregational church followed by a sweaty stint in the church kitchen along with the rest of the ladies making ready the big Christmas Day dinner.

"I think I shocked them," she confided to Mike that night. "I asked about getting some of the men in to help, and they said very kindly, well, they'd just as soon not have any men cluttering up the kitchen."

"Menfolk," Mike corrected. "They must have said menfolk."

"That's right, they did. But you share our housework without either of us mentioning it. What I wonder is, if you were raised in this Spruce Pond atmosphere, why aren't you a male chauvinist pig?"

"You know, I never thought of the possibilities. Now that you mention it—"

"Forget I mentioned it," said Amy.

Euphoria time.

Until that week before the Scoville-Lang Easter holiday break when the roof fell in. Four kids caught pushing Quaaludes of all goddam poisonous stuff, the proper penalties exacted, and then the double-cross by headmaster George Oliphant. No suspensions, said George, no penalties. A stern lecture, a gentle

28

Christian forgiveness, that was the medicine in this case.

"No good, George. We can't let a set of success-happy, coke-sniffing parents make up our rules."

"Michael, in running an institution like this there are practical considerations which—"

"Parental clout? And you don't think all our kids won't understand you're making a joke out of me and the rules? In that case—"

"Yes, Michael?"

"Then this isn't the place for me anymore. It can't be."

That was it. Almost ten years at Scoville-Lang, then suddenly no more Scoville-Lang.

Rose DelVecchio was furious at him. "You idiot, you hand him an ultimatum like that when he's looking to trim the faculty budget? Now he can replace you cut-rate and be a real hero to the board."

"I wish him the best, Rosie."

"He won't wish you the same. And what do you think'll happen to Amy now? That he'll keep her around to remind him what a son of a bitch he was?"

Still, there was a heroic quality to the deed those first few days. An angry outcry from some of the students and even a few of the parents. A petition—though eight of its thirty words were misspelled—presented by the students to their headmaster. Who, Amy reported, received it graciously, remarking that while some of the school community were not clear on the situation he was pleased it knew how to exercise its rights of petition.

It was Rose who reported, however, that if there was anything to recharge George's fangs with venom, it was that petition. And how right her judgment proved when slowly, inexorably, frighteningly, it dawned on Mike—his job applications turned down one after another—that George was responding to queries about this applicant by sinking the fangs all the way in.

Score extra points for George, too. His victim hadn't been fired, he had quit, so there was no unemployment insurance forthcoming. And Amy, steadily wilting under it, was getting a lot of George's personal attention. Classroom auditing at odd times every other day, public analysis of her maverick syllabus at

29

faculty meetings. On the final day of the term, Amy wearily said good-bye to all that and joined the party.

No favorable response to job applications, no unemployment insurance there either. She signed up for temporary jobs — receptionist and painstakingly slow and accurate typing her specialties — and Mike set to work on the novel-in-progress, an expanded version of the short story really, the narrative of the farm boy finding himself in the big city. It went badly. The financial pressure still wasn't all that acute — there were a couple of thousand in the bank at the start of that summer — but at the typewriter his concentration was faulty, blurred by the images of calendar leaves flipping over, clock ticking, bank balance wilting, credit accounts demanding.

Panic time set in when he sat at his desk with the bank book before him, its perforations pronouncing *Account Closed,* and beside it the now inoperative credit cards. With no way of getting back into the private school system, with the public school system not hiring, it was change of vocation time.

The Sunday *Times* employment section became his bible; sitting in waiting rooms became his routine where, always judged overqualified or underqualified, he found that he was a superfluity on the job market, one of a number of such white-collared superfluities. He grasped at odd jobs as an almost last straw — demonstrating kitchenware at Bloomie's; door-to-door commission selling of a children's magazine guaranteed to get anyone's kid into Harvard; grinding out thesis papers for a thesis mill that was suddenly padlocked by the law — and then, as the genuine last straw, driving a cab. Last one in, night shift was his stint, ten to twelve hours a night, six nights a week, sometimes seven, enough to almost make a living at it when the take was added to what Amy brought in. A few months of it until Amy found out about the gun shoved into the nape of his neck, and that settled that.

The BMW finally had to go, and since he got a fair price for it that money helped for a few months. Then, bit by bit, using the bulletin board in the lobby of the Thompson Street house where such notices indicated that the building's middle class was now taking a beating all around, the less essential furnishings of the apartment went for what they could bring. No complaint from Amy about any of this, nor about the fact that with his nerves tight he had to take frequent refuge in what were now expensive six-packs.

Nor even any complaint from her about the way that unemployment, like some kind of evil spell, seemed to make him incapable now and then of delivering the goods in bed.

Nor about the way, with his pride bruised, Amy was stuck with the wheedling of the landlord and the local storekeepers into extending credit another inch. Or had to be the one at crisis times to apply for the charity that their good neighbors, guardian angels, tenants of the duplex upstairs, were always ready to bestow on them. Loans, so called. Charity, de facto.

The angels were Abe Silverstone, professor of economics at NYU, a few blocks over on Washington Square, and wife, Audrey, proprietress of Custer's First Stand, that West Eighth Street boutique that had become such a hot number. They had been Mike's devoted friends pre-Amy. When she arrived on the scene they took to her with delight. When hard times arrived they became the generous providers at the drop of a hat.

"What the hell," Abe said, "it's survival money for people who matter to us. Look. I lived through the big depression—the 1930s—figuring I'd never get steady work. The end of the world is here, prepare to meet thy doom. But of course it wasn't the end. So the name of the game is survival. For one more week and one more after that. Because you never know what'll turn up or when."

Exactly one week after that what turned up was a handsome Cadillac limousine in front of the playhouse on Sheridan Square, a somehow familiar figure in chauffeur's livery polishing its already gleaming hood.

Mike, on his way to the supermarket with grocery discount coupons tucked in his pocket, stopped short with the realization that the figure was definitely familiar. Charlie Philbin. Upper School social studies teacher at Scoville-Lang for a stretch until, a chronic rabble-rouser at faculty meetings, he had been eased out by George.

Hung up with embarrassment, Mike saw that Charlie had

31

recognized him. Charlie gave him the flip of the hand and a wry smile. "Hiya, teacher."

"Charlie?"

"Call me comrade. One of the proletariat. Surprised?"

Mike stood in uncertain balance for a moment, one foot headed down the block toward the market, the other aimed at Charlie. What the hell, he thought, it would be good to open up to another sad case. He walked over to Charlie and they shook hands. "No surprise at all," Mike said, biting the bullet. "Matter of fact, I don't even rate proletarian. Strictly unemployed. Maybe unemployable. George and I had a falling-out."

"You? I thought you had lifetime tenure. When did that happen?"

"Almost two years ago. No school jobs open, so I did this and that, hacked a cab, am now open to any offer."

"Hard times, as Mr. Dickens put it. Well, one consolation is you weren't the marrying kind, as I recall, so there's no—"

Mike shook his head. "Married three years ago. Very married. It doesn't do much for the morale that she's carrying the load right now."

"You don't have to describe it to me, friend. I've been there. Wait a second. You drove a cab?"

"Yep. Until a couple of armed robberies convinced me otherwise."

"A sound instinct for self-preservation, I call it. But what I'm getting at is, would you mind getting behind the wheel of a gaudy object like this, in a costume like this, in public?"

"It depends. My wife doesn't make much. Even add chauffeuring to it, Charlie, and it still—"

"Hold it, friend. Think hard. What kills is not the pitiable income but the painful outgo. I'm a family chauffeur. Nice people out on the Island. I'm not paid any fortune, my dear wife is not paid a fortune for being cook and chief bottle-washer there. But we have three rooms over the garage that would cost a mint here in the Village, we dine royally on the house, we have practically every goddam expense you can think of covered. We are a choice live-in couple, and to those aristos of Oyster Bay who cosset us, we are worth our weight in platinum. Get the scenario?"

"Just about," said Mike.

"Good enough. Now there's this agency on Fifth Avenue up-town called Domestique. You pay no fee, the employer pays all. Let me tell you about it, Mike. And how to get in with them. After all, you never know."

And, as it turned out, you really don't.

THEY stood on the corner where the cab had let them out and surveyed the building. This luxurious stretch of Madison Avenue at quarter of eight on a September Sunday morning was almost deserted. There was nothing to distract from the survey.

"Massive," Mike finally decided. "What's the first word comes to your mind?"

"Grand Central Station."

"That's classic imperial. This, it so happens, is a Gilded Age palazzo designed for a James Hamilton Durie in 1900 by the architectural firm of Trowbridge and Livingston. Observe that the tops of those ground-floor window frames are arched to soften the heavy effect of the stone-block outer walls. And that the windows of the floors above are trimmed with rococo stonework to make the entire façade more graceful."

"Oh? Where'd you pick that up?"

"The library, Friday. Out of one of those 'Good Old New York' picture books. Impressed?"

"Not really. I'm still trying to comprehend that this is a house. Just a house. Where people live."

"And where we now live, darling. It is our little nest where we will eventually hatch a gigantic nest egg."

"Yes, we will," said Amy.

"In that case, how about getting this luggage inside by the stroke of eight? First impressions, you know."

There was quite a load piled up on the sidewalk. Six well-worn suitcases, one duffle bag with the heavy winter gear, one carton containing Mike's old Underwood, another laden with type-scripts and personal papers. The unsold remainder of the Thompson Street household — TV set, stereo components and tapes, a few cartons of books and bric-a-brac — were now stashed away among the detritus of a century in the attic of the farmhouse at Spruce Pond.

As Mike hefted a couple of suitcases Amy said, "Remember what Mrs. Bernius told us. The service entrance. It must be that iron gate down the street there."

"Shouldn't I leave one hand free to tug the forelock with, dear?"

"The service entrance," said Amy, pointing.

In fact, on the iron gate was a small brass plaque inscribed *Service Entrance* and luckily, considering the weight of the suit-cases, the concrete walk behind the gate was a steep downward slope to basement level where a massive door opened on to — from what Mike could make of it through glass curtains — a pantry. Still, even with that slope making the cartage easier, by the time he had all their belongings stacked outside the door he was well winded. He motioned Amy to ring the bell.

A young man answered the bell. A large, enormously stout man, black and of cheerful mien — a veritable black Bac-chus — he wore a full-length apron and a chef's toque pressed flat on the crown of his head like a starched white beret. "Lloyd and Mrs. Lloyd?" he said. The voice had in it the lilt of the Carib-bean isles.

"Lloyd and Mrs. Lloyd," said Mike.

"Very good. You are expected. I am Mabry. No," he said as Mike reached for a suitcase, "don't bother about them, mon. They will be attended to."

He led the way inside, and Mike saw that what he had guessed to be a pantry was indeed a well-stocked pantry about the length and width of a railroad car. Beyond was another door opening

34

into a kitchen that could have engulfed the entire Thompson Street apartment. Judging from its display of machinery, cookware, and cutlery, it was equipped to serve a battalion of gourmandizers. Also on display was a very youthful female, fresh-faced, blond, blue-eyed, ripe of figure, who, in willow-gray uniform and decorative little apron, looked as if she had just stepped out of a nursery rhyme. Little Bo-Peep herself. She studied these strangers narrow-eyed, her forefinger in her mouth.

"This is O'Dowd," Mabry said by way of introduction, and O'Dowd, without removing the finger, said something that sounded like "Mrf."

"She is waiting to take you to Mrs. McEye," said Mabry. "And when she sees Mrs. McEye"—he cocked an eye at O'Dowd—"she will also tell her that these people have baggage down here so Swanson must deliver it to their rooms. The only question is, can O'Dowd remember all this?"

O'Dowd removed the finger from her mouth. "Blow it," she said to Mabry in level tones.

"She will remember," he assured Mike and Amy. "The service elevator is there, in that foyer. Trust O'Dowd to operate it most stylishly. She is an expert at it."

The service elevator could have transported a grand piano with room left for a few passengers; its walls were hung with protective mats; it was operated by buttons. O'Dowd pressed the top button—third floor—then stood with her back against the wall, her face blank.

"That chef," Mike remarked to her helpfully, "is quite a tease, isn't he?"

"Him?" O'Dowd said scornfully. "He's not chef, he's cook." As Mabry's voice had the flavor of the Caribbean, this one was redolent of old Erin. "All brass only when chef's not around."

"I see," said Mike. "One does not take liberties with chef."

"No," said O'Dowd, "one does not."

The elevator door opened. A corridor stretched into the distance, one wall studded with doors, the opposite wall with windows. A shorter and narrower hallway—though not all that short and narrow—diverged to the right and appeared to be the

35

route to a corridor paralleling the one O'Dowd was marching them along. So the building would be an immense quadrangle constructed around a courtyard. Mike drifted close to a window to get a look through it and saw that he had guessed right. Stone walls on all four sides made a ponderous enclosure for a cobblestoned courtyard below, where on display was a formal garden.

No sign of any garage though, and that was a puzzle. Not puzzling, however, were two of the doors they passed midway down the corridor, one displaying a skirted figure in silhouette, the other a trousered figure. Public toilets. Evidently, la Bernius in describing a pleasant little apartment as one of the job's perquisites had choosen not to mention it was minus a bathroom. Of course, la Bernius didn't get where she was by always telling everything she knew.

At the far end of the corridor was another service elevator and beyond it a stairway. Up to here the hardwood floor was uncarpeted, but here, as they made a right turn down the traverse narrower hallway, they trod on carpet. An unsubtle sign perhaps that they were now in upper-echelon territory.

O'Dowd knocked on a door. The woman who opened it was stocky, with a flattish red face, thin-lipped, snub-nosed, slightly pop-eyed, her gray hair in a braid around her head. She wore a tweedy suit and what could only be called sensible shoes.

"The new people, ma'am," said O'Dowd. "And Mabry says will you call Swanson to bring their things up."

"Indeed? Try again, O'Dowd."

"Sorry, ma'am. Will you *please* call."

Oh, boy, thought Mike. No private toilet. Five miles to the nearest exit whatever direction you turn. Will you *please* call, ma'am. We are off to a galloping start, we are.

"That's better," the woman told O'Dowd. "And Mabry will be getting the trays ready now, won't he?"

"Yes, ma'am," said O'Dowd, and with what could only have been a defiant switch of these well-rounded hips she marched off.

"I'm Mrs. McEye," the woman informed the new help. "The housekeeper. In charge." She motioned them into what was plainly an office. Desk with several phones and revolving index on it, filing cabinets, a duplicating machine, a typewriter on a stand, a tabletop computer. There was a businesslike swivel chair behind the desk, two straight-backed chairs already planted before it. Mrs. McEye pointed at the chairs and when Mike and Amy seated themselves she settled down in the swivel chair, which somewhat dwarfed her, and made her phone call to Swanson in the fewest possible words. She replaced the phone, then drew a pack of cigarettes from the desk drawer and lit one. She made a broad gesture with the cigarette that encompassed the room. "The nerve center here, so to speak. A difficult job." The voice was thin and hard, the enunciation exaggeratedly refined. "Especially since we're shorthanded. Eight in residence and a permanent staff of only sixteen. Including you two."

Only sixteen, Mike thought. My goodness, it's like camping out.

"So," said Mrs. McEye, "I'm glad to have you with us. You're new to all this, I know, but Mrs. Bernius believes you'll take hold quickly." She drew deeply on the cigarette and let the smoke filter out between her teeth. "One word in advance. Confidentiality. Staff will always respect and maintain the family's privacy. It will always remember that the family's domestic life is not the business of outsiders. Anyone forgetting that must be prepared for the consequences.

"Such as?" Mike asked.

"Notice on the spot, two week's dismissal pay, no favorable reference. That's it. So take notice, both of you. Newspaper and magazine people may try to get information from you about family. May even offer payment for it. Don't be tempted."

"Under no conditions," said Mike.

"None," Mrs. McEye said flatly. "Now for protocol. Members of the family are addressed by surname. Mr. Durie. Mrs. Durie. Miss Durie. However, 'sir' or 'ma'am' does quite as well. That applies also to a family member not in residence but who may visit, the Principessa di Sgarlati. Miss Margaret—that is Miss Margaret Durie, the senior of the family—does not want the principessa, her sister, addressed by title."

"Why not?" Mike asked. Miss Margaret, according to

Domestique, would be Amy's personal boss. She began to sound interesting.

Mrs. McEye's regard of him made clear that he had stepped out of bounds. "Just curious," he said.

"Don't be. Do — not — be."

"No, of course not."

"We really are very new at this," Amy pointed out.

The pop-eyes softened a little. "I'm taking that into account, Mrs. Lloyd. What you must take into account is that I am always between the rock and the hard place. Neither of you will ever be reprimanded by family for whatever you do that displeases it. I will be reprimanded."

"Lesson number one for us," Amy said gravely.

"I would say so." Teacher was almost mellow now. "Where was I? Oh, yes. Except for the principessa and Mr. Craig's married daughter, all family members are surnamed Durie by either birth or marriage. So to avoid confusion you will refer to them by their given names. Miss Margaret. Mr. Craig. Mr. Walter. And so on. As for the staff, our protocol here is that they be addressed or referred to by given name only. Miss Margaret once remarked to me that good form always stems from practical need, and, of course, this is a case in point."

"Of course," said Amy.

Cooing like a dove, Mike thought. Charming this biddy right out of her sensible shoes. That new Amy hairdo didn't hurt either. Hitherto those flaming tresses — the original turn-on, let's not forget — had always been draped over her shoulders or piled up into a sort of hit-or-miss arrangement. Now, both of them having sweated over it before dawn, it was an awesomely sleek chignon. The perfect sycophantic hairdo.

"However," said Mrs. McEye emphatically, making it two words, "I am Mrs. McEye to staff, and you are Mrs. Lloyd."

"Because there are two Lloyds," Amy said.

"Well, more to the point, Mrs. Lloyd, you'll have certain administrative duties. And staff must recognize your status."

"Administrative? But Mrs. Bernius didn't —"

"Please." Mrs. McEye tamped out the cigarette in an ashtray and immediately lit another. "Let me explain. My days off are

Thursdays and Saturdays. Those days I must have someone in this chair to, so to speak, hold the fort. This also means that your days off are Wednesdays and Sundays. Lloyd's too, as a convenience for you both."

"Thank you," said Mike.

"Well, couples-in-service do require certain considerations. Oh, yes, and there are no holidays off. But you get vacation the entire month of July." Mrs. McEye glanced at her wristwatch. "Just enough time to clear up the other essentials. You'll want to freshen up in your apartment before introductions. So"—she held up a clenched fist, thumb extended—"you are not to seat yourselves in the presence of the family. Good manners there." She extended a forefinger. "Two. You will not pointlessly wander around family areas, that is, the two lower floors. You will be there only in the line of duty. The basement and third floor are the staff areas." She extended a middle finger. "Three. Use service elevators only. There's one at the northeast corner of the building right down this hallway, another at the kitchen end. Of course, this does not apply when you accompany family. Their instructions always come first." She looked inquiringly at Amy. "Mrs. Bernius did inform you about Miss Margaret's infirmity?"

"Blindness?"

"Yes. A tragic business. An accident not long after her presentation party. Her coming-out. From what I've been told, she was a beautiful and most talented young woman. Really tragic. We must be extremely sensitive to that, Mrs. Lloyd."

"Oh, yes."

"Extremely sensitive." Mrs. McEye again glanced at her watch. "So all that's needed now are your signatures on these insurance forms. Mrs. Bernius already sent me your other completed forms, so this takes care of the lot." She was already out of her chair and ready to go as they signed. "Now let's see your apartment. There's not much time to spare before introductions."

"Just introductions," Mike said. "No interviews and such."

"Correct. Again a matter of good manners and practicality. We all like to know who these strangers are in our home, don't we?"

A policy, Mike reflected, which would just about wipe out a large part of Village social life. Then he had another thought. "What about having family or friends in? On our own time?"

Mrs. McEye shook her head vigorously. "Under no conditions. Staff does not invite any visitor into this house for any reason. Security is difficult enough as it is. That would make it impossible. We have two security men on premises at all times—they room on this floor—and on patrol at night. If you ask them, they'll explain the problem to you."

"No need," said Mike.

"Good. Then let's be on our way." Mrs. McEye pointed at the door behind her. "That is my apartment. Yours is down the hall just beyond it."

She steered them out of the office and along the transverse corridor to a door that, previously shut, was now wide open and displayed a living room with the familiar luggage in it.

Magic, Mike thought. You make one quick call to a Swanson and your wish is instantly granted.

Mrs. McEye ushered them in. The room in furnishings and decoration, Mike took note, was good old Holiday Inn. He crossed over to the window and saw Madison Avenue below. Since it was Sunday morning there were no signs of life in that stretch of boutiques and galleries.

"Please," Mrs. McEye called sharply, and Mike found that she and his sycophantic wife were already in the next room, the bedroom. He walked in and saw more Holiday Inn. But visible behind yet another open door was a sight to gladden the eye.

"A bathroom?" he said.

Mrs. McEye looked surprised. "Of course."

"Sorry," said Mike, "but when I saw those lavatories along that main hallway—"

"The North Hall. Yes, for other staff. Especially convenient for the housemaids. Four of them. They each have a single room along there. That reminds me, Lloyd. These girls come highly recommended but they are young and impressionable. You won't take offense, I trust, if I advise you never to get the least familiar with them, so to speak."

"No offense at all," Mike said. He found himself bemused by

40

the image of four Little Bo-Peeps playing Delilah.

Amy tugged his sleeve. "Mrs. McEye asked me if this double bed was all right, or if we wanted twins. I told her this is what we're used to."

"That we are."

Mrs. McEye nodded approval. "My feeling, too." Her expression became wistful. "And my late husband's. Gone three years now. He was butler here. A good man, a good marriage. And an excellent butler. The family hasn't been able to replace him any more than I have."

"So there is no butler now?" Mike said.

"None. Mrs. Bernius hasn't had any luck there. She told me she doesn't believe there are any of the old-fashioned butlers left, the ones with proper competence and style. The one man who did fill the position last year . . . well."

That Jack Benny *well* spoke volumes.

"Yes?" said Mike.

Mrs. McEye wrestled briefly with discretion and lost. "I'm sure you'll hear about it anyhow," she said, and though there didn't appear to be another pair of ears within hearing distance she lowered her voice. "Staff here is a rumor mill as you'll find out. However. Mr. Craig got word from friends in England that a certain well-regarded butler in a Great House there was ready to make the move to the States. So Mr. Craig arranged for his employment here. After only two months it came out — no need to say how — that this creature was having an obscene affair with a houseboy he took into our service. Had actually seduced him, and almost every night in this very apartment — well, I don't imagine I have to describe it to you."

"Not really," said Mike.

"Of course," said Mrs. McEye, "since Mr. Craig held himself responsible, he attended to the matter personally. And vigorously. That, keep in mind, is the actual story no matter what version of it you get from staff." She made a gesture of dismissal. "But let's get back to business. That white phone on the night table is the in-house phone. A direct line to all family rooms and the office — I really should say *from* all family rooms, because you never call family yourselves, you phone me to do

41

that. The black phone provides an outside line. Local calls won't be charged to you; long distance calls will be.

"And"—she held up a hand in warning—"a word to the wise. Don't let the maids use your outside line, no matter what excuse they concoct for it. They don't have outside lines in their rooms, but there are a couple for their use—for staff use—in the staff hall downstairs. Do a favor for one, you'll wind up doing it for all. Be wise in advance."

"As much as possible," Mike said.

"At least that. There's also a folder of vital information in your desk drawer. Go through it carefully. Right now—this isn't in the folder—I must clear up the matter of dress. Appropriate dress for you, Mrs. Lloyd; the livery for you, Lloyd."

Amy looked down at herself with approval. "Well, I think that the kind of dress I'm wearing—"

"Yes, very nice. But the color and pattern, well, they are a bit emphatic, so to speak. On duty, pastels are in order, and no patterns. Separates are also acceptable. White or pastel waist, dark skirt. Hemlines always at knee-length even if styles raise them. Never excessively high heels; those casuals you're wearing are perfect. Not that you indulge in high heels, I imagine, with your height."

"No, I don't," Amy acknowledged. "An overdose of *Drink Me,* I'm afraid."

Mrs. McEye looked bewildered. "I beg your pardon?"

"From *Alice in Wonderland,*" Mike said. "Sort of a family joke."

"I see," said Mrs. McEye, who obviously didn't. "Well, strictly between us, Mrs. Lloyd, your height is all to your advantage. One requisite for secretary that Miss Margaret laid down was height."

"She's this tall herself?" Amy said.

"No, no, quite the contrary. But the family feels—and I agree—that the more frail she becomes, the more she needs the assurance of being served by someone physically imposing."

Mike looked at his wife. Imposing? Willowy was the word.

"However," Mrs. McEye told the willowy one, "the point is that I have no duties for you tomorrow. Take what time you

42

need to arrange for a wardrobe as specified. And Lloyd — "

"Present," said Mike, and knew as soon as it was out that it was a mistake.

"Another family joke?" Mrs. McEye inquired drily.

"No. Just high spirits, I guess."

"Are they? Well, bear in mind, Lloyd, that *this* family may not appreciate any such display of high spirits."

"I will bear that in mind, Mrs. McEye. Depend on it."

The repentance evidently struck the right note. Mrs. McEye now looked merely reproachful. "Not that I don't have a sense of humor, Lloyd. But there is a time and place for everything, so to speak."

"I understand."

"That's what I must depend on. Well, then. Your livery. Actually demilivery. Always to be worn on duty. As Mr. Craig put it, family does not want its chauffeur to advertise it. So instead of the standard livery, our jacket is simply a double-breasted business-style, hard-worsted in neutral gray, and with trousers to match. Black shoes and socks. White shirt, black tie. The cap is standard, gray with black peak. Two suits, caps, pairs of shoes and gloves. Half a dozen of each other item. Is that clear?"

All too clear, Mike thought. He heard cash registers sounding off around him like fire alarms.

"Yes," he said, "but that kind of investment — "

"Oh, no." Mrs. McEye almost smiled. "All this is charged on the household. And tomorrow at nine you have an appointment with our clothiers downtown. Hale & Hale. On Broadway near Wall Street. They'll see to everything. And have it ready the next day."

This was awesome indeed. "Twenty-four-hour service?" said Mike.

Mrs. McEye's smile broadened, revealing very small, even, and yellowed teeth. "Exactly."

One thing was plain, Mike thought. The little lady thoroughly enjoyed putting on her show for the bedazzled villagers.

"Hale & Hale," he said. "Nine, tomorrow morning."

"Yes. Now I'll leave you two alone. I'll see you in ten minutes."

With that she departed. The new help looked at each other.

43

"Well?" said Mike.

"I have to go to the toilet," Amy said. "I've had to go since we got here."

Mike followed along and stood in the open doorway. "Any thoughts on the all-seeing McEye, my dear?"

"Yes. I think there won't ever be any butler here again. Not if she can help it."

"Why?"

"Because," Amy said, "don't butlers outrank everyone else on staff? Isn't that how it was in 'Upstairs, Downstairs'? He was the one really in charge?"

"I didn't watch that show. I have to go by *The Admirable Crichton*. And all those Astaire and Rogers late-night shows with butlers. Eric Blore. Come to think of it, McEye does look a lot like Eric Blore in braids, doesn't she? Pop-eyes and all."

"Maybe. But he wasn't a butler, he was a valet. What is it butlers really do anyhow? And no," Amy quickly added, "don't tell me they go around sodomizing houseboys. I mean in the line of duty."

"Buttle, of course. Which is all kind of irrelevant, isn't it, dear? Because I am not a four-star butler. I am a one-stripe chauffeur. In demilivery."

Amy flushed the toilet. "All right," she said shortly, "it's your turn," and left him to his privacy. When he came out of the bathroom she was tensely waiting for him. "You know we've been waltzing all around the real subject, don't you?"

"Do I?"

"No more evasion, Mike. After we meet the family we cannot walk out on that woman. If we do it, we do it now as soon as she's back here."

"Why would we?"

"Because you're extremely troubled, now that you see what this is all about. This kind of life for us."

"Aren't you?"

Amy shook her head. "No. But then I'm Mrs. Lloyd while you are Lloyd the chauffeur. You said we could handle this by role-playing, but now you know that role is not for you. And when you're unhappy, I am. I won't live that way."

44

"A purveyor of sweet and sour truths, aren't you, baby? All right, let's say we walk out. Where do we walk to?"

"The farm. I've thought that out. Your folks would love us there with them, and we wouldn't be any drag. I'd help out full time and you'd write full-time. You know how proud your father is about your writing. Get the book published, and his cup runneth over."

"Maybe. But writing full-time? While he's out there trying to get his pot-smoking hired boys to help him turn the compost over? No, I've still got some conscience left. The farm is out. Better Lloyd the chauffeur than that."

Amy said in despair, "But if you're going to—"

"I am not going to. If you mean hanging on here and being bitter about it. Wait. You've made me do some hard thinking right now. At this time and place."

"About what?"

"For instance," Mike said, "why should I feel humiliated and resentful about this job when I didn't while I was driving that cab? Or playing patsy for George Oliphant all those years. Only because of what Bernius warned us about. It's the flunky factor. And this weird protocol crap with all its fine print. If some drunk looked like he was ready to heave up in my cab, I could tell him to kindly remove himself or get removed. If Mr. Craig or Mr. Walter or whoever else here heaves up all over my handsome livery, I take it and like it. Abject flunkyism. Everything on an intensely personal basis. See what I mean?"

"Yes, and it's what I meant, too. That's why—"

"Let me finish. At the same time, I just got a coldly objective look at this Lloyd the chauffeur. He hit bottom, he miraculously found a way out, and now he began to feel maybe it was just too much perfumed manure for him to handle, really, my deah, altogether impossible for such a sensitive fellow. Fact?"

"No," Amy said. "Not the way you're putting it."

"Precisely the way I'm putting it. Remember my reaction when Bernius painted the picture for us? I said it was unreal?"

"Yes."

"Well, I was wrong. Our money troubles are real, this house is real, the people in it are real. This is the present reality. I wasn't

45

prepared as well as I thought to face it. Now I am. Without being bitter. In fact, by taking a healthy interest in it. That, and a healthy sense of humor—"

"But not for public consumption," Amy said. "Please?"

"How wise is the elegant Mrs. Lloyd. No, the humor will be strictly for our private consumption."

"Then we are staying?"

"That we are."

"I didn't think we would," Amy confessed. "I really do love you. You are a unique and excellent human being."

"Well, you're kind of unique and excellent yourself. By the way, did you notice there's a handy little refrigerator in the corner of the bathroom?"

"No."

"Well, there is. With a card on its door saying 'For non-alcoholic beverages and fresh fruit only!' Exclamation point. How's that for explicit?"

Amy grimaced. "Mrs. McEye. Mike, do you think she has a key to this place and sneaks in to check on things like that?"

"Want to bet?" Mike said.

WHEN Mrs. McEye returned she produced a pair of keys to the apartment, one for secretary, one for chauffeur. Mike held his up. "Good for the outside door, too?" he asked. "The service entrance?"

"No, no, no. Absolutely not. Except for our security men staff has no keys to any outside door. Just ring the service entrance bell and someone will let you in. One of the security men if it's after hours. They make the rounds every hour on schedule, so you can time it and avoid having to wait outside. A bit of a nuisance but it does work. In all my twenty-two years here, we've never had a break-in."

"A record for the Big Apple," Mike said.

"It may be. And now—" Mrs. McEye reached up toward Amy's head and when Amy involuntarily drew back she was addressed sharply: "We do want to look our best, don't we, Mrs. Lloyd?" Mrs. McEye reached up again and tucked away a strand of hair that had escaped from the chignon. "There now." She looked Mike over, and, he thought, probably itched for a close inspection of his ears and fingernails but didn't have the nerve to carry through.

She led them past the service elevator at the end of the hallway down the staircase there. "Much more convenient when it's only one flight down," she remarked. "Family apartments are on the second floor."

Since the stairway was sharply pitched, and each step— unyielding iron plate with a floral design etched into it—seemed steeper than the ordinary, this route, Mike thought, might be more convenient for Amy and him but hardly for the stumpy-legged good soldier ahead of them. It suggested that the lady, without making protocol of it, was indicating that for short trips between floors one depended on leg power to make proper speed, not on any mechanical devices that would take their own sweet time about it.

The second-floor hallway they emerged on provided a different world from the one upstairs. The ceiling here, Mike saw, really soared. No mere windows on the courtyard side either, but vast expanses of glass from floor to ceiling, vertically framed at intervals by slender marble pillars, the whole arrangement diffusing daylight through the corridor as well as offering a full view of courtyard and garden below. And along the polished hardwood floor here was an array of oriental carpets, pale green and rose predominating in their varying patterns. The Janus effect, Mike thought. Outside, that view of the building around the courtyard was of forbidding gray stonework. Inside all was gracious invitation.

47

There was traffic in this corridor, a housemaid approaching in that willow-gray uniform and minute apron. Unlike O'Dowd, this one was lean and plain-featured, and, even more unlike O'Dowd, she appeared to be of amiable disposition. "Good morning, Mrs. McEye." There again was the lilt of old Ireland. "A gratifying pleasant day, isn't it?"

"It is, Nugent. This is Mrs. Lloyd. And Lloyd." Mrs. McEye turned to them. "Nugent is senior housemaid. And quite good at it."

Nugent smiled self-deprecatingly. "At least as much as I can be. I am very pleased to meet both of you and that you'll be here."

Before either could respond in kind, Mrs. McEye took charge. "You're to be in the office now, Nugent."

"I'm on my way there, ma'am," said Nugent, and moved off briskly.

Mrs. McEye steered her party back on course. "You can see the problem. I have to depend on her to take my place at the phone while I'm away from it, and good as she is at her work—and keeping an eye on the junior maids—she's really not up to that kind of thing."

"Mind if I ask a question," Mike said, "on garb? She's not wearing any headpiece. That kind of dressy little cap or whatever. Neither was that other maid we met. O'Dowd. I had the impression that—"

"Oh, that." Mrs. McEye shrugged dismissively. "Mrs. Jocelyn—she's Mr. Craig's wife—felt that those frills were unnecessary and rather stagy, so to speak. That somehow they made the younger girls especially a bit pert in appearance. That reminds me. I didn't explain about the laundering and tailoring here, did I?"

"No," said Amy.

"Well, you'll make up your own rooms of course and draw whatever fresh linen you require. That and your personal laundry is picked up Tuesdays and Fridays by our service and returned next pickup day. Just bag laundry and dry-cleaning separately, mark each bag with your name, and leave it in the old laundry room in the basement. Plastic bags are available in the laundry room. Staff, by the way, is not charged for the service."

"At all?" Amy said.

She looked positively dazzled, Mike saw, and why not? In all her brow-furrowing calculations as family accountant and banker she hadn't allowed for this bounty.

"No charge at all," said Mrs. McEye. "However"—she bore down on it heavily—"kindly take heed. This service is not for the benefit of one's relatives or dear friends. A word to the wise?"

"Is more than sufficient," Mike assured her.

"I trust so." Mrs. McEye pointed at the hallway bisecting the corridor. "That is East Hall. Our Madison Avenue side. Mr. Craig's apartment is there, Miss Margaret's beyond. We'll call on him and Mrs. Jocelyn first."

There was traffic in the East Hall, too. A man emerged from a door of the interesting Miss Margaret's apartment and headed their way. In his mid-thirties, he was rigged out in tennis whites and sneakers and carried a couple of rackets under his arm. Tall, tan, and terrific, Mike thought. At least a couple of inches taller than even Amy, suntanned to glossy perfection, and obscenely fit. That long, narrow, high-bridged nose and those curiously downward-slanting eyes would certainly have their appeal for the ladies, too.

Mrs. McEye seemed disconcerted by his presence. "Good morning, Mr. Durie. But it was my impression we had arranged—"

"So we had, Mrs. Mac. The apartment, sometime after breakfast. But"—he patted the rackets—"a surprise invitation. Anyhow, here I am, and here, I believe, are our newcomers."

"Yes." Mrs. McEye did not sound altogether mollified. "This is Mrs. Lloyd. She'll be Miss Margaret's secretary. And my assistant."

"Both you and Aunt Maggie are fortunate."

"And this is Lloyd. He's replacing Wilson."

"Our insurers will be delighted to hear it," said whichever of the male Duries this happened to be. And, Mike noted, he said without removing his eyes from Mrs. Lloyd and looking pretty damn interested in what he saw. "Well," said the Durie, "I do wish both of you the best of luck."

49

Mrs. McEye waited until he was out of sight before she responded to the two inquiring faces confronting her. "Mr. Glendon. Mr. Craig's son." And as if to indicate that she recognized unwanted byplay when she saw it: "Mr. Glendon can be somewhat — well — casual at times."

So, thought Mike, a vocabulary takes form. Staff is pert. Family is somewhat casual at times.

"Mr. Glendon lives here?" Amy asked.

"He and Mrs. Dorothy. Their apartment is North Hall." With those quick, short steps Mrs. McEye brought them up before a door and halted them there. "Observe," she said.

Never mind the winsome Mr. Glendon, Mike thought, here comes that ole protocol again.

Mrs. McEye lowered her voice. "You knock twice and wait. If there's no answer after a reasonable time, you repeat. You never enter a family room without invitation."

"Suppose there is none?" Mike asked.

"I'm to be informed of that at once. Actually, this applies to Mrs. Lloyd and other staff. Our chauffeur does not accompany anyone to the car, he always remains right there with the car. Wilson will fill you in on all that. And now, Mrs. Lloyd" — Mrs. McEye graciously indicated the closed door — "if you please."

A test run, Mike realized with mixed disbelief and delight. Behind their mentor's back he gave his wife a tight-lipped nod of mock encouragement, and in return got a baleful look from her. She firmly knocked twice on the door and no repeats were needed. "Come in," said a voice, and they came in, Mrs. McEye in the van.

The room was spacious, with paneled walls the same pale green that predominated in the carpets outside and in the pair of carpets here. Deeply recessed, multipaned windows. Bookshelves — an up-to-date library, judging by some of those jacketed copies — set in an arched recess. Obviously a working fireplace, what with the basket of kindling ready beside it. And, Mike saw with a pang, the furniture — chests, tables, highboy, desk, armchairs and side chairs — was all beautifully proportioned Federal, every piece with the mellow patina that comes

50

with a long, long time of tender loving care. Mouth-watering.

The man in the winged armchair, a section of the Sunday *Times* in hand, other sections scattered on the floor, suggested the same patina, human variety. Probably closer to seventy than sixty, he was trim-looking with ruddy complexion, silvery hair, neat military mustache, and looked fit as a fiddle. He had that long, narrow nose and those down-slanted eyes too. He nodded at the company arrayed before him. "Good morning, Mrs. Mac."

"Good morning, Mr. Durie. Ma'am." This last was directed at the gray-haired woman in dressing gown who sat at the desk near the window, pen in hand. Madam Chairperson, Mike thought. Handsome, hard-faced, and well-kept. No nod there. And no good-morning. Just that look of frowning concentration.

Somehow—it was interesting to see how prettily it was done—Mrs. McEye, while addressing the master, managed to make plain that she was also addressing the mistress. "This is Mrs. Lloyd. And Lloyd."

"Yes, of course," said Craig Durie. "And things are all settled now, are they?"

"I believe they are, sir."

Madam Chairperson, eyes on Amy, appeared to have doubts. "You're very young, aren't you, Mrs. Lloyd?"

"Not really," said Amy. "Ma'am."

"You are—?"

"Twenty-five. Ma'am."

"You don't look it," Jocelyn Durie said accusingly. Which in this case, Mike saw, was a real conversation-stopper. Jocelyn Durie, however, didn't allow blank silence to prevail too long. "You do understand about Miss Margaret's condition, Mrs. Lloyd? That she is unsighted?"

"Yes, I do."

"Then you will also understand that there may be moods at times. And you must be very kind to her at all times, but especially at those times." Jocelyn Durie aimed the pen at her housekeeper. "Your responsibility, Mrs. McEye."

"Yes, ma'am."

"But before you go, Mrs. Mac," said Craig Durie, "a word in private."

Mrs. McEye nodded assent and motioned her charges out. "Wait there," she ordered, and closed the door against them. They stood in the hallway looking at each other.

Amy whispered. "Something has definitely gone wrong."

"How?"

"That Jocelyn. I think she was signaling him she does not favor me, and he got the signal. Now he's passing it on to McEye."

"Knock it off, baby."

"Mike, if that's what's coming, it'll be awful. You have to get back to writing."

"Baby, the writing is supposed to be my obsession, not yours."

The door opened and Mrs. McEye walked out, closing it behind her. No way of reading the news from that expressionless bulldog face.

"I didn't get around to telling you people," she said, "that wages are paid here each Friday. In cash."

Oh, no, Mike thought at the sight of his stricken wife.

"However," said Mrs. McEye, "Mr. Craig is concerned that you might wish an advance against the first week's wages. If so, I'm to arrange it. Shall I?"

"No," Mike said promptly.

Amy found her voice. "Still, if it's customary—"

Mrs. McEye shook her head. "Quite unusual, in fact."

"Oh. But then why would he—I mean Mr. Craig—?"

"Well, he is a very considerate person, Mrs. Lloyd. As you can now see for yourself."

And what had Craig Durie just seen, Mike wondered. That his new team members—not your average from the look of them —must really be losers to have signed on here? Granted that there was kindness in his offer, it wasn't a kindness easy to swallow.

If Mrs. McEye, her eyes on him, wasn't a mind reader she came close it. "Very considerate, Lloyd. And very much pleased that Mrs. Lloyd appears to be exactly the kind of young woman Miss Margaret had in mind. Physically tall, mentally superior. There had been concern, so to speak, about finding a suitable person, and meeting Mrs. Lloyd made Mr. Craig feel much easier about it."

"An unco guid man," Mike said.

For an instant Mrs. McEye seemed to freeze up, then thought better of it. She nodded. "Nicely put, Lloyd. And the advance?"

"Not necessary," Mike said.

"It's your decision to make. Now we'll pass by Miss Margaret here for the time being and see Mr. Walter. A widower for many years. Sad when he lost Mrs. Durie, especially for Miss Camilla. Their daughter, that is. She's North Hall. She was only three years old when it happened."

"How awful," Amy said.

"Yes. We go to the end of the hall here and turn right. That is South Hall. Mr. Walter's apartment is the first one. You are getting these locations clear, Mrs. Lloyd?"

"Oh, yes."

"Very important to do so; it means no wandering around in all directions. You'll find the plan of each floor in your desk folder." Mrs. McEye made sweeping gestures with both hands, herding them along. "It is a large building," she acknowledged.

"Very," Mike agreed. "How many rooms are there in these apartments?"

This was a subject Mrs. McEye obviously relished. "In Mr. Craig's and Mr. Walter's, two bedrooms, two baths, sitting room and an adjoining small room. Mr. Craig uses his as an office away from his office. Mr. Walter refers to his as his den.

"It's much the same with Miss Margaret's except that the wall between the two bedrooms was removed long ago to make one room. And her small room is occupied by Hegnauer. That is her female attendant who's most expert in body conditioning. The equipment for it is also there. And here we are. South Hall, first door."

Since Mrs. McEye must have established to her satisfaction that her physically tall, mentally superior new assistant knew how to knock on a door, she attended to that herself now and immediately drew a melodiously soprano, "Come in, but watch how you come."

Except for some variation in choice of furniture and its

53

placement, this sitting room, Mike saw on instant appraisal, was much like the one they had just left. The lone occupant of the room was a pretty and shapely young woman, mid-twentyish, befrocked but barefoot, who was kneeling on the floor waving the company to keep its distance.

Hey-ho, Mike thought, an elderly widower's life can still have its sweet consolations, but then, disappointingly, the young woman said in that melodious voice now charged with dark drama, "Daddy's contact lenses again, goddammit. No, no, Mrs. Mac, don't help, don't move. I think I just felt it. There!" She rose to her feet triumphantly, something invisible resting on the tip of her extended forefinger. "Daddy!" she called, breaking it into two syllables that Verdi might have scored.

The call brought a man into the room, and here again were the Durie nose and down-slanted eyes. This Durie, however, was on the hefty side, a big, solidly built, aging jock with close-cropped gray hair, a half-lathered face, and razor in hand. There were also spots of lather on the T-shirt he wore above un-belted tweedy slacks. He smilingly nodded at Mrs. McEye. "Ah there, Mrs. Mac, right on schedule as ever."

"Yes, Mr. Durie. Miss Durie," said Mrs. McEye, who seemed anxious to get on with introductions while Miss Durie, forefinger extended, said defeatingly, "Take this damn thing, will you, Daddy. Just wet your finger and pick it up."

Daddy obeyed and now stood with his forefinger extended. "And these are our new people, Mrs. McEye? The marines have really landed?"

"So to speak, sir. This—"

"And wash it before you use it," Camilla Durie ordered her father.

"No, darling. I'm putting them away. They don't work. You were saying, Mrs. Mac?"

"Yes, sir. This is Mrs. Lloyd, Miss Margaret's secretary and my assistant. You'll remember that was the arrangement. And Lloyd. He's replacing Wilson."

"They do work, Daddy," Camilla Durie said menacingly. "And you *will* use them."

Really a luscious creature, Mike thought. And powerfully

54

single-minded. Daddy's own half-orphaned little treasure, God help him.

"Darling," said Walter Durie, "I will not use them. I am quite beautiful enough without them. So Wilson is actually in retirement, Mrs. Mac? No more comic adventures for us?"

"I'm sure not, Mr. Durie. Lloyd comes highly recommended."

"You will use them, father dear"—the little treasure was really leveling now—"because, in case you don't know it, any sort of eyeglasses make you look obscenely ancient."

"So I am," Walter Durie said amiably.

His daughter turned impatiently to Mrs. McEye. "Will you kindly tell him, Mrs. Mac, that he's just being perverse?"

Mrs. Mac continued to play wooden Indian. "Well, Miss Durie, if Mr. Durie feels—" and that was as far as she got, because Camilla Durie flashed out, "Oh, you're as stupid as he is!" and stalked into the corridor, regal even in those bare feet.

And the most fascinating aspect of this, Mike found, was that neither injured party reacted to it at all. Mrs. McEye stood there apparently emotionless and Walter Durie remained his amiable self. "Anything else, Mrs. Mac?"

"No, sir."

"Then thank you."

Company dismissed.

So, thought Mike, if a tree crashes down in Durie Forest with only servants in earshot, does it make any sound? No, it does not.

Mrs. McEye held her course along South Hall, and here was an elevator, its gate bronze grillwork, the gate bracketed by the head of a staircase winding downward. "Family elevator," said Mrs. McEye. "For your use, Mrs. Lloyd, when you accompany Miss Margaret. Beyond it there is the principessa's apartment. Always kept ready for her. Now we turn down West Hall here, and these are guest suites. All unoccupied at present, thank heaven. And behind that pair of doors is our other service elevator. Always use the service elevator nearest the apartment you're called to."

They moved along almost at a trot until they turned into what Mike gratefully judged to be their almost final lap. "And here," said Mrs. McEye, "is North Hall. Mr. Glendon obviously won't be in, but Mrs. Dorothy may be."

So she was, and following her hoarse instructions, they wound up at the doorway to her bedroom. Although the room, its blinds drawn, was shadowy, the occupant of the bed put on dark glasses as she sat up to take stock. A few years older than cousin-by-marriage Camilla, Mike estimated, and not in Camilla's pretty-pretty class, but seen even in chiaroscuro she gave the impression, dark glasses, tousled hair and all, of strong-featured good looks.

"Of course," Dorothy Durie said. "Your latest finds, Mrs. Mac. Aunt Maggie's new secretary, our shiny new chauffeur."

"Mrs. Lloyd, ma'am. And Lloyd."

"Have you shown off our recruits to Aunt Maggie yet?"

"Not yet, ma'am."

"No? Then if you move fast you may find Mr. Durie with her. He told me he'd visit her before tennis time."

"Yes, ma'am. We met him as he was leaving."

"Well, good for you. Cigarette, Mrs. Mac? I'm out."

Mrs. McEye produced cigarette pack and lighter and saw to the lighting up. "I'll leave the pack on the night table here, ma'am. Is there anything else?"

"One thing. Mrs. Lloyd, have you been told about Miss Margaret's blindness?"

"Yes, I have," Amy said. "Ma'am."

"Then try to understand this. Never for an instant let her feel that you pity her. She does not regard herself as pitiable, although some dull-witted people can't seem to comprehend that. Don't be one of them. And that is my Sunday morning homily, Mrs. Lloyd. Bear it in mind."

"Yes, I will," said Amy. "Ma'am."

There are subtle currents stirring through these halls, Mike reflected. Some dull-witted people? How about Madam Chairperson for one — Miss Dorothy's mother-in-law, Mrs. Jocelyn, that would be — whose own sentimental little homily had taken the opposite tack?

Out in the corridor Mrs. McEye said, "Now this next apartment is Miss Camilla's. She's already met you. And the one beyond—" She stopped there, apparently caught up in some troublesome considerations. She came out of it abruptly. "Yes. Well. That is Mrs. Gwen's apartment. Mr. Craig's daughter. Mrs. Daniel Langfeld. To be addressed that way. Mrs. Langfeld."

Which, Mike thought, was inarguable. Mrs. Langfeld was Mrs. Langfeld.

"What concerns me," said Mrs. McEye, "is that you may hear gossip by staff about Mrs. Gwen, so, much as I dislike going into such matters, I think it's wise to give you the facts. Mrs. Gwen and her husband are temporarily separated. A very cordial separation. Absolutely nothing scandalous about it. Is that clear?"

"Yes, indeed," said Mike.

"Good. And if either of you is misled by the name into thinking Mr. Langfeld is a Jew, no, he is not. In fact, the senior Mrs. Langfeld is an officer of the DAR."

"Neither of us would give the matter a thought," Mike lied cheerfully. "Not for a moment."

"I mentioned it just in case, Lloyd, because staff will gossip. My husband wouldn't tolerate that past a certain point. Any staff caught at malicious storytelling was fired on the spot. Here's your final pay, good-bye and good riddance. Unfortunately, it's not the same nowadays. Not when anyone discharged from staff knows that certain magazines would pay a handsome price for any possible scandal about family they're offered."

"Has that ever happened?" Amy asked.

"Never," said Mrs. McEye grimly. "And one of our jobs is to make sure it never does."

So this snowy banner shall never be sullied, Mike thought. Blab to the media and next thing they're dragging the river for your body. And this in an era when most of the high and mighty yearn only to catch the public's eye no matter how. Fact was, whatever reservations one might have about Clan Durie, it did shape up as a class act.

The guardian of the snowy banner, her self-starting temper

apparently geared back to neutral, moved her convoy along to the door of the nonscandalous Mrs. Gwen and knocked on it but drew no response. On second try, however, the door was partly opened by a diminutive young woman, moonfaced, snub-nosed, and pallid, dressed in a caftan. Behind her, Mike caught a glimpse of blue-jeaned figures seated on the floor, their heads drooping low on their chests.

The young woman regarded her callers with vague wonderment, then said in a soft little voice, "We're in meditation, Mrs. McEye."

"Oh?" Mrs. McEye made a futile effort to peer around the caftan. "Well, I wasn't informed about it, Mrs. Langfeld. And we had arranged—"

Gwen Langfeld pressed an admonishing forefinger to her lips and slipped through the door, drawing it shut behind her. "If we must, Mrs. McEye."

Mrs. McEye looked relieved. "Thank you. This is Mrs. Lloyd, Miss Margaret's new secretary. And Lloyd, who's replacing Wilson."

By now the almost legendary Wilson, Mike thought.

The moonface turned up to get a proper view of Mrs. Lloyd then briefly took in Lloyd. The luck of the genetic draw, Mike thought. Pure Durie stock but without the least sign of the distinctive Durie nose and eyes. Gwen Langfeld said gravely, "They appear quite suitable, Mrs. McEye. Now if you don't mind—"

"Of course not, Mrs. Langfeld. I'm sorry to have bothered you."

"No, I should have told you about the gathering." Gwen Langfeld turned the doorknob, then released it. "But then you don't know about Peters, do you? That he's sharing meditation with us?"

Mrs. McEye couldn't seem to grasp this. "Our Peters? The houseman?"

"Yes. When I called your office for someone to arrange the furniture Nugent sent him up. And he seemed so much interested in the meditative process when I explained it that I invited him to share it."

"To share it," Mrs. McEye echoed feebly. "But he is on duty, ma'am, and might be needed. If you don't mind telling him now—"

"In a while," said Gwen Langfeld, and this time opened the door to its necessary minimum and disappeared behind it.

Mrs. McEye, a pillar of salt, remained facing the door. Then there were signs of life. She raised an arm and pressed her fingertips to her forehead. And once again, Mike thought, the best thing for those present to say is absolutely nothing. After all, according to the rule book none of this had really happened.

The face Mrs. McEye finally turned to her charges suggested that none of it had. She glanced at her watch. "Nearly ten," she said, "and Miss Margaret expects us at ten sharp. One never keeps Miss Margaret waiting, so let's move right along."

Really the final lap, Mike thought, when, having circumnavigated the rectangle of hallways they now for the second time made their way down East Hall, past Craig and Jocelyn Durie's apartment to what shaped up as the most significant door of all.

Mrs. McEye knocked, the door was opened by a stalwart, middle-aged blonde who motioned them in, they entered, and there in the center of the brightly sunlit room, seated in a low-backed armchair, sat a woman smiling in their direction. She was small and slight, with snowy hair in a mannish cut and with those Durie facial characteristics shaped here to greatest advantage. Never mind that fold of aging flesh at the throat or the lack of focus in the gray eyes, Mike thought, Margaret Durie was a strikingly beautiful woman. In her youth she must have been an absolute heart-stopper.

"Mrs. Lloyd, ma'am," said Mrs. McEye. "And Lloyd."

Margaret Durie's head shifted a little in the direction of the voice. "Good-morning, Mrs. Lloyd."

"Good-morning, ma'am."

"And," said Margaret Durie, "good-morning to you, Lloyd." It sounded almost teasing.

"Good-morning," Mike said. "Miss Durie."

"And now, Mrs. McEye," said Margaret Durie, "you and Lloyd may go. And Hegnauer."

The stalwart blonde immediately moved toward the door.

59

Mrs. McEye did not. "But I thought, Miss Durie—"

"Yes. But you're not needed, Mrs. McEye."

Mike hung back, for what reason he didn't know, and Mrs. McEye started him on his way with a poke in the spine. In the corridor he said to her, "What happens in there now? An introductory session?"

"I really don't know. What I do know, Lloyd, is that at eleven you're to meet with Wilson and a Mr. Sidney Levine at the garage. All procedures will be explained to you there."

"A Mr. Sidney Levine?"

"The cars are kept in a public garage on Third Avenue. He's the owner. And he and Wilson are going out of their way to meet with you, so be on time. You can start unpacking in your apartment now, but do watch the clock. After you've gotten all necessary instructions about the cars, you're free for the day. As Mrs. Lloyd will be when Miss Margaret dismisses her. And remember tomorrow morning, the arrangements with Hale & Hale for your outfitting."

"First thing after breakfast," Mike said. "And talking about breakfast—"

At four in the morning in the kitchen of the farm, after not much of a night's sleep, he and Amy had managed to get down some coffee and toast, and the emptiness in his innards was making itself felt.

"Mabry's on duty in the kitchen," said Mrs. McEye. "The cook. He'll attend to you. In that case, take the service elevator to the basement, then walk straight through to the kitchen."

"Thank you. Do you have any idea how long Mrs. Lloyd'll be in there?"

"Lloyd, the sooner you get it into your head—"

"Of course. Mrs. Lloyd is responsible to Miss Margaret, not me. Technically we are married when off duty, not otherwise."

Mrs. McEye grimaced. "And since you have gotten that much into your head, it would help if you now got it into your system, so to speak. Mr. McEye and I were a couple-in-service so, believe me, I do know the problem. A matter of adjustment. And the quicker the adjustment, the better."

"I'm on my way to it now," Mike assured her solemnly.

Mrs. McEye showed those tiny, yellowed teeth in a smile. "The

60

garage at eleven. Straight down to Third Avenue, and it's on the corner there. And Lloyd."

"Yes?"

"Mrs. Lloyd is not really alone in a lion's den right now. As a matter of fact, she may be having a rather pleasant time of it."

Which, Mike reflected on his way down to the basement in the elevator, still didn't ease his guilty feeling that he, a Daniel, had somehow slid to safety between the bars of the lion's cage leaving Mrs. Daniel to cope. And that he was on his way to nourishment while she, a hearty trencherperson, would have to abide with hunger pangs until the lion—no, make that lioness—was in a mood to release her.

How much of a lioness? Well, judging by that shoulders-back posture and the suggestion of steel behind that sweetly modulated voice, enough. And from the bits and pieces picked up during that tour of the second floor, it was obvious that Margaret Durie, as sister, as aunt, as doyenne of the household, had a lot of people devoting a lot of thought to her well-being. A beautiful young girl blinded for life just as she was entering womanhood. And, no fool she—one look at her told you that—she'd know just how to exercise the tyranny of the handicapped.

A delicate flower, said chilling Jocelyn Durie. A tough one, said handsome Dorothy Durie in her Sunday homily. And one way or the other, said wisdom, she'd get exactly what she wanted from anyone in her orbit.

And that room, Mike thought, as the elevator trundled basementward, what was there about it? He narrowed his eyes trying to see past the image of the old lady in the low-backed armchair and suddenly recognized what it was. Not Federal, not traditional, not anything seen in any other Durie apartment. Art Deco, for God's sake. Right out of all those Fred and Ginger movies. The obtrusive curves of the glossy white furniture. Chromium trim. Tubular chairs. White carpeting. The whole thing as purely and extravagantly Art Deco as the spire of the Chrysler Building.

And for someone who couldn't even see it?

The elevator hit bottom with a small thump.

* * *

THERE was a slender cane leaning against the arm of Margaret Durie's chair, ebony black, tipped with silver, and with a mother-of-pearl knob. Margaret Durie took it in hand, reached out, and pressed its tip into the carpet.

"Stand there, Lloyd."

Amy followed orders with a feeling that, really, treading on this snowy-white expanse of carpet she should be doing it shoeless. That Durie face now seen close up revealed a fine web of wrinkles at the corners of the unseeing eyes and on the upper lip, a mesh of them taking the smoothness out of the cheeks. The facial makeup was curious, the lips too brightly red, a circular patch of rouge imprinted on each cheekbone. Still, Amy thought, this was a remarkably beautiful woman.

The tip of the cane moved, touched Amy's shoe and was withdrawn. "Some advice, Lloyd," said Margaret Durie. "Always walk firmly in my presence. I'll never be put off by good firm footsteps, only by furtive sounds. That doesn't mean thumping around to indicate where you are. I'll know where you are. Despite my age, Lloyd—I am seventy years old—I have extraordinarily acute auditory and tactile senses. Compensatory. Do you know what all that means?"

"Yes, ma'am."

"What does it mean, Lloyd?"

"Well, that as compensation for your—your blindness, you've developed an acute sense of hearing and touch. Ma'am."

"Very good indeed, Lloyd. But learn not to stammer when referring to my blindness. It always conveys to me—I don't pretend to speak for all blind souls on earth—that one is indicating guilt for not sharing another's misfortune. That *is* foolish, don't you think? You wouldn't want to share it if offered the opportunity, would you?"

"I—well, no, ma'am."

"Very sensible. And it leads me to warn you about those back stairs you may use at times. They can be deadly dangerous if you're in a flighty mood running down them. Detachment of both retinas was the price I paid for that mood, Lloyd. And where sometimes the operation to repair this may succeed, sometimes it may not. So always keep a hand on the rail when you use that staircase, Lloyd. More to the immediate point, I prefer to speak bluntly, whatever the subject, and I want to be spoken to bluntly. I regard any other kind of communication as verbal tiptoeing. Let's have none of it."

Easy for you to live by, ma'am, Amy thought; perhaps not so easy for the likes of me. Try bluntness at the wrong moment, and the next thing you have your head handed to you on a platter. Poor Mike had undergone a couple of such wrong moments with the McEye, each time giving his ever-loving wife the feeling that her stomach had been abruptly dislocated.

"Now, Lloyd." Margaret Durie gave evidence that the cane was not needed for support by rising effortlessly from her chair. She held out an arm, fingers extended. "Take my hand and place it on your shoulder. No, no, don't take it as if you're preparing to clamp handcuffs on it. That way. Yes."

The slender fingers moved lightly along Amy's shoulders as if determining their span, then were withdrawn. "You *are* tall, aren't you, Lloyd?" There was satisfaction in the voice. "Does that make you feel any the less feminine? Truthfully."

"Truthfully no," Amy said.

"Because your husband is even taller than you? And well set up?"

As if it's any of your business, ma'am, Amy thought. "He is well set up, ma'am. But not taller than I am."

"Oh? A man of firm self-assurance, I'd say. Is he?"

This could be a trap, Amy thought. She said cautiously, "He is very mature, ma'am."

"A pretty tribute, Lloyd, if delusory. No male, however he may huff and puff, ever attains true maturity." The fingers fluttered, dismissing the subject. "Now seat yourself there." The fingers fluttered in the direction of the low-backed armchair.

"Ma'am?"

"Sit down, Lloyd. In that chair."

Amy gingerly sat down on the edge of the chair.

"Let me explain something, Lloyd," said Margaret Durie. "Before my blindness I demonstrated talent as an artist. Authentic talent. Do you recognize the name John Singer Sargent?"

63

"Oh, yes. I've seen—"

"What is relevant, Lloyd, is that when Mr. Sargent was shown a few of my youthful efforts he remarked that I might have more than an innocent flair for art, I might actually have a true talent, the kind to be nurtured by proper instruction. *En passant,* he brought up the name of Mary Cassatt and her youthful demonstration of talent, a glorious compliment I was then too young to appreciate. Have you also heard of her?"

"Yes, ma'am."

"How pleasing. Not only bright, but with at least a smattering of culture."

What made this a little less offensive, Amy found, was that her condescending majesty did sound pleased.

"What I'm getting at," said majesty, "is that when I reached age seventeen and the talent remained quite exceptional I was given instruction by an artist who had been one of Mr. Sargent's protégés. An instructor who demanded both talent and a passionate dedication to art. When I demonstrated both it became evident that, in my turn, I would become his protégée. This should make clear to you, Lloyd, that I may have been on my way to becoming a Mary Cassatt or, considering the period, a Georgia O'Keeffe. Another name familiar to you?"

"Yes, it is," Amy said apologetically.

"I am impressed. But the point is that while my eyes are dead my mind is not. Given the necessary clues, I recreate a vivid world in that mind. The fingertips provide those clues. I trust you won't object to my learning your features through those fingertips."

"Learning my features?"

"Seeing them through touch, Lloyd." A hint of impatience there. "Drawing a mental picture of you that way. Now just guide my hand to your forehead. That's right. You do learn quickly, don't you?"

What she was learning quickly, Amy thought, was that the darkly handsome, tousle-haired Dorothy Durie had something there when she warned against pitying her old Aunt Margaret. A tough old birdie, auntie, a falcon permanently blinded, but a falcon to the bitter end.

Margaret Durie stood behind her, a hand resting on each of her shoulders. "Sit straight, Lloyd. But at your ease."

Amy shifted a little to indicate, untruthfully, that she was at her ease. She closed her eyes as those fingertips met in the center of her forehead, then parted and traced the outlines of forehead, eyelids, cheekbones, and the line of the nose. A not unpleasant sensation really, but a little creepy in a way. An insinuating feathery searching, which, if you wanted to let your thoughts ramble off in that direction, hinted at the sensuous. Let them ramble far enough and you might nervously wonder if Ma'am here, never mind her age and condition, didn't have Sapphic inclinations.

Didn't have? Observe that the room had been cleared of all other company. Observe that it was the campiest Art Deco kind of room. And, Amy thought with mounting tension, if those fingers worked their way down to check Mrs. Lloyd's brassiere size, Mr. and Mrs. Lloyd would be giving up this employment any minute now.

She went rigid as the fingertips moved along her jaw to her throat and then, not fingertips alone but the whole hand cupped the throat. Under the pressure Amy gulped, and the hand was instantly removed.

"There now," said Margaret Durie. She touched her subject's ear, then surprisingly tweaked it. "The ordeal is over. But what about your coloring? Your hair?"

"Auburn," Amy said. It came out as a croak of relief. But because that tweak of the ear had been no grope at all, only a display of goodwill, she felt an amendment was due. "Actually, it's quite red. Natural red. Ma'am."

"Learn to say Titian red. And your eyes?"

"Hazel, ma'am. My husband says sherry-colored."

"How poetic. Fair complexion, of course? With a tendency to freckle under sunlight?"

"Some. Yes."

"So, Lloyd, I now see you clearly. Good strong features, a bit irregular. Fine large eyes. A slightly receding jaw that helps avoid unpleasant heaviness there. All in all, quite charming. Would you dispute any of this?"

"Not really, ma'am. I never dispute any compliments that come my way."

"Indeed? That answer speaks well for you, too, Lloyd. Yes, we're going to get on very well. Now I'll reclaim my chair."

Amy leaped from the chair almost knocking over the cane leaning against its arm, and Margaret Durie seated herself. Suddenly she seemed drained of all energy. The cheeks became even paler against the patches of rouge, the nostrils flared, the mouth gaped. Amy found that her immediate reaction to this was a shameful one: Oh, God, I'm just settling into the job, and she's going to drop dead on me! Shameful and calculating for that instant, but as the hoarse breathing became more labored she felt only an overwhelming concern for this suffering old woman. She kneeled down and took the flaccid hands in hers. They were icy cold.

"Miss Durie?" she pleaded.

The hands were abruptly snatched away. The face became fully alive. The voice was flint hard. "What do you think you're doing, Lloyd?"

"Ma'am," Amy said helplessly, "I thought —"

"Fatigue, Lloyd, that's all. Stupid of you not to recognize it, wouldn't you say?"

Amy felt overwhelming concern become overwhelming outrage. "No, Miss Durie," she heard herself say, "I was frightened for you. I wouldn't call that stupidity."

But, she thought numbly, talking back like this sure was. Warned by Bernius of Domestique that servants show no feelings, enlightened by the McEye's demonstrations of how not to show feelings, no matter the provocation, she had simply blown it all on the very first test. And with the luggage not even unpacked.

Margaret Durie, lips compressed, was maintaining an alarming silence. Finally the lips parted. "Are you on your knees, Lloyd?"

"Yes, ma'am."

"A ridiculous position, isn't it, for any confrontation with a fierce old dragon? Do stand up."

Amy got to her feet. "I'm standing, ma'am."

Margaret Durie sighed. "I'm aware of that, Lloyd. Now let's have it. Do you find me a fierce old dragon?"

"Not really. But when you misread good intentions—"

"I don't, Lloyd. I'm stifled by them. I've lived with them for more than half a century and sometimes they drain all the air out of my lungs. Therefore I sometimes respond to them ungraciously. Do you understand?"

"Yes, I do, ma'am."

"And you will not carry any of this—or anything I ever confide in you—past that door? That I would regard as unforgiveable."

"Yes, ma'am."

"Then tomorrow morning you'll familiarize yourself with your duties here. Eight o'clock promptly."

"Oh, dear," said Amy.

"Oh, dear?"

"Mrs. McEye told me that tomorrow morning I'm to shop for the kind of wardrobe that's required here."

"Ah, yes, those sumptuary laws. However, I'll attend to Mrs. McEye, and you'll present yourself here at eight. The kitchen first, so that you can bring my breakfast tray—cook will prepare it for you, coffee and brioche, *ça suffit*—and a copy of the *Times*. I'll need your services for only a little while, and then you'll attend to your shopping. Exactly what did Mrs. McEye find unsuitable about your present wardrobe?"

"Well, she felt this dress was a little too colorful. Most of my dresses are like that."

"My turn for an apologetic 'Oh, dear,' " said Margaret Durie. "And now you're smiling, aren't you?"

"Yes, I am," Amy said, a little surprised to find that she was.

"And you're wondering how I know you are. White magic, Lloyd. Close the door firmly when you leave."

Amy closed the door firmly. And, she thought, taking in the empty length of East Hall, what happens now is that a white rabbit comes into sight, apprehensively glancing at its watch and muttering, "Oh, my ears and whiskers."

"Oh, my ears and whiskers," Amy whispered. With no McEye in the offing, no duties scheduled, the logical thing was to head back to the apartment and help Mike, poor hard-beset darling, unpack the luggage. But just how far did logic extend down this rabbit hole?

Never mind all this mental nattering. The thing to rejoice over despite various confusions was that Miss Margaret—Super-ma'am—had given this Mrs. Lloyd at least a passing grade on first acquaintance.

Sufficient unto the day . . .

MIKE pulled open the elevator gate and stepped out into a cool, damp world of whitewashed stone. Close by was a pit in which were installed a couple of mighty oil burners and a quartet of huge water tanks. The apparatus murmured contentedly, gauges clicked fitfully. The ceiling was solid with rows of pipes—red, green, black, white—which made an entertainingly jazzy sight extending down this spacious tunnel into what appeared to be infinity, and here and there along the way smaller-gauge stuff ascended through the ceiling from the main lines to areas above. Everything looked as if it had been freshly polished or painted first thing this morning.

Xanadu, thought Mike. And here, folks, since you must have wondered what they look like, are those caverns measureless to man.

A few steps along the way he found life in the caverns. Behind a wire mesh was a workshop that looked, from the display on its walls, like a prosperous hardware store. Added to all the gimickry, sheets of glass stood in a rack against the wall, and a tall, leathery-skinned oldster was bent over a pane of glass on a worktable, trimming it with a cutter. A much younger man in a rumpled dark suit was watching him, hands clasped behind his back. The outline of a holstered pistol showed plainly under the jacket. The man looked up as Mike stopped at the door of the fencing. "You in the right place, mister?" he asked doubtfully.

"On my way to the kitchen," Mike said. "Mike Lloyd. I'm the new chauffeur. Straight ahead does it?"

"Straight ahead. Wait a second." The man strolled out to take stock. "I'm Inship. Security. You don't mind, I'd like to see some ID. House policy, you understand."

"Sure." Mike handed over his chauffeur's license and Inship, after close inspection, returned it.

"Good enough," he said. "But you're live-in, ain't you? You and your wife. She's Miss Margaret's secretary, right?"

"Right."

"Then better get the change of address on that license soon as you can." Inship turned to the glass cutter. "Hey, Borglund, say hello to the new chauffeur. Wilson finally got his ticket out. See what happens when you get that old?" He winked at Mike. "Borglund's even older'n Wilson. And been here even longer."

Borglund tapped a fringe of glass free of the pane and looked up. He said to Mike, "You know how to use your hands, mister?" The voice was a Scandinavian fluting. "Some plumbing, some wiring?"

"I was a farm boy," Mike said.

"Yah? That could do it. I will let you know when." He returned to the glass.

"You mean," Mike said to Inship, "I'm down for handyman, too?"

"Only in the clutch. Mrs. Mac gets calls for too many rush jobs all together, and you're just watching a ballgame on the tube, you're a handyman."

"Live and learn," said Mike. He pointed. "Straight ahead?"

"To the end of the line. The double-doors there."

At wide intervals along the way to the end of the line were closed doors, some padlocked, and at the end of the tunnel Mike found himself confronted by a massive pair of doors, not padlocked. He pulled one open and was in a long room, glass-doored cabinets mounted on chests occupying much of the wall space, a well-worn rectory table in the middle of the floor, and

69

some familiar company scattered around the table sharing a nosh. Among it were the testy and pretty O'Dowd and amiable, plain-featured Nugent of the housemaid department, and the muscular Hegnauer, the body builder or whatever. One diner was unfamiliar, a middle-aged, thickset man in soiled overalls who bore a vague resemblance to Borglund. This, Mike conjectured, had to be the hitherto unseen Swanson, the helping hand who had seen the Lloyds' luggage up to their apartment so promptly. Kin to Borglund probably, and with a team like Borglund and Mrs. McEye on his tail, promptness would have to be his style.

"Good-morning," Mike said to the faces turned his way and got a nod from O'Dowd and Swanson, nothing from Hegnauer, and a cheery "Good-morning again to you, Lloyd" from Nugent.

"And how does one sign on for breakfast?" Mike asked her.

"Oh, there's no signing up," she said seriously. "Those swinging doors there are the kitchen doors, and cook'll attend to you nicely."

Behind the swinging doors Mike found Mabry, the large, rotund black cook, trussing up some small fowl on a worktable. "A bite to eat, mon?" he said in response to the question. "That can be arranged. How big a bite?"

"The minimum. I'm due at the garage, so I'll have to settle for toast and coffee."

"Then leave the toast to me, and if you look closely around the staff hall you will find a sideboard with a coffee maker always ticking away on it."

"Thank you. And where is the staff hall?"

"You have just walked through it, mon. It was the servants hall, but since these are democratic times it is now the staff hall." Mabry wiped his hands on his apron. "That is where you dine. Then you bring your soiled dishes and cutlery here, hose them down at that sink to get the gumbo off, and deposit them in that dishwasher."

"And the dining comes when? Does staff have a schedule for that?"

Mabry removed a couple of slices of bread from a bin and popped them into a toaster. "Breakfast is come when you can.

70

For lunch and dinner, staff gets its turn after family. However, this jim-dandy kitchen is open to staff twenty-four hours a day, manned or unmanned. Hands off that small fridge there, which contains various specialties, but you are free to help yourself to whatever you want from that big one. If you do a bit of your own cookery, just make sure to leave the premises so blindingly clean that no one could guess you had even used them. Chef is a dear old chap, but with delicate nerves. If he detects one little crumb on his floor, he reaches for the carving knife. One crumb, one ear. That's the way he scores it."

"Almost biblical," Mike said. He watched with admiration as Mabry, in a series of balletic movements, flipped the perfectly browned toast onto a plate, slid the plate onto a tray, added knife, coffee spoon, and linen napkin, then handed over the load with a flourish.

"Butter, jam, and necessaries are all next to the coffee maker. I gather Mrs. Lloyd is not yet at table?"

"Eventually," Mike said. "Mind if I ask a question outside the line of duty?"

"If you don't mind that toast getting cold," said Mabry. Mike took note that he looked wary but interested.

"It's about Miss Margaret's previous secretary. The one Mrs. Lloyd's replacing. Was she retired or fired?"

Mabry shook his head. "But there was no previous secretary, mon. Sometimes a female masseur like that Teutonic dreadnought inside, sometimes a maid to particularly fuss over her, sometimes a very highly qualified nurse to get her through the worst of the bad times"—again that shake of the head—"but never any secretary. Mrs. Lloyd is the first. Perhaps, if all goes well, the only."

"Perhaps," Mike said. He felt stirrings of uneasiness. "But bad times? What kind of bad times?"

"Ah, that. Have you been told about that accident on the stairs?"

"Yes."

"Well, after that came the bad times. Morbid times, mon. Like a hurt animal. Doesn't take it out on you, you know, just crawls off into the corner. It was like that when I started

71

here—oh, about four years ago now—and from what I heard it was that way all those years since the accident. Can't blame the woman, can you? Fine-looking, spirited girl—Golightly and Borglund and Wilson knew her that way—and I've heard tales about the young society cockalorums flocking around her. And she had a real talent for being an artist—that's the story—so that even her father went along with her plans for it, and that, mon, was not customary for old-line people like him. All of that, the whole world right in her pretty little hand, and then"—Mabry snapped sausage-thick fingers like a pistol shot—"blackout. Total blackout forever and a day. No man to warm your bed, no child to bring up, no fine pictures to paint. And that toast is cold now. Throw it in that can, I'll make you some fresh."

"No, it's all right," Mike said. "But she didn't seem like that when I saw her. Morbid, I mean. Matter of fact, she seemed in sort of a jokey mood. Not in what she said, just the way she said it. Nothing like morbid."

"You think I'm stretching the truth, mon? Not a bit. Because what you met is our new-model Miss Margaret. Like Lazarus, back from the grave. About a year ago. Reborn."

"Found religion?"

"Not likely, mon." Mabry shrugged broadly. "Those older ones here are not much for religion, especially the born-again style. Give generously, so I hear, to that Presbyterian church down Madison Avenue, but when you chauffeur them to church it will only be for weddings and funerals. If they happen to esteem the wed or dead. No, we all have ideas about why the lady came back to the land of the living, but they're only ideas, mon. There are more things in heaven and earth—you know the line?"

"Yes."

"Then this is one of those things. But whatever the cause, we are one and all grateful for the results. No more zombie under this roof. This is now a lady living the full life. That is why she found herself in need of a secretary."

"I see," said Mike, then was moved to ask, "It doesn't worry you that you are, by Mrs. McEye's way of thinking, telling tales out of school? And to a comparative stranger?"

"But harmless tales, mon. Even morally elevating." Mabry grinned broadly. "Besides, I like your style. Refreshing, mon, after a bellyful of empty-headed Hibernian females, not to mention their empty-headed male counterparts. And that cold and clammy toast should not—"

"It'll do fine," Mike said, backing away as Mabry reached for the tray. "Not enough time anyhow. And I thank you for your many courtesies."

"They come natural to me," Mabry said, straight-faced.

And jest or not, Mike thought as he pushed through the swinging doors, they probably did. A handy chap to get close to, cook Mabry, especially when it came to filling in bits and pieces about the Durie lifestyle. And when they were all filled in? Mike felt a tickling sensation in the midriff, sometimes the signal that literary inspiration was dawning. Dawning to what purpose, however, wasn't clear.

Only Hegnauer remained at the long table now, and she gave him a fishy eye as he filled a coffee cup, spooned marmalade on a piece of toast, covered it with the other, and, defying any local propriety, gulped down this second makeshift breakfast of the day standing there. While at it he took notice that each of those ceiling-high, glass-doored cabinets around the room displayed collections of china and glassware. Risking Hegnauer's disapproval, he pulled open a chest drawer a few inches, and sure enough there was an array of cutlery nested in black velvet. So the staff hall was not just staff's dining room but also family's chinaware and cutlery department. For dinner service tonight, Jeeves, we'll try catalogue number A-100.

With hunger pangs falsely soothed, he brought his service—definitely not catalogue number A-100—back to the kitchen and was about to give it the requisite hosing down when Mabry nudged him aside.

"You're in a big rush, mon, I'll take care of it. And when you eat so fast, you can work up a hurtful stomach even on toast and coffee."

"I thank you, sir," said Mike.

Mabry gave him that grin. "Style," he said. "You see how easily I am victimized by it?"

73

THE garage was a big one, combining a repair shop and a four-story parking setup. Mike found Levine, the kingpin himself, in the street-level office of the parking setup, and Levine, a hard-eyed man with his lips shaped into a permanent little smile of all-knowingness, introduced this newcomer to the almost legendary Wilson. Who, Mike took notice, was obviously not going to let the weight of his years get him down. A skinny little antique, conspicuously false teeth agleam, he was done up in expensive-looking tweeds and lizard shoes like something out of a geriatrics issue of *Esquire*.

"Floyd?" he said to Mike on introduction.

"Lloyd."

"Yeah?" Wilson sounded as if he doubted this. "Who'd you used to drive for?"

"The public," Mike said. "I drove a cab."

Wilson turned unbelieving eyes on Levine. "You hear that? The worst drivers on God's green earth."

"There's all kinds of cabbies," Levine said equably. He shrugged at Mike. "Don't mind him. After fifty-three years on the job he still can't see why they put him out to grass. And too stupid to know how lucky he is. Fat pension, nice rent-free apartment—"

"Three dinky rooms," said Wilson.

"Dummy," said Levine, "those rooms on the East Side here would cost you fifteen hundred a month if you paid rent like other people. Now let's go look at the cars and you tell this man the ground rules. Then you can retire for keeps and open your mouth to somebody else. Get yourself a wife and drive her crazy."

He led the way to the rear of the garage where a small disappointment awaited. There were some impressive items parked there—Caddie and Mercedes stretch limos—and a little apart from them were lined up three custom-built Buick sedans, Park Avenues, two black, one gray, and a station wagon, a black Chrysler Town-and-Country. Quality stuff, Mike thought, smooth-riding, high-powered, but nothing to turn heads as they went by.

Levine read his expression. "Expecting something like those Pullmans?"

"Well—"

"Not with your people. Don't like anybody taking notice. I buy that myself. When you know you've really got it all you don't have to advertise it."

"Yeah," Mike said, "but four cars and one chauffeur?"

"Mrs. McEye'll let you know when you need extra drivers. You give me an hour's notice, I'll fix it up." Levine turned to Wilson who, Mike saw, was regarding the Durie transportation with mournful eyes. It was, in a way, touching. "All right, dummy," said Levine, "tell the man what he has to know."

"Oh, sure." Wilson still came on testy but some of his fire seemed to have been banked. "Fifty-three years worth in five minutes." He said to Mike, "You know the staff hall?"

"Yes."

"McEye puts up a bulletin board next to the coffee machine there every night. Or whoever's on duty in the office. It's got next day's orders. You go by that. Nine-thirty every morning except weekends is getting Mr. Craig and Mr. Walter down to the office on Broad Street. Four o'clock you get them home. All around that you could have heavy days, you could have light days. You work it out and Levine here backs you up."

"So," said Mike, "what with one thing and another, I'm admiral of the fleet."

"And captain of the dawn patrol. That wagon there's for when Golightly, the head cook, goes marketing. You drive him. Early up and early out. What with one thing and another, Floyd, it's a tough job."

"Lloyd."

"Yeah. Because there's a right way and a wrong way for every little thing, and family wants it strictly the right way."

"Like how?"

"Like you always walk around the back of the car when you open the door for people. With the old lady you might think you give her a hand, but you don't unless she asks."

"Miss Margaret."

"Yeah. And you wait right by the car with her until somebody

75

takes over. You never leave the car. You always stay right with it."

"Does she do much driving around?"

"Well," said Wilson, "she never did any all these years, but now she's starting to tool around some. Like to the Plaza Hotel. The doormen there know her; they'll take care of her fine. And a couple of these high-toned art galleries around the neighborhood here."

"Art galleries? Miss Margaret?"

"I know, I know," Wilson said irritably. "But don't you go ask her what the point of it is. Fact is, Floyd, you don't talk to anybody you're driving unless they talk to you first. And whatever you hear them say to each other, you forget it as soon as you hear it. Get the message?"

"Loud and clear," Mike said. "But about those art galleries —"

"Now what the hell! I just told you —"

"Cool it, friend. I'm not asking whys and wherefores. I'm just seeing myself pull up someplace without any doorman, and I'm supposed to stay with the car. Then who do I turn the lady over to? The first kind stranger that passes by?"

Levine hooted, and Wilson glared at him. He said to Mike, "I was just getting to that. Any such place, McEye makes a phone call in advance and they have somebody waiting. If you knew McEye, you'd know they damn well better have. Simple?"

"It's the only way to live," Mike said. Art galleries? he thought.

Wilson cut into this line of thought. "Another thing is about tickets. Parking tickets you just hand to McEye, they're not your worry. But any moving violations are right out of your paycheck. That means any cabbie ideas you got, get rid of them fast. And anybody crowds you on the road, no loudmouth stuff. And you keep your hand off the horn. I'll tell you this much, Floyd. If it was all family chauffeurs on the road, you'd never hear any horn sound off in the whole city. So now you know something about what's expected."

"Any questions?" Levine said to Mike. "This could be your last chance to ask them."

"One," said Mike. "I understand I can use a car for myself sometimes. When is that?"

"Days off," Wilson answered. "And whenever you ain't on duty and there's a car free. Only thing, Floyd, you better handle that machine like glass. You land it in the body shop on your own time, McEye'll take the heart right out of you."

"Like glass," Mike said. "And, come to think of it, who takes over for me on my days off?"

Wilson pointed at Levine. Levine said, "Wednesdays and Sundays off. I've got regulars booked for that. No problem."

"All right?" asked Wilson, then answered himself: "All right. And since I ain't needed any more, good-bye."

"You'll be back," Levine said. "Don't make it sound like forever."

"You'll see," Wilson said and walked out into the street without a backward glance.

Levine shook his head sympathetically. "Fifty-three years," he said. "A long time all right. He even knew the old man himself, old James Hamilton Durie. But he can't say those people weren't good to him. He was washed up at least a couple of years back, and they still lived with it. Getting deaf and forgetful to where they had to kiss him off. With full salary as pension for life and a real class apartment in one of their buildings. But that's the way they are."

"Nice people," Mike said.

"In more ways than one. There's something Wilson didn't bring up, in case you've been wondering."

"Such as?"

"Well," said Levine, "I hope this is no big letdown, but there's no vigorish goes with this job."

"Vigorish?"

"Kickbacks. Payoffs from me to you for your business."

"Suppose I told you, Mr. Levine, that the thought never entered my mind?"

Levine's fixed smile broadened. "It's your mind. Anyhow, that's how we do it here."

"Only for the Duries?"

"That's for me to know and you not to worry about. But definitely for the Duries. And that goes back to when my father opened this place and old Mister James Hamilton Durie was his first customer. Mister Northeast Colonial himself."

"Mr. Northeast Colonial?"

"You didn't know that was the family shop? So now you know. Northeast Colonial. Hell, they own this whole block. And a lot of others all over town. Old man James Hamilton himself met with my father personally and told him if there was ever a whisper of payoff to the chauffeur, he'd have him and the chauffeur out in the street next day. He was quite a character that one."

"Father of the present Craig and Walter, I take it."

"And Margaret. That's right. And they're a lot like the old man some ways. Except not so much Moses on the mountain, the way my father said the old man was. Cast iron. No bend in him at all."

"Glad I'm working for this generation," Mike said.

"That's a fact. Mind my asking how come you are driving for them? There's a lot of chauffeurs in and out of here, and you do not shape up as the usual."

"Came down in the world," Mike said. "Or maybe up. I'm not sure yet."

"Depends where you came from. Corporation desk? They're doing a lot of letting go these days."

"Schoolteaching. Private school. As they say, supply right now exceeds demand."

"Things'll change," Levine commiserated, and it struck Mike how readily those who are making it hand this line to those who are not. "Meanwhile," said Levine, "you're in with good people. Know how to talk to you. Don't put on any fancy show." He motioned with his head at the stretch limos. "A lot of big-money characters are disgusting. That's the only word for it. Disgusting. So you play it smart with your people, you got something good going."

"With no vigorish," Mike said.

"I phony up no bills, I pay no graft, we all sleep better at night. At least I do. Oh, yeah, and another thing for you," Levine said warningly, "prompt is the magic word. They tell you show up at nine minutes after zip, they mean nine minutes after zip. You know that joke about the rich guy, he never worried if there was a chair around, he just started to sit down wherever he

78

wanted, and bingo! there was a chair under him?"

"Cecil B. DeMille, I think," said Mike.

"Whoever. What's your name, by the way? Not the Lloyd part."

"Mike."

"Mike. So all you have to keep in mind, Mike, is any time one of your people wants to sit down in one of those cars it better be right there ready for him. Or her. Which reminds me. You meet any of the younger set? Like Glendon and Camilla?"

"Just to say hello."

"Then you ought to know that Glendon's got a Jag XJ-S parked upstairs—twelve-cylinder monster you have to see to believe—and Camilla's got a Fiat Princess, which is the latest in a whole string of heaps she busted up. And orders are you never drive either of those cars for them, even on request. That's the rule."

"I see. Any special reason for it?"

Levine shrugged. "Could be they don't fit the family image. Could also be they're not on the family account. Strictly personal property, billed personally. Could be both. By the way, you get a good look at that Camilla?"

"Well, medium good."

Levine's smile broadened. "And?"

"I briefly lusted after her in my mind," Mike said. "But my wife happens to be Miss Margaret's secretary, living right there with me. And between you and me, Mr. Levine—"

"Sid."

"Between you and me, Sid, outside those curves my wife rates a lot higher with me than curvy Camilla."

Levine held up a hand in protest. "No offense, Mike."

"None taken," said Mike. "I'll bring her around sometime so you can judge for yourself."

"Anytime," said Levine. "Believe me, after that commercial I can't wait to see the product."

* * *

IT was Mabry who unbolted the service entrance door. "Ah, there, chauffeur Lloyd, ready now for a proper lunch?"

"Not just yet, cook Mabry. If my wife is available, I'd like to renew acquaintance with her first."

"Available she is, mon. A few minutes ago I had a lunch delivered to her at her telephoned request. Breast of chicken on white with mayo, coffee, and a basket of assorted fruit. And several bottles of seltzer water. By any chance does she like to bathe in fizz water?"

"Not usually," Mike said. "Champagne by choice."

"I believe that. She speaks in sweet and gentle tones that make it plausible. And obviously she is home to you now."

"If I wanted a lunch sent up to me —?"

Mabry shook his head ever so slightly. "A problem arises. Mrs. Mac's instructions specify only your lady for room service. You see, she is administration. Such as you and I are not."

"But since she and I share an apartment —"

"So you do. But your tray-bearer knows that Mrs. Lloyd has already been served, so this portion must be yours. Mrs. Mac would soon be told that staff is grossly overworked by having to fetch viands to the chauffeur."

Mike resigned himself to this quaint logic. "Well," he said equally, "considering the dimensions of the old homestead, staff may have a case."

Mabry looked scornful. "Mon, you think our Hibernians and housemen do the cleaning up here? Not when we have an army of experts attend to it every other Friday. Excluding, of course, staff's personal rooms."

"Of course. An agency?"

"You came here by way of an agency called Domestique?"

"Yes."

"Because that is the filter through which we all flow. It also operates Domestique Plus. Very efficient. Ready to take on Buckingham Palace if requested to. So where does that leave the Hibernians and housemen? None of them, mon, with blisters on their hands. Or working up a sweat at their cruel labors. I am the one with the blisters and the sweat to show."

"I can appreciate that," Mike said, trying for just the right note of sympathy.

"Yes, you and your lady would, because" — Mabry tapped his head — "there are brains working there. Not the usual donkey's view of the world. Refreshing to meet here, mon, I can tell you. As for your lunch, if you care to carry your own along with you —"

"Thank you, but, no, I'll be down later."

"And if I'm not here, you know the procedure." Mabry indicated the kitchen with a gracious sweep of the arm. "Eat, drink, be merry, and leave no crumbs."

Mike found his lady standing in the middle of their sitting room studying empty wall shelves, half a chicken sandwich in each hand. A couple of the suitcases had been unpacked and lay open and empty. The typewriter was already on the desk, what there was of the novel in progress and the notes for its completion planted beside it. Sort of a nudge in the ribs from the concerned wife, Mike thought, that beckoning typewriter.

When he embraced her she held her arms wide to keep mayonnaise from marring his good suit, and after swapping a couple of chicken-flavored kisses she asked, "All done with the garage?"

"How'd you know I was there?"

"When I got back here I called the McEye about where you were. And when I asked how you get anything to eat here she told me to call Mabry. And he told me you only had a piece of cold toast on your way out to the garage." She thrust half a sandwich at him. "Here. And there's coffee in that pitcher."

He bit into the sandwich while pouring the coffee. The chicken breast was perfection. Melted in the mouth. He asked, "How do you stand with your schedule now?"

"Fine. The McEye said we're both free for the rest of the day."

"Free! Free! Oh, Lord!"

"Clown," Amy said. She pointed at the wall. "But look at those shelves. We could have brought the TV and stereo and some books along with us instead of packing them away at the farm. Now —"

"No problem." Mike looked at his watch. "There's the family station wagon on standby, and if we get moving now we can be up to the farm and back well before Cinderella time."

"No, we can't. I already called to make sure Abe got the van back"—the van had been rented on the Silverstone credit card and had, after the trip from the farm, been parked on Thompson Street so Abe could return it to the agency—"and he said he and Audie'll be waiting for us. He said he did some scouting through the NYU stacks yesterday and he's come up with stuff about the Duries that might interest us."

Mike tried to put aside the vision of that big wagon and the inviting open road. "Want to leave the unpacking and head for Abe and Audie right now?"

"Nope."

"Funny, funny woman." Mike hefted a couple of suitcases. "I'll lay these out on the bed and we'll work from there. Meanwhile, let's hear about Margaret Durie. I've been wondering."

Amy followed him with the duffle bag. "I like her." She sounded defiant.

"All to the good. What makes her so likable?"

"I didn't say she was, I just said I liked her. I'm not even sure why. She comes on unbelievably arrogant and condescending and sharp-tongued. And for a minute she had me scared out of my wits. She sat me down and traced my features with her fingertips. She said that way she could get a vivid picture of me in her mind."

"And that scared you out of your wits?"

"No, but right afterward she had some kind of attack. Glassy-eyed, hyperventilating, the whole thing. Looked like a stroke. Then when I showed natural concern she came right out of it and really landed on me. Let me know my concern wasn't wanted, thank you."

"So naturally you like her."

"I know. But something funny happened. I talked back. And she didn't seem to mind."

"Maybe the novelty of it got to her," Mike said thoughtfully. "Probably nobody's dared talk back to her for the last fifty years. Spoiled rotten since then. By the way, did you know you're dealing with the new-model Miss Margaret? Apparently lived most of her life since the accident in morbid retirement. Then about a year ago magically snapped out of it. Which dresser is mine?"

"That one," Amy said. "Your clean shirts are already in it. And what do you mean, snapped out of it?"

"Oh, took a passionate new interest in life. Hired a personal secretary for the first time. Because you are indeed the very first."

"I am?"

"Yep. And people who hire secretaries usually do it because they're making contact with the world out there. Also, Ma'am now comes and goes. Like, to the Plaza. And to art galleries."

"Well, art galleries," Amy said, then did a double take. "What would she be doing in art galleries?"

"A good question."

"Of course," Amy said reflectively, "she is obsessed with painting. Still has dreams of what might have been if—"

"A sad if, baby."

"But still she might go to galleries just for the atmosphere. Even if she can't actually see anything."

"Awfully masochistic, isn't that? Oh, well." Mike carried the flight bag with the family toiletries into the bathroom, where the refrigerator caught his eye. He opened its door and saw the bottles of seltzer and the assorted fruit. He said from the doorway, "Another good question is why all the soda water? Mabry asked if you bathed in it."

"For his information," said Amy, "and yours, I can't see the maids making deliveries up here one bottle at a time."

"They're supposed to do that for you. After all, dear, you are administration. As Mabry and I are not."

"I don't like the way you put that, Mike."

"It's a fact of life. There is a well-defined pecking order here. First requirement for happiness is to know your place in it. Otherwise confusion sets in."

"Right now," Amy said, "more than confusion. You're making me very unhappy."

"Hell, baby, you know better than that."

"No. Whenever you make me feel this way you mean to, whether you know it or not. And I'm insecure enough without that."

"About what?" Mike asked, honestly concerned.

"Plenty. Like, if I'm an administrator, why is my first job tomorrow to fetch Ma'am her breakfast?"

"Does that bruise your pride?"

"Well, I tell myself it shouldn't with the kind of money I'm getting. But there's more than that. I have the feeling there's some very edgy interplay among these people when it comes to Ma'am."

"True," said Mike.

"And there's that attack or whatever she had. Nobody even mentioned she's subject to that kind of thing. I'm not sure anybody even knows about it. But the one thing she demanded was that no notice be taken of it. Absolute confidentiality prevails. So where I probably should at least tell McEye about it I just don't have the nerve."

"Understandable."

"Yes," said Amy, "but what do you advise? Seriously."

"Seriously. Well, you know the players now but not the play. Wait it out. Eyes and ears open, mouth shut. If real disaster impends, yell like hell. You can't be fired for that."

"Maybe not. But how do I know if it's real disaster?"

"You'll know. And remember I'm standing by. As the sage Mrs. Bernius remarked, couples in service have one thing going for them, they have each other to confide in. As a matter of fact—"

"Yes?"

Mike waved a dismissive hand. "No, not yet. Later on when I get my thoughts about it unscrambled."

"Now you've got me curious."

"I've got myself curious. And wheed up. But I don't want to talk about it just yet."

Amy apparently recognized the symptoms. "Something to do with your writing?"

"Yes. But not now. Right now what my case calls for is a couple of stiff drinks. The kind Abe and Audie'll have waiting.

Look, there's no law says we can't go over there now and finish packing later, is there?"

"No, I suppose not. But early home. I have to be up at seven."

"No problem. And on the way out I have something to show you. Caverns measureless to man."

"Xanadu?"

"The basement here. And I'll bet Sam Coleridge never knew it."

SEEN objectively, as Mike had once explained, his friendship with Abe Silverstone was solidly built on the dislikes they shared. Conversation Boston-style about what you like can be dull. Conversation New York-style about what you detest—politically, economically, socially, or the management of the Yankees—never loses its edge. It was what Damon and Pythias must have shared.

"Sounds bilious," Amy had objected, "and neither of you is of bilious disposition."

"Yes we are. In partnership."

But it was her theory that Abe and Audrey, now married for twenty-eight years and childless, had simply seized on the Lloyds as surrogate offspring. Certainly they were parental in their concern for their downstairs neighbors in the Thompson Street roost. And certainly they were almost embarrassingly generous in gift giving—good givers, awkward receivers—and especially when the Lloyds hit bottom, out of work, out of money, out of expectations, the upstairs neighbors made it plain that they were always ready with the trusty checkbook. Definitely parental,

Mike had to admit, although that didn't make the taking any easier.

When it came to this touchy issue, however, Amy steadfastly argued that for one thing repayment would eventually be made, and for the other thing, well, since Abe and Audrey were backing a writer who would one day make them proud they lent a helping hand when needed, they couldn't find a better investment for some of the overflow from their already overflowing cup. Consider Sylvia Beach.

"Sylvia Beach?" Mike said.

"You know. That bookstore woman in Paris who practically supported James Joyce. Who'd even remember her now if it wasn't for him?"

Mike addressed the ceiling: "My poor wife. Driven mad by privation she now dreams she is wed to James Joyce. Not even Hemingway or Norman Mailer, Lord. Joyce, no less."

"I'm serious, Mike. Abe thinks you are one hell of a writer."

"On the basis of one published story and one unpublished novel. And various incomplete odds and ends."

"Well, if you wrote more, he'd have even more basis. But you know he means what he says. He does not conceal his feelings about things that matter to him. Like writing."

True, Mike thought. And like the wedding. Of course, the Silverstones had been invited; Mike had seen them as the back-up team he needed in Boston; it had come as a jolt when Abe announced, in no wise apologetically, that he had no intention of spending a day in Boston in the company of middle America. What he recommended in this case was an elopement such as he and Audrey had wisely arranged for themselves way back when. A clerk at City Hall, a couple of strays picked up as witnesses, and a twenty-four-hour celebration party afterward. Which, said Abe, the Silverstones would be glad to provide.

So he and Audrey had not attended the Lloyd wedding, but a week later did provide a celebration party that in the end seemed to involve most of the Village and large segments of Chelsea and SoHo.

Easy to forgive people like that.

And, as Mike reflected after that James Joyce passage, his wife

86

was certainly right in one regard. Abe and Audrey did have the Midas touch. Not only had Abe been doing all right as an NYU economics professor — at least by the Lloyd standards — but he had then produced that economics text for the layman, a book about America's future so wild-eyed pessimistic that it was calculated to send any reader right up the wall. *The End of the Dream.* Which had, after a slumbrous period, become a thundering best-seller, six months on the list, fantastic paperback sale, invitations to address panicky audiences from coast to coast at top dollar.

"And the moral of it is, kiddies," Abe had pronounced, "pessimism pays."

Amy was troubled. "The way you say that — but don't you believe what you wrote? That the country is economically living on the slopes of a Vesuvius?"

"Sure."

"I don't see — Well, close up you don't come on terribly worried about it."

"Look, darling. The sun will probably be extinguished in five million years. If my life expectancy was ten million years, I'd worry about that. Since it isn't, I don't."

"But Mike and I might be around. I mean, for that Vesuvius eruption you're predicting."

"Well, I won't be. So all I can do is wish the best to you dear people."

That was soon before Vesuvius, in the form of George Oliphant, headmaster of Scoville-Lang, had erupted all over Mike and then caught Amy in the lava flow, after which Abe had done a lot more than just wish them the best.

As for Audrey Custer Silverstone, she had retired from a long-term job as a Macy's women's-wear buyer to housewifery, but after a spell of boredom had risked some of Abe's best-seller bounty on Custer's First Stand, a boutique on West Eighth where, she announced, she'd stay exactly twenty-four hours ahead of any prevailing fashion. In this she had struck oil, Custer's First Stand now being *the* boutique in the West Village and drawing a heavy trade of heavy spenders from uptown who were apparently mesmerized not only by the trendy stock but even more by the most chilling saleswomen in captivity. Sure they are, Audrey had placidly acknowledged. Let the customers feel you're doing them a favor and they eagerly pay for the favor.

"At least tell me," Mike pleaded, "that you lose a large number of customers that way."

"Only a few terribly secure ones," Audrey answered. "You'd be surprised how few there are."

Come to think of it, Mike reflected, having found a parking space for the wagon a couple of blocks away from Thompson Street and now following Amy up the three flights to the Midases' duplex nest, could any of the Durie women be ranked among that terribly secure few? Ma'am? Hard-jawed Jocelyn? Curvy, poisonous Camilla? Slugabed, darkling Dorothy? Moon-faced, meditative Gwen?

Hell, cross any one of them and walk out of the room with your head tucked underneath your arm.

Poor Amy.

On the fourth-floor landing, before she could knock on the Silverstones' door, Mike took her in tight embrace and engaged her in a lingering kiss.

"Very nice," she said at last. "Any special reason?"

"A whole complex set of them. They all add up to one four-letter word."

"Now? Here?"

"The word happens to be love, not the one you think. As much agape as eros."

"In exactly that proportion?"

"Don't nitpick," said Mike. "Just knock on that door three times. Not twice. We're not on duty here."

It was Abe who answered the knock, luxuriantly gray-bearded and with shaven pate gleaming. He drew them into the room, where at the wet bar Audrey, the perfect hostess, was already pouring bourbon into a tall glass. Success had not physically reshaped Abe, who remained wiry lean, but Audrey, who had struggled during her Macy's years to maintain a size seven, was now plainly heading toward a size fourteen.

For Mike the bourbon properly watered. For Amy a Perrier. "Horse doves," Abe explained as Audrey headed for the kitchen.

"The cold kind because we didn't know when you'd show up. But non-Japanese." He had the same shuddering distaste for Japanese cuisine that Mike did. "Now sit, sit, and wet your whistles. You've got some talking to do about life with the highly."

"First I have to settle something with Audie," Amy said, and as soon as Audrey reappeared with the tray of hors d'oeuvres Amy said to her, "Clothes."

"Clothes," Audrey echoed through a full mouth.

"Yes. I'm all wrong now. It has to be pastel dresses, no patterns. Or white waists, dark skirts. All hemlines at least knee-length. I'm supposed to look subdued."

"Sounds to me," Abe commented, "that whoever laid down those rules is more concerned with keeping the gentlemen of the household subdued."

Mike had a fleeting glimpse of hard-jawed Jocelyn Durie at her writing desk, eyes narrowed in contemplation of the new secretary. *"Touché,"* he said.

Audrey was now looking Amy over with professional interest. "When are you free tomorrow, doll?"

"Not in the morning. Later on sometime."

"You phone me at the shop when you are, and I'll meet you at this wholesale place on Thirty-fifth. Off-the-rack but quality. And they'll do any fitting while we wait. No problem."

"Except for the money."

"A housewarming gift," said Abe.

"Oh, no. A short-term loan."

"Now look, darling—"

"Abe," Audrey said, and Abe took the warning.

"You know," Amy said, "we do love both of you for your generosity. We'll love you just as much after we repay everything. Even more. You realize that a debtor always has a shadow over him."

"What I realize," said Abe, "is that I love to hear you talk. Say something else in Victorian."

"Abe," Audrey said mechanically. She dropped down beside him on the couch and planted her legs on the coffee table. "What I want to hear," she told her guests, "is the uptown story. What there is of it so far."

89

It was Mike who told the uptown story, and it was a long time—two more drinks, two trays of hors d'oeuvres—in the telling. When it was all told Abe said, "Protocol. Confidentiality. Sounds like you're working for the State Department. Incidentally, aren't you already violating confidentiality by giving us these domestic details? Harmless as they are?"

"Seriously," Mike said, "I wouldn't expect either of you to use them as table talk anywhere." Charged up as he was by his own narrative, he was a little disappointed in the flat response to it. "Anyhow," he said, "don't you think all those details add up to something a touch Byzantine?"

Abe nodded. "A touch. With that housekeeper lady the head Byzant. Quite a woman though. America can put a man into space but can it get anyone in to clean the house properly, including windows? Hardly. But your Mrs. McEye can. How do you two feel about being her genies?"

"Tired and confused," Amy said.

"Interested," Mike said.

"In the way she plays her role?" Abe asked.

Mike shrugged. "In everything about the place so far. Actually, I think it's mostly that family. They're real people, Abe. Human beings."

Abe feigned great astonishment. "No!"

"All right. Obviously they are. But today, after the introductions and with all those heavy warnings about confidentiality, it suddenly struck me that I had been plunked down backstage at a marvelous show. Real flesh and blood people insulated by millions of dollars against the world outside and all the more driven to an intense interplay among each other. Very human people when you see them with their hair down. Chekhovian almost."

This was sneaky in a way, Mike knew, because when you mentioned Chekhov to Abe he melted. He sat forward. "The Duries as literary material?"

"Yep."

Amy, the day having caught up to her, had been struggling to keep her eyes open. Now she opened them wide and said accusingly, "Is that what you had in mind to tell me sooner or later? About using the Duries in a book?"

"Yep."

"But you're already halfway through the book about George Oliphant and the school." She looked really distressed.

"I know. But I seem to have cooled off on that. Look, baby, I started writing that as our vengeance against George. What I found out lately is that vengeance isn't the kind of fuel I can operate on. The bile is all thinned out."

"Two years of work," Amy said mournfully.

"And," Abe said, "all of one day on this new job. What novel do you see emerging from the one day?"

"It'll be a lot more than that, Abe, before I start the actual writing. First comes a close study of these people until they become understandable. Three dimensional. A great big fat daily journal on them."

"Meanwhile, sonny, keep that journal locked up tight. One hint to them that they might wind up as characters in their chauffeur's novel—say, they don't know you're an aspiring author, do they? You didn't put that into any resumé?"

"Nope. Glum I sometimes am. Suicidal never."

"At least," said Abe, "until publication time. After which, if your text is closely drawn from identifiable sources, you could wind up facing a big fat libel suit."

"I doubt it," Mike said. "Murder maybe, suits for libel never. Not the way the Duries see it. They're acutely publicity shy."

"Indeed?" said Abe. "Then listen closely, because I did a mite of research on them yesterday and came up with something pertinent. In 1920, a James Hamilton Durie—he'd be papa of the present brood—put aside fears of publicity to defend the family honor. Seems his wife was deeply involved in some churchly good works. And the lady she had ousted from the good works committee—its previous chairperson—proclaimed loudly and recklessly that if the dominie of the church wasn't so young and attractive, Mrs. Durie wouldn't be so committed to Christian charity. James Hamilton then sued for slander, risking all that nasty publicity, and won hands down. Fifty thousand old-fashioned American bucks. Quite a pile then. Mrs. Durie, the family's honor restored, then contributed the money to the good work. Interesting?"

91

"In the light of the book Mike plans," said Amy, "oh, yes."

"Baby," Mike protested, "by the time there is publication we'll be independently wealthy. If there is publication. Remember that nest egg we'll be hatching? But if you want me to give up all ideas of doing this book—"

"No," said Amy. "And don't use that tactic on me."

"Talking about wealthy," said Audrey, the peacemaker, "I wonder what that Mrs. McEye must have accumulated by now."

"Awesome thought," said Abe, "but she'll never catch up to the family. You know, Michael, you've been referring to their millions. But from what I picked up in my research yesterday, you'll have to think bigger. Try billions."

"Billions?" Mike said. "Fact, not fancy? Nine zeros?"

"Nine. Now keep them in mind while we turn time backward. We focus on the Duries, prosperous colonials. They buy land, then lease out what they buy. Got it?"

"Got it," said Mike.

"Stay with it. Before the Revolution they owned big chunks of lower Manhattan. After the war, when land held by the Tories was confiscated and put up for auction, the Duries were usually right there with the winning bids. Cash flow required in those early days was provided by a family they united with in marriage. The Cheathams. Rum distillers. Their distillery was on ground leased from the Duries. Marriage was inevitable."

"How romantic," said Audrey.

Abe gave her a look. "Anyhow," he said, "that accumulating disposition—it seems to have been in the blood—went on generation after generation. Last year when *Forbes* magazine published a study of America's wealthiest, there in the top percentile was the Durie family. Estimated net worth? Three billion. Source of wealth? As with the inevitable Getty and Rockefeller, inherited. Certainly your new bosses are the good stewards."

"Nine zeros," Mike said.

"But why do they keep piling it up?" Amy asked. "I think that when you've got more wealth than you could ever dream of spending—"

"Because," Mike said, "it's not the spending that's fun, it's the getting. And highly moral. Calvinist morality."

92

Amy looked doubtful. "I didn't hear of any of them going to church this morning."

"Because the Lord has already given them the nod." Mike turned to Abe. "Anything about their Northeast Colonial company in those records?"

Abe raised his brows. "Without going into any records I can answer that one. A very conservative brokerage house, more investment slanted than speculative. In the shadows behind it is a network of agencies devoted to land development. No soil as fertile as what they till, is there?"

"Probably not," said Mike. "Now, aside from the name Durie there's that other name I dropped along the way. Langfeld. Gwendolyn's faraway husband. Somehow it seems familiar. Does it ring any bell for you? Daniel Langfeld?"

"Oh, yeah," said Abe. "Haven't you ever noticed how many of our educational TV shows are brought to you courtesy of the Daniel and Francine Langfeld Fund?"

"Hell," Mike said, "of course. That's why the name was familiar. But Daniel and Francine? Not Gwendolyn?"

"Daniel senior," Amy pointed out. "It has to be. And Gwen's husband is junior."

"Sounds like it," Abe said. "No billions, the Langfelds, but nevertheless formidable."

"Jewish?" said Mike.

"When they emigrated here from Germany around the Civil War, yes. Converted long ago. Why? You got a whiff of anti-Semitism up there in Durieville?"

"The merest," Mike said. "By way of Mrs. McEye who wanted it known that the Langfelds are distinctly not Jewish. And that Gwen's separation from Daniel is all good clean nonscandalous fun."

"Although," Amy said, "why there should be any family reaction to any religion when Gwen comes on like a Hare Krishna—"

"You see?" Mike said to her. "You're catching it too. Questions, questions, intriguing questions."

"Uh-huh. And what I'm to do is go around and help dig up answers, answers, intriguing answers."

"Yep. If you can stay awake along the way. Right now, if you let your eyes close completely I'll lead you to the bedroom where you'll take a necessary nap."

Amy closed her eyes. "I can stay right here and listen."

Audrey stood up. "The guest room," she said. "The bedroom's a mess. Come along, honey."

"I am really not that sleepy," Amy said as Audrey nudged her through the door.

She rejoined the party two hours later looking, Mike saw, much more her fresh-faced self. On the way downstairs for a paella orgy at Julio's Restaurant around the corner, when they passed the door of the old apartment Abe, the irrepressible, asked, "Miss the old homestead?"

"Abe," said Audrey.

"Just curious, dear."

"It's all right," said Amy, "because I really don't feel any pangs about it."

"No streak of sentimentality at all?" Abe said.

"No," said Amy. "Almost none at all."

"Live and learn," said Abe.

THE party adjourned at ten o'clock, but early as this seemed to be, only a pallid night-light showed through the curtains of the kitchen door at the foot of the service entrance. Mike rang the bell, and the man who eventually opened the door wore a shoulder holster, gun butt displayed, over a T-shirt. "You're Lloyd?" he said. "And Mrs. Lloyd? Right?"

"Yep," said Mike.

"I'm Krebs. Security. I have to ask for ID first time out, you understand." He looked over the driver's license Mike proffered and handed it back. "You ought to get a change of address on that," he said as he bolted and chained the door behind the new help. "You folks know your way upstairs? Straight up, no sight-seeing."

"We've been told," Amy said.

"Figures. Oh, yeah, and Mrs. Mac said to make sure you check the board before you turn in."

"I know where it is," Mike said. "Staff hall."

"Right. See you around, folks," said Krebs, and moved off, friendly as a guard dog to its keepers.

The staff hall was in darkness. Mike located the switch inside the doorway and under the light the large cork-faced triptych on the coffee table looked grotesquely out of place. Too businesslike somehow. Slips of paper were pinned to each panel here and there.

"Alphabetical order," Amy reported, squinting closely at them. "And models of brevity. Here's you. And me."

Mike peered over her shoulder. The slip of paper headed *Lloyd* read *9 A.M.: Hale & Hale, clothiers.* The one headed *Mrs. Lloyd* read *8 A.M.: Miss Margaret D.* When Amy pulled the papers free of the pushpins he said, "Sabotage?"

"No, this had to be what you do with them to show you've seen them. There's only a few left. Those could be staff who haven't checked in yet."

"Or out," Mike said. "Here's O'Dowd. Off duty, it says. Same for Mabry. Which leaves us short one cook tomorrow. Maybe Bernius drops in from Domestique Plus to whip up breakfast and lunch."

"Domestique Plus?"

"Oh, I forgot to tell you. It's an adjunct service that provides total housecleaning here every other week. I bet you've been wondering how the folks could get along with only sixteen live-in help. That's the answer. I got it from Mabry. You know, he might be a veritable mine of information."

"Like me," said Amy.

"Hey, baby, are you heating up again about my little reve-lation? About this place as a book?"

"These people, don't you mean?"

"Naturally."

Amy took her time working it out. "I don't know," she said at last. "One way I'm all for it. I can see what a milieu like this offers a writer. For that matter, I can even see the pleasure in a literary sense of vivisecting somebody like that Camilla."

"Pretty little thing though," Mike couldn't resist saying.

"I'm serious," Amy said.

"Well," Mike said, "I suppose I'm trying to fend off what I suspect is coming. Miss Margaret is pitiable. You like her. You don't want to be two-faced with her."

"I suppose not."

"But what makes you think she won't have a sympathetic role? A beautiful and talented girl of eighteen tragically blinded, spending the next fifty years in morbid and self-isolated darkness, now suddenly determined to make the rest of her life worth living. And that's the way it really is, mind you. It's not soap opera."

"Even so, Mike. When I told you she's also an arrogant, sharp-tongued bully I saw how you reacted. Not that I didn't somehow like it. I mean the feeling that if anyone comes down on me you're ready to commit mayhem. But in this case it could be literary mayhem where I'm an accomplice. After all, you do have a way of—who said it?—writing with a quill dipped in venom. Not that it isn't fine writing."

"Waldo Lydecker. Out of *Laura,* by Vera Caspary."

"Oh? I thought it was somebody more eighteenth century."

"Twentieth. But Lydecker was eighteenth in spirit all right. Matter of fact, I think he said goose quill. But your mistake was natural. Because, dear Amy, we ourselves are right back in the eighteenth century now, aren't we? While out there beyond these walls ghostly Duries and Cheathams are buying land and distilling rum and waiting for a War of Independence that will—"

"Mike, you are somehow changing the subject."

"Well, it is a pretty unlikely subject, isn't it? Almost as unlikely as our situation. That coffee machine is winking at us, by the way. Want a cup of coffee while we hash out the subject?"

"No. I should have realized that with all you had to drink—"

"After all, dear, I have to drink for two. If you'd reform your Puritan ways—"

"—that you're high and getting steadily higher. You will now catch up on your sleep, Michael, while I finish unpacking and laundry sorting. And I have to be up before seven to bring Ma'am her breakfast."

"An hour's allowance?" Mike said.

"I know, but I have the feeling that if I'm one minute late—"

"God help you," Mike said. "A flogging in the public square at the very least."

"There you go again," said Amy.

*   *   *

PART TWO

Ma'am

MIKE never stirred when the alarm went off at seven, and when she tiptoed out of the room he was still sound asleep. There were no signs of life along the corridor on the way to East Hall elevator, but at the junction near the elevator could be heard the rhythmic grumble of hard rock from one of the maid's rooms. O'Dowd's kind of music, Amy surmised, certainly not the prim Nugent's. But of course there were a couple of still unseen housemaids on the premises. For that matter, and a little spookily, nobody was to be seen along the whole route to the staff hall by way of the basement. The explanation came when she pushed open the door to the staff hall and found quite a company gathered around the table dining in style. There was a buffet breakfast on a sideboard and, instead of last night's bulletin board, on the coffee table were now a toaster and basket of sliced bread. The most welcome sight, however, was the cheery face of Nugent.

It was Nugent who made the introductions. Walsh and Plunkett were obviously from their uniforms the hitherto unmet housemaids, met at last. Both were fresh-faced colleens who could have passed for a buxom sixteen but were more likely just closing out their teens. Borglund, custodian, looked as ancient and forbidding as the Old Man of the Mountain; Swanson, assistant custodian, was a middle-aged version of Borglund. Peters and Brooks, housemen, were neat, trim, and fortyish in vest and black bowtie, and yes, Amy recalled, that had to be the Peters recruited yesterday for Gwen Langfeld's meditation circle. And finally there was Krebs, security, the one who had let her and Mike in last night, and among this silent, unresponsive company, thank God at least for his nod of recognition. The others couldn't exactly be called unfriendly, but they certainly weren't warm and welcoming. Not surprising really, Amy assured herself, because for better or worse she rated administration, whatever that meant, and on early acquaintance they'd naturally regard administration with a wary eye.

Not that Nugent mentioned administration during introductions. But what she did say certainly took care of that. *Mrs. Lloyd.* The formal touch, the protocol at work. *And this is*

101

Mrs. Lloyd. Ridiculous, this medieval codifying of the pecking order. And yet—and yet—just the least bit gratifying. Enter this strange new school, and because you bear the imprimatur of your wedded title you start right off as blackboard monitor.

Confide that to Mike and see what he makes of it.

Nugent solicitously followed the new hand into the kitchen. "Breakfast, ma'am? There's almost everything you'd be wanting in those hot plates out there."

"Thank you, but I'm supposed to bring Miss Margaret her breakfast. Mine can wait."

Nugent glanced at the wall clock. "Right now, ma'am, she'll be getting her exercises from Hegnauer, and then there's the bath and the settling down and all. You'd best have your own breakfast while you can."

"You're very kind, Nugent."

Nugent turned pink. "Well, it does take a bit of time to learn the way around. So all you do right now is help yourself to breakfast out there and then put the dishes into that washer. I'll attend to the washer."

It was, Amy found, not the most convivial kind of breakfasting. She had the feeling that before her appearance the gathering must have been sharing some conversation. Now whatever of it there had been was restricted to an occasional whispered remark, a nod, a shrug. It was a growing relief when one by one the staff departed, the youthful maids trundling along carts with covered dishes, and finally only Nugent was left.

Amy said to her worriedly, "About preparing Miss Margaret's breakfast. If Mabry is off duty today—"

"Yes, ma'am. But when he's off I do breakfast and lunch."

"Isn't there another cook? Golightly?"

"Chef, ma'am. Only does dinners and special lunches. He's blue ribbon."

"That's very impressive."

Nugent appeared to be evaluating this and, for that matter, evaluating Mrs. Lloyd. Then, after glancing around the empty room, she leaned forward to offer her judgment in confidence. "I'll tell you, ma'am, him being that, and serving here from the time Miss Margaret and the gentlemen were young people, well, it does make him hard to get along with. You don't mind me saying so?"

"Not a bit. He doesn't make things hard for you, does he? You really are so efficient and helpful."

Nugent turned pink again. "Thank you, ma'am. But he is a prejudiced one, forgive me for saying so. Does not take to the Irish at all. For all he's a blackie he's old-fashioned Jamaica-British, and he does see everything the British way."

"Oh. And you and the maids are all Irish."

"Of course, ma'am." Nugent seemed surprised. "Couldn't very well pass for anything else, could we?"

Not very likely, Amy thought, feeling a little foolish. "What I meant," she amended, "is that it's not altogether coincidence."

"Oh, no, ma'am. Mrs. McEye didn't much like the kind of maids starting to show up from the agency—blackies and Spanish, you see—so that Mrs. Bernius at the agency made this arrangement with the Dependents' Society in Belfast. Girls whose fathers were killed in the trouble there could be brought to the States for training in good houses. And have part of their wages sent back home."

"And that happened to you?" Amy said. "Your father was killed?"

"Oh, yes, ma'am. Done in by the Orangemen. Same for the others, except I was the first here and I chose to stay on, while the others so far keep coming and going. Get a bit homesick, I daresay, much as they like it here in the States. But all of them are in training really, and that's what Golightly won't allow for. He's so long in the tooth he's a bit dotty at times. And Mabry's no help either with his nasty talk about Hibernians."

"That's really too bad," Amy said. Which, she realized was a pallid way of communicating the depression she suddenly felt.

"Yes, ma'am. Like the priest put it when my father was laid away, we must believe God created the Orangemen but we will never understand why." Nugent looked alarmed. "Ma'am—Mrs. Lloyd—if you don't see the politics of it that way—"

Mrs. Lloyd? Oh, the name, Amy thought, the name. "Lloyd's

103

my husband's name," she said. "Welsh. A long time ago. Not British."

Nugent looked relieved. "A very good people, the Welsh. And it is getting on time for Miss Margaret's tray, isn't it? Brioche and coffee is no matter at all. I'll fix it up."

"Oh, please. I can do it myself."

"My pleasure, ma'am. You don't mind me saying it, it's good to have you here."

"I don't mind in the least, Nugent. In fact, I need it."

"I had a feeling you did, ma'am. Now all you do is fetch Miss Margaret's service in here, and I'll make everything ready. It's the Spode for her."

"The Spode. Nugent, I'm not sure I'd know Spode from Tupperware."

Nugent giggled. "You do have a way of putting things, ma'am. The Spode's in that third cabinet down the line there. Cup, saucer, small plate, very small plate for butter. Cutlery's in the first big drawer below, and napkins are bottom drawer."

"Spode," Amy said with apprehension. "What happens if I break one?"

"Well, ma'am, I can't say there's rejoicing over it, but they do break. Just tell Mrs. McEye about it frank and open, and she'll make a bit of fuss and hope it won't happen again. But most likely it will."

"You have a way of putting things yourself, Nugent," said Amy.

*   *   *

THERE had to be, she discovered, some trick to turning doorknobs while gripping that damn tray with both hands and with the morning's *Times* — the blessed Nugent had remembered it at the last moment — under an arm. This discovery came at the end of the basement corridor — Xanadu — when after passing Borglund and Swanson leaning over something on the worktable in their screened-in shop she came up against the door to the foyer of the East Hall elevator. The door of the staff hall had offered no problems; it was just a case of shoving it open with a hip. This one, however, was a real stinker. A shove of the hip didn't move it, and an attempt to grasp the knob while juggling the tray with a few hundred dollars worth of fragile china on it made everything on the tray shift alarmingly.

The realization struck Amy that she should never have tucked away that full breakfast herself, what with the way her stomach now seemed bent on rejecting it.

"Hell and damnation," she said to the door.

A response came from the workshop. "Yah?" said the ancient Borglund.

Amy carefully made a half turn and saw that he and Swanson were regarding her with puzzlement.

"I'm stuck," Amy told them. "I can't open the door."

"Just turn the knob," Borglund said. It came out *yoost toorn.* "It works good."

"Yes, but while I'm holding this tray?"

A flicker of amusement passed over those otherwise stolid Scandinavian faces. Then Swanson came forward. He removed the tray from Amy's deathlike grip, pivoted her hand palm up, and planted the tray on her outspread fingers. "Like this, lady."

"With one hand?"

"Sure. You think they do like this in the restaurant for fun? Easier this way."

And, in fact, it was easier, even if more terrifying. Holding her breath, Amy turned the doorknob and pushed open the door. "I do thank you."

"You're welcome — Mrs. Lord?"

"Lloyd."

"Any time, Mrs. Lloyd."

After that, there was no trouble dealing with the elevator, and so pleasing was the image of one-handed authority presented Amy by her reflection in the glass wall along East Hall that she passed right by The Door and had to reverse course to get back to it. She knocked twice according to prescription and what was surely the burly Hegnauer's deep growl commanded, "Come in, come in."

Amy came in. The sitting room was empty, and with its drapes wide open everything in it was tinted gold by the morning sunlight. Hegnauer stood in the open door to the right motioning for more speed, please. Amy walked by her, tray held daringly high, and here was a spacious Art Deco bedroom also golden with sunlight. Ma'am, in negligee, was propped up against several pillows in the bed. And, Amy took note, not yet made up. Even more strikingly beautiful without those bisque-doll dabs of rouge on her cheeks and the blood-red lipstick. Amy also took note that Hegnauer was silently mouthing something at her. She suddenly realized that what those writhing lips were communicating was *Good-morning. Good-morning.*

Of course, she thought, the protocol. Apparently the servant supplied the ice-breaking hello on arrival. She cleared her throat. "Good-morning, Miss Durie."

"It seems to be, Lloyd. Place the tray here. You may go, Hegnauer."

Hegnauer did not go. From that look in her eye, Amy thought, she's waiting for me to make a mess of this waitress act. Knock over the coffeepot, drop the newspaper, and faint away. The hell with her. Amy lowered the legs of the tray and set it on the silvery quilted counterpane over Ma'am's knees, then wondered what to do with the newspaper. There were night tables on both sides of the bed, but this one close by was cluttered with a pair of telephones and two large flat plastic control panels studded with push buttons. Trusting she wasn't violating any house rule, she gently balanced the newspaper on the edge of the bed away from those outstretched legs.

No rules violated it seemed because "Off you go, Hegnauer,"

106

said Ma'am. This time there was a warning in the voice, and this time Hegnauer did go. The sound of the hallway door probably meant that she was on the way to the staff hall for her own breakfast now.

The sightless eyes pivoted toward Amy. It was disconcerting, she found, that they were directed well below her own eye level, a misjudgment there. And the realization that blindness would make this room pitch black, everything in it concealed by impenetrable blackness, suddenly struck her like a small sharp blow to the diaphragm.

Ma'am made no move toward her breakfast. "Difficult at moments, our Hegnauer," she remarked, "but refreshingly direct in answering the direct question. I asked her what you looked like. She said," — the fluting voice dropped to a simulation of Hegnauer's guttural — " 'She is tall and skinny with red hair and she will not win any beauty contest.' Not a bad quality, that outspokenness."

Not unless it's aimed at you, ma'am, Amy thought with irritation. And what would you know about that?

"Now," said Ma'am, "tell me what she looks like."

"Ma'am?"

"You heard the question, Lloyd. Don't make me repeat it while you contrive an answer. Do you know the advice Alice was given in that situation?"

Alice. Alice? "Oh, Alice in Wonderland," said Amy. "Yes. 'Curtsey while you're thinking what to say.' "

"Well, now." Ma'am did seem pleased. "You are well informed in some ways, aren't you? But never mind the curtsey. How would you describe Hegnauer?"

A trap, Amy thought. I am Alice going headlong down the rabbit hole and when Mike kept saying unreal, unreal he knew what he was talking about. And how do you describe Hegnauer anyhow without putting your size-ten foot in your mouth?

"She looks very strong, ma'am."

"And she is. But with remarkably gentle hands. The strong can afford to have gentle hands, can't they? The weak cannot. You brought the paper, Lloyd? You placed it on the bed here?"

107

"Yes, ma'am."

"Good." Ma'am pointed. "Now draw that chair up. Observe its imprint on the carpet; it must be returned to exactly that place. Be careful. It's heavier than it looks."

It was heavier than it looked, flat white leather pads for seat and back mounted on shiny metal tubing. Amy placed it beside the bed and was poised to sit on command when Ma'am pointed again. "That birdcage. Just to prevent distraction, cover it."

The ornate birdcage — it appeared to be a minipagoda made of silver wire — hung from a stand in a corner of the room. Its occupant, Amy saw when she peered closely, was a canary that looked absolutely wretched. It stood on a perch, eyes closed, head thrust down into its shoulders, if that's what they could be called. When Amy worked a finger through the wiring and along the perch it made no move.

"Playing with it, Lloyd?" Ma'am said uncannily. "I only asked you to cover the cage."

"Yes, ma'am."

The cover dangling from a cross-piece of the stand appeared to be made of a section of discarded garment, wildly patterned and crudely stitched together into a cylindrical piece. While Amy was working it down over the cage Ma'am remarked, "The bird's name is Philomela, Lloyd. Do you think it a suitable name?"

"Well, ma'am, Philomela was a bird, so it's not unsuitable."

"Indeed? What kind of bird?"

"A nightingale, ma'am."

"Yes, go on."

"But a girl originally. Then raped by her brother-in-law, who cut out her tongue so she couldn't tell about it. In the end, the gods avenged her and then turned her into a nightingale."

"Avenged her how, Lloyd?"

Back to school, Amy thought. Friday morning orals in Greek mythology. "Well, ma'am, the rapist's wife did find out what happened, and she killed their son and served him to her husband as dinner."

"Very good, Lloyd. An adequate vengeance, would you say?"

"Perhaps more than adequate, ma'am."

"Not at all. A just vengeance can never be more than adequate. It must be all-consuming, all-fulfilling. That is why the original Philomela is immortal. My niece gave me that bird as a well-intentioned gift, Lloyd. Have you met her? Mrs. Langfeld?"

"Yes, very briefly," Amy said, and waited with trepidation for what was coming.

What does she look like, Lloyd? How would you describe her?

The meditative one, ma'am? Well, to put it as succinctly as possible, she looks like Miss Piggy. In a caftan.

But it didn't come. Ma'am said, "She and I once had a discussion where I explained why I dislike small animals about me. Pets, so-called. Dogs are always blundering into one, cats slyly get underfoot. But Mrs. Langfeld is kin in her way to Saint Francis, passionately in love with all of God's little creatures. She gave me that bird as my Christmas portion last year, perhaps as a means of investing me with the spirit of Saint Francis. Now tell me, Lloyd, do you think he would have caged one of those birds he so much loved?"

Another trap, Amy thought. Even deeper than Alice's rabbit hole. Answering yes didn't make any sense here. But answer no, and next thing, this merrily malicious old woman could pass that judgment along to Gwen Langfeld, who'd then have her own score to settle with this beleaguered waitress-secretary-adminis-trator-whatever.

Ma'am cut in on the thought. "Prefer not to answer that, Lloyd?"

"Well, it does seem rather a rhetorical question."

Ma'am laughed deep in her throat. "You are a clever girl, aren't you? Now sit down and find the obituary section of the paper. I want you to read me the obituary index, never mind the encomiums."

"Yes, ma'am." Amy reached for the *Times* on the edge of the bed and took notice of the tray. She screwed up her courage. "If you don't mind, ma'am, your breakfast. I'm afraid it's getting cold."

Ma'am dipped her head in acknowledgment. "Quite right. Kind of you to remind me of it, Lloyd."

109

Amy sat back with a glow of self-satisfaction to scout out the obits. Then as she opened the paper to them the glow faded. Preening herself at age twenty-five, she wondered, because she had just gotten a pat on the head from the unpredictable mistress?

She folded the paper for easier reading of the boxed column listing the late departed, then found herself fascinated by the unpredictable mistress's handling of her breakfast tray. Those fingertips, the nails scarlet, explored the tray, lightly brushing over everything on it with a butterfly touch. Then nerve-rackingly the coffee was poured—

"Lloyd?"

"Oh, I'm sorry," said Amy and bent to her labors. *"Abrams,"* she read. *"Beaufort. Benedict. Dolfman"* and so on to the end, taking notice along the way that Ma'am, neglecting coffee and brioche, was now lying back against the pillows, eyes closed, face a mask of concentration.

Anticipating bad news? Amy wondered. An old friend dying? Or good news? An old enemy dying. Although it was hard to conjecture what enemies Margaret Durie could have made in her fifty years of darkness. After the reading was over and apparently no name had struck a spark, Ma'am's reaction suggested that this, in fact, was the good news. No name. Nobody there for her to mourn. She sat up briskly, bit into the brioche although it couldn't have been that tempting anymore.

She patted her lips with the napkin. "You read well, Lloyd. Tell me, do you find this a macabre procedure?"

"No, not really."

"Wise of you, because in the midst of life we are indeed in death. At my age especially, familiar names show up more and more on that page. That means, Lloyd, that each day you're on duty, we'll start this way. Regrettably, on your days off Hegnauer must attend to it. Do you read braille?"

"No, I don't. But I'm sure that if I—"

"I'm not asking you to learn the method, Lloyd. I'm quite fluent in it myself. I was merely curious. Is there any art news in this edition? Art, meaning the fine arts."

Amy located the section. "Not much, ma'am. A few paragraphs and a few advertisements."

"Nothing about the Jason Cook Gallery?"

Amy looked closely. "No, there isn't."

"A newcomer," said Ma'am. "Brash. A bit scandalous. But mark that name, Lloyd. The Jason Cook Gallery. Do you object to the scandalous in art?"

It was not only dizzying to be subjected to these conversational gambits, Amy thought, but tiring. She had the feeling she was getting winded just keeping up with them. Although what was the worst that could happen if she didn't keep up with them?

What, indeed. Off with her head, the Red Queen would order McEye.

Even so. "I'm afraid," Amy said, "I don't know that much about art, ma'am."

"Possibly. What do you feel about the feminist movement? Do you find that scandalous? Or are you a partisan of it?"

Here, Amy thought, I take my stand, I can do no more. "Well, ma'am, I *am* a working woman."

"Hence a partisan?"

"Yes, ma'am." And, thought Amy, never having waved that flag before I pick this time and place to wave it. Self-destructive all right, this Mrs. Lloyd.

This turned out to be a misjudgment. Ma'am said, "You have spirit, Lloyd. No polite lies about matters of conscience. And of course you're right in your position. But a married feminist? Does your husband approve?"

"Yes, he does, ma'am." Which was the truth, allowing for Mike's occasional teasing about the lunatic fringe of the movement. And of course Abe was no help, pointing out betimes that Audrey never needed any membership card to do well on her own, Audrey making it all the worse by coming on very smug about it.

"You're fortunate in your marriage, Lloyd. What is the name of the art gallery I asked you to keep in mind?"

"The Jason Cook Gallery, isn't it?"

"Yes. The proprietor—an anomaly perhaps?—seems devoted

111

to the works of talented women. I understand his showings will be restricted to those who haven't yet won the public they deserve. Do you know what happened to Mary Cassatt when she returned to America after achieving fame in France as one of its finest impressionist painters?"

"I'm afraid I don't really—"

"She was described by the press here, Lloyd, only as the sister of Alexander Johnston Cassett, president of the Pennsylvania Railroad. That was all. Not a word about her superb achievement. I take pleasure in the knowledge, Lloyd, that the railroad eventually went bankrupt while Mary Cassatt's paintings are now national treasures. Does that knowledge please you?"

"Well, ma'am, I never knew there was—"

"What other duties has Mrs. McEye assigned you today?"

"Only shopping, ma'am. She feels that my wardrobe—"

"Yes, she's explained that to me. Do you feel she's presumptuous in the matter?"

"No, ma'am."

"Your tone indicated you do. But bear in mind that Mrs. McEye reflects the older generation here. A stickler for the proprieties. And intensely male-oriented. The male as dominant species. So a word to the wise, Lloyd. Be circumspect in your dealings with her. On my behalf as well as yours." The pale, scarlet-tipped fingers motioned. "Now open the doors of that cabinet, Lloyd."

The cabinet against the far wall stood between long, low bookcases filled with what appeared to be bulky leatherbound albums. Of course, Amy thought as enlightenment struck, works in braille. What those tall, thin volumes were on one shelf, however, couldn't be that smartly figured out. She opened the cabinet doors and found herself confronted by the components of an elaborate hi-fi set, phonograph, tape deck, speakers, the works. In a way it looked as out of place in this Art Deco territory as did the bulletin board in the oak-paneled staff hall. But if nothing else, it did explain those remote-control panels on the night table.

However, this was not to be a musicale. Ma'am said, "Mrs.

112

McEye has been attending to my mail delivery. The mail pouch is placed in the pantry by the postman. Mrs. McEye sees to its sorting and distribution midmornings, but you are to do that for me from now on. That is, to extract anything addressed to me and bring it here along with my tray. Starting tomorrow."

Good-bye seven o'clock rising, Amy thought. And just how long would it take to sort out the family mail? She had the sinking feeling that this family got a lot of mail.

"Yes, ma'am," she said, but it was the grudging unspoken thought, not the spoken words, that Ma'am responded to.

"It won't take long, Lloyd. I'll have one of the staff assigned to help you. And that's all for the present. You're free to go."

Amy hesitated. "Hegnauer's not back yet, ma'am."

"I'm aware of that." The voice became sharp. "Is it your impression that I require someone at my side every minute of the day?"

"Sorry, ma'am."

"Indeed? More heated than sorry, from that tone. Foolish of you, Lloyd." The voice was now teasing. "After all, we can't afford to have both of us in bad temper at the same time, can we?"

Amy found herself smiling. The miserable old charmer, she thought. "No, ma'am."

"Of course not. That will be all, Lloyd."

A ND now that you've shot the rapids, Lloyd, Amy asked herself on the way to the staircase, what do you make of them?

Well, the bottom line is that she's blind, poor thing. Can't read faces, can't read body language, can't get clues to people that way. So she throws those non sequitur questions at you. And

113

clever as she is, she quickly knows more about you than you might want her to. But, fair exchange, she does let you know surprising things about her.

Margaret Durie a woman's libber? And wary of the McEye? The older-generation, male-oriented McEye? Something rankled Ma'am there, going by her choice of adjectives. Older-generation male had to mean Craig and Walter Durie. Was she jealous of them as the unblind masters of the house? While she, suddenly emerging from those years of self-imposed isolation, found that time had passed her by, that she was not her younger brothers' equal but their pet?

Could be. Certainly there were signs she didn't like those brothers. And didn't really trust the McEye, who was—had been for so long—much more their vassal than hers. But she did seem to trust this Mrs. Lloyd, the rank newcomer. Take that mail thing, for example . . .

In fact, thought Amy, from the signs and portents, things didn't shape up too badly for the rank newcomer.

She climbed the stairs up to the third floor, the curlicued iron-work banging underfoot, and felt an uncomfortable sensation at the head of the stairs. This, she thought, was the last thing Margaret Durie ever saw, this staircase. Then she opened her eyes to darkness. For the rest of her life, that maddening darkness.

If it were me, Amy thought, Mike would probably be very kind to me afterward, and I might come to hate him for it.

Craig and Walter were probably very kind to their older sister, and she came to hate them for it.

Or was that an oversimplification?

Philomela, indeed. If that sad-looking canary sang—and who makes a gift of a canary that doesn't—it had to be a male. Philomela was a female name; on those grounds alone all wrong.

When she entered the apartment Mike had already gone his way to Hale & Hale, clothiers, leaving the bedding neatly turned down for airing and the windows wide open to the mid-September breeze. In the living room she observed—Mike must have heeded Abe's warning—that the manuscript and notes had disappeared from beside the typewriter. Wisely hidden away somewhere, just in case the McEye did have a spare key for this door and was inclined to make covert tours of inspection. An unpleasant thought, but evaluating the McEye in Ma'am's terms it made sense.

The McEye was, after all, the next-door neighbor on this hall, and as bulldog guardian of the proprieties she'd probably feel righteous about putting an ear to the wall or an eye to the keyhole. Which might explain what had happened to the last butler here. Foolish of him to go around seducing houseboys right next door to the family's busybody conscience.

Amy helped herself to a bunch of grapes from the bowl in the refrigerator—the grapes in their perfection had to be a hothouse variety—and while at them phoned Audrey at Custer's First Stand about the shopping expedition.

"Meet you at eleven, doll," said Audrey, and gave her the address. "Right near Herald Square."

Now for the McEye. The other phone that would be, the house phone. In the desk as promised was a bulky folder, the first page of which provided a listing of in-house numbers. Others, Amy saw as she flipped through them, were the plans of all of the building's floors, including the basement, each room area identified in neat, tiny print, and there followed pages headed *Important. Staff Information.* Considering the McEye's fussiness, Amy thought, this must be the comprehensive text on the subject. Look under *p* for *picayune*.

On the phone, however, the McEye came through affably. "Of course, Mrs. Lloyd. Take whatever time you need. Your schedule has been kept open to allow for that."

"Thank you."

"And, by the way, Miss Margaret just phoned me to report most favorably on you."

"That's very kind of her."

"Yes." The voice changed subtly, a coolness setting in. "She also explained about your attending to her mail. You'll have one of the staff to help you with the sorting out. I'll attend to the rest of the distribution."

"Yes, Mrs. McEye."

"And remember that tomorrow morning is pickup time for

your laundry and cleaning. And Mrs. Lloyd"—the voice smoothly reverted to affable—"you do seem to have gotten off to a good start. That's most gratifying." *Click* went the phone.

Touchy about her prerogatives all right, Amy thought. And a mite wary of me now, but playing it down. Because, comes to bottom lines, it does look like whatever Ma'am wants, Ma'am gets.

The same also appeared to be true about Audrey when the time came. The loft she led Amy into was crowded with dress-manufacturing equipment and deafening with activity. Its shirt-sleeved, sweating proprietor, introduced as Maxie something-or-other, looked skeptical when Audrey said, "For the trade, Maxie. Wholesale."

He motioned with his head at Amy. "This is the trade?"

"So to speak. She's model-size anyhow. It'll be just some hems for me to pin up and a little needlework for one of your ladies."

"Even so, darling, not now. Look around. You can see not now."

"In fifteen years at the big store, Maxie, I never once said to you not now, did I?"

Maxie threw up his hands. "All right, all right, there's the line on those racks over there; go help yourself. But we do the hems only after you do all the fitting. The pins are free."

Going by her own shopping technique—take the first thing that fits and try not to look too closely in the mirror at those damn bony clavicles—Amy had estimated that about an hour should do it. After two hours, however, most of it spent standing in bra and pantyhose in a beat-up little dressing room while Audrey, her mouth full of pins, scurried back and forth between racks and dressing room, there was still a long way to go. The trouble was, Amy saw, that Audrey was really enjoying this, every bit of it, even that getting down on her knees for the endless pinning while her client's belly crawled with impatience.

But Audrey did have her limits. "Lunch break," she finally announced. "There's a great deli right next door. We can finish this later."

In the deli she maneuvered them to a corner table, and after their orders were delivered she said, "Another thing is, this gives

116

us a chance for some woman talk. You know how Abe monopolizes the table talk when we're all together. And I have something on the mind."

"What?"

"You and Mike yesterday. Granting you were dead tired and all, when he brought up that business of your helping him get material out of the Durie family for a book you came on way too cranky about it. There was something between you two I never saw before. What was that all about?"

"I was being stupid. It's that old woman, Audie. I did have the feeling that Mike was somehow asking me to betray her."

Audrey looked disbelieving. "Oh, come on."

"I know. But she did have that affect on me. She's extraordinary and overwhelming."

"Overwhelming," said Audrey. "She and Abe ought to get together. That should make a great match."

"He'd come up against what I do. She's blind. And for all she's outspoken about it and brave about it, there it is. Perhaps it's because I never dealt with anybody blind before, but it throws me. No matter how much she keeps putting me in my place I find myself pitying her terribly. I keep wanting to say something comforting or whatever. Which would really be the wildest kind of mistake."

"Besides," Audrey said, "she's got a family for that."

"Except there's an alienation there. At least on her part."

"But," Audrey said, "there's none between you and Mike, is there? Everything—allowing for him being the imperfect male —is the same as ever?"

"Oh, yes."

"Good. Because in case you didn't know it, doll, Abe and I have a stake in you two. Not financial. That part is just a token stake. Don't ever let it cloud your day."

"It doesn't, now that we can make repayment. Including for these dresses and things. And while we're on this, Audie, how much will this stuff cost? And no cheating in my favor. Really how much?"

"It's all billed to the shop, doll, at full discount. You'll get the bill when I do."

"I'd like to be prepared for it. You know how I am."

"Yes, a size-nine worrywart. Well, figuring dresses, skirts, waists, and all, minus discount, you can put down seven hundred bucks in that little black book."

"Oh, Audie!"

"But consider, doll, you now live among the implausibly rich where seven hundred hardly pays for that little sweater in the window. And take it from me, the perfect dress—even if it's just a simple little workaday number—is a great spine-stiffener in that company. So the subject is closed. The real subject is the emotional stake Abe and I have in you and Mike. By the way, that classical hairdo is very good. Whose inspiration was it, yours or Mike's?"

"Both, I guess."

"See? There you are. Both."

"What about it?"

"Mostly," said Audrey, "it's about the way your marriage is working out. Not only bedmates but trusted best friends, right?"

"The same as you and Abe, Audie. Except you've been married a lot longer."

"Twenty-eight years, doll. And spent too damn much of it watching a whole egomaniacal generation foul up their marriages rather than turn off any of that egomania. You know, when Mike first showed up in our building Abe and I went for him right off, he was so genuine and so minus egomania. The country boy in the big town but with a sense of humor. I mean, really refreshing when you consider everybody else around. He hasn't lost that either, has he?"

"Nope," Amy said firmly.

"Ah, the voice of authority. Still, as the years rolled on we started to worry about him. He'd come up with some really all right females now and then, but there was never a sign of commitment to any of them. Fact is, he seemed a lot more committed to that BMW he drove than to any woman. What is this, we wondered, another me-generation Peter Pan in the making? Another aging babe in toyland? Our Mike? So when you came along—our country boy had found his country girl—it was a happy day for us. Commitment was in the air. Real maturity was in the making."

Amy simultaneously felt touched and a little miffed. "Boston is hardly the country," she pointed out.

"You know what I mean. And what matters is that you and Mike — there aren't many like you around — are still holding high the Silverstone banner. The working marriage forever. And nothing better happen to yours, or you'll have to answer to us."

"You're both darlings," said Amy.

"Well, we do have our moments. Now how about we attend to these sandwiches and get back to the fitting room? And don't look like you're being invited to stretch out on the rack. We'll civilize you if it takes all day."

In fact, it did take almost all day, and when the bulky boxes, contents all nicely hemmed and pressed, were handed to them Audrey announced that since there was no way of getting that load aboard a bus and no chance of getting a cab around Herald Square during rush hour she'd phone Abe to pick them up in the car. "He'll be glad to," she said in response to Amy's halfhearted objections. "He's dying to see which of those uptown palaces is yours."

Abe amiably responded to this call to duty and eventually double-parked on the Madison Avenue side of the palace. They all got out to unload the boxes, and Amy was gratified to see that he was visibly impressed by the building.

"Talk about conspicuous consumption," he said, "those were the days. Interesting family, too, in its way. I mean, with all this how inconspicuous they've managed to be."

"Decorous," said Amy, hefting the boxes. She pointed upward with her chin. "That's our sitting room. Top floor. That window where the curtain is blowing."

"Naturally," said Abe, "the Lloyds' curtains have to provide the common touch. Well, Rapunzel, any time you want to let your hair out of that window Audie and I will be glad to climb up and look around. Meanwhile . . ."

At the door of the service entrance Amy had to set down the boxes to ring the bell. The man who opened the door was, to her surprise, unfamiliar, though she was sure that, allowing for the head chef, she had by now encountered all the staff. Certainly he appeared to be staff, dressed as he was in that waist-length tight little black jacket and white bowtie. On the other hand, he was young, handsome, lithe, and looked as if he put in a lot of time with a hair blower.

He smiled engagingly. "Well, hello there."

"Hello," Amy said. "I'm Mrs. Lloyd."

"And I'm Harold. Let me help you with those boxes. It has been a day for shopping, hasn't it?"

The kitchen, Amy saw when she followed him into it, was a sort of controlled chaos. Another Harold type was doing something to bowls of fruit on the drainboard of the sink; the junior maids, Walsh and Plunkett, along with Peters the houseman, were chopping and slicing away at edibles on the long worktable; a woman in apron and white, antiseptic-looking hairnet was busy at the ovens; and somehow dominating the scene was a very tall, skeletally thin, wondrously wrinkled old black man in chef's hat dipping into pots on the stove. Regal, Amy thought. And mean-looking. From all descriptions, it had to be chef Golightly, the great man himself.

And of course these unknowns must be Domestique Plus. Emergency help. The ubiquitous Mrs. Bernius strikes again.

Harold helped tuck the boxes under her arms, and as she tried to get a tight grip on them Golightly took notice of her.

"Lady, there is no room for you here at this time." The voice had the same Caribbean lilt as his stout and cheerful assistant Mabry's, but unlike Mabry's basso this was a high, thin, coldly challenging voice. "You will please remove yourself and those packages."

"Yes, of course," Amy said, and was tempted to throw a little weight around. "I'm Miss Margaret's secretary."

"And I am Mister Golightly." He came down hard on the Mister. "Which makes neither here nor there. Now remove yourself and give my people room to work." He aimed his stirring spoon at Harold. "Young man, the lady can attend to herself. You have work to do."

120

"The old darling," Harold said into Amy's ear before leaving her to her own devices.

Using her hip, she awkwardly worked her way through the swinging doors into the staff hall and found that here was action too. The refectory table was now covered with a green baize cloth from end to end and more Harolds were stacking plates and arranging cutlery on it. A panel of the wall behind the coffee table gaped open, exposing a dumbwaiter. Mrs. McEye stood at the dumbwaiter, clipboard in hand, cigarette dangling from her lower lip. She squinted through its smoke at Amy.

"Ah, Mrs. Lloyd." She frowned at the boxes. "Oh, dear. This is a dinner for eighteen. I don't see how I can call on anyone now to—"

"No, it's all right, Mrs. McEye. I can get these upstairs myself."

"That would be best. Then tomorrow morning at eight. And, oh, yes, remind Lloyd that his schedule will be posted on the board too, will you?"

"Yes. What time is the board put up, by the way?"

"At ten every evening. You'll attend to that on my days off. We must make time tomorrow for me to explain the procedure. That is essential. I'd suggest you somehow convey this to Miss Margaret."

"Perhaps if you took care of that, Mrs. McEye," Amy said.

"Well. Yes, perhaps I should. Good evening, Mrs. Lloyd."

"Good evening," said Amy and moved on her way to Xanadu. Close call, she thought, but sometimes, Mrs. Lloyd, you do think on your feet. Convey orders to the dangerous Miss Margaret indeed. If anyone were going to throw oil on those embers, let the McEye do it.

Mike was in their bedroom, and the sight of him gave Amy that familiar sense of gratification, of comfort, of this part of life being pretty much all right, no matter how troublesome other parts were.

"I'm sorry it took me so long," she said.

"I just got in myself." He helped unload the boxes onto the bed. "A day of achievement, baby. Got measured for work

121

clothes, stood in line at Motor Vehicles for the change of address, handed in our new address at the post office. And what
was your day like?"

"Not mine. Audie's. She did everything. Including having Abe
drive me back here."

"That's where I had the edge. Namely, the station wagon. I
also found out what demilivery is."

"Mike, this stuff cost seven hundred dollars. Do you know
what that does to our repayment schedule?"

"Extends it a few weeks. Anyhow, demilivery is not full livery.
Full livery is that tunic with rows of buttons and dog collar.
Demilivery is just folksy double-breasted. It makes you look like
the chauffeur for a terribly humble billionaire."

"Seven hundred dollars," Amy said mournfully. She observed
that next to her boxes on the bed was another, this one imprinted with a heraldic coat of arms featuring winged lions.
"That can't be your whole order," she said.

"Just one costume. The rest gets delivered tomorrow, and then
I really spread my wings."

"Sooner," said Amy. "The McEye hinted that you're scheduled for something heavy on that bulletin board downstairs. She
posts the schedules at ten every evening. By the way, did you encounter Golightly on your way in?"

"No encounter. I just got a look at him."

"You're lucky," Amy said. "Mine was an encounter. He put
me down hard for merely setting foot in his precious kitchen
during business hours. He made the McEye look charming by
contrast."

"Maybe," said Mike, "he took you for another Hibernian.
What struck me is that he's practically antediluvian. I mean old,
old. Talk about faithful retainers, what we have here appear to
be faithful employers. Anybody who'd make do with three
dinosaurs like Wilson and Golightly and Borglund—"

"Well," Amy said, "both Craig and Walter do seem like
people who'd be considerate to anyone who serves faithfully and
well. Don't you think so?"

"Sure. But something curious happened at the garage when I
brought the car back. Wilson was taking his ease in the office

and driving Sid Levine right up the wall."

"Wilson? I thought he sort of walked off into the sunset."

"Yesterday. This afternoon he walked right back to the old corral, along with a six-pack. Evidently decided to make the garage his home away from home. And Levine's at a loss because if he tossed the old guy out he's not sure how the family would take it. So he's stuck. And when I brought the wagon in I got stuck."

"The ancient mariner and the wedding guest," said Amy.

"Just about. He nailed me for half an hour with curses against Mrs. Mac for tossing him on the junkpile. Blames that on her, along with the family. And pointed out that if the late McEye, the butler she wed in his dotage, was still around, she wouldn't be so high and mighty. Butler McEye, it seems, had all the staff, including his wife, right under his thumb. A tough man. The only one in the house Wilson rated tougher was Big Daddy himself, Mr. James Hamilton Durie. Nobody, said Wilson, ever tried on Mr. James for size and lived to tell about it. And his butler was evidently cast in the same mold. Perfectly attuned to each other, master and man."

"Then as I see it," said Amy, "Wilson is an ingrate. I mean, the way these people kept him on after he proved incompetent. And this fantastically luxurious retirement they've provided him."

"Right. I gently suggested this to him. His response was interesting."

"Yes? You don't have to milk it for effect. My legs are killing me, standing here like this. I'd like to get into a bath. What response?"

"Well," said Mike, "he looked downright contemptuous at my suggestion that the family had been exceptionally kind in their treatment of him. Then he put on a wise face and said to me, 'Kind? Hell, there's a lot more to it than that, sonny.' "

"More than just kindness?"

"Good question. Which I then put to him in those exact words, and he just clammed up tight. Curtain down. *Exeunt omnes.*"

"Making himself important," Amy said. "And now I am

123

exeunting into the bathtub." She shed clothing along the way, Mike drifting after her. He watched appreciatively as she pulled a handful of pins from her hair and shook it free. The old-fashioned tub on claw feet was long enough when filled to float her full length. Mike leaned against the doorway, contemplating the delicious picture she made.

"How did it go with Ma'am this morning?" he asked.

"Swimmingly. Matter of fact, she even told Mrs. McEye what a nice young lady I am."

"Oh? And how did you earn that accolade?"

"Read the obits in the *Times* to her. Hunted through the art page for mention of the Jason Cook Gallery. Ever hear of it?"

"Nope."

"Well, Jason Cook seems to be highly supportive of painter-type woman's libbers. For that matter, so is Margaret Durie. She made that pretty plain."

"No," Mike said admiringly. "Why, bless her radical old heart. Look, did she give you any hint as to how after fifty years of morbid solitude, she suddenly got back on the rails again?"

"Nope," said Amy.

"Reassuring in a way," Mike said, "but is there any chance she's into pick-me-up pills? Something used to get her out of the morbid phase and that she's now hooked on?"

"I'm almost sure not. But how would I know?"

"Because," Mike said patiently, "you're right close to her. Could Hegnauer be her Doctor Feelgood maybe? Her connection? She's in perfect position to provide a connection."

"Mike darling, you are going overboard with this drug thing."

"Because I'm exercising foresight. That old lady hardly knows you, yet here she is clutching you to her bosom, involving you in a conspiracy against the family. Why?"

"Because she must sense I can be trusted to help her move toward independence from the family without giving the game away. Besides, all of this theorizing is no help to my handling some real worries about the job."

"How real?"

"Enough," said Amy. "Look, there's the McEye—and clipboard—at the dumbwaiter in the staff hall ordering up the proper chinaware and crystal for a fancy dinner party for eighteen. And cutlery. Did you notice there's about half a dozen different sets of china in those cabinets?"

"No."

"Because it wouldn't matter to you. But it does to me. Anyhow, I know Spode from this morning and Wedgwood because everybody knows Wedgwood. But beyond that? And cutlery? And someday when the McEye is off duty I will be stuck with that damn clipboard and that kind of dinner party. Then what?"

"Well, if I know Mrs. Mac, there's an instruction book ready for you. If not, you could just faint away and be carted off to your bed, a pitiful and appealing figure."

"Great," said Amy. "Then get ready for a lot of fainting. Ma'am's already been at me about feminist art, which I know nothing about, and Greek mythology where by sheer luck I came up with a passing grade. But who knows what comes next and when? That's what's on my mind, not any sinister drug ring operating on the second floor."

Mike regarded her kindly. That look, Amy thought, always roused in her the same mixed feelings. The urge to sling something handy at him—the scrubbing brush she was holding would do nicely in this case—and at the same time that pleasant, though probably degrading, sense of being cradled in paternal protectiveness.

"Darling," he said, "listen to wisdom. Miss Margaret wants you bright but not summa cum laude. If she wanted that, she'd go out and buy it. This way whenever you're at a loss you just say, 'Sorry, ma'am, I'm at a loss,' in a properly apologetic tone. Then relax."

"Good. I'll start relaxing as soon as you depart and close the door behind you."

"First, one final question."

"What?" Amy said warily.

"I'm starved. Aren't you?"

"Well, now that you mention it—"

"Right. But what do we do about it? I can't see exercising

kitchen privileges right now, the way things are down there."

"No. But we've still got fruit left and soda water."

"A veritable Garden of Eden."

"Then," said Amy, "after the McEye posts those schedules, you go down and pick up ours along with an aftertheater snack."

"If need be. On the other hand, there's a delivery-type pizza joint near the garage. Suppose—just suppose—I phoned them for a pie, one of those cartwheels with everything on it."

"You're daft," said Amy. "Anyone who walks in with that pie will have it shoved right in his face by Golightly."

"I was just supposing. But now you take somebody here like that sultry Dorothy—"

"Oh?" said Amy. "And what makes her sultry? Dark glasses and a hangover?"

"Whatever. At the same time she seems human enough to crave a pizza now and then. Do you mean even she couldn't get one up to the second floor while Golightly's on duty?"

"Possibly not."

"Pathetic," Mike said. "Talk about a bird in a gilded cage."

It was meant to be funny, Amy thought, and while it was, it wasn't. Sultry? Yes, to be honest Dorothy Durie rated sultry. And that curvy, poisonous little Camilla spelled temptation. For that matter, so did the overblown, mean-tempered housemaid O'Dowd, who looked as if she'd be more at home horizontal than vertical. And those two junior maids, Walsh and Plunkett, fairly bursting out of those cute outfits. A whole houseful of temptation with more bedrooms than you could count. Ridiculous? Not quite.

"Hey, lady," Mike said, "are you by any chance mentally sucking a particularly juicy lemon?"

"No. Now go away. If you want to make yourself useful, you can unpack those dresses and put them on hangers."

"Not me. When I put dresses on hangers they slither right off. What I will do is remove the bowl of fruit from this refrigerator—thus—and take it along with me to the typewriter. Want an apple? Or the rest of these grapes?"

"The grapes. What'll you do, work on the book?"

"Sort of. Notes, descriptions, questions, *pensées*. Emotion recollected in tranquility."

And that's the way it goes, thought Amy. He stirs up everything, then goes off to be tranquil. Writers. On the other hand, this book and all those others to follow were what it was all about, wasn't it? She said, "You put away the pages of the other book somewhere, didn't you?"

"Bottom of my dresser drawer, under my shorts. I doubt Mrs. Mac'll invade our privacy that much."

When Amy finally got out of the tub she could tell from the clacking of the typewriter in the sitting room — Mike was a fast, inaccurate, two-fingered typist — that he was hard at it, very good news because he hadn't been at it like this for a long time. And when she was finished using the hairdryer and with the hanging up of Audrey's bounty he was still at it.

And going by her gut feeling whenever she read pages he handed her, and by Abe's coldblooded judgment, he was a hell of a writer.

And going by logic, he would, as staff, be invisible to the Durie females. After all, invisibility was the name of the game, wasn't it?

And since Mrs. Lloyd was administration, these housemaids wouldn't dare make advances to her husband, would they?

And . . .

She woke up to find the bedroom lights bright in her eyes and Mike standing there in the doorway. "Room service, lady." He looked her over, and she realized she hadn't bothered to put anything on when she stretched out on the coverlet. "And you can come as you are. You look delectable."

He was a darling.

She slipped into a nightgown and squinted at the clock. Ten-thirty. So much for what was intended to be a couple of minutes of shut-eye. Which reminded her to set the alarm for the morning, allowing time for the private mail service the conspiratorial Miss Margaret demanded.

In the sitting room a laden cart was pulled up beside the table, and Mike was setting places from it. "Observe," he said. "This is tableware, not silverware. And this is crockery, not Spode. However"—he drew covered platters from the oven of the cart—"here we have some potted shrimp, poached fillet of sole Mornay, roast Aylesbury duck, and trimmings. This jug is coffee. How will that do for an aftertheater snack?"

"It'll do for an aftertheater banquet. You mean you just walked into the kitchen and loaded up?"

"By Mrs. Mac's invitation. They're all down there in the staff hall, including her. And that slew of temporaries. It seems that when invited guests upstairs have gorged sufficiently, the help downstairs gets the leavings."

"They're not leavings. They're perquisites."

"When you raid the refrigerator, that's perquisites. When you eat the remains of a family dinner party—"

"Of course," said Amy. "And when you've finished analyzing that one, you can work out how many angels can dance on the head of a pin." She seated herself and started filling her plate. "While I find out what Mornay means. And Aylesbury."

Mike stood looking down at her. "Did I ever mention that you were overqualified to be my wife?"

"Just now." She could see that he was in one of those edgy states where the mood could turn either way, dark or bright, and the job was, as ever, to gently shoulder him toward bright. "Sit down and eat, please. It's lonely this way. And what was it like downstairs among the varlets? Sort of a roistering spirit?"

"No roistering," he said. "Not with Mrs. Mac present. Decorum prevailed. Except—and she can be a pain in the butt—when she needled those two kids—that Walsh and Plunkett—about their table manners. 'Elbow off the table, Walsh.' 'Not such huge mouthfuls, Plunkett.' With everybody else, including that outside help, carefully not taking notice, of course."

"Be fair," Amy said. "They're training, and she's supposed to polish up their manners, isn't she?"

"Not in front of people. When you had those kindergarten classes, did you correct the kids that way?"

"Yep."

"I should have known," Mike said, but the mood was definitely bright now.

"Well," Amy said, "if I'd waited to get them alone after class, they wouldn't know what I was talking about. The average kindergarten child has a memory that goes back as far as two minutes. By the way, those temporaries are Domestique Plus, wouldn't you say? Bernius people?"

"Bernius people? Oh, you mean those beautiful young men. Have to be. And between theater jobs, of course. By the way, McEye also gave me some instructions. First one of us down tomorrow wheels this thing to the kitchen and puts the dishes and cutlery into the washer. So, according to the schedules I have here—" He held up two slips of paper.

"The schedules," Amy said. "I forgot all about them."

"I didn't. According to them, you're first one down. Mrs. Lloyd to Miss Margaret D. at eight A.M. However, to even it up, I already took down our laundry and dry cleaning. Basement room next to the staff hall."

"What did you take down?" Amy asked in alarm.

"Trust me. None of your new things. Everything else with the least wrinkle. You think those jeans'll come back starched?"

"No. What does your schedule say?"

Mike focused on the longer strip of paper. "We open at nine-thirty A.M. Mr. Craig and Mr. Walter from *R* to *O*." He looked up. "*R* means residence, *O* means office."

"How do you know that?"

"By asking Mrs. Mac. Whereupon she said—not unkindly—that I had obviously not studied my information folder and I really should. So I just did. Also *G* means garage and *W*— What do you think *W* means?"

Amy considered this briefly. "Wait."

"I love you," Mike said. "Especially when I think what life might be with a short, fat, slow-witted wife." He turned to the paper again. "Then after delivery I come back and *W* at *G*. At eleven-thirty, Mrs. Jocelyn from *R* to Bonwit Teller and *W* for return. At four, Mr. Craig and Mr. Walter from *O* back to *R*. At five— Are you listening closely?"

"I am."

"At five, Mrs. Langfeld and *L*—luggage—from *R* to British Airways, Kennedy Airport. Interesting?"

"Assuming the flight's to London," said Amy. "In that event, Gwen's going to join her separated husband."

"Where," said Mike, "a reunion may be impending. You know, it's stuff like this that fevers up gossip columnists."

"Well, resist the temptation to fever 'em up. And there's something else. Maybe this means Gwen is being exiled for that meditation gathering yesterday. At least for inviting a houseman to be part of it. Don't you think the McEye reported that to mama and papa?"

"I don't doubt it," Mike said, "but somehow papa Craig strikes me as the typical father who'd be at a loss in dealing with a freaked-out daughter. On the other hand, I must admit that mama Jocelyn definitely shapes up as hellfire and brimstone."

"She does, doesn't she. Still, this is all conjecture."

"But fun."

"Sleazy," Amy said, "but undeniably fun."

"That brave kid, flying alone across the Atlantic to exile."

"Or to rejoin her yearning husband."

"Which reminds me," said Mike, "it's been a while since we've made passionate love. Do you think that tonight —"

"Any time," said Amy. "Any place."

TWO firm raps on the door. Open sesame. Open, Hegnauer. And here was Ma'am in the sitting room, upright in that low-backed armchair—really inspiring square-shouldered posture there—the chair drawn up to a small, round table, the black cane with mother-of-pearl knob resting against an arm of the chair.

"Good-morning, Miss Durie."

"Good-morning, Lloyd. Off you go, Hegnauer," and Hegnauer tarried not.

Ma'am wore a dress that was sweet, expensive simplicity itself. She was fully made up, with those roundish patches of rouge high on each cheek and that gooey scarlet lipstick slightly askew at one corner of the mouth. Evidence, so it would seem, that she applied her own makeup.

"Well, Lloyd, don't stand there like a ninny."

"Yes, ma'am."

Amy wheeled the cart beside the table. Nice to have mastered the tray, but the cart was obviously the sensible conveyance. On top of it were the breakfast service and silver coffeepot, the *Times,* and the packet of mail. In the heating unit, two brioches. Her decision. If there was going to be that abstracted break-fasting where brioche number one grew cold, number two would be waiting.

"My mail, Lloyd?"

"Yes. Right here."

"Any difficulties with it?"

"No, ma'am."

True, Amy thought. Though there might be difficulties in the offing. Depending, of course, on O'Dowd's good sense.

O'Dowd had been the one appointed to help her with the mail sorting. Had, in sullen mood, led her to the outside pantry, showed how the sack was to be emptied on a broad shelf, the contents spread out and gone through and then—excluding whatever was addressed to Margaret Durie—replaced in the sack. Nothing was said as they worked side by side at this. Amy couldn't think of anything to say that wouldn't come off as a transparent effort to cozy up to this blank-faced creature, and O'Dowd did not seem disposed to break the ice. Until, taking Amy by surprise, she held up an envelope. "Mrs. Lloyd, ma'am?"

"Yes?"

"This one is for me. Could I please have it now?"

Strange she should even ask, Amy thought. "If it's for you," she said, "why shouldn't you have it now?"

131

"Well, ma'am, Mrs. McEye don't—doesn't let staff take letters out of turn when she tends to the mail. I was wondering if you'd feel a bit different about it."

Look before you leap, Amy warned herself. "Out of turn?" she said. "What does that mean?"

O'Dowd looked surprised. And, Amy saw, she really was a very pretty girl when she forgot to be sullen. "Because then we'd be getting our letters before family gets theirs."

I don't believe it, Amy thought heatedly, believing it. Protocol again. And where it could make some sense—keep that machinery oiled—here it was at its most idiotically mean-spirited.

"You keep that letter, O'Dowd," she heard herself say with heat, and then in response to the warning bell sounding off in her head, "but you won't mention this to anybody. I'm in no position to change rules here, so it's strictly between us. Understand?"

"To be sure, ma'am. It's very good of you."

"Reasonable is the word."

"Ah, yes, ma'am." That wicked grin, Amy thought, suggested a certain cleverness behind the dolly look. "Reasonable, too," said O'Dowd.

So, Amy thought while setting Margaret Durie's table in what she hoped was the same pattern as yesterday's tray, telling Ma'am there had been no difficulties about the mail was wisdom. A feminist the lady might be, but not likely one now ready to raise the red flag for a housemaid. Not yet at least.

And it proved to be wisdom. Ma'am leaned forward, nostrils flaring. "You don't use a scent, do you, Lloyd?"

Hell and damnation, Amy thought in panic, was it possible that even after this morning's shower— "Just soap and water, ma'am."

"Well, your skin has a most pleasant odor. Now and then a maid here will attempt to conceal a vile body odor under bottled scent. I won't tolerate that near me. If you encounter it, warn the offender at once. Show her how to use soap and water, if necessary. Tell me, Lloyd, when those girls drench themselves with cheap scent do you think it's a matter of laziness? Or could it be, however nauseous, a misguided effort to be sexually enticing?"

132

Here we go again, thought Amy. Question-and-answer time. Not to mention physical intimacy time. She said, "I really wouldn't know, ma'am."

"I suppose not, since both the laziness and the sexuality are equally natural to certain alien types. But as for yourself, Lloyd—now listen closely—never use soap on the face. Never. Use only a cosmetic cream. I've never used anything else." Disconcertingly, she tilted her face upward. "Do you see the results?"

Amy dutifully looked close. The fine wrinkling of the pale skin was made conspicuous this way, but wrinkling of this sort, she thought, was far better detected by the eye than the fingertips, so Margaret Durie could not really have a picture of herself in her aging. The more luck to her in that. The unseeing eyes touched a raw nerve however. And that smear of lipstick at the corner of the mouth painting a grimace there . . .

"If you don't mind, Miss Durie—"

"Mind what?"

"The lipstick is smudged. At the corner. Just a bit."

"Then repair it. Stupid of Hegnauer not to have taken notice. There are tissues on that desk behind me."

Amy carefully made repairs on the face trustfully offered her. Trustfully, she thought, had to be one of the more heartbreaking words in the book, poor darling.

"There now," she said.

"Good. I was a watercolorist, Lloyd. Competent at oils, but much more than that at watercolors. A challenging medium. You can repair a misjudgment in oils the way you can a smudged lipstick. You can't do that with watercolors. Fortunately maquillage is only a form of oil painting, isn't it? Do you understand what I'm saying?"

"Yes, ma'am."

"And you have today's newspaper?"

Maquillage to today's *Times*. "Right here, ma'am."

"Then draw up that chair"—the stick pointed unerringly at the twin of Ma'am's small armchair—"and let's attend to business. The obituary index."

Amy leafed through the paper and then was caught up by the sight of those slender fingers fluttering over the table service, taking inventory there. Yesterday, it had been unnerving to watch the pouring of that steaming coffee into the cup—first, the precise positioning of the spout over the cup, then the pouring to the exactly right level—but now it was mesmerizing.

"Lloyd!"

"Sorry, ma'am."

Reading the list, Amy observed that Ma'am, stick planted before her, hands resting on the knob, was listening with tight-lipped intensity. And when the reading was over she sat back with every sign of relief. Good for her. Rumor had it that old folks, on getting word of some friend's death, might feel a pang of regret but that the pang was usually salved by a sense of triumph. Well, I've outlived another one, thank God. Nothing like that here. Margaret Durie, at least, didn't seem to look for triumphs of that kind.

Next, the art page, but, as Amy discovered, today there was no art page. Word, if any, about gallery owner and woman's lib supporter Jason Cook would have to wait.

"Very well," said Ma'am, "now the mail. There's a letter opener on that desk where you found the tissues. Bring it to me. And the wastebasket."

The letter opener was a flat, narrow, not very sharp blade set in a mother-of-pearl handle. Amy placed it in the outstretched hand and saw that the breakfast had so far gone uneaten. "Your brioche must be cold, ma'am. If you don't mind, I have another here all heated up."

Since one could never be sure which way this cat would jump, the response was gratifying. "You are foresighted, aren't you, Lloyd? No, I don't mind at all."

But then when the switch was made, as if to demonstrate its futility, Ma'am disregarded the heated brioche and turned to opening her mail. This was something to see, too. One snick, and dull as the blade was, the envelope was slit as neatly as if by machine. Ma'am placed it aside and motioned at it with the opener. "Read the message, Lloyd. Correspondent's identity to start with."

Most of the messages were charity pitches, and these got short shrift. A couple of lines, and Ma'am would say shortly, "Dispose of it, Lloyd," and into the wastebasket it would go. There were a couple of notes, however, handwritten invitations to some occasion. "Answer in one phrase, Lloyd. *Miss Durie will be unable to attend.* Over your signature as my secretary. Do not embellish the message. It's common knowledge that I haven't attended any social event since losing my sight. Do you think, Lloyd, that these people really seek the pleasure of my company? Or are they acting out of shameless curiosity?"

And now, Amy thought, we're into multiple choice. "After all, ma'am, I don't know these people."

"All humanity is of a piece, Lloyd. But let us attend to our muttons. This mutton now."

It was a note on embossed stationery. *"Castello Sgarlati, Bologna,"* Amy read. Of course, she thought. The principessa.

"Castello," Ma'am commented drily. "My sister, Lloyd, is its chatelaine. The Signora Enid di Sgarlati. Read it."

"Yes, ma'am. *Dearest Margaret, I am well and Enzio is well. What more is there to say except that I pray you'll continue your improvement and look forward to visiting you soon. Devotedly, your Enid.*"

"My prayerful Enid," Ma'am said chillingly. "Did you know, Lloyd, that all titles of nobility were rendered null and void by the Italian government after the last war those stupid people involved themselves in?"

"No, I didn't."

"Null and void. Bear that in mind."

"Yes, ma'am. And how do I answer this?"

"Very simply, type at the foot of that paper *Message received and contents noted* and return it to the sender."

And, Amy thought with apprehension, just how long would it take the principessa to learn just who committed that rudeness? "Miss Durie, I'm not sure—"

"I don't care to repeat myself, Lloyd."

"Yes, ma'am."

"Nor have I enjoyed a lifetime of my sister's urgings that I gracefully yield to my misfortune because it was God's will. Never having known any misfortune, she is topheavy with Christian forbearance. I take pleasure in testing it now and then.

135

Of course"—the cane was raised in a series of small arcs toward Amy's arm. She sat rigid as it pressed the arm, then moved up to rest on her shoulder. It was an uncomfortable feeling. Not actually threatening but not far from it. "Of course," Ma'am repeated with emphasis, "this is all said in confidence. It is between you and me, Lloyd, and no one else."

No one else, Amy thought, and that's how it goes. Open the day by entering a little conspiracy with O'Dowd, work up to another with Margaret Durie, and take it from there. Secrets. And that business of Wilson confiding to Mike that he had a Durie secret he was keeping to himself. And the McEye sometimes came on pretty furtive about this and that, probably sorting out the secrets from the public domain stuff while she talked to you.

If you want to create a miasma, Amy thought, that's the way to go. And heighten it with a stick laid on the shoulder, which was not the way to do anything. That was really out of line.

She carefully took the silver tip of the cane between thumb and forefinger and removed it from her shoulder. It briefly wavered in the air, then was returned to the floor. If Margaret Durie had any reaction to this mutiny, she concealed it. "Understand, Lloyd, I am neither hardhearted nor softheaded. Do you think I was hardhearted in dismissing those appeals for my charity?"

"I suppose you had reason to dismiss them, ma'am."

"I did. I don't contribute to institutions my family's endowments may already finance. But I do give to the deserving. For your information, Lloyd, I virtually support the Upshur Institute for Braille with personal funds. Two most deserving people, that's all, working out of their apartment. A husband and wife—Mr. Upshur is blind, Mrs. Upshur is not—splendidly efficient in their instruction. I speak from experience. Mrs. Upshur was the patient angel who gave me a command of braille not long ago."

"Not long ago?" Amy said. "But I thought— Oh, I'm sorry."

"No, I understand your confusion. Offered braille instruction many times over the years, I rejected it—I'm almost embarrassed to say—angrily. Learn from that, Lloyd. This is a fascinating and challenging world. Don't let any handicap have you withdraw from it."

Like the handicap of a family, Amy reflected, who with all good intentions helped you to withdraw. So Margaret Durie, resisting them, needed a partner in her little war of independence, and here in this Mrs. Lloyd she had found one. And that cane laid on the shoulder was not a threat, it was in a way the knighting of the squire, the sealing of the partnership.

"No, ma'am," Amy said. She realized it came out a little more fervent than she had intended, but that was all right too.

"Nor," said Ma'am, "does my charity go unrewarded." She smiled. "Mrs. Upshur has the dire conviction that I'll backslide without her prodding. Become dependent again on being read to where the writing can be found in braille. That's why you'll now and again find messages from her in my mail done in braille. Firm admonitions to keep in practice. What do you think of an instructor like that, Lloyd?"

Amy felt a pang of jealousy. "She seems very capable."

"She is. Capable, highly principled, and, I'm sorry to say, absolutely incompetent in handling her business affairs. Could that also be said of the ancient Greek philosophers walking the groves of academe? Fortunately for the Upshurs I do provide for them generously. Do you know about the groves of academe, Lloyd?"

"Yes, ma'am."

"Well, we shall now tread our own groves. Have you seen our galleries yet?"

"No, I haven't."

"You shall now." Ma'am stood up easily, without any support from the cane. There was a sudden vivid youthfulness in her face. Off on an adventure, Amy thought, and delighted about it. "Come along, Lloyd."

Amy looked at the two uneaten brioches. But no, she warned herself, you mustn't mention them. This wasn't a child to be urged into eating her breakfast. This was a spirited woman who'd been treated like a child for too long. Which must have been exactly the point Dorothy Durie—smart if sultry—had been making with her homily about too much pity, too much protectiveness.

137

Ma'am moved on sure feet to the door, cane tip never touching the carpet, and Amy opened the door. She followed along as Ma'am crossed the corridor to the interior window overlooking the courtyard and halted there, fingertips against the glass. "Have you taken notice of my little garden, Lloyd?"

"Yes, it's lovely," Amy said, though the vista wasn't improved by a couple of grimy-looking men working on it with spades and shears. Domestique Plus again?

"My garden, Lloyd. Only scented flowers are cultivated in it. My father arranged it as a gift for me after my mishap. I'm going to introduce you to him now."

"Your father?"

That startled reaction was evidently what Margaret Durie had hoped for. She looked mischievously pleased with herself. "You'll see. Do come along."

No guiding hand or cane was needed as she led the way toward the elevator midway down East Hall. A couple were standing there at the elevator, Amy saw, the tall, athletic-looking Glendon Durie and wife Dorothy, she with cigarette in hand. And one look at her in full light, Amy knew, settled all doubts. Dorothy would definitely rate sultry. Dark hair, dark eyes, full lips, high cheekbones—trust Mike to have gotten the picture at once although that bedroom where introductions had been made was so shadowy. And that husky voice didn't hurt either. "Good-morning, Auntie. You do look well."

"Dear Aunt Margaret," said Glendon. There was a teasing note in it. "Off to the races?"

From Ma'am's expression she didn't mind this. She held up her face in invitation, and simultaneously nephew and niece delivered a polite kiss on each cheek.

"You're smoking, Dorothy," Ma'am said. "If you don't mind—?"

"No, darling," said Dorothy. "But only one puff."

"I'll watch for the cops," said Glendon.

Dorothy carefully placed the cork tip of the cigarette to Aunt Margaret's lips. The glowing end glowed brighter, and Dorothy removed the cigarette. Smoke jetted from Ma'am's patrician nostrils. "Heaven," she said with rich contentment.

"Poor darling," Dorothy said. "I'm glad I haven't your will-power."

"My priorities require willpower, child."

The elevator car appeared behind the bronze grillwork gate. The Duries turned to face it, and then Amy saw that Dorothy was frowning at her. Oh, God, Amy thought, the protocol again. She hastily pulled open the gates and stood aside. The car was wide and shallow with a red-cushioned bench extending the width of its rear wall. The family party arranged itself in a row, rejecting the bench, Ma'am in the center.

Amy stood there holding the gate. Now what, she wondered. Do I come aboard without invitation or just wave good-bye? The McEye in all her spelling out of details had overlooked this one.

"What are we waiting for, Lloyd?" Ma'am said sharply, and Amy with vast relief said, "Sorry, ma'am," and stepped aboard.

Glendon pressed the button that started them downward. "I imagine you've gotten the word?" he said to Ma'am.

"Almost at once, I daresay. I'm surprised you prevailed."

"So am I," Glendon said. "A riddle, Auntie. What's harder than adamantine?"

"That is not correctly a riddle, Glendon, but yes, I know the answer. Your father."

The elevator came to a stop at the ground floor. Amy pushed open the gates and stood aside in attendance. The family party broke up after one more puff on the cigarette for Auntie, and Glendon and Dorothy Durie went their way across the marble foyer to the front door.

Frustration time, Amy thought. All right, Glendon had prevailed over his father about something, but what?

"Your arm, Lloyd," said Ma'am.

Amy placed her wrist — the lesson well remembered — under the hand extended toward her, and this way they moved across the marble floor. The cane was used here, not tapping the floor, but searching from side to side a little above it. The second floor, Amy thought, could be kept clear of unfamiliar obstacles at all times, but not this open territory.

They halted a short distance from a huge pair of doors. "The West Gallery," Ma'am said, and as Amy pushed open a door, a

139

little surprised at how easily it opened, Ma'am's arm moved free of hers. Back on sure ground again, evidently, even though there were obstructions here and there through the broad sweep of the gallery. Statuary. Marble figures, some much larger than life-size, all gleaming in the light coming through the high French windows that made up part of one wall of the gallery and offered a view of the courtyard and garden outside.

Some of the statuary appeared to be Ma'am's old friends. As she moved along, the tip of the cane would find a pedestal—not by accident, Amy had a feeling, but seeking it out—and there Ma'am would stop, fingertips moving lightly over the surface of the stone, then a hand pressing against a curve of it, the woman obviously taking a sensuous pleasure in the pressure.

"Houdon," Ma'am said. "Maillol. Mr. Daniel Chester French. If they're unrecognizable to you, Lloyd, it's for good reason. None has ever been on public exhibition. Nor are reproductions or photographs permitted. Do you think that dreadfully selfish of the owners?"

"Well, ma'am—"

"No need to be diplomatic, Lloyd, because it is selfish. My instructor in painting once confronted my father on this. He learned on the spot what a mistake that was. But you still haven't met my father, have you? Well then"—the stick pointed —"there he is."

The aim of the stick wasn't altogether accurate, but there was no mistaking which portrait it indicated, the centerpiece and largest one on the wall. The strikingly beautiful woman in the foreground, dressed in an Edwardian full-length gown of white satin, could have been Margaret Durie herself in her early womanhood, the resemblance was that strong. So, thought Amy, that was who today's Duries inherited those strange, downward-slanting eyes from, and that disdainful, narrow nose— their mother. But in a way the face was disappointing. Characterless compared to Ma'am's.

The same could not be said of the man standing at the woman's shoulder. A brooding, strong-featured face, all command. James Hamilton Durie. A very revealing portrait, Amy decided. A man with urgent matters to attend to was dutifully but impatiently taking part in a project he found a waste of time.

"Do you recognize the artist?" Ma'am asked.

"I think so," Amy said. She had sufficient clues, she felt, to take a chance on it. "John Singer Sargent?"

"Quite right. Mr. John Singer Sargent. Are you looking at the portrait?"

"Yes, I am."

"My father and mother. Mr. Sargent had an eye for charming women. She was to be the main subject here, my father supplementary. And what happened? He defeated Mr. Sargent." Ma'am's voice was scathing. "Not easy to do, it was not done with intent, but he did it. Do you think it a fair match, Lloyd?"

"She seems very lovely," Amy said.

"Indeed she was. But even loveliness of that order isn't much help against the visage of Jove. Would you recognize the painters of any of these other works?"

Here, Amy thought, was where Mike had recommended the comic "I'm at a loss, ma'am," but on the grounds that the biblical Daniel himself had not likely tried out comic repartee on the lions it seemed good policy to settle for an apologetic "I'm afraid not."

"Trumbull, Inman, Inness, Chase, Eastman Johnson — those names mean nothing to you?"

"I'm afraid not."

"Interesting, Lloyd, that my instructor once said that those names would soon mean nothing to even the comparatively well informed. A passionate man, he was passionately devoted to the modernists. Demuth, Stuart Davis, Hartley, Marin. He idolized Joseph Stella. Are those names familiar to you?"

"Most of them, ma'am," Amy said, grateful that she could say it.

"Then, since I regard you as comparatively well informed, he was correct in his judgments. Although *modernist* is an awkward word in this context. Yesterday's modernists these were. A long yesterday ago. Now tell me, Lloyd. I remarked on a certain gallery owner to you. What is his name?"

"Jason Cook, ma'am."

"Very good." The cane pointed. "That door, Lloyd. Let's see what's behind it."

When Amy drew the door open what turned out to be behind it was the dining room, still in some disorder from last night's dinner party. The table was almost cleared, but under Nugent's supervision the two junior maids were bundling together linens and stowing empty wine bottles into a carton. The open door across the room exposed a service area with dumbwaiter ready to be loaded. Which meant, Amy thought, that this dining room was located right above the staff hall and far from the kitchen where invisible agents prepared the dinner.

The room itself was extravagantly large, but since unlike the West Gallery its ceiling and the walls were wood-paneled its dimensions weren't oppressive. But like the gallery its centerpiece was the portrait of a Durie, a life-size study that compelled the eye at a glance.

Margaret Durie herself sitting there, Amy thought. It had to be. Not only was the resemblance acute, but presented in her late teens she was wearing a dress—low-waisted, short-skirted, the rounded knees gleaming in silk stockings—which was a giveaway to the early thirties, when she would have been about eighteen. Before her accident? Yes, because even seen from this distance those eyes were clear and lustrous and altogether alive.

"Your arm, Lloyd," said Ma'am, and with a hand resting on it moved into the room.

The two juniors froze in their tracks at the sight, but the cheerful Nugent said, "Good morning to you, Miss Durie. And Mrs. Lloyd. We're not in your way, are we?"

Amy had a kindly "Not at all" on the tip of her tongue, but there it stuck when Ma'am said, "Who's with you, Nugent?"

"Walsh, ma'am. And Plunkett."

"Then you will all find something else to occupy yourselves with for a few minutes."

"To be sure, ma'am," said Nugent, and like a mother hen herding its chicks, she steered the apparently terrified juniors into the dumbwaiter area and pulled the door shut behind her.

More secrets? Amy wondered as Ma'am, that hand still lightly on her arm, the other using the cane as a guide by tapping it against chair legs along the way, circumnavigated the table. They stopped before the portrait, and seeing it close up Amy had a feeling that time really had been made to stand still here. That same boyish haircut, those ovals of rouge on the cheeks, that crimson lipstick — But then, somehow depressingly, there was the brightness of those eyes and the extraordinary warmth of that expression. Margaret Durie, age eighteen, ready to take the whole world in her arms and hug it tight.

While this Margaret Durie, her dead eyes raised to her youthful image, looked like a brooding, hard-faced reflection of that image.

"My gift, Lloyd, to my father. I gave it to him soon after he made me a gift of that scented garden. An exchange of gifts. A way of letting him know my feelings for him. Do you think it made an appropriate gift?"

"Oh, yes. It's a marvelous picture. Who painted it?"

"One does not refer to a painting of merit as a picture, Lloyd. Nor indulge in that sickly adjective *marvelous*. It was painted by my instructor. Signed by him on the reverse of the canvas, if you're wondering. It was his theory that if the casual viewer must judge a masterwork by its signature, it is no masterwork. An interesting theory, isn't it?"

"Yes, it is," Amy said.

"Yes, it is," echoed Ma'am. "You'll also observe, Lloyd, that this work has place of honor here. I insisted on it. Do you think that was vain of me?"

"I think," Amy said, working it out carefully, "you were honoring the artist, ma'am, not the subject."

"Nicely put, Lloyd. I'll wait while you take time to look more closely at those other works on view. Some of them are also unsigned."

Amy made the round, trying to make it not so fast as to indicate careless viewing and not so slow as to have the boss start tapping her shoe on the floor in impatience. But, as she discovered, slow had to be better. These were all smallish watercolors of marvelous — no, splendid — quality. You didn't need signatures to identify Winslow Homer. And here was Sargent again in some heated scenes of apparently Arabic streets. And there were some signatures that should have been familiar but weren't. And finally there was an unsigned series of paintings, all, under closer inspection, done by the same hand. New York City long ago. Fifth Avenue, Battery Park, other avenues back when elevated trains still ran overhead — each painting vividly suggesting the scene, the people in it barely suggested by a stroke or two of the brush.

Amy studied them with a growing sense of discovery. An excitement growing along with it constricted her stomach. It became impossible to bottle it up. And again there were clues to go by, weren't there? Hell and damnation, she thought, even if she were wrong about it, it couldn't do any harm.

She turned to the brooding figure across the room. "Miss Durie?"

"Yes?"

"These New York scenes are yours, aren't they?"

"Very discerning of you, Lloyd. How did you know?"

"Well, they are unsigned, and after what you said about signatures— And you also said that you did favor watercolors—"

"I see. A process of deduction."

"And"— Amy found with dismay that her tears were rising and her voice choking—"I had the thought that if the girl in that portrait of you was a talented painter, this is how she'd paint."

"And so she did. Come here, Lloyd."

As Amy came up to her, Margaret Durie reached out a hand. It touched the proffered arm, moved up and rested against the damp cheek. "You are a dear thing, Lloyd, but spare me the tears. I've wasted enough of them in my time. And they are wasteful. What matters is only the setting of a goal and the moving toward it. Do you understand?"

"Yes, I do."

"Good. Now accompany me upstairs, where you'll pick up my correspondence and attend to it in Mrs. McEye's office. I assured her I'd release you to her when convenient, and she understands that my correspondence is your first obligation. Oh, yes, and tell Nugent and company to get back to their duties. Otherwise, they'll have an excuse to do nothing the rest of the day."

Which didn't seem quite fair to Nugent really, thought Amy, but the thought was tempered by this suggestion that Nugent and company were what they were, while Mrs. Lloyd was a dear thing. Hardly the most charitable reaction, but one could live with it.

Mission accomplished, she moved with her charge across that marble expanse of foyer toward the elevator. Passing the West Gallery, Ma'am, who seemed to know exactly where she was in the expanse, motioned at the massive doors.

"Did you find our little tour instructive, Lloyd?"

"Oh, yes. But one thing—if you don't mind?"

"Don't fuss, Lloyd. Just ask your question."

"Well, are these all American artists?"

"Those who did the works in oil, yes. However, it wasn't always the case. My instructor once persuaded my father to purchase some meritorious French impressionist works. Including a Mary Cassatt, whom my father chose to regard as more French than American. One of her finest studies. All disposed of by him very soon after."

"Disposed of? But why?"

Ma'am smiled a wintry smile. "Oh, one might say that for his own reasons he found them offensive. So what is left of the oils is all domestic art somewhat past its prime, though its commercial value is on the ascendant. Is it possible"—Ma'am seemed amused—"that you're considering an investment in it?"

Hardly sensitive of her, Amy thought, to make it so plain that what she had to sell this dear thing could not possibly afford to buy. Sensitivity in Margaret Durie did seem to work on an uneven current. Amy said, "What I had been considering is whether I shouldn't get some books on these painters—"

Ma'am cut that off sharply. Almost contemptuously. "Art as an intellectual exercise, Lloyd? Don't bother."

Definitely, that sensitivity worked on a very uneven current.

*　*　*

FROM the sublime to the ridiculous. Or, Amy thought as Mrs. McEye, cigarette glued to her lower lip, set about showing her office procedure, at least from the sublime to the mundane.

Like stepping down from Olympus to till the potato field below.

However, with the typing of the answers to Ma'am's correspondence, the shadow of sublimity—willful, unpredictable, all-powerful—did briefly reappear. When that *Message received and contents noted* was neatly appended to the foot of the principessa's letter Mrs. McEye, happening to glance over the typist's shoulder, was momentarily transfixed. Then she snatched the letter from the typewriter. She had to squint at it one-eyed because her lips were now so tightly compressed that the cigarette tilted upward and the other eye was right in line with the rising smoke.

"Really, Mrs. Lloyd. Is this what you were told to respond? On the letter itself? Without signature?"

"That's right, Mrs. McEye."

"You're sure?"

And yet, Amy thought, the McEye did know about Ma'am's dislike for her sister—her refusal to acknowledge her title, for instance. However, she didn't seem to know the dislike could extend to this show of witty bad manners. Amy put on the face of innocence. "If you want to ask Miss Margaret about it—"

Mrs. McEye instantly stepped on the brakes. "Well, I don't see any need for that, Mrs. Lloyd. Of course I take your word for it."

Of course, Amy thought. Ho ho ho.

But, as she had to admit to herself while being guided through the office routine, there was much about this pop-eyed, chunky little martinet to admire. The routine entailed the mastery of details piled on details, and the McEye seemed to have every one of them at her fingertips, especially the delicate maneuvering of staff and temporary help so that the family dwelt in a plastic bubble—no, make that a crystal bubble—maintained by flawlessly operating machinery.

To this end there were these duty rosters and daybooks for each day's assignments, present and future, with plenty of blank

146

space in them for the unexpected. And this battery of phones to arrange comings and goings, and the record sheets to record them. It reminded Amy of that time Mike had been briefly and unwillingly drafted as radio dispatcher for the cab company, trying to keep the widely scattered fleet of cars making the right moves. Like playing blindfold chess, he had explained, except that he was playing on a board the size of metropolitan New York and with three times as many pieces. Watching the McEye at the phones as she guided staff through its paces, Amy suspected that even on a board that size and with that many pieces she'd be a dandy chess player.

Abe Silverstone—or was it Audrey?—had been right. What became clear was that the word *housekeeper* was pretty meaningless in this context. What we had here was a grand vizier. Housekeeper all right, but also personnel director, building manager, transportation agent, typist-secretary, and bookkeeper, even though these figures scrupulously transferred to an account book and toted up there were monitored each month by CPA's from the family's business office.

There were a couple of calls from the outside world. A contractor for a cornice repair. One for an electrical installation. Each evidently had a large chip on the shoulder, each finally wound up waving the white flag. During negotiations Mrs. McEye's voice never rose. In fact, it became almost a purr—*what a funny fellow you are in your tantrum*, said that purr—and somehow sounded all the more dangerous for it.

After the second call, a long one, she said to Amy, "You got the gist of that, didn't you?"

"Yes, I did."

"They try to cheat people in this position, you see. A philosophy of soak the rich, so to speak. Unfortunately, there must be many well-to-do people easy to take advantage of."

"I suppose there are," Amy said. "Will I be handling contracts like that, too?" Nice if she could, she thought. A way of paying off some of those arrogant contractor types who took pleasure in soaking that formerly insignificant Lloyd couple down on Thompson Street.

"Possibly. All in good time." The McEye smiled pleasantly,

and the wonder of it was not only the unexpected smile but that in her position she had never had anything done about those discolored teeth. "You know, Mrs. Lloyd, I can see why Miss Margaret is so taken with you. Mannerly and intelligent both? Believe me, an unusual combination nowadays, if you know what I mean. It's been difficult with Nugent replacing me here when she must. Mannerly, yes. But when things get hectic she does tend to lose her head."

"She's been very kind and helpful to me," Amy said, not quite sure why she felt compelled to hand out this bouquet.

The McEye didn't take umbrage. "Oh, she would be. And she'll still be the one to call on when you're tied down here. I've arranged her days off to coincide with yours for that reason. Now it's time for lunch, isn't it? Mine is always sent up here, and I could have yours included. However, if you prefer the staff hall—"

There was something almost wistful about the way she said it, Amy realized, something that suggested she very much wanted her assistant's company at lunch.

"I'd very much like to have lunch with you," Amy said, stretching it considerably.

The McEye was obviously pleased. "That would be nice. I'm having a salad. Mabry prepares a special salad I can recommend. Would you care to try it?"

It was indeed an excellent salad, Amy found, a gigantic bowl of exotic flora, crabmeat, avocado, and spiced croutons. Along with it came a basketful of rolls and what appeared to be a small tub of butter. Peters, the houseman who seemed to have been forgiven for having been briefly hijacked into Gwen Langfeld's meditation circle, arranged a service on each side of the desk, poured coffee, and departed. To her coffee the McEye added enough thick cream so that its residue floated palely on the surface. She was buttering a roll with slow voluptuous pleasure when a phone rang.

"Oh, Lord," she sighed. Then she gave her assistant a look that, Amy thought, could only be described as ponderously mischievous. "Time for you to try your hand at it, Mrs. Lloyd. I'll be standing by." There was something about this, Amy felt, of the flight instructor wishing the student good luck on her first solo.

But she knew there had to be an augury in this trial run when she heard Mike's voice: "Mrs. McEye? Lloyd here."

It would be too weird, she thought, to address him as Lloyd even though the McEye, the protocol freak, was sitting there all ears. Besides, the McEye was practically twinkling at her. "Mike? It's Amy. Where are you?"

"In the garage. As instructed. Hey there, Mrs. Lloyd, how's it going?"

"Very well. Mrs. McEye is showing me the ropes, and we're now having lunch." She observed that the McEye was still twinkling. "Come to think of it, what are you doing about lunch?"

"Believe it or not, baby, I'm Wilson's guest. Couple of sandwiches he went out for and a dip into his six-pack."

"Wilson?" Amy said. "You mean he still—?" She suddenly saw that the McEye had stopped twinkling.

"Wilson?" said Mrs. McEye.

"Wait a second," Amy said into the phone, then reported to that now forbidding presence, "It's Lloyd. He's at the garage as instructed. Wilson's there, too."

"He is, is he?" Mrs. McEye thrust out a hand and Amy placed the phone in it. "Lloyd? What's that about Wilson?" She listened intently, in the process lighting a cigarette and deeply inhaling. Furious, Amy saw. The cigarette smoke, when she ejected it, appeared to eddy not only from her nose but her ears as well. She finally said, "Yes, I understand. But, Lloyd, listen to me. Don't get close to him socially, if you know what I mean. He'll make a nuisance of himself, and you'll regret it."

She listened again. "Yes, yes, he's right about that much. You do report here whenever you complete a trip. Now you're scheduled to pick up Mr. Craig and Mr. Walter at the office at four and to take Mrs. Langfeld to the airport at five, but there may be an interim call, so you remain there. Good-bye, Lloyd."

She put down the phone looking angry and troubled and tamped out the cigarette in an ashtray with a hard pressure of the thumb. "The old fool," she said.

"I beg your pardon?" said Amy.

"Wilson. He's making himself thoroughly at home, so to speak, in the garage office. And your husband's in the way of becoming his victim. He had to be warned about it. I trust he'll take the warning to heart."

Victim, Amy thought. She didn't like the sound of it. "Well, he did say Mr. Levine's not too happy about having Wilson there. If you let Mr. Levine know that you don't either—"

"No." It came out short and sharp. "I don't require Mr. Levine to serve as my deputy. And Wilson can be very difficult."

"But you said victim. What sort of victim exactly?"

"Of gossip. About family. Wilson's served here most of his life, and he's full of distortions and fabrications about family matters, if you know what I mean. Much too shrewd, I'm sure, to try them out on any outsider, but now that he sees Lloyd as staff— You do understand, don't you?"

"Yes, of course," Amy said.

Except, she thought, for one curious aspect of it. The lady herself had previously hammered home that any staff caught in just such distortions and fabrications about the family would get canned on the spot for it. And since Wilson was marked as a long-time offender, why, instead of having been summarily dismissed somewhere along the line, had he been royally pensioned off?

There was that miasma again.

"Aren't you forgetting something, Mrs. Lloyd?" asked the McEye, and for an instant Amy had the feeling that her thoughts were visible. But no, Mrs. McEye was indicating the record sheet on the desk and her expression was once again almost pleasant. Gently reproving, but almost pleasant.

"Sorry," Amy said, "I almost did forget."

She reached across the desk and under the most recent entry on the sheet she wrote—Mrs. McEye craning her stout neck to follow this—*1 P.M. Lloyd at G.*

Mrs. McEye nodded approval. "We now know at a glance —Nugent too for that matter—where to reach him. If his schedule suddenly becomes tight, he'll then have Mr. Levine supply a temporary to help out. Not difficult at all, is it? Though Nugent does have her difficulties with it."

"Well," said Amy, "you did mention that the pressure does mount pretty high at times."

"So to speak. But I can't see it getting the best of you, Mrs. Lloyd." Mrs. McEye went through that business of leaning forward and lowering her voice. "It doesn't seem to trouble you in serving Miss Margaret. And she does have a way of putting one under pressure, doesn't she?"

That warning bell sounded in Amy's head. This growing chumminess was all very well, but the McEye was—no matter how chummy—the representative of the brothers Durie in their too tender oversight of their sister, freedom fighter Margaret. And in that opaque conversation in the elevator, the one thing that hadn't been opaque was Margaret Durie's acid comments on brother Craig and his wife.

Still, Amy thought, there were signs that the McEye was in a confiding mood, and if she didn't take advantage of it, Mike would never forgive her.

She picked her words carefully. "Well, I don't really feel I'm under pressure from Miss Margaret"—the McEye looked skeptical, and that was all that was needed for Amy to proceed—"but she is changeable of mood."

Obviously, this is what the McEye had hoped for, the honest statement. She nodded broadly. "Yes, indeed. Most temperamental. Hard to keep up with at times."

So far, so good, Amy thought. But as Audrey had succinctly put it in describing life in the Big Store, one must always take care to cover her ass. "Most temperamental," Amy said. "But I think that's because she is so intelligent and quick-minded and well informed. She probably finds it hard to understand why I can't always keep up with her."

Mrs. McEye looked sympathetic. "Among many, Mrs. Lloyd."

"Cultivated," Amy said. "That's the word. But how does one become that cultivated when for all those years she cut herself off from the world? And was in such a morbid state. Because she was, wasn't she?"

"Oh, yes. A permanent depression, so it appeared. Withdrawn. Would come downstairs now and then but her only interest seemed to be making sure those pictures in the West Gallery and the dining room were right there as always. Painful really, to watch her go along testing their frames with her fingers to make sure of that, poor dear."

"And she had no tutoring, no private instruction all that time?"

"Wouldn't stand for it," Mrs. McEye said. "Nothing in the way of any instruction until last year, when she came out of that bad time and took up braille. But she did listen endlessly to cultural things on radio and recordings. And did want to be read to. Old plays especially. And news about the theater in the *Times.*"

"The theater?" Amy said. "Not the art news?"

"No, I imagine art is a touchy subject there, Mrs. Lloyd, considering she had a fine talent that was suddenly no use anymore. But Mr. McEye told me that she loved to go to the theater as a girl. Her father—that was Mr. James—had copies printed up of all the plays she ever saw, and that's what she usually wanted read to her. I used to do it for her myself sometimes. Not lately however. Not since she did make the turnaround, so to speak. Has she asked you to read any of those plays to her?"

Careful, Amy thought. Ma'am's intense interest in art—especially feminist art—was not a secret to share. "She hasn't asked me yet," she said.

"Well, sooner or later perhaps." Mrs. McEye returned to her lunch. She ate with almost excessive neatness, pressing a napkin to that overflowing embonpoint with two fingers. Amy suspected from her frowning concentration that mastication was being accompanied by some deep thinking. So it proved. Mrs. McEye said, "Very strictly between us, Mrs. Lloyd, the family is concerned—we all are—about her emotional state. I mean, now that she's miraculously come out of that dreadful depression, could she be going too far the other way?"

"Other way?"

"Yes. Too volatile, so to speak. She seems to be living in a constant state of—well, I suppose you could call it excitement. And at her age she does have just so much energy to spare. She is frail. One look makes that plain enough."

Amy seized opportunity. "You mean there's something physically wrong there? Fainting spells—something like that?"

152

"Oh, no," said Mrs. McEye with assurance. Which, thought Amy, does put me one up on her. And the family. Ma'am's terrifying, glassy-eyed blackout had the look of something concealed from all but Mrs. Lloyd. Not that there was any joy in this little triumph. It was made even worse when Mrs. McEye leaned forward and reverted to the lowered voice. "You see, Mrs. Lloyd, there's a feeling in the family that Miss Margaret is—it's awkward trying to find the words—well, that she's involving herself in some matters beyond her experience. If you know what I mean."

Amy hesitated only the flicker of an eye. "Not really."

"Oh, dear, it is hard to explain. But I can tell you that after never setting foot outdoors all those years she doesn't hesitate now to be driven off somewhere by herself. Wilson would give Mr. Craig the addresses in confidence—a certain office building, the Plaza Hotel, various art galleries—but of course he couldn't go inside with her and report on what she was doing there. Who she was meeting there."

Whom, Any corrected silently. "But," she asked, "why assume she was meeting anyone?"

"Oh, no question about that. Wilson reported that her manner when she entered those places was, well, very purposeful. And when Mr. Craig finally put it to her in the nicest way she flew into the most frightening rage. Far beyond what might be expected at such a natural question. Believe me, Mr. Craig knows her moods very well. Her response on that occasion made him greatly concerned. And then—"

Amy waited. "And then?"

"Well, there was her asking me to hire a private secretary for her. And the way over the past month she rejected several suitable applicants just on my description of them."

Signally honored, Amy thought, that's me. She said, "Is there something so strange in her wanting a private secretary?"

Mrs. McEye held up a hand in protest. "Believe me, Mrs. Lloyd, this is no reflection on you. But why a private secretary all of a sudden with family and staff attending to her with such devotion? What troubled Mr. Craig and Mrs. Jocelyn most—and this is very much between us—was her repeated emphasis on a private secretary, a confidential secretary."

"Just a way of putting it," Amy suggested.

"Yes, but it did seem to mean sharing confidences with an outsider—again no reflection on you, Mrs. Lloyd—rather than with her family. I'll tell you this, I feel it was the best of good luck that you came along just when you did. And Lloyd, too, of course. He appears to be a most desirable addition to staff."

Both Lloyds signally honored, Amy thought. She had the uncomfortable feeling from the McEye's almost intensely sunny regard of her that there was more to come. An invitation to the waltz. Confidential secretary to Ma'am, confidential agent for her terribly devoted family.

Hell and damnation.

Mrs. McEye leaned over farther forward than usual. "I'm sure I don't have to ask whether you share the family's concern for Miss Margaret."

"No, of course not."

"Well then, you can see how much they'd appreciate your help in assuring that well-being." She pressed a hand to the embonpoint. "I for one certainly would. You do understand what I'm getting at, don't you?"

"I believe so."

"Yes. Then if she does communicate—through correspondence, through visits—with people who are strangers to the family, and she shares this with you—"

"I then share it with you," said Amy. "But I really—"

"Please. You must see that this is not a betrayal of Miss Margaret's trust in you. Not one bit. After all, Mrs. Lloyd, you have the family's trust, too. And consider that Miss Margaret after all those years out of the world, so to speak, doesn't realize how it's changed for the worse. Doesn't appreciate how easily she can be victimized by unscrupulous people. In that regard, she is childlike, so to speak. So the family's deep concern is quite natural and proper, isn't it? If you saw a child pull away from its parents and prepare to run out into traffic, the least you'd do is warn the parents, wouldn't you?"

Casuistry lives, Amy thought. "Of course," she said. Unless,

154

she thought, the child happened to be a highly intelligent, fiercely independent woman of seventy.

Still, it seemed from the churning inside her that she wasn't really made for this game. And it could get to be quite a nasty game, too. She had a vivid picture of Craig Durie in his armchair and Jocelyn Durie behind her desk and the McEye with that perpetual hovering, all of them confronting her with a demand for some solid information about God knows what nonsense. But it was Ma'am's private and treasured nonsense whatever it was. As for the idea that Margaret Durie could be readily victimized by anyone, that provided the only comic touch to the business.

Meanwhile, none of this was relevant to the case of Amy Lloyd. The bottom line was that even if she weren't made for this game she'd have to play it as best she could. The stakes were simply too great. Let the Lloyds knock on Domestique's door again, this time with dismissal notices in hand, and it wasn't likely that door would be opened.

The McEye seemed to be well satisfied with the way things had gone. "Now then," she said, "on my Thursdays and Saturdays off, Nugent will attend to the office here as well as she can, and you'll take over as soon as you've finished with Miss Margaret. Which means that early in the evening you'll draw all necessary information from next day's calendar and any additions to it along the way and post the next day's duty rosters on the board. Any questions about that?"

"None that I can think of," said Amy.

"Then let me ask you a question. One of the staff reports illness. Malingering possibly, but staff gets the benefit of the doubt there. Still, that leaves you with some assignments and no one to attend to them. What do you do about it?"

"I suppose," said Amy, "I phone Mrs. Bernius and ask for a suitable temporary to be sent over."

Mrs. McEye regarded her fondly. "Yes, indeed," she said. "You do learn quickly, don't you?"

* * *

MIKE took one more quick reading of Mrs. Mac's handy schedule reminder. No mistake about it: *5 P.M. Mrs. Langfeld and L from R to British Airways, Kennedy.*

So here he was at five-fifteen, dutifully standing beside the parked car at *R* and still no sign of the lady and her *L*. Dead, he thought. Lying upstairs like Elaine, the Lily Maid of Astolat, dead of unrequited love, and nobody had bothered to let him know it. How long did he wait here like this? Or did the chauffeur dare ring that doorbell and inform whoever answered that Gwen Langfeld had better get a move on if she expected to catch her plane?

Of course, a car phone would solve all such problems. It was Wilson who had brought up this car phone thing, and then with a typical Wilsonian mixture of pride in the family's strange ways and irritation at his own martyrdom under them had noted that the family had once tried car phones until Mr. Craig got a troublesome call from his office while on the road and promptly had all the phones removed.

"Quite a temper," Mike had remarked.

"Don't show it," said Wilson, "but don't let that ever fool you."

At five-twenty, thank God, Gwen Langfeld did at last emerge from the building. She looked even smaller than she had appeared to be on introduction—she was really on the tiny side—and was wearing a caftan, a bulky gray cardigan over it, sandals on stockingless feet, and a babushka tied around her head. With that moonface and snub nose, Mike observed, the babushka did nothing for her. As she seated herself he also observed that there was something missing from the scene. *Mrs. Langfeld and L,* said the schedule, but aside from a large pocketbook made of some kind of unfinished leather, there was no luggage.

He addressed her through the open door. "Your suitcases, ma'am?"

She made a vague gesture. "No, it's all right."

"Yes, ma'am." And, he thought when he got the car moving, there was a certain style in walking aboard a transatlantic flight with only a pocketbook as luggage. In her own daft way, Gwen Langfeld had style.

She said nothing until they were well into Queens, crawling through the worst of the rush-hour traffic. Then Mike became aware that she had shifted over in the seat and appeared to be studying his profile. Finally she said in that small voice, "What's your name?"

"Lloyd, ma'am."

"That's right. And you're married to the new housemaid, aren't you? The very tall one with the red hair."

"Yes, ma'am, but she's not a maid. She's Miss Margaret's new secretary."

"She is? I didn't know Aunt Margaret had a secretary. Why would she need one?"

"I believe you'd have to ask her about that, ma'am."

"I suppose. But she's always saying how much she hates people clustering around and helping her. Have you met her?"

"Yes, ma'am. Briefly."

"Then you must have seen how forceful she is. She believes the only true gratification of the spirit lies in setting some goal and moving in every possible way to achieve it. Of course she's wrong. That way can be very destructive to the spirit. Do you know anything about transcendental meditation? In group?"

Oh, boy, Mike thought, here it comes. An invitation to a soirée à la Peters, the erring houseman. He said, "I've heard of it. I'm afraid that I —"

"It means above all — What is your name?"

"Lloyd, ma'am."

"It means above all, Lloyd, that you find your center. You are within the universe, the universe is within you. When you find your center you feel the oneness. Acutely. When I'm home again I want you to share in my gatherings so you can search for that feeling. I think you'd be very responsive. Your wife, too. It'll help her counter that flow of negative forcefulness she must be meeting in Aunt Margaret."

"I'll mention it to her," Mike said, then moved almost as much by concern at the nonflow of traffic as by the feeling he'd better haul himself out of this metaphysical quicksand: "I hope you won't miss your flight, ma'am. This traffic makes slow going."

She made that vague gesture. "No, it's all right. Mrs. McEye made the arrangements."

Now that's real faith, Mike thought. Mrs. Mac, the infallible. Still, there were limits to infallibility as in this case where once they docked at the terminal this moon maiden could wander off somewhere in search of her center and never be seen again. And who would take the rap for that? Well, since his orders were never to leave the car, Mrs. Mac would.

Enlightenment came as soon as he pulled the car up to the curb of the departures area. Before he could open the door, an anxious-looking gent, middle aged, dressed impeccably, emitting a distinct whiff of VIP, had opened it and was helping the passenger out. If not the manager of the airport, at least the manager of the airline. Right behind him was a younger model of VIP on the rise. Also on hand was a redcap standing by an empty handtruck and involved in something of a hassle with travelers who would plant their bags on the truck only to have them immediately pushed off.

Add it all up, Mike thought, and one thing was clear. Mrs. Langfeld — no, make that any of the clan Durie — would never be found wandering off alone at any airport.

The VIP led Mrs. Langfeld away. The younger man pointed at the trunk of the car. "The luggage, man," he said in purest Oxbridge.

"No luggage," said Mike. "None at all."

He strove for a tone that would indicate surprise that anyone could imagine Mrs. Langfeld traveled with luggage. Young Oxbridge actually looked apologetic. "Ah, then," he said awkwardly, and as he moved off was clearly attempting to cover the awkwardness by making a firmly dismissive gesture at the waiting redcap. The redcap, taken aback in his turn, rallied just in time to give Oxbridge the finger as he disappeared through the door.

Just another couple of cases, Mike thought cheerfully as he got back into the car, of people who hadn't found their centers.

* * *

"WELL," said Amy, "luggage or no luggage, she is not checking into a hotel in London."

She was helping Mike put away the order delivered on schedule by Hale & Hale, clothiers: the livery sheathed in a black plastic bag, the rest in boxes of various sizes, everything with that winged lion crest on it. With the dresser here and the closet there, they were making a sort of gavotte of it while Mike described the trip to Kennedy.

His wife's authoritative tone interested him. "Do tell," he said.

"No hotel. The family owns a house in London. According to the McEye, a loverly Georgian town house in Belgravia, all staffed. And I'm sure that whatever Gwen needs is all laid on there for her."

"It's the only way to live," Mike said. "Once folks realize how easy that makes travel, everybody'll be doing it."

"And," Amy said from the recesses of the closet, "they also own an estate in Scotland and another one on Gonquit Island off Maine—the whole island is theirs—and another one in Aiken, South Carolina. All staffed and waiting."

"And an oceangoing yacht berthed down the block to complete the ensemble."

"No yacht," Amy said. She emerged from the closet, her face bright with pleasure. "I'm glad you brought that up. The best part is that the McEye was so humorless about it."

"The no yacht?"

"Yes. All because of James Hamilton Durie. When the Morgans and other nouveaux riches were going in for yachts he refused to. Want to guess why?"

"Too easy," Mike said. "The old gent was subject to seasickness."

"Oh, no. That's terribly plebian. The reason was he felt—and I quote the McEye—that motor-yachting was vulgar. Isn't that beautiful?"

"It is. But sailboating?"

"His thing. That's why he bought that island off Maine. He and his wife did a lot of sailing there. Matter of fact, that's where they and the boys were when Margaret went down those stairs. I

159

suppose the worst of it for them was that they were so far away when it happened. They didn't get back here until the next day."

"Double misery," Mike said.

"It must have been. Especially the way James Hamilton felt about her. The McEye said that while he could be hard on the two boys, there was nothing he wouldn't do for her. Like her taking up painting seriously. He didn't like it, but when she came on stubborn, he just buckled at the knees. Anyhow, that's how Mr. McEye described it to the McEye. She hadn't started working here yet when it actually happened. Of course, as butler he'd be in the middle of everything, ears fanned wide."

"Just where she is now," Mike said. "Come to think of it, what made her so chatty about all this? You must have really captivated her."

"Oh, I did," Amy said. "For the wrong reason."

Her tone was suddenly bitter, Mike noted, her face troubled. He recognized the symptoms of a downer in the making. He seated himself on the edge of the bed and patted the coverlet. "Sit."

She sat down against him and he put an arm around her waist. "Speak."

"Hell and damnation."

"Not very enlightening. How did you captivate her for the wrong reason?"

"Because she asked me to report back on Ma'am's private little doings, and I let her believe I would. After that, she couldn't have been friendlier."

"I see. But you don't intend to oblige?"

"Of course not. Ma'am's explicit orders are not to oblige. You can see she's right about people snooping and reporting back on her. Since she insists on confidentiality, I'm not going to be the one to violate it."

"You realize," Mike said, "that the family put Mrs. Mac up to this. And that they do have a legitimate concern."

"Only up to a point. What's it their concern if she wants to go woman's lib or immerse herself in trendy art or whatever? Or meet outsiders she's interested in? If they want to keep an eye on her every minute, let 'em hire a private detective to do it."

160

"Never. Definitely not the Durie style. Terribly déclassé."

"It's not funny, Mike. It's ugly. If the McEye presses me for the latest about Ma'am's doings and saying, I have to be the vague, evasive liar. For that matter, so do you. You don't believe the McEye asked me to become her pet snoop without knowing I'd go to you with it, do you?"

"No, I guess not."

"So?"

"So," said Mike, "you're still the one in the direct line of fire. Look. Suppose you went to Ma'am with this and asked for sanctuary? It even proves to her how trustworthy you are. Then—"

"Oh, please. If I tell her about it, she'll head for a confrontation with Craig and Walter that'll knock the roof loose. After which the McEye will be out for our blood. Remember George Oliphant?"

"Yes."

"Well, the only difference between him and the McEye is that she's fantastically competent at her job. I'll give her that much."

"But no information about Miss Margaret's secret life."

"None," Amy said flatly.

"It's up to you," Mike acknowledged. "But I still can't see anyone so competent at her job taking you to her bosom—and what a bosom—just because you agreed—"

"Seemed to agree."

"—seemed to agree you'd be her snoop. There must be more to it than that. You did all right as assistant administrator of the works, didn't you?"

"Yes."

He squeezed her waist hard. "Let's not be excessively modest. Or is that job just low-level routine?"

"All levels. What really made her cup overflow was when she left me alone midafternoon—she went inside for a quick nap, I suspect—so that I was stuck with some significant correspondence. Each of those other four places they own has a manager who writes a full report on staff and maintenance every month. What goes on, what's needed, and so forth. The letters I was handed to trim down and collate for Walter's reading—"

"Walter?"

"He's in charge of those places. Anyhow, the letters were all a jumble, and two of them, the ones from Aiken and Maine, were in impossible handwriting using native dialect. When the McEye saw how I had filtered out all the worthwhile information and collated everything in just two pages, tears came to those pop-eyes. Well, not really tears, but they did shine with gratitude."

"So they should. By any chance, was there a hint in the London letter that Gwen's not-quite-separated husband is occupying that apartment there?"

"No. But when I was on the elevator this morning with Ma'am and Dorothy and Glendon—"

"Going where?"

"To the ground floor with Ma'am. She wanted to show me the dining room and West Gallery. Both loaded with paintings. There's a full-length portrait of her in the dining room that's really dazzling. She's about eighteen—that must have been soon before the accident—and even in that freaky Jazz Age outfit she's meltingly beautiful. All aglow. There are also—"

"Hold it," Mike said. "We're off the track. What happened in the elevator?"

"Oh, that. Well, they were talking about some kind of showdown Glendon had with his parents, and I think it had something to do with Gwen and her husband." Amy looked at his face. "Not very satisfactory, is it?"

"Not very." Mike stood up. "You know, if we got the tape recorder down from the farm—"

"No, Michael. I do not speak to tape recorders. Only to people."

He recognized from her tone that this was not negotiable. "All right, you won't mind if I take notes while you tell it to me, would you? Mrs. Lloyd's day at length?"

"Not really. But first supper. Then I want to take a walk with you. I want to get outside awhile before claustrophobia sets in. Don't you feel that way?"

"I'm not shut in most of the day," Mike pointed out. "What I feel is an itch to get these rewarding little details down on paper. However, right now I'll settle for that pizza joint near the garage."

"We do get free viands downstairs."

"The pizza joint," Mike said. "Then a walk. Then we come back and you tell all."

"But not tonight. We're off all day tomorrow, so—"

"So tomorrow," Mike said, "we'll be driving up to the farm to reclaim the TV set and stereo and tapes and some books. After all, if this place is home, it should be a little more homey. Right?"

"I suppose."

"Then right now, baby, we eat, drink, and be merry. We walk. Then we come home and you tell all. And it's early to bed because tomorrow the bugle sounds at dawn. We have a lot of mileage to cover in one day."

"Oh, God," Amy said. "On my day off."

THE Massachusetts expedition went well, eased by traffic along the way that was at least tolerable and colored by bursts of crimson New England autumn foliage. With Amy at the wheel for the final Boston-to-New York run they didn't make the speed they might have—as she pointed out, she had a feeling she wasn't supposed to be behind this wheel at all—but still they were back home by midnight.

Security man Krebs let them in, and at Amy's request—Mike wondered what the response would have been had he made it—Krebs kindly unlocked the workshop door so that a handcart could be obtained to fetch the TV set, stereo components, and cartons of books from the car. When Mike had brought back the wagon to the garage and returned on foot he found that his wife had whipped up a platter of sandwiches, located a couple of wedges of extravagantly rich cake, and had set places at the table in the staff hall for them. She was already hard at work on a sandwich.

Mike poured himself a cup of coffee from the machine and joined her. He looked into a sandwich. "What is this stuff?"

"Lobster salad," Amy said thickly. "And that looks like Black Forest cake, doesn't it?"

"It does. And this is your idea of what to go to sleep on?"

"Don't worry, I'll sleep." Amy shoved over the two slips of paper before her. "Tomorrow's schedules. Kind of interesting."

Hers, he saw, was not the interesting one: *8 A.M. Miss Margaret.* On the other hand, his, besides the expected office trips, had two items of interest. At eleven-thirty, there was Miss Margaret, no destination entered. At three P.M. Miss Camilla to Locust Valley, Long Island.

"Tell me something," Amy said. "Why, if Miss Camilla has her own cute little car, does she need to be chauffeured out to Long Island?"

"Don't know. Maybe her car is in the shop getting yet another body job. According to Sid Levine, she's that kind of driver."

"Is she?" Amy said, eyebrows raised. "Well, talking about body jobs —"

"Yes, dear. I grant that Camilla is state-of-the-art. I also suspect that her daddy Walter has been the only real love of her life since her mother died. As you are the love of mine."

"True," Amy acknowledged. "But that girl is something to behold. And there is an aura of decadence about her. I just want to post a warning. You look very good in that uniform."

"Role-playing," Mike said. "Trust me. Now how about the more interesting item here? Miss Margaret at eleven-thirty, no destination. No destination for the record? I imagine that's what stirs up the family. Has them put Mrs. Mac and her snoops on it."

"We could be facing some questions," Amy warned.

"We could. In that case, what do I answer?"

Amy thought it over. "Nothing really untruthful," she decided. "You could say that the one to ask is Miss Margaret, isn't it? All innocence."

Mike curled his lip at her. "First that gaudy line you handed your mother about my wild success as private tutor. Now this. And you told me you didn't have a talent for dissembling."

"You know I don't. Or do I?" Amy gave this some thought too. "I suppose if I am developing a talent in that direction, it's because that's how you survive here. And you know what Abe said about survival."

"Yep," Mike said. "It's the name of the game."

When, with the sandwiches and cake wiped out, they made their way up to the third floor Mike trundled the handcart into the sitting room. He looked around. "Home," he said. "Pretty cozy at that."

Amy nodded. "It is, isn't it? I just wish the McEye wasn't right next door."

"You can't have a picnic without a gadfly," Mike said. "Hey, has it struck you that she's located right over Ma'am's apartment? What's chances she's got a hole drilled in her floor and keeps an eye on Ma'am odd hours?"

"If Craig or Walter asked her to," Amy said. "But they wouldn't. Besides she married into that apartment. It used to be McEye's when he was butler. Oh, yes, and who do you think occupied ours? I'll give you a clue. A painter."

"Easy. John Singer Sargent himself."

"Oh, no. He'd be on the second floor swimming in luxury. Think," Amy admonished. She looked aggrieved. "Now what was the use of my sitting here telling you everything I picked up during the day—and you were taking notes, too—and then you don't remember any of it?"

"Darling, that's why I take notes. They're my memory bank. Wait a second. A painter. Obviously in residence. Could it be the one who gave young Miss Margaret her lessons?"

"None other. And painted that great portrait of her. The one in the dining room. This room was his studio."

"Artist-in-residence," Mike said.

"So he was. Anyhow, this whole apartment was his, and it was kept empty all those years after he left until we moved in."

"Aha," said Mike. "And that explains the strange experience I had last night when I woke in the small hours."

"You slept like the dead all night."

"I woke and sensed a presence. I tiptoed to the door and looked in here. And there was this transparent ghostly figure—male—wearing beret and string tie, standing at a transparent easel, but he wasn't painting. Would you like to know what he was doing?"

Amy compressed her lips but, Mike knew, it was just a case of waiting her out. At last she said, "All right, what was he doing?"

"Laughing his head off. Peals of silent laughter filled the air."

"Silent laughter?"

"Naturally, coming from a ghost. And do you know why? Because, if memory serves, he was the one who advised James Hamilton Durie to collect French impressionists. And Mary Cassatt. Which collection James quickly sold, thus dishing his descendants out of a few million dollars worth of great art. True?"

"That part of it. But how could he tell at the time?"

"He couldn't. Because, my dear, despite the awe he inspired, he was just your typical small-minded, uncomprehending Philistine."

"Not typical," Amy said. "He evidently was awesome. Moses on the mountain."

"I think that you may—"

"Awesome," said Amy. "I saw that portrait of him and his wife. Even John Singer Sargent felt it and couldn't get out from under it."

* * *

A sort of death watch, Amy thought. Ma'am's face was expressionless as she listened to the roll call of obituaries, but she was obviously wound up tight, the hands bearing down hard on the knob of the cane propped before her. From that degree of tension it couldn't be just random bad news that was anticipated. There had to be a particular concern here about someone Margaret Durie would not name. Perhaps speaking that name aloud might be too painful. Which suggested, however illogically, that this daily reading of the obit index was simply a roundabout way of hearing that name, if and when it was listed.

Devious if true. And touching.

"That's all there is," Amy said, and saw her auditor visibly relax. "The art news now?" It would be a relief to do the art news. At least one knew what to look for in it. Jason Cook.

"Yes," Ma'am said. Then abruptly, "No. Wait a moment." The slender fingers fluttering over the packet of yet unopened mail were against the bottom envelope, the largest there, the kind Mike used for mailing short stories. "Who is this from, Lloyd?"

Amy looked closer. "From the return address, ma'am, the Upshur Institute."

"I thought so." The voice hardened. "You should have let me know it at once. I told you about Mrs. Upshur. Foolish of you not to understand I'd regard any message from her as urgent."

Amy felt resentment start to percolate. "I didn't think it was my place to read the return addresses on your mail, Miss Durie."

"Indeed? Then from now on —"

A phone on the desk rang. Blessed instrument, Amy thought. A heaven-sent call to allow tempers to cool.

"Answer that," Ma'am said, her tone indicating that this intrusion was no cooling agent. "Whoever it is, I'm not available."

"Yes, ma'am," Amy said. White phone in-house, she reminded herself; black phone outside line. She picked up the black phone and the white one continued to ring. She made the change to white, discovering in the process that there was a strip of white felt along its handpiece. Of course. A means of iden-

167

tifying which was which for the blind. But an in-house call to this apartment? On the McEye's day off? "Mrs. Lloyd here," she said with trepidation.

"It's Nugent in the office, ma'am. A troublesome matter for you, so it looks to be."

Amy realized her hands were trembling. A troublesome matter, and there was Ma'am glaring in her direction. "Yes, Nugent?"

"A call from Mrs. Jocelyn of a sudden," Nugent sounded panicky. "She wants a car at ten prompt. And Lloyd—your mister that is—I mean Lloyd, ma'am—well, he's not to be found. Not in his room nor staff hall nor the garage. And he has to arrange for the extra driver."

Curse Mrs. Jocelyn, Amy thought wrathfully. From the first look at Madam Chairperson she could be marked as nemesis. But Mike not to be found? The light suddenly dawned. He hadn't come to bed with her, but had headed for the typewriter instead. And as sometimes happened when he had this fever, he might have been at it till dawn and, tuned in only to the alarm clock, was now sleeping it off.

Let Ma'am glare her impatience, she thought, there wouldn't be any dereliction of duty on Mike's part while she was filling the McEye's shoes. "Nugent?"

"Yes, Mrs. Lloyd?"

"Is there a spare key to that apartment?"

"Well, yes, ma'am," said Nugent, thus settling that little question, "but I don't really—"

"He's right there, Nugent. Take a minute off, use that key, and attend to the matter personally. Do you know what I mean?"

"I think I do, ma'am."

"Personally. At once. Thank you, Nugent."

Amy firmly put down the phone and braced herself for some hostile questioning, but Margaret Durie apparently had not the slightest interest in the mysterious workings of staff. "If you're quite finished," she said coldly, "bring me the letter opener."

Amy placed it in the outstretched hand. The envelope had been doubly sealed with a strip of tape over its glued-down flap.

Ma'am found the edge of the tape and deftly slid the blade under and along it. She motioned at the breakfast service before her. "Clear this away. And no need to remain standing."

Amy sat down and hastily moved the service to her side of the table. There was a change in the atmosphere, she sensed. The tension was still there, but there was no more bile in it. Now there appeared to be a taut eagerness. The poker player's eagerness in drawing cards with a big pot on the table.

And, in fact, Ma'am did remove two cards from the envelope. Neutral-colored, large — about half the size of a sheet of typing paper — and they were speckled all over by almost invisible little dots. Braille. Of course. And there was a greenish slip of paper accompanying them, easily identifiable as a check.

Watching those fingers search out the message of the dots, Amy decided that the poker-playing analogy was pretty accurate really, especially if one had in mind the kind of player who, after drawing the cards, could mask all reactions to them.

The mask fell away as Ma'am finally put aside the cards and rested her fingertips on the check. Although the blank eyes were disconcertingly focused below Amy's, the face, thank God, was friendly. At its most charming, Amy thought with some irritation. The old woman may not have seen herself in the mirror for fifty years, but she must sense that when she turned on that charm it was enough to make the birds sing. Possibly excluding Gwen Durie's gift canary in the bedroom, which never did seem to sing.

Ma'am smiled. "Our dear Mrs. Upshur," she remarked. "Full of sage advice, and" — she shook her head pityingly — "confusion when it comes to her accounts. Are you confused in the handling of your accounts, Lloyd?"

"I don't believe so, ma'am."

"Indeed? Perhaps we ought to make you treasurer of Mrs. Upshur's Institute. It would do her good to deal with someone not as beholden to her as I am. However, since I am treasurer by title, I suffer the obligation. On my desk, Lloyd, a ruler and a pen. Bring them here."

Amy brought them. The ruler was rather an unusual one, she

169

observed, silver from the look and heft of it, a flat six-inch square with an open slot along its center. The pen was a heavy, old-fashioned silver fountain pen which could have been a family heirloom.

Ma'am rested the cane against the arm of the chair. "Now stand here at my shoulder, Lloyd. That's right. And do exactly as I instruct. Make sure this check is face up and place the ruler over the appropriate spaces so it will contain my margins. Then you'll guide my hand as I write. I have a tendency, so I've learned, to crowd my letters."

Pathetic pride, Amy reflected, as she followed orders. It would have been so simple for her to fill out the check, after which Ma'am could attend to the signature. But pride—that fierce sense of independence—wouldn't allow for it.

Centering the ruler on the check below its imprint *West Side National Bank* followed by *The Upshur Institute,* Amy took that slender hand in hers and in the process of writing became aware that she was not merely guiding it, she was controlling it.

"Payable to cash," Ma'am instructed: "three thousand dollars."

She signed her name with little difficulty however, and on the reverse of the check signed again in endorsement. She carefully replaced the cap on the pen. "A nuisance," she said, "but a self-imposed one. Do you think, Lloyd, that one has the right to complain about a self-imposed nuisance?"

"I suppose not, ma'am."

"Quite right. I was rude to you a little while ago, wasn't I?"

Amy's tongue clove to her palate. She finally managed to say, "Well, I should have understood that certain mail—"

"I was rude, Lloyd. I am at times. A bad habit fostered by the insensitive people I deal with so often. Hegnauer, for example, has a rhinoceros hide. You are certainly not in that category. But she did, in line of duty, demonstrate a means of soothing away emotional soreness. Sit down, Lloyd."

Amy sat down and suddenly found their positions reversed. Ma'am now stood behind her, fingers moving from her upper arms to her shoulders. "I forget how tall you are, Lloyd. Now bear with me."

The fingers—surprisingly strong fingers—moved to the back of her neck digging in, probing, massaging. "Soothing?" Ma'am asked.

"Oh, yes." And, Amy thought, embarrassing. Mike sometimes provided this treatment, but it was different when he did it. This was more like mental portrait-painting time all over again, a repeat of that introductory session. And kind as its intentions were, it somehow had the same creepy effect as the first time. Especially when, with thumbs probing the back of the neck, the fingers came to rest a little too snugly against her throat.

Mercifully, it didn't go on very long. "There now," said Ma'am, "that did have a beneficial effect, didn't it?"

"Yes, thank you," Amy said. With the hope of getting back to comforting routine, she asked, "Shall I look through the art news now? I mean, for anything about the Jason Cook Gallery?"

"No, don't bother. I told Mrs. McEye I may want the car this morning. Has that been arranged?"

"Yes, it has." Actually, Amy thought, that schedule hadn't indicated *may want* but *did want*, so it appeared that in Margaret Durie's case final decisions could be made on whim. "It'll be waiting at eleven o'clock."

"Plenty of time then. Come along."

Talk about emotional highs and lows, Amy thought, the woman was plainly in a state of exhilaration as, with the Upshur cards in hand, she led the way into the bedroom. At the dresser there she opened a drawer and drew out a pair of scissors with long narrow blades. With the same unerring hand she had demonstrated in wielding the letter opener, she sheared the braille messages into narrow strips which scattered on the dresser. Enjoying herself at it, Amy suspected. Happily venting the last of her temper this way on the irritating Mrs. Upshur's irritating message.

Ma'am returned the scissors to the drawer and fluttered her fingers at the mound of scraps. "Dispose of that, Lloyd. Then draw the windows. All of them."

Amy disposed of the scraps in the wastebasket and drew down the windows, avenue side and street side. Tall and wide as they were, they slid down effortlessly. With the last one closed, she

171

became aware of how insistent the sound of the morning traffic had been. Now the silence was like a pressure against the ears, the only thing disturbing it a tentative chirping from the canary Philomela.

Ma'am grimaced. "Do cover that birdcage, Lloyd."

Amy unwillingly did so. Another sample of that occasional and curious insensitivity in Margaret Durie. Poor Philomela, apparently with no songs left, was condemned to darkness for a few hopeful chirps. And never mind what Mike might remark about the Pathetic Fallacy. This was insensitivity, especially in someone who herself lived in blackness.

Ma'am arranged herself on the chaise longue near the avenue window. It was satin, white as everything else in the room was white, and against its cushions the pale face became almost all sightless eyes and glaring red lipstick.

"I want you to read something to me, Lloyd. You've had sufficient education to read a play aloud?"

"Well, not education in dramatic arts, I'm afraid."

"Just as well." Ma'am sounded amused. "I don't require dramatic performance, just a reading. Those bookshelves there, beside that electronic device. The lowest shelf to the right."

Amy kneeled before the designated shelf. The tall, slender volumes arranged here were bound in limp leather, their titles in gold on their spines. Going by the titles, Amy saw, they all appeared to be plays. Actually, from the look of them, bound playscripts.

"Which one should I read, ma'am?"

"A fair question. What do you have to offer?"

Oh, yes, Amy thought, when she's in a rollicking mood it's game-playing time for all. "Well, there's *Cynara*, ma'am. And *Reunion in Vienna*. *Private Lives*. *The Barretts of Wimpole Street —* "

"Yes, that one. Now bring a chair close to me and make yourself comfortable. And don't emote, if that's the word for it."

Amy seated herself and took a deep breath. Footlights on, she told herself as she started reading in what, to her ears at least, sounded like clear and well-modulated tones. She was immediately pulled up short by a directional forefinger aimed at her.

"I asked you not to emote, Lloyd. And kindly do not read the name of the character preceding each speech. A brief pause and the least change of inflection will inform me that someone else is now speaking."

"Yes, ma'am."

"In my time, Lloyd, I saw all these plays when they were first presented on the stage. All. Some of them several times. I'm not asking you to recreate those experiences for me. I will do that myself. You will simply provide the wherewithal. That's not too difficult to understand, is it?"

"Not at all, ma'am," Amy said. And, she thought with feeling, it wasn't the words that moved her, it was the appeal in that voice, the shade of wistfulness that was evidently always there right under the surface of this otherwise fiery creature.

With that settled, the reading went well until the end of the first act when she found herself getting winded. But one act at a reading appeared sufficient for the audience.

"Nicely done, Lloyd. Now tell me. Did you know about the romance between Robert Browning and Elizabeth Barrett?"

"Yes, I did."

"Very good. So you realize marriage impends in this case. Would you approve the marriage of a shaggy-haired poet, however talented, to the well-bred daughter of a prosperous merchant, if you were that merchant?"

"Well, ma'am, I don't believe this involved class. Wasn't it more a matter of an unhealthy relationship between father and daughter? An intense possessiveness on his part? I don't think Mr. Barrett would have tolerated any man who came courting his daughter."

Ma'am smiled. "A wise child. You give me hope for your generation, Lloyd. Did you ever hear of Brian Aherne and Katherine Cornell?"

"Katherine Cornell, I think, ma'am. An actress?"

"The actress of her day. She *was* Elizabeth Barrett as Aherne was Browning. Magnificent. I suspect there's no one like that performing today. But it's going on eleven now, isn't it?"

"Yes, ma'am."

"Then get yourself a coat for street wear and join me here.

You're coming along on a little business trip. Mrs. Upshur's business, dear incompetent that she is."

When they emerged from the building Mike was waiting beside the car, and, Amy surmised, after his first surprised view of her he had to be role-playing like mad. He ushered mistress and secretary into the car with frozen-faced gravity. "Where to, ma'am?"

"The West Side National Bank, Lloyd, at Broadway and Eightieth Street. And you do drive carefully, don't you? I dislike the unexpected start and stop."

"Very carefully, ma'am."

Luck of the draw, Amy thought. Once Ma'am was left to her banking, she'd have a chance to renew acquaintance with her husband. And, having turned it over in her mind, she felt she did owe him an apology for her handling of Nugent's panicky phone call.

But the apology was not to be delivered yet. Ma'am, given a hand out of the car at the bank, said, "Mrs. Lloyd and I won't be long, Lloyd. You'll wait here."

"I will, ma'am."

Regrettable, Amy thought, but nevertheless complimentary that she herself was to be part of Margaret Durie's confidential business. But then, what were confidential secretaries for?

Inside the bank she observed pityingly that Ma'am's demeanor underwent a subtle change. The same brave front but shaded with uncertainty. The hand did not rest lightly on Amy's wrist but gripped it hard in this foreign territory. The cane tapped on the floor and sometimes moved searchingly in little arcs.

"I understand that the manager is a Mr. Fontaine," Ma'am said. "Have someone inform him I'm here."

Amy passed this on to a sour-looking guard. He disappeared for a while, and when he reappeared he was all sweetness. With him was a deferential young man. "Miss Durie, I'm glad to finally meet you. I'm Mr. Fontaine."

"You do have an office?" Ma'am said.

Fontaine seemed momentarily caught off balance by this direct approach. "Yes, of course. Of course."

He led the way to it and saw the ladies seated before his desk. "Coffee?" he inquired. "Or if—"

"No," Ma'am said. She withdrew the check from her purse. When she held it up Amy took it and placed it on the desk.

Fontaine studied it. "Cash? In any particular form? I mean, denominations? Hundreds?"

"Quite a bundle that way, isn't it?" Ma'am said coldly. "You do have thousand-dollar bank notes?"

Again Fontaine seemed caught off balance. "Yes. But there is— Well, that does mean some red tape. I mean, we register the serial number of each note of that denomination when we pay it out, and that might mean some bother for you. I mean—"

Ma'am cut this short. "I know what you mean. And I'm not here to be engulfed by your red tape. If I ask for five-hundred-dollar notes—?"

"No problem at all," Fontaine said with relief. "None. If you ladies don't mind waiting?"

He took off, obviously glad to do so, and Amy found her emotions somewhat tangled. On the one hand, poor Mr. Fontaine. On the other hand, oh, what a pleasure to deal with stuffy institutions the way Margaret Durie could.

Ma'am remarked, "Idiotic is the word for it, Lloyd, don't you think? A woeful species of bank, this. But I don't have much choice. Mrs. Upshur lives nearby. It's convenient to her."

Poor Fontaine must have moved like a bandersnatch. He very soon rejoined them, money in hand. He sat down, a little breathless. "And here we are," he said brightly. He held out the money midway between his client and her secretary. Amy took it and touched it to Ma'am's fingertips. The fingertips rejected it.

"All five-hundred-dollar notes, Lloyd?"

The notes appeared to be freshly minted and were hard to separate from each other. Amy painstakingly went through each. "Yes, ma'am."

This time when she offered them they were not rejected, and Ma'am made a careful count. "An envelope," she said.

Fontaine hastily produced one from the desk and passed it along by way of Amy. Ma'am placed the notes in the envelope, folded it in half and tucked it into her pocketbook. Amy, watching this, felt a sudden discomfort. Being asked to confirm the denominations of the bills and now that careful counting of them by Ma'am. Was it possible—a mean thought, but was it remotely possible—that the reason the confidential secretary hadn't been asked to make out that check herself, not including signature, of course, was that the secretary was not entirely trusted? Impossible. Then why this feeling that the hand she had guided through the writing process might have been there just to make sure of what she was writing? Especially the amount being entered.

Really a horrid thought. Grossly unjust.

Mike opened the car door. "Home, Miss Durie?"

"No. Central Park, Lloyd. Inside the park. It's possible to make a complete circuit of it that way, isn't it?"

"Yes, ma'am."

"Then do so. Then to the Plaza Hotel. Mark the time. My lunch reservation at the Palm Court is for one o'clock."

Life's surprising little rewards, thought Amy. First partners with her boss in her banking, then on to lunch with her at the Plaza.

Wrong.

This time, when Ma'am was guided to the sidewalk before the hotel entrance, the doorman spurning everyone else in sight to trot over and take her in hand, she said to secretary and chauffeur, "You'll both wait here. Stay close by, Lloyd," and that was that.

Mike opened the front door of the car and Amy sulkily got in. He pulled the car up a few lengths to unblock the entrance and cut off the motor. He squeezed Amy's shoulder sympathetically. "Poor baby. You thought you were going to lunch with her majesty, didn't you?"

"I did not think any such thing," Amy said with acerbity.

"Yes, you did. But never mind, you'll get there. According to the view in this mirror, Margaret smiles on you very tenderly now and then. Meanwhile, explain something to me. What was she doing in that bank? With people in the family ready to handle such sordid details. Not to mention Mrs. Mac and the family accountant."

"Because this looked like highly personal banking. It was for that Mrs. Upshur, the Institute lady. Ma'am's treasurer of the Institute, and for all I know the family doesn't even suspect it. I

176

think it could be her way of proving to herself she's just as competent in business matters as Craig and Walter."

"If not on the same scale."

"Obviously," said Amy. "But you know—"

"Yes?"

"The banking she did was strange. Cashed an Institute check for three thousand dollars, put the money in her purse, and that was it. I thought she was going to drive over and give the money to Mrs. Upshur, but she didn't. No Mrs. Upshur, just Central Park and here."

"Meaning," said Mike, "that she's now gallivanting around with three thousand dollars in that purse. Could it be that she's simply a very heavy tipper?"

"Not that heavy. It's all in five-hundred-dollar bills. That's strange too, isn't it? Hardly what you use for pocket money. I find it all somehow disturbing."

"Don't," Mike advised. "Just consider that Hemingway may have been wrong when he said that the rich were the same as everybody else except they had more money. They also seem full of surprises. Take the case I have under consideration. Camilla. Remember little Camilla, the living Barbie doll? Daddy Walter's precious prize package?"

There was a way men had, Amy thought, of confiding to you their low regard of that girl across the room they couldn't keep their eyes off. "What about her?"

"I'm to drive her out to Locust Valley at three o'clock. And if you're going to remind me that I'll never make it back in time to take Craig and Walter home from the office, I've already arranged for an extra driver with Sid Levine. The point is, why is Camilla going out to Locust Valley?"

"All right, why?"

"Not for fun. From what her father and uncle had to say when I drove them in this morning, she's making a business call on a Miss or Mrs. Laura Sandoval. Laura, as she's known to the Duries, turned over a huge portfolio of securities to them last year. They've been reorganizing it—winnowing out the dogs, as Walter put it—and Laura doesn't understand what they're doing and might withdraw the portfolio. And who is delegated to ex-

177

plain everything to her and make sure she doesn't withdraw the portfolio? Camilla."

Amy knew she was being unfair in seizing this opportunity, but she seized it. "If you're surprised," she said, "it's because you still believe deep down that any pretty blonde can't be more than a dumb and incapable sex object."

"You were surprised, too," Mike said. "It showed on your face. How about an apology for that slur?"

"Half an apology. No, wait, I do owe you one. For the way I had Nugent wake you up ahead of the alarm clock this morning. I should have phoned Sid Levine myself, not laid that on you."

"And subjected Nugent to such embarrassment as I have—"

"Miss Durie's car." The doorman was looking in at the window. "Okay, you can back it up."

Mike hastily backed it up. "Twenty minutes?" he muttered during the process.

"She's there all right," Amy said. "Perhaps she couldn't get a table."

"Miss Margaret Durie? With a reservation?"

But as Ma'am was guided into her seat there were no recriminations. In fact, Amy observed, she looked all aglow. "Now we'll go home, Lloyd," she said.

On the way she reached out a hand and found Amy's knee. Her fingers dug into it. "Describe our itinerary, Lloyd. Wisely."

Wisely? Amy thought. But of course. "We went for a long drive through the park, ma'am. Then we went home."

"And that was all?"

"That was all, ma'am."

"So it was," said Margaret Durie.

*   *   *

178

LIKE her meditative cousin Gwen, Mike learned, Camilla Durie was not one to be ruled by the clock. Twenty minutes overdue, she finally emerged from the house followed by houseman Brooks carrying a weekend bag and an attaché case. Even done up in that conservative suit, Mike took note, she was as pretty and curvy as remembered. And as peremptory.

"Old Haywain Road, right past Locust Valley, Lloyd. Follow it to the gates there. Now let's move it."

But unlike her cousin, she was not inclined to be chatty en route. As soon as the car was on the move she opened the attaché case and drew from it what appeared to be yards of computer printout. Pencil in hand, she worked at them with total absorption. What is this world coming to, Mike marveled after a couple of furtive glances at the rearview mirror. A Barbie doll with brains. Anyhow, business brains.

That oddity digested, he turned his thoughts to his own intriguing business. The book. The work eventually in progress. He was at the point now—the best part of writing—where just considering the project gave him a charge. But it was a shapeless project so far, the Duries, individually and collectively. And the way they remained under one roof—even granting the size of the roof—when they could easily live separate lives. It would be ironic if concern for Margaret Durie, the eldest, bound them to this way of life, because she herself so detested that concern.

And there seemed to be another force operating here, the shade of the Jovian, long-dead James Hamilton Durie himself. The book could begin with this generation, then flash back to him. Or, tempting thought, could it be a massive generational story starting way back with those colonial Duries and Cheathams, real-estate hustlers and rum distillers? And following that grim Scotch Calvinist drive—there had to be fascinating bends in it here and there—to its three billion.

A generational novel, solidly grounded, vividly colored. The trouble lay in the amount of research required, because the catch to chauffeuring like this was that you couldn't schedule library time. For that matter, according to the rules the chauffeur couldn't even do sight-seeing around that museum like ground floor. Amy's description of it had been sketchy at best. Which was hardly her fault. It was hard to examine the scenery closely when you had to keep on eye on the boss every instant. Still, if all went well Mrs. Mac might soften the rule a bit.

No, not Mrs. Mac. Margaret Durie had taken to Amy, no question there. And, not too subtly, had also made her chauffeur her co-conspirator. Given some time . . .

Concentration on this was abruptly broken as they rolled into Nassau County. "You can make better time than this, Lloyd."

That ringing soprano in throbbing recitative, Mike thought, was really wasted on an audience of one. He didn't need to check the speedometer but made a show of doing so. "We're right on the speed limit now, Miss Durie."

"What of it?"

Well, Mike thought, like for instance speeding fines come out of the chauffeur's pocket and speeding violations entered on the chauffeur's license. The trouble was that she had to know this and obviously didn't give a damn. Make an issue of it, and next thing the case would be adjudicated by Judge McEye, who knew which side her bread was buttered on.

He compromised by speeding up a notch beyond the limit, but that didn't serve very long.

"You're a lousy driver, Lloyd."

"Sorry, Miss Durie."

"No sorrier than I am, considering I'm stuck with you. But then"—the tone became reflective—"you're not really a professional, are you, Lloyd? Do you know what I think? I think you're a middle-aged chorus boy who found there wasn't any more career left for him on the stage. Not even in road companies. So here you are."

Mike glanced at the mirror. Printouts in hand, she was actually leaning back and smiling. He smiled into the mirror. "If you say so, Miss Durie."

"I do. Now try to get me where I'm going this week. And arrange for someone else to pick me up for the trip home tomorrow."

Where she was going turned out to be a Georgian mansion at the end of a lane that wound through picture-book landscaping.

As soon as the car pulled up before the portico of the house, a white-haired little woman came out to greet Camilla warmly, so warmly, in fact, that the pair of them appeared to melt into each other's arms.

"Camilla, my dear."

"Laura, darling."

Really wasted, Mike thought. Given those looks, that voice, and that temperament, there was an opera star manqué here. Utterly phoney, utterly convincing.

Away from the estate, he pulled the car off the road and drew out the small notebook kept for this purpose in the breast pocket of his jacket. The notebook was already well filled, but there was still room in it to enter the Camilla episode in his own makeshift shorthand. The dialogue verbatim, then impressions and reflections. Therapeutic too, he had advised himself from the start, to get things down on paper rather than let them stew in the gut. This time, however, the therapy didn't quite work.

Back at the garage he phoned the office, and his wife took the call.

"Reporting in," Mike said. "Hey, aren't you putting in an awfully long day?"

"Well, I have to make out everybody's schedule for tomorrow and post it. When you get back here stop in the office."

"Sure. What about supper?"

"I just had mine here," Amy said. "You'd better have yours in the staff hall. But first stop in here."

"Trouble?"

"Not exactly. Just something strange."

"See you in ten minutes, ma'am."

He found her standing at the desk and, as if laying out a hand of solitaire, arranging schedule slips in a row. "No errors allowed," she explained, "and I have to take into account who'll be off duty tomorrow. You know, I'm starting to get corrupted."

"How?"

"Well, when the McEye complained there were only sixteen people for staff I thought it was funny. I mean, only sixteen. Now I'm beginning to think she was right. Those two housemen are also valets for Craig and Walter when there's heavy dressing-

181

up, and those two junior maids are nice kids but slow, slow, slow —"

"Then for Christmas," Mike said, "I'll buy you another house-man and two fast maids. But this isn't what you meant about something strange, is it?"

"No. It's that money Ma'am took out of the bank. The three thousand dollars. It's gone."

"Hell, if she's holding you responsible —"

"Oh, no, nothing like that. I don't think she even wants me to know it's gone."

"Sit down," Mike said, and when she held up the handful of schedule slips to show why not he said firmly, "Sit. Then start at the beginning."

Amy sat down. "When we were in the bank she got that three thousand in an envelope. She put the envelope into her purse. Then we went to the Plaza, and then we came back here. Hegnauer wasn't in, so she asked me into the bedroom to help her out of her dress. Before that, she opened the purse on the dresser and took out a couple of used tissues she told me to throw away. I did. But that envelope with the money was not in that purse."

"You're absolutely sure?"

"Mike, I was standing right next to her. And it isn't that big a purse. You saw it."

"All right then, how about somewhere along the way she put the envelope into a pocket?"

"No pockets. None in the dress or the coat. And when I helped take her dress off, no envelope underneath."

"Then obviously," Mike said, "she gave it to someone at the Plaza. Whoever she had lunch with."

"And you really think she had lunch?" Amy asked. "Going, eating, and coming, all in twenty minutes? That was the Palm Court, Michael, not McDonald's."

"Look, you've had more time to ponder this than you've allowed me to have, so maybe you're right. We assumed lunch. We took the dear old lady at her word. We did not assume she was setting up a rendezvous with someone to hand three thousand dollars to him. Or her. But she probably did just that. Which, darling, is her privilege. Going by her relationship with

182

that Mrs. Upshur whoever, she does have her charitable side."

"Mike, that was the Institute's own money. And it takes charity, it doesn't give it." Her voice became intense. "There's something else too. That was cash. Now what kind of institution—?"

"Whoa, baby," Mike said.

Amy drew a deep breath. "I'm sorry. I shouldn't get so emotional about it."

"Well, I can think of two reasons for that. One is that your sense of proportion is slightly skewed. Three thousand dollars would rate about two cents in Ma'am scale of values. If she wants to play games with her two cents, that's her business. The other reason is—and this is what bothers me—you're being grossly exploited by Ma'am and Mrs. Mac. They may have divided you up, but each of them is laying a full workload on you. Has it struck you that you are now into a twelve-hour day?"

"I don't mind."

"I do. So as soon as you tack those schedules on the board we retire to our own private quarters and watch something trivial on TV. That's an order."

"Even so, I still have to type up all the pay envelopes for tomorrow. It's Friday payday."

"And when do I ever get to see you again?"

"Soon as I'm done here. Anyhow, we're off Sunday. Sleep late, go over to Abe and Audie—"

"Ah, yes," Mike said. "That day off."

"What about it?"

"Well, I was about to add my name to your list of exploiters. Library duty. Get into those stacks to do some research for the book."

"I'll be glad to help. You know that."

"I do. You are a very special case."

"We are," Amy corrected. "Which reminds me. How'd you make out chauffeuring Camilla?"

"Ah, Camilla. All business, that girl. When the time comes to take over daddy's business interests she'll be ready."

"I'm sure. Now go have supper. It's very good. Pot au feu."

"Leftovers again," Mike said. "And to think that's what we bartered our souls for."

183

HE woke in pitch darkness, tried to get back to sleep before the brain started whirling, and found the whirling headed into high gear. After a few minutes of this he lifted Amy's arm from his chest, went into the sitting room, carefully closing the door behind him, turned on the desk lamp and sat down at the typewriter. He rolled a sheet of paper into the machine and sat squinting at it with one bleary eye. Finally he typed *Friday: pick up washing and cleaning*.

He laid the paper beside the typewriter and rolled in a fresh sheet. One advantage of this domicile, he told himself encouragingly, was that since its walls were constructed as solidly as those of the stony Chateau d'If, the clatter of the machine never penetrated them. Bang these keys here with creative fervor all night, and no one would come knocking to complain.

It was the creative fervor, muzzled and handcuffed, that had cause to complain. You knew that the first lines you wrote would be all wrong, destined for the wastebasket, so why write them? Yet something clamored to be written.

He heard Amy open the door, and then—he realized it was to make sure he wasn't startled—she knocked on it twice. That double knock must be habitual to her by now. The servant's password in Castle Durie. And yet, wasn't that a nitpicking view of it? Born out of frustration because this damn blank page confronted him so defiantly?

"Come in, love," he said, and when Amy crossed the room he patted his knee in invitation. She perched on it and draped an arm around his neck. It felt good, and to make it even better, where any other wife would now have asked, however gently, "Are you going to be at it again all night?" this one didn't. She looked at the page in the typewriter, then at the one on the desk. " 'Pick up washing and cleaning,' " she read. "That's right. I forgot about it."

"You've got other things on your mind."

"Perhaps. And from the way you look, so do you. Such as?"

Mike sighed. "Three thousand missing dollars. You've infected me."

"I'm sorry. As you said, it really isn't my business."

"I'm not so sure anymore. I don't know whether I dreamed it or not, but I suddenly woke up with a theory that won't let go."

"About what happened to that money?"

"Partly," Mike said, "but it goes way beyond it. I have a feeling that Ma'am is using the Upshur Institute to wash her private funds. Know what that means?"

"Yes. It means concealing the source and disposition of money. Usually cash, I suppose."

"Henry James couldn't have phrased it prettier. And I believe that Ma'am, a sort of Jamesian character, is washing her money through Mrs. Upshur's Institute."

Amy shrugged. "I don't think there's any secret about her giving the Institute a lot of money."

"True. But she certainly is hush-hush about drawing out chunks of it, courtesy of Mrs. Upshur, who sends checks to be cashed. Blank checks. Get the picture? They go through the bank and right back into Mrs. Upshur's files. Since she's boss of the Institute and Ma'am is treasurer, those canceled checks are nobody else's business. All the family can know is that dear Margaret seems to be excessively generous to the Institute. But then why not? She's deeply grateful to it for bringing her braille."

"She really does seem to be," Amy said. "And you keeping saying checks. As far as we know, there's only been one of them."

"Even one makes a case. And there's been a structure set up to take care of more than one. Look how you were suddenly ordered to attend to her mail delivery personally. Making you the only one to know she got that little package from Mrs. Upshur. And the way you described the making out of the check and the cashing of it. And her arranging for the car without any destination entered. And the lunch at the Plaza, which doesn't seem to have been any lunch at all. Where — and this is what it led up to — that cash could be handed over to some person unknown. Anything to dispute there?"

Amy thought it over. "No. I suppose that's what's been troubling me. I've been seeing all this without wanting to. But it could be just well-meant game-playing, couldn't it? Her way of proving to herself that she can function apart from the family."

"That would depend on who got the cash. Harmless or harmful is the question."

"Harmful?" Amy said apprehensively. "In what way?"

"Blackmail."

Amy stood up. "That is ridiculous. Margaret Durie? After hiding away from the world all those years. Who could possibly blackmail her? And for what?"

"Darling, if we could answer that we'd be having a heart-to-heart talk with Craig Durie about it right now."

"Well, we won't because it can't be blackmail. Look at her mood all day. Contentment. Does anyone paying blackmail go around feeling contented about it?"

"I guess not," Mike admitted. "She was in a sunshiny mood, wasn't she?"

"Don't knock it," Amy said. "I've seen her other moods close up."

P AY time, according to both their schedules, took place in the office at noon, so by prearrangement they met in the corridor outside the office and entered together. If not hand in hand, Mike thought, still most definitely a couple-in-service.

The office was a fog of cigarette smoke, Mrs. McEye at her desk the center of it. She handed each a pay envelope and saw to the signing of the payroll sheet.

"There is time to go to the bank now?" Amy asked. "I mentioned to you we'd like to open an account there."

"Very sensible. Just inform any bank officer there that you're on the staff, and they'll attend to you most cordially."

And, Mike took notice, Mrs. McEye herself appeared to be brimming over with cordiality. She raised eyebrows at Amy. "Any difficulties in the office yesterday?"

"Not really."

"So it seems. You did very well indeed."

"Thank you. But you did make everthing so clear there couldn't be any serious problems."

My wife, the fledgling sycophant, Mike thought fondly.

Mrs. McEye turned her attention to him. "Miss Margaret ordered the car for yesterday morning. She did use it?"

Oho, Mike thought. "Yes, she did," he said.

"I'm glad to hear that. It's good for her to get out, so to speak. But it can be fatiguing. Were there any signs of that?"

Mike opened his mouth, but it was Amy who said, "No. None at all."

The chair swiveled back toward her. "You were with her then, Mrs. Lloyd?"

"Yes, I was."

Mrs. McEye did not seem to be displeased by this revelation. "Most encouraging. That would be a first for her, if you didn't know. Inviting company on a drive. And where did she want to go?"

"The park," Amy said. "Just all around Central Park. She seemed to enjoy it very much."

There were unexpected depths to this woman, Mike thought. Prevarication with trimmings, for example. Cool as the proverbial cucumber too, although she had to know she was now in the process of burning her bridges behind her. His, too, for that matter.

"Just a drive around the park?" said Mrs. McEye. "No stops anywhere? I mention it only because it was so near lunch hour. Last time, she did stop at the Plaza for lunch."

And, Mike calculated, Wilson, despite orders from his passenger, then brought this information right back to the office for transmission to the brothers Durie. Who, on broaching it to sister Margaret, carelessly let her know that she was under surveillance and had damn well better turn on the guile full force if she wanted to get around it.

187

Last chance to come clean, he thought, as his wife—that tall, well-bred Bostonian in whose mouth butter would obviously not melt—said, "No, there wasn't any stop for lunch. I'm sorry. I should have suggested it to her."

There go the bridges, Mike thought.

"Well," said Mrs. McEye, "the suggestion would be kindly, if you know what I mean, but Miss Margaret is extremely sensitive to what she regards as—well—nagging on her behalf. Now you'll want to be about your business, I'm sure. You'll take over the desk when you return, Mrs. Lloyd. And, Lloyd, Mrs. Jocelyn is entertaining friends at lunch. She wants the car here at two so that one of them may be driven home. And yes, I must say both of you have been doing very well."

In the corridor Mike said, "Of all the—"

"Hush," said Amy.

"Come on, nobody says hush anymore."

"Until we're outside," Amy said, "hush."

However, on the way out they were waylaid by the stout and smiling Mabry in the kitchen. "Ah, good people. Let me make a guess. Your destination is the bank."

"Yep," said Mike.

"Good. Then if you do me a favor today, I will return it any time on demand." He reached under his apron. "Here is some money for deposit and here is the deposit slip. All you need return is the slip, properly stamped."

"You put such faith in strangers?" Mike said.

"Hardly strangers. Friends, who toil under the same yoke. Honesty shines in their eyes. Especially the lady's. I make her overseer of this project."

Outside, Mike waited until they had made the uphill ascent to the sidewalk then said, "Oh, boy. If he had seen the lady's sneaky performance—"

"I was waiting for that," Amy said. "He gave you the perfect opening for it, didn't he?"

"He didn't have to. But I must say I admire your style. About your truthfulness I'm not so sure anymore."

"She shouldn't have questioned us that way," Amy said. "You don't set servants to spying on the family."

"Family's orders," Mike pointed out. "And she sees her position as clear-cut. Yours, since you've developed this crush on the old lady, is ambiguous. In a way, Mrs. Mac is righter than you are."

"I don't see that. And it's not a crush. It's an intense sympathy. Sometimes when I'm walking down a hall I try a few steps with my eyes tight shut just to sense what it's like that way, and it's terrifying. With all that brave front, she is so pitifully helpless. Besides, it's not the whole family that's allied against her. When I was with her this morning Glendon and Dorothy came to call. They get along fine with her. There's a sort of teasing that goes on, and I think she likes it."

"Sounds hilarious. Any interesting talk develop?"

Amy nodded broadly. "About Gwen. She is in London now trying to convince her husband—that Daniel Langfeld—to give her a polite divorce. That's what Craig and Jocelyn don't like. Any kind of divorce. And Dorothy said the only reason is they're afraid there could be some publicity. In this day and age, can you imagine?"

"Well, knowing the Durie phobia about publicity, any day and age, I can. But do you really mean that it's Gwen who's dumping Daniel?"

"Yes. And according to Dorothy, it's because Gwen found Daniel too earthy."

"Lovely," Mike said. "And where were you when all this frank talk was going on? Hiding in the closet?"

"Sitting right there at the desk sorting mail. But invisible all right."

"I know. Ma'am couldn't see you, Glendon and Dorothy wouldn't. But come to think of it, if we find Ma'am's secret life getting troublesome, that couple might be the ones to turn to."

"Not at all," Amy said sharply. "They're family, aren't they?"

"Did you actually say family with a capital *F?*"

"I'm serious, Mike. They are family, and they could be acting for the family in this cozying up to Ma'am. In getting her off guard."

"High-level spying."

"Whatever. And since you're so impressed by Dorothy's earthy quality—"

"Me?"

"—let me tell you that she's nobody's sex object. It so happens that Northeast Colonial puts out some kind of newsletter—inside advice to investors about stocks and bonds—and Dorothy Durie is its editor and chief researcher. That's what Ma'am admires her for. Inside that earthy exterior is an astute businesswoman."

"Kind of fits Camilla, too," Mike pointed out. "Is it these strange times doing it, or is there something about that house that infects the occupants with the commercial bug? Is there a possibility that eventually you and I—?"

"That's why we're there," said Amy.

"So it is. Did you do any other business with Ma'am besides eavesdropping?"

"Same as usual. Read her the obits, sorted the mail, and after Glendon and Dorothy left I finished reading her *The Barretts of Wimpole Street.*"

"Moving her to tears."

"No, I don't even think she was listening. She was far away and long ago. I think I was just sort of background music to whatever she was thinking."

"Moody thoughts? Morbid thoughts?"

"No," said Amy, "just as I told you. Far away and long ago."

"Funny you put it that way. You might have hit it right on the head. About her kind of thinking, I mean. You know those plays you told me she has lined up there? Not only the *Barretts,* but *Cynara, Private Lives,* and so on?"

"Yes."

"Well, it struck me that they all date back to the early 1930s. Very close to when she went down those stairs. Possibly even that season. My guess is that they were the most memorable occasions for her just before she lost her sight. So it wouldn't only be the plays that matter to her, it would be the time, the place, the occasion itself she's reliving. Does that make sense?"

"Yes," Amy said in a strained voice. "Too much. I'm sorry you told it to me."

190

"Baby, don't be like that. You can't live her emotional life for her."

"I know. And I don't even want to. But I can't help it. Especially after seeing that portrait of her when she was a girl. When you see it you'll know what I mean."

"I'd be glad to see it. But I've been given to understand that chauffeurs aren't invited to ramble around on sight-seeing tours of the palace."

"Then I'll just talk to the McEye about it." Amy frowned at him. "Or would that suggest to her you're taking an undue interest in the family's private lives? On the other hand—"

"Whenever you work it out," Mike said, "just let me know."

L ATE Sunday afternoon, after a stint at the Forty-second Street library, they made it down to the Silverstones of Thompson Street on foot. Abe and Audrey greeted them fondly, and Audrey, Mike took note, after surveying his wife with a professional eye was obviously smitten by her own handiwork. "I knew that dress was a winner as soon as I saw it on the rack, doll. But what did you do, swear off jeans for keeps? I thought this kind of costume was strictly business."

"I know. But it didn't seem fair to let the family have all the benefit of your good judgment."

Audrey looked startled. "You mean Mike's folks are in town?"

"God forbid, bless their hearts," Mike said. "No, dear, family happens to be the generic term for the Duries."

"Oh? Well," Audrey said to her favorite client, "you look enchanting. All the better you've gone off slouching, too. It's about time."

191

"Generic term for the Duries," Abe said. "Good God."

But Amy, Mike saw, was not to be diverted by this. She said to Audrey, "The Margaret Durie influence. Shoulders squared, back straight whether she's sitting or standing. And even though she can't see me, I have the feeling that if I slouch she'll immediately say something about it. Anyhow"—she dug into her handbag and came up with the check she had prepared—"this is for you and Abe with gratitude. First payment, more to follow."

Abe took instant possession of the check. He glanced at it. "Too much. Ridiculous." He tried to thrust it back into Amy's hand and she firmly resisted.

"It is not ridiculous, Abe. And I've already mailed out payment for the back rent here and payment in full to Mike's father. And we still have some money left over."

"Look," Abe said, "a schedule of payment must be reasonable. If you—"

"Take the check, Abe," Audrey said. Mike observed that she had been watching Amy's face. "Just take the check and bring our friends their drinks."

"Capital idea," Mike put in. "Remember I'm restricted to beer while on duty. I need a total relaxant."

"But no snacks." Audrey warned. "We found a good new place for dinner down in SoHo, and it's made for overeating."

"And separate checks, I trust," said Mike.

"No, I don't want my husband to start climbing the wall. This is our party to celebrate your payment schedule."

Abe handed Mike a bourbon and water, Amy a Perrier. He fixed drinks for Audrey and himself and turned an inquiring eye on Mike. He was evidently still in a mood. "Well, friend, what's the latest about your generic Duries?"

"Actually," said Mike, "the earliest. We were lining up bibliographies in the library today. Anything mentioning the name Durie, anything in depth on colonial New York. Just scratching the surface so far."

"And," Amy said accusingly to Abe, "Mike put me on *Who's Who,* and I found out something. You're in it and you never told us."

"You never asked. And why, Amy darling, were you researching me? All you had to do was come to the source."

"She's serendipitous," Mike said. "She was supposed to be doing Craig and Walter."

"And they're not in *Who's Who,*" Amy said, still accusatory. "Why not? Don't they rate?"

"By my reckoning," Abe said, "they do. But I suppose you don't have to be listed if you don't want to be, and after what you've had to say about them I'm not surprised the Duries reject the invitation to join the club. For one thing, unlike us mere mortals, they don't need printed assurance that they rate. For another thing, they seem powerfully compelled to stay out of any limelight. But behind the scenes at the manor house what goes? Your Mrs. McEye carry out her coup and seize power yet?"

"Well—" Mike said and caught Amy's small warning frown. Tough, he thought, after all the years of being open with the Silverstones, to lock off even one small corner from them, but Amy, really the one in the front-line trenches, had the say-so there. This double-agent thing she was involved in had to be closed off to any outsider, no matter how near and dear. "Well, the more I know our Mrs. Mac, the more I think that while she'd be an unknown as presidential timber, she'd make a hell of a one-woman cabinet. And my wife is now heading in the same direction. Along with being the perfect secretary and companion for dear old Miss Margaret."

Amy gave him a quick smile—an *A*-plus for diplomacy. "It's not that big a deal," she assured Abe and Audrey.

Abe looked dissatisfied. "Interesting how everything is now all sweetness and light. No deeper thoughts? No sober reflections on exactly what the very, very rich are, and why? Is it possible, for example, that people like the Duries—all that very old money —have no consciousness of being rich?"

"Hard to tell," Mike said. "But I do have one ongoing reflection about them, and maybe you'd have an answer. This business of their sharing the same house. Father, mother, and unmarried children, yes. But here we have a couple of brothers and a sister, and their adult children, married and otherwise. Granting there's more than enough space for everybody to live the full life without banging elbows, is this a customary mode for such as the Duries?"

"Hotel style," Audrey suggested. "Same as if they bought their own hotel and used different suites in it. Why not?"

"Except," Mike said, "this is very much a private home occupied by one very private family. And the staff is not like hotel staff. In a way it's part of the family. Especially the old-timers. Highly privileged. The chef, the building custodian, even that chauffeur I replaced. No, the hotel analogy does not fit the case."

"The Kennedys," Abe said. From his tone Mike recognized that, even though he wasn't controlling the conversation, he was interested in it. "Didn't they set up in family enclaves?"

"For a specific purpose," Mike said. "Aggression. Taking over. Right up to the presidency. But there's none of that in the Duries. Not the slightest whiff. If anything, their enclave is completely defensive. Pull the door shut and block the world out. Business done at the office, some entertaining of the chosen in the house, that's it."

"It isn't bad," Amy put in, "once you're used to it. Comfortable in a way."

"You agree?" Abe asked Mike.

Mike thought it over. "I don't know if comfortable is the word. There are family conflicts you become aware of, volatile elements at work. But I know what Amy means. Once you settle in you do undergo a change. Like when we were walking here from uptown and I felt that everything along the way was just too damn noisy and dirty to tolerate. Sometimes even threatening. In the Durie house you're totally cut off from the confusion. Do your job, keep your nose clean, and you're sort of invulnerable to that mess out there."

"I see," Abe said. "Then you polish up the car nicely, the boss pats your head, and you're doubly gratified. Of course, along the way you could lose that cold objectivity that is supposed to be the writer's prime instrument."

"I doubt it," Mike said. "All I've lost so far is the sense of money pressure that made writing damn near impossible. I mean, watch the calendar and wonder if you can get up the rent on time, and you can't really concentrate on your beautiful prose. Right now, the way things are, I can."

"We're going out to dinner now," Audrey said loudly. "Finish your drinks, all of you, and place your glasses on the coasters, not the woodwork. Especially you, Abe."

"Hey," Abe protested, "we were just getting into—"

"Chug-a-lug, Abe," Audrey said sweetly.

Since the host continued in his mood the dinner at the good new place in Tribeca didn't go too well. It was, Mike recognized, like doing white water in a canoe, Audrey paddling stern and struggling at every shift in current to keep them afloat.

When it came time for the party to break up there was a hassle about transportation. Abe announced that he was driving his guests home, Mike, despite aching feet, the walk downtown having caught up with them, insisted that the guests could just as easily take the bus almost to their back door. In the end, out of regard for Audrey, who looked as if she were ready to climb the wall, he conceded the point. Abe dropped them off at the Madison Avenue corner of the building, and where Audrey's farewell was heartwarming, his was just on the edge of being chilling.

O'Dowd opened the service door and greeted them pleasantly, and when they stopped to pick up their schedule slips a gathering around the table in staff hall was no less pleasant in manner. This, Mike found, only added to his resentment of Abe's carrying on. He held back his private thoughts until he and Amy were in the apartment. An advantage of this kind of marriage, he knew, where the partners shared a single thought under duress was that you didn't have to spell anything out. The basic code did fine.

"What the hell was going on?" he demanded of Amy.

"He's jealous of the Duries," she said.

"Abe?"

"As soon as I referred to them as family. He and Audie are our family, that's how he wants it. And he didn't like our paying back as much as we did. I think he'd just as soon we didn't pay back anything. He might have even felt somehow that since it's Durie money we're paying with, they're taking possession. And one way or another, everything said after that only made it worse. Underneath, it was all jealousy of them."

Mike tried to see this. "But since he's just as bright as Audie and you can't apply any of this to her—"

"She's not as insecure as Abe. Anyhow, as soon as they're back home Audie'll call up. And put Abe on to apologize."

She was almost right. A half hour later Audrey did call, but it was she who made the apologies. Abe did not get on the phone.

"Hell," Mike said, "he is a stiff-necked people, isn't he?"

"He'll come around," said Amy.

ALL the same, she found herself thinking during the days that followed, she might act casually about it for Mike's benefit, but it would be rough if the friendship with the Silverstones was in the process of being broken. Or even badly bent. And it was all up to Abe really, who, like Achilles, still sulked in his tent.

Finally, while on office duty Friday Amy phoned Audrey at the boutique.

"The extrasensory perception kid," Audrey said. "I was just about to take a chance on your house rules and call you. Wednesday's your other day off, isn't it? I kind of thought you two would be dropping in for potluck."

"When Abe invites us, Audie. You understand, don't you?"

"Oh, yes." Audrey heaved a long sigh. "You're making life very complicated for me, doll. Why not just come over Sunday and let the men go into the study and work out their problems that way?"

"Because it wouldn't be fair to Mike. He's the one on the bottom of the pile, and he's being completely well balanced and courageous about it—there's a lot of pride to swallow—and he shouldn't have to swallow any more because of Abe. What got into him anyhow?"

Audrey sighed again. "He says he detected symptoms in both of you of character change. He says you're being overwhelmed by your new condition in life and you're not even aware of it. When I told him I didn't believe that for a moment he cooled off on me for a couple of days. Make of him what you will."

"What I will," Amy said, "is that he's worried the Duries are taking his place in our lives. Don't you think that's what it is?"

"It could be, doll. And when you hear his voice on the phone you'll know he caught wise to it himself. Meanwhile, you keep in touch, hear? Never mind my neurotic husband, I need that."

"So do I, Audie."

The whole thing would have been funny, Amy knew, if it didn't cast such a pall. Yet the whole week seemed to be pall-casting time. Spell of emotional fair weather with sudden dark passages, the dark passages moving in not only from out there where Achilles sulked but from right in here where Ma'am was doing her thing, whatever it was.

Take the repetition of that furtive banking and Plaza Hotel excursion, this time plainly tied in with another packet from the Upshur Institute in the mail. The only differences were that this check had to be made out for two thousand dollars, and instead of an immediate calling for the car, that was put over a day.

While the car was waiting outside the hotel the thought of now five thousand dollars secretly dispensed within a week to God knows whom for God knows what was too much to live with. Amy announced to Mike, "I'm going in there. After all, she can't see me, can she? And the Palm Court's not a room, it's a wide-open space. I'll be able to see her without getting close."

Mike looked doubtful. "Baby, with that hair and that height, you are the world's least likely private eye. You show undue interest in the lady, and whoever she's with might describe you to her."

"I have an excuse all ready. I had to go to the ladies' room. And you said yourself she's involving us in this thing. I am not happy just sitting here and wondering about it."

After warily skirting the perimeter of the Palm Court, making careful inspection of the chattering lunch-hour clientele, she found she really had something to wonder about. She headed back to the car full-tilt to report this.

"You're absolutely sure she's not there?" Mike said.

"Absolutely. She must be somewhere else around the hotel.

But she clearly and distinctly said the Palm Court."

"Indicating," Mike said, "that she doesn't trust us completely. And who can blame her when her confidential secretary stealthily sets out on her trail?"

"Oh, don't be so self-righteous about it. And I can't altogether blame her for not trusting us. She must know she was being reported on by Hegnauer and Wilson and everybody else around her. So until she does learn to have faith in us—"

"And here she comes now," Mike said. "Not quite twenty minutes, same as last time. It had to be a payoff, not a lunch."

"You see?" said Amy.

But it was a depressing triumph at best. Another pall maker. And now this Friday morning came that thing with the canary Philomela.

There had been fair warning from the McEye that Miss Margaret would not be in good mood this morning because it was an alternate Friday, when Domestique Plus took over the housecleaning.

"They're quick and thorough, Mrs. Lloyd," said the McEye, "but they do use noisy machinery and they do create a sort of confusion, so to speak. Miss Margaret finds this all very disturbing. If you could persuade her to breakfast in the dining room this morning it would be to your advantage as well as hers."

Fair warning. The actuality of the impending noise and confusion came clear to Amy while she and O'Dowd were sorting mail in the outer pantry, and she had a view of the legions entering, young men, middle-aged women, a fair number black or Hispanic, all in neat dark-blue coveralls, each having ID's checked at the door by Inship and Krebs, the security men. And with the legions came an impressive assortment of motorized houscleaning equipment.

Distraction from this scene was provided by O'Dowd's holding up a couple of letters, the petitioner who, though having been granted special privileges when it came to getting mail out of turn, still politely renewed the privilege each time. "All right if I take these, ma'am?"

There was something about the way she said it, Amy thought. "Yours, O'Dowd?"

"Well, not exactly, ma'am. This one's for little Walsh, and

198

this other's for Peters who's going to valet for Mr. Craig so mail can't get to him for a while, and both are in staff hall right now."

"O'Dowd, no one's supposed to know you have the privilege."

"I'm sorry, ma'am, but we must have been seen at it here, because some do know. Not Mrs. McEye or Nugent though. So it could do no harm surely if poor little Walsh—"

"That is pure blarney, O'Dowd."

O'Dowd grinned. "Just a bit of it, ma'am."

Amy gave up. And, in fact, as time had gone by all the staff had steadily warmed to her, administration though she might be. Nor could this secretive mail privilege nonsense be regarded as a bribe for their goodwill, Amy decided, since already O'Dowd was no longer sullen in her presence, nor junior maids Walsh and Plunkett timid to paralysis, nor housemen Peters and Brooks stony-faced. And any protocol about staff's mail delivery was nonsense.

However, in trying to lure Miss Margaret down to the dining room for breakfast until Domestique Plus had its way with her room, Amy found she lacked O'Dowd's hand at blarney.

"I will not be dispossessed by these people, Lloyd." Ma'am had to raise her voice to be heard over the roar of vacuum cleaners from her bedroom. "Never mind the tray. Bring the newspaper into Hegnauer's room. Intolerable, really. When I was young one's home wasn't converted into a factory to keep it clean."

Almost predictably, Hegnauer's room turned out to be spartan, half of it given over to basic personal furnishings, the other half to body-building equipment: massage table, heat lamp, shelves of towels and linens, and a glass-doored cabinet in which were arrayed—worrisomely—large bottles of pills, none showing labels. If these were pills that shouldn't be here, Amy thought, there could indeed be five thousand dollars worth of them. Unfair really to consider any such possibility, but there it was, planted by Mike somewhere in the brain cells.

She saw Ma'am to the straight-backed chair at the foot of the bed and seated herself close by on the bed to read the obits above the racket in the sitting room and bedroom. Ma'am, leaning close, eyes shut, lips compressed, listened with the familiar absorption. At the conclusion of the reading she sat back, her mood plainly brighter.

"So many deaths," she remarked. "It's surprising there's anyone left alive in the city. Describe this room, Lloyd."

Amy looked around. "Well, there's this bed — a single bed — and that chair, a bedside table with lamp, a chest of drawers—"

"Any attempt at decoration?"

"No, ma'am. I'd say the only things not strictly utilitarian are a television set on a stand and magazines on the bedside table."

"Indeed? What sort of magazines?"

Amy craned her neck to see. "Movie fan magazines, ma'am."

"Of a garish nature?"

"Well, yes."

Ma'am smiled broadly. "When I asked Hegnauer about it, she was so evasive I suspected something like this. From her demeanor and that unpleasant guttural speech, one would suspect she's deep into Ibsen and Strindberg. What else does she have to offer?"

"Across the room, the equipment for massage. And" — Amy nerved herself to say it — "a cabinet of pill bottles. So many pills," she added disingenuously.

"Hegnauer is a great believer in what she calls megavitamins, Lloyd, and I permit her to feed them to me. It makes her feel like a ministering angel. I doubt it does me any harm."

Or, Amy wondered, is this lady protesting too much?

The noise of machinery suddenly ended. Blessed silence prevailed.

"See what's going on, Lloyd," Ma'am said.

Amy went into the sitting room where a Domestique Plus squad was in the process of departure. It appeared to be under the command of a tall, gray-haired black man.

"All finished?" Amy asked him.

"All done, lady." He jerked his thumb over his shoulder at the bedroom. "You know that little birdie in there?"

"Yes."

"Well, I put the cover on the cage so he wouldn't get fussed while we was there. You ought to look at that birdie."

"Something wrong?"

"You just look at him, lady." There was reproach in the voice.

Amy watched him depart, then returned to Hegnauer's room. "All clear," she reported.

"Good," said Ma'am. "What was that man complaining about?"

"Not complaining exactly. He thought I should look at the bird. At Philomela."

"Why?"

"I don't know. He did seem concerned though."

"Then do look now. If they've hurt the creature with that machinery—"

Ma'am led the way into the bedroom and stood there poised. Amy lifted off the cover of the birdcage and peered within. The misnamed Philomela, she saw, did look worse than ever, hunched on its perch into a little bunch of bedraggled feathers, its beak gaping. When she looked closer she realized there was a gray film over its eyes. She poked a finger along the perch and the bird didn't move but simply yielded to the pressure of the finger. One more little push, she thought, and down it tumbles.

"It does seem very ill, ma'am," she said.

"Birds and beasts are not ill, Lloyd, they are sick. Well, what do you recommend?"

"Perhaps a veterinarian, ma'am?"

"To what purpose?"

The purpose should be obvious, Amy thought with annoyance. "Well, ma'am, I wouldn't know how to—"

"Neither would a veterinarian, Lloyd. That creature's been sickly since the day it was thrust on me. My niece is an arrant sentimentalist, Lloyd, the kind who buys the runt of the litter out of misguided charity. Then, unable to bear the sight of it, makes a gift of it to someone unable to see it. Do you know what I mean?"

"Yes, ma'am. But I don't think Miss Gwen—"

"Did you bring in the newspaper with you, Lloyd?"

So much for any kind words about meditative Gwen, Amy thought. "No, ma'am."

"Then bring it here and lay a page of it on the dresser."

Ma'am was at the dresser when she returned. A forefinger indicated a cleared space there. The other hand was loosely clenched around the pathetic Philomela exposing only its head. Amy folded a sheet of newspaper and laid it down. Ma'am rested the clenched fist on it. Then with her free hand she opened the drawer and drew out those long narrow shears. She opened the blades wide and guided by the flat of one blade against the thumb restraining the bird she snipped off its head. One quick purposeful snip, Amy saw, not quite sure she was seeing it, and that was that. The head lay there, and the body, released from the executioner's grasp, lay nearby. The claws contracted a little and then were still.

Dead, Amy told herself. Quite completely dead.

And it must have been almost bloodless all along. There was one small spot of blood and a few specks of it on the paper. When Ma'am laid down the shears a red stain showed midway on one blade.

"Dispose of it, Lloyd." The voice was indifferent.

"Ma'am?"

"What's wrong with you? Wrap the remains in the paper and dispose of it in the wastepaper basket. Then call a houseman to clear away the basket and that cage. And do wash the shears thoroughly in the lavatory with very hot water."

Amy found that while she couldn't remove her eyes from the remains, neither could she bring herself to touch the paper. Those ears tuned to her every move, so it seemed, must have helped Ma'am to reconstruct a vivid picture of her plight.

"You're behaving very oddly, Lloyd." The voice took on a sardonic edge. "Squeamish?"

"I'm afraid so. I'm sorry."

"Indeed? Do you feel it would have been kinder to allow that thing to continue its suffering?"

"No, I don't."

"No, you don't. Then you evidently feel that the proper course would have been to foist this duty on one of the other servants. Someone of coarser grain. We ourselves are too fine to confront the uglier aspects of life."

Amy found that anger could be a potent antidote to squeamishness. "No, I don't feel that. I'll take care of everything."

"Good. And bear in mind that when necessity can be dealt with only by a sharp blade, the one concern is to wield the blade efficiently. Don't expect others to do it for you."

"Yes, ma'am."

It wasn't until late that night that all this could be shared with

202

Mike who, these past evenings, had been on duty driving various Duries to the theater or to concert halls at Lincoln Center, waiting and returning.

His response was irritating. "There wasn't any reason to react like that, baby. You've seen my father and me chop off chickens' heads at the farm. No big deal."

"I saw it just once, thank you. And that was you and your father, not Margaret Durie."

"Yes, but the impression you've given me is that she's a very tough and efficient little lady."

"Oh, yes. Efficient with those shears all right, even without eyes. Same with that dagger thing she uses to open the mail. Absolute certainly. Zip, zip."

"Fifty years of practice there," Mike pointed out. "And she was right in what she said. She could have asked you to do it, and if you didn't have the nerve, one of the other staff would have been stuck with it. But instead of dumping on anyone else, she did it herself. Give her credit for that."

"Except that she didn't say one of the other staff. She said one of the other servants."

"Oh? And the terminology bothers you? Baby, I thought you were over that right there in Bernius's office. Remember? She asked how the word *servant* struck us, and you just shrugged it off."

"I know," Amy said unhappily. "But this is the first time Ma'am ever applied it to me. Or maybe it was because she made me feel like such a frail, useless flowerlike type. Anyhow, I was so shaken up—"

"And now it's time to unshake. You've passed it along to me, I'll get it all down on paper, it's no longer your experience to ponder, it's mine. The Michael Lloyd therapeutic method. No charge."

"Mike, you're not going to sit down to that typewriter now. With all these evening calls you're not getting half enough sleep as it is."

"Plenty of soothing naps in one of the cars whenever I get clear of Wilson. Or right on our own couch. So I'll now type myself to sleep and evidently you'll read yourself to sleep." He pointed at the encyclopedia-size ring binder she had laid on the bed. "What is that thing?"

"Oh, that. Kind of interesting really. The building's inventory. The permanent stuff. The McEye let me borrow it from the office." She opened it at random and read, *"Floor two, room eight C: one Philadelphia Chippendale camelback sofa, canted back, scrolled arms, molded square legs. Designated Marlborough. One Massachusetts block front, kneehole chest—"*

"That's enough," Mike said. "Fascinating, but I'll wait till they make the movie."

"Yes, but it lists all the chinaware too. Mabry and Nugent laid some out and explained it to me this afternoon in the staff hall. I know five kinds by sight already. Spode, Royal Doulton, Wedgwood, Haviland, Minton. And formal service, with fish and without."

"But fried shrimp is finger food," Mike said. "Don't let anybody try to tell me different."

"I'm serious. I feel much easier this way about what can happen when the McEye's off duty. And there's something else. Your book. It can't hurt to have this inventory right here as a reference source. With this and the floor charts, it's all right in front of you."

"That's a fact," Mike acknowledged. "What's in the refrigerator?"

"Seltzer water and ginger ale. Steak sandwiches. A dish of sensational chocolates."

"Contraband?" Mike said. "You know, if Mrs. Mac decided to make a tour of inspection here—including that fridge, which for some weird reason is supposed to contain only fresh fruit—"

"Let her. I'm perfectly willing to make an issue of any such nonsense. But, Mike, there are all those notes you're accumulating. And the Duries are identifiable in them, aren't they?"

"Very clearly. But we now own a shiny new fire-retardant safety box. The writings go into it. It goes into the closet. Both keys will always be in my pocket. I spent about half of my this week's allowance on that thing, by the way. Any chance of reimbursement?"

"None. But it is a shame that in our own private apartment—"

"C'est la vie Durie," Mike said. "Or should that be *la vie* McEye?"

IT rained through the weekend. It was still raining Tuesday.

Ma'am didn't like it.

"Too much of a good thing, Lloyd." She stretched out on the chaise longue, ankles crossed. "That playscript of *Camille*. We'll start on it now. It's suitable for this weather."

As Amy arranged herself for the reading, Ma'am addressed the ceiling. "Eva Le Gallienne, Lloyd. Is that name familiar?"

"No, it isn't."

"So much for the stars of yesterday. She starred in *Camille*. She was sufficient. But the next season Lillian Gish— Do you know that name?"

"Yes, ma'am. From old movies.

"Let us be grateful for small bounties. But the very next season—my own last season in the sun—Lillian Gish starred in the play. Without the same grasp of technique she was much more than sufficient. Deeply moving. She was the living and dying lady of the camellias. Get on with the reading, Lloyd."

It wasn't all that easy, Amy found, with that *my own last season in the sun* tightening the throat. She started badly, recovered herself, and was hitting her stride when ma'am abruptly sat up, feet planted on the floor. "That's enough. Look through the window. Can you see any possible break in this weather?"

"No, ma'am. I'm sorry."

"It's hardly your fault. Where would Lloyd be right now?"

"Back at the garage, ma'am. He takes Mr. Craig and—"

"Phone him. Tell him I want the car here at noon promptly."

This, Amy thought, must be handled with a maximum of tact. "Yes, ma'am. But I think I'd better do it through Mrs. McEye."

"Indeed?" The voice was coldly challenging. "Why?"

"Because the office keeps an ongoing record of where everyone on staff is at all times. That way orders can be carried out so much more efficiently."

"I see. It was my impression that procedures here were for my benefit, not Mrs. McEye's. However, have her attend to it. Who am I to stand against her peculiar concept of efficiency?"

Mrs. McEye responded in lowered tones as if the boss were

standing there at her shoulder. "Of course, Mrs. Lloyd. Any destination mentioned? It couldn't be a drive around the park in this rain, could it?"

"I'll ask," Amy said, and turned to the boss. "Mrs. McEye would like to know the destination." Then as Ma'am's lips narrowed dangerously, Amy hastily improvised, "That would be a matter of knowing how long Lloyd would be required."

"Then inform the efficient Mrs. McEye that the destination is lunch at the Plaza. The Palm Court. And while she's at it, she's to reserve a table for two."

Confusion, Amy thought, was the name of the game. No more mystery about the Plaza? The cards were now to be played face up? Then, with the McEye's response to these further instructions, an added possibility was introduced. "For two, Mrs. Lloyd?" The voice dripped curiosity. "And you are to be the guest?"

Hell and damnation, Amy thought. The possibility was fascinating, but presenting this question to Ma'am in her immediate mood would be like seeing how long you could hold a lit stick of dynamite in your hand.

"I'll report to you as soon as I'm free, Mrs. McEye," she hedged, and instantly put down the phone.

At its click, Ma'am said impatiently, "Sit down, Lloyd. I must now speak to you most seriously. And, to repeat what has already been emphasized, I am speaking in utter confidence."

Amy sat down, braced. "Yes, ma'am."

"Do you remember the name of that art gallery I expressed particular interest in?"

"Yes. The Jason Cook Gallery."

"Correct. You are going to be my emissary there on a matter of importance. I'll explain it in the car so that I won't have to repeat it for Lloyd's benefit. Remember, neither of you is to mention a word of this to anyone. Do you understand?"

"Yes, I do."

"Good. And since I imagine you share excellent rapport with Lloyd, I leave it to you to see that he does not make any slip in this regard. Do you share excellent rapport with him?"

To say the least, Amy thought. "Yes, ma'am," she said.

"Very good. Now let's get back to *Camille*."

But it soon became clear during the reading that Ma'am's thought were far from *Camille*. She lay there, apparently holding communion with herself, a most pleasant communion, never mind what was happening to poor Camille.

She abruptly cut the reading short well before the first curtain. "Put it away, Lloyd. And in the topmost righthand drawer of the dresser you'll find a watch case. Bring it to me."

A watch case? Amy thought as she followed orders. To what purpose? An antique watch, a memento of that last season in the sun?

However, the wristwatch Ma'am drew from the case certainly did not look antique. The design of the face and hands seemed smartly up to date, the case was unadorned gold, the strap a black ribbon. More than ever, to what purpose? Ma'am had demonstrated an uncanny time sense, and when unsure about it simply asked the time.

"One of the miracles of our age, Lloyd. It requires no winding." Ma'am extended an arm, and as Amy wonderingly strapped the watch to the fragile wrist, Ma'am said, "What time is it by your watch?"

"Just about ten after ten," Amy said.

Ma'am pressed the stem of her watch, the glass sprang open, she lightly rested the tip of her forefinger against the face. "Quite right," she said. "And if you're wondering, Lloyd, the numerals are braille and the hands can't be damaged by this contact. A gift from my niece Dorothy. She does have more discrimination in her choice of gift than some."

Which, Amy thought, had to mean blobby, meditative Gwen, donor of the luckless Philomela. In any competition with sister-in-law Dorothy, whether for Glendon's favor or Aunt Margaret's, poor Gwen didn't stand a chance.

And give Dorothy credit. The gift watch assured Aunt Margaret that while she did have a handicap, she was still a going and doing independent woman who'd need a timepiece to keep her on schedule. Useful and subtly flattering, all in one neat package, that gift.

207

The car at noon promptly, Ma'am had said. At twelve noon promptly, houseman Peters holding a huge umbrella over the ladies, Amy getting the benefit of only a fraction of it, transferred them into the care of Mike, who was waiting at the open door of the car, also with an umbrella upheld. He saw his passengers inside and got behind the wheel, but before he could start the motor Ma'am said, "Wait. As Mrs. Lloyd knows, I must explain something to both of you." She reached out the cane, found Mike's shoulder with it and gently pressed the tip into the shoulder. "Are you listening closely, Lloyd?"

"I am."

Ma'am withdraw the cane. "Then note. You will take me to the Plaza Hotel and leave me there. You will then drive Mrs. Lloyd to an art gallery—the Jason Cook Gallery—on Prince Street at West Broadway." She turned toward Amy, the sightless eyes in line with the rain-drenched car window. "My information is that this Mr. Cook has opened a showing today of an artist who interests me. A young woman who made something of a *success de scandale* in a showing out of town last year. According to report, she has talent, courage, and a profound concern for the female condition. Vilified by some critics—male, of course—she steadfastly answers to her own conscience. You can appreciate my interest in her, Lloyd."

"Yes, I can," Amy said, and when Mike turned to look at her, casting his eyes to heaven, she bared her teeth at him in a silent snarl. A darling, yes, not really a male chauvinist pig, but there were times when that good old Spruce Pond backwoods masculinity seemed to addle his wits.

"The artist's name," said Ma'am, "is Kim Lowry. What is her name, Lloyd?"

"Kim Lowry," said Amy, and this time, when Mike mimed amazement at such a display of intelligence, she aimed a menacing forefinger at him. Enough, he had to understand, was enough. She also had the uncomfortable feeling that Ma'am, sensitized to every current of air, might be tuned in to this byplay. Impossible, but yet . . .

Of course, she thought, part of Mike's mood must stem from his recognition of the same thing she recognized. Those Upshur messages, the secretive banking, the handing over of large sums — all were connected somehow to the career of an artist who had stirred old Margaret Durie's youthful spirit. A persecuted female artist — a *succes de scandale* suggested more notoriety than reward — had found herself a rich, reclusive, sympathetic ally, never mind that certainly Craig and Jocelyn Durie, probably Walter Durie, would have a fit if any of that notoriety splashed publicly on fiery Margaret. Would lead them to nip that career as avant-garde fellow traveler right in the bud, however they could.

Ma'am found Amy's hand and took a firm grip on it. "You will approach Kim Lowry as my representative — my agent, one might say — bearing in mind that I insist on remaining incognito. You understand what that means?"

"Yes, of course."

"I take for granted you have sufficient tact to convince her of my bona fides without identifying me. She must be given to understand that any effort to identify me means the prompt withdrawal of my patronage. That will be costly to her, because I am prepared to buy her work at her price."

"Yes, ma'am. But buying does mean bills of sale and making out checks, so that incognito — "

"I'm not a fool, Lloyd. Payment will be made in cash, bills of sale can be made out to your name for that matter. The only problem you may face is in gaining the confidence of the artist. She must be made to know that I — unnamed — am her good friend. To that end, ingratiate yourself with her. I believe you're entirely capable of that."

"Yes, ma'am," Amy said without assurance.

The slender little hand squeezed hers hard. "Then let's be on our way. The Plaza for me, the gallery for you. I deplore this weather, but the car can wait for you right outside the gallery. On your return from it, you'll pick me up at the Palm Court. I'll wait there as long as necessary."

Mike turned in his seat. "One thing, ma'am. Anyone curious enough about an identity can trace it through a license plate. In case that comes to your mind later, I want you to know I'll park out of sight of the gallery."

Ma'am was openly delighted. "How clever of you, Lloyd. Yes, see to that. By that way, you do know about things mechanical?"

"Things mechanical?"

"Such as telephones. I understand that phone conversations may be listened to by third parties who give no notice of this. In that event, would an otherwise inexplicable clicking on the line result?"

"I don't believe so, ma'am. The device for tapping—that's what it's called—is supposed to be foolproof that way."

"Supposed to be, Lloyd, isn't altogether reassuring. But thank you. Now the Plaza."

Which, Amy thought resentfully, was really something. Faithful Mrs. Lloyd had never gotten a thank you. Lloyd, however, gets handed one just like that. A fiery feminist Margaret Durie might be in her secret life, but on occasion there was still the leaning toward the male.

At the Plaza, after their charge was delivered into the care of the doorman, Amy climbed into the seat beside the chauffeur.

"Michael, darling."

"Oh, oh," Mike said.

"Michael darling, one request. When the three of us are together, don't mime your emotions for my sole benefit. Considering that the women in our charge is blind, it's not merely discourteous, it's crude and juvenile. And it bugs me."

"Sorry. And what bugs me is the way she talks to you. By now she must know you're not a drooling idiot. Why does she make you repeat to her whatever she just told you?"

Chivalry in any form, Amy thought, must not be put down. She found herself softening. "It's just her way, Mike, and I don't mind it. What I do mind is this weird assignment we're on. I mean weird."

"Ah, yes. We meet at midnight in the old cemetery. Masks and capes will be worn."

"Not far wrong," Amy said. "Although it does settle one thing. I mean, that those supposedly tender messages from Mrs. Upshur are really reports on this Kim Lowry, don't you think?"

"By braille and mail. Avoiding the use of that treacherous telephone. Yes, it seems likely."

"Which could also mean that those cash payments so far have been going to the gallery man himself. Jason Cook. For all we know, it was Ma'am who set up this Kim Lowry show. So the only one who doesn't know her identity is Kim Lowry. For good reason she's to be kept in the dark about it."

"What good reason?"

"The obvious one," Amy said. "Kim Lowry—who seems to be a scandalous figure—might take pride in having won Margaret Durie over to her side and tell the world about it. I'm not sure about Walter, but can you see Craig and Jocelyn opening their *Times* and reading all about it there? They're even terrified to have it known that Gwen might be on her way to a perfectly proper divorce."

"Delightful," Mike said. "I can see old James Hamilton Durie spinning in his grave. But didn't our Miss Margaret broach another possibility? Suppose this Kim Lowry is a truly feisty spirit who'd detest being patronized by some unknown fat cat?"

"Oh, please, not that," Amy said with feeling. "I'm the one up there in the line of fire."

"So you are," said Mike.

IT was another one of those grim blocks south of the Village, which, as Abe liked to point out, was being engulfed by cute. Even seen through the sluicing rain, the cute was indomitable. A shop titled Things 'n' Such with an antique wickerwork baby carriage prominent in its window, then a coffee shop titled The Burning Bush, then the Jason Cook Gallery. The display window of the gallery was curtained across with black monk's cloth on which was inscribed in white flowing scipt *Ars longa, vita brevis*.

In the shelter of the doorway Amy closed the umbrella Mike

had thrust on her as she had prepared to dash from the car, waited a few seconds to steady her nerves, and walked in. At first glance she recognized that there were no surprises here. The familiar little neighborhood store converted with a minimum of investment and a maximum of optimism into the familiar little showplace for the latest in art. Half a dozen huge paintings on the walls—easy to count because there were three paintings on each side of the room—linoleum floor, rickety-looking table with leaflets and guest book on it, and visible through the open door in back what appeared to be a combination kitchen and storeroom. Track lighting overhead glaringly focused on each of the paintings.

There were several people in the room—one male among them—all wearing jeans and either T-shirts or flannel shirts, and they all turned to look at her as she stood there wondering what to do about the water puddling on the linoleum from the umbrella. Then the male came forward, and this, Amy decided by simple elimination, had to be Jason Cook. He was, despite the heavy beard, obviously youthful. He was also very short and very fat, the black T-shirt with the white *Ars longa, vita brevis* on it overflowing his belt line.

"Here," he said, "we can put these in the bathroom," and led the way to a closed door in back. He hung the umbrella and sopping raincoat over a shower-curtain rod already bending under the weight of umbrellas and raincoats, then regarded Amy keenly. He aimed a stubby forefinger at her. "The press," he said. "Right?"

"No."

"Oh. Friend of a friend of Kim's?"

"Well, no."

He looked pleased. "Just dropped in to see the show? I'm Jason Cook, by the way. And I do apologize for the weather. It's a killer when it comes to an outpost like this."

"Amy Lloyd. And yes, I would like to see the show and then talk to Miss Lowry. She is here, isn't she?"

"Right there. That tall, dark, and vastly talented one and the paintings are all yours for the looking."

Emerging from the bathroom, Amy took furtive stock of the

tall, dark and vastly talented one and found her heart going out to her. Very tall indeed — another six-footer — hunched forward in that familiar way to make conversation with her unequals. Olive-skinned, a saturnine face, and that frizzed hair of all styles, Amy thought, was a distinct mistake adding yet further inches to the height. If nothing else however, she and Miss Lowry would be literally seeing eye to eye.

Ingratiate yourself with her, Ma'am had ordered. Looking at the streetwise face under the mop of hair, Amy had a feeling that this was easier said than done. To forestall the moment, she crossed over to the table with a sense of eyes on the back of her neck and picked up a brochure from the pile there. Actually not a brochure but a single-page leaflet recounting some history.

Reading it, she found, was reading to chill the blood, especially with the images of Craig and Jocelyn Durie vividly before her. The inflammatory showing in Cleveland two years ago, the wrathful assault by some local Association for the Promotion of Decency, the entrance of woman's lib in trying to withstand the assault. The hotly controversial set design for the off-off-Broadway production of *The Bacchae* last year ("Stole what there was of the show" — *New York* magazine), which led to sometimes violent audience reactions led by various factions, male and female, of the gay community. And now these six most recent works by this artist who has a statement to make and will not be deterred from making it. Six titles. *Marjorie. Toni. Deirdre. Bren. Helena. Joan.* Prices available at the desk.

Margaret Durie, thought Amy, dear, unseeing Margaret Durie, I know how I got into this, but how did you get into it?

Whatever the answer, the thing to do now was put on a solemn, art-viewer's expression and at least make a round of the six works. She did so, checking off each title against the leaflet in her hand, wondering as she went what this list of apparently all female names had to do with the works. The paintings were of uniform size, taller than she was and considerably wider. Seen close up like this, the canvases were heavy-laden with a thick, buttery impasto in swirls and globs, predominantly pink, red, and white, with varying patches on each of black, brown, or yellow.

Abstract expressionist, Amy thought with relief. Certainly a long way from those pictures in the Duries' West Gallery and dining room, but — especially since abstract expressionism was now ancient history itself — nothing to work up a fever about. So why the scandal and controversy?

When she stepped back to get a longer view the answer leaped at her. What she was now seeing, she realized, was what any gynecologist sees when he has the patient on the table, legs up in the stirrups. No, to be precise, what Gulliver would see if he had been a gynecologist and had a Brobdingnagian female on the table. The view varied in each painting, right side up, upside down, sideways, but in each there was no mistaking it. Only the one title *Joan* differed drastically. Here the torso appeared to be chained to something while a burning brand wielded by a manifestly male hand was being thrust into the center of interest.

Amy became aware that Jason Cook was at her elbow. "Of course you get the statement," he said.

"Joan," Amy said. "Joan of Arc."

"Right. Beneath all the establishment cover-up, the truth. A devasting *aperçu.*" He took her by the arm. "Kim, this is Amy Lloyd. She wants to talk to you."

Kim Lowry detached herself from her companions and drifted over. "Yes?"

"In private?" Amy said.

"Oh?" Kim Lowry studied her with great deliberation from head to foot. "Look," she said, "let's get this straight. If you're here to save my soul — "

"No," Amy said. "Only to discuss something to your advantage. But it must be in private."

"Kim," said Jason Cook, "the chip off the shoulder. Please?"

His client curled her lip at him, then gestured with her head at the storeroom. "Back there," she said to Amy.

The storeroom was still occupied by a stove, refrigerator, and kitchen sink. Unframed canvases, faces to the wall, were stacked everywhere. Kim Lowry waited until Amy had picked her way through this to a small clearing, then closed the door behind them. "Private enough?" she asked. Amy had the feeling that she wasn't so much hostile now as wary. So the quicker one came on as Santa's helper, the better.

She said, "I represent someone who's intensely sympathetic to your work, Miss Lowry, and what it stands for. She's ready to buy some of that work. I'm to make the arrangements."

"For someone intensely sympathetic to me. What's the someone? Institutional or human?"

"Definitely human. A woman who for good reasons does not want to be identified."

The wariness was gone now. The expressive lips quirked in amusement. "A closet collector. And female? Amy Lloyd possibly?"

"No, my employer. She's elderly—you might say grandmotherly—but very spirited really. More to the point, she's very wealthy and very supportive of you. But she does want it known that her buying your work depends on your willingness to let her remain unidentified."

"You mean," said Kim Lowry, "this is on the level? Mysterious granny and all?"

"Yes, it is. I suppose describing her as grandmotherly would raise doubts, but that was my mistake."

"Don't you believe it— Mind if I call you Amy?"

"No."

"And I'm Kim. And don't you believe for a moment, Amy, that I take any position against grandmothers. For one thing, most of them are women who in their time have seen it all, done it all, suffered it all. For another thing, I was raised by mine from cradle up to this moment. Talk about spirited, you ought to meet her. I am whatever I am only because of her. My best friend, and I think I'm hers. Does that sound too far out for you?"

"No," said Amy. "I like the way it sounds."

"I'll take your word for it. But getting back to your mystery lady, does she have any idea of my prices? I assume she knows they are not Washington Square, open-air exhibition prices."

"I'm sure she does. What are the prices?"

"For that," said Kim, "we have to call in Jason. He not only operates this place, he's my agent. And you don't have to worry about him keeping your lady's secret, not if money's involved. This is not to say he's a moneygrubber, much as I sometimes wish he was. But he's sunk his life's blood into this project—along

215

with a few quarts from a couple of the gay cultural asso-
ciations—and he's really desperate for cash flow." She
grinned and shrugged in self-deprecation. "That doesn't make
me too smart either, does it? I mean, letting you in on this. But I
can tell you it doesn't give you bargaining rights. The prices are
fixed. Jason and I agree on that much at least."

Amy thought it over. Her instructions, after all, did not
preclude a third party's entering the scene, not as long as the
buyer's anonymity was maintained. She said, "If you'd explain it
to him very clearly—"

"Trust me," said Kim.

She called in Jason, and when he had wedged himself into
what remaining space there was, she explained it to him clearly
and succinctly. His instant reaction was unconcealed pleasure.
This was followed by concern. "The price," he said. "You ought
to know that it's six thousand for each painting in the show. By
the way, which one are we talking about?"

"I'm not sure yet," Amy said. "Besides, there may be more
than one."

"At that price?" Jason seemed increasingly suspicious. "And
then you know like there's this anonymous thing. Like any check
has to be made out by somebody who—"

"Payment would be in cash," Amy said.

Kim raised her eyebrows. Jason looked stunned. "Cash?"

"Yes," said Amy. Right or wrong, she thought, just saying it
with this cool authority gave her the pleasant feeling that the
cash in question was hers.

"At least," Kim said to her agent with malice, "if this goes
through, it looks like you can pay for that lighting before they rip
it out."

Jason was deaf to the malice. "At the very least," he said happily.

Kim turned to Amy. "What's the next step?"

"I report back on this. Then I should be meeting with you
—and Mr. Cook—very soon."

"With the payment?" said Jason.

"I imagine so. Yes."

"And," Kim said, "you still haven't settled on which painting?

216

You don't mind my asking, but will some very rich grandma-type lady be sneaking in here to take a look around before decision time?"

"Definitely not."

"So she must have seen my Cleveland show. Or was it that set I did for *The Bacchae?* You can't blame me for being just a touch curious, can you?"

"No," Amy said, "but I'm not supposed to tell you more than I have. It's embarrassing for me, but it can't be helped."

"It's all right," Jason assured her. "Nothing to be embarrassed about. Not a thing."

AMY had just managed to wrestle the umbella open when the car pulled up before her. She closed the umbrella and climbed in. The car instantly took off. There are elements of low comedy in this, she thought, Bonnie and Clyde and the quick getaway.

"How'd you make out?" Mike asked.

"All right. But one thing. You know we thought perhaps Ma'am was handing over that money to Jason Cook? Might even have paid for this showing? Not so."

"You asked about that?"

"Of course not. But what came out was that this is a very meager operation. Not much money to start with and none left. This Jason Cook doesn't seem to have any business head. Certainly Kim doesn't think he has."

"Kim is it? So you two did get along nicely."

"I think so. She's at least as tall as I am, so I could sympathize right off. We even got into grandmothers, believe it or not."

"Grandmothers?"

"Anyhow hers," Amy said. "She has one who's been mother, father, and guiding light from way back. They're very much devoted to each other. You have to admit that kind of thing does soften the image."

"If you say so," Mike acknowledged. "What about the paintings you're shopping for?"

"Oh, God."

"You intrigue me," Mike said. "Porno?"

"No. Just the opposite to my way of thinking. Huge vulvas, one and all. It's like getting ready to drive into the Lincoln Tunnel. Or is it vulvae?"

"Whichever. But huge? Where the hell can they possibly be hung without stirring up a riot in the house?"

"I have no idea. But maybe the price will put Ma'am off. They're six thousand each."

"Pocket money, baby," Mike said.

"Well, I can hope, can't I? How she even got interested in Kim to start with—"

"Yes?"

"You know," said Amy, "it just struck me where it could have started. For a while I had to read the art news in the *Times* to her every morning, looking for something about the Jason Cook Gallery. Then that stopped suddenly. It could have stopped because those messages from Mrs. Upshur had whatever news Ma'am wanted about the opening of Kim's show. Does that make any sense?"

"In a crude way," said Mike. "But it still doesn't explain how she got hooked on this Kim Lowry."

"Oh, that. Well, I just remembered the McEye telling me that up to about a year ago she used to read the theater news to Ma'am. Not art news, theater news. That would be about the time *The Bacchae* opened here and made a scandal. The scandalous part was the set design by Kim. So the *Times* could have had reviews and interviews and such, which set Ma'am off. A woman artist getting jumped on because of her feminist outlook. Does it still make sense?"

"It does," Mike said. "And it still leaves me wondering what

218

happens when those masterpieces are carted into the house."

"Oh, God," said Amy.

At the Plaza she found Ma'am seated alone at one of the small, round tables in the Palm Court, the remains of a plate of finger sandwiches and a tea service before her.

"Miss Durie?"

"Sit down, Lloyd, and have the waiter arrange a service for you. It would be wasteful to leave these sandwiches uneaten."

Amy was about to offer a gentle reminder that the car was waiting when it struck her that of course this would only be the chauffeur's concern. She followed orders and applied herself to tea and the remainder of the sandwiches.

Ma'am checked the time, finger against the face of the wristwatch. "You weren't too long about it," she said. "You did meet with Miss Lowry?"

"Yes, I did."

"And explained matters to her? Discreetly?"

"Oh, yes."

"And she was properly receptive?"

"I believe so."

"Good. And her paintings? Describe them to me. Briefly."

Amy drew a long breath. "Very large. Impasto. The same subject in all of them. The female organ displayed very close up."

Ma'am's face remained expressionless. "And their quality? Professional, would you say?"

"Well, I really don't know enough, ma'am, to make any—"

"You're mumbling, Lloyd. And nonsense at that. I quite realize I'm not addressing a Bernard Berenson."

"Well then, yes, they do seem professional. The trouble is that wherever they'd be on display they'd have a very strong impact on some people."

Ma'am smiled. "And we should not distress those people, should we? But I have no objection, Lloyd, to the artist keeping possession of any of her works I may buy. After all, I can't see the works. Describe her to me."

"Very tall," Amy said with relief. "Rather Hispanic-looking. Quite frank about herself and her situation. Almost emotional about her grandmother, who she feels is the important influence in her life."

219

"Indeed? In what sense?"

"I'm not sure," Amy said. "But whatever happened to her parents, her grandmother evidently brought her up. And would seem to have been very supportive about her career."

Ma'am nodded. "I imagine one could become very much devoted to a talented grandchild. What are the paintings priced at?"

"Six thousand dollars each. I did make it clear that if any are bought, payment would be in cash and the buyer must remain unknown."

"Precisely. There should be a phone nearby, Lloyd. Call Miss Lowry and inform her that I will buy three of her paintings under those conditions. I want her to reserve three she especially favors. Payment will be made in three parts, the first next week."

"Yes, ma'am. Do I also tell her she's to have the paintings in her care even after they're sold?"

"No reason why not, Lloyd. Now attend to the call."

"Yes, ma'am," Amy said, but as she was about to get to her feet she was stopped short.

"One thing, Lloyd. How did we spend this afternoon, you and I?"

It took a moment to get the point. "We had lunch at the Plaza, ma'am."

"And a very pleasant lunch it's been, Lloyd. Now attend to that call."

THE weather turned up sunny and cool on blessed Sunday, the day off. They slept late, breakfasted luxuriously in the staff hall, then returned to the apartment, where Amy seated herself at the desk to make out the weekly payment-schedule checks.

"Before you start," Mike said. He removed the thick folder of house inventory and Mrs. McEye's information folder from the drawer. "I want to look through the floor plans in the folder and the art works listed in the inventory. Put 'em together with my copious notes and see what comes out."

"No library today?"

"Nope."

"But we won't be stuck inside all day, will we?" Amy pleaded. "I'm sure the McEye can do without me on our days off, but if she knows I'm right next door to that office—"

"Fact," Mike agreed. "We'll definitely be going out. But I'm also thinking that if Abe's gotten around to missing us as much as I miss them, he could be on the phone about it this morning. I mean, another Sunday where we don't all get together? So don't prepare to mail him his check yet. You might be hand-delivering it."

This sound judgment was verified an hour later when the phone rang. Abe said, "Look, Audie tells me I'm supposed to apologize for something, God knows what, so I apologize. Now when'll you two be over? How about lunch?"

"We just had a very late breakfast," said Mike, spirits on the rise.

"Not bagels, lox, and cream cheese, that I'll bet on. Besides, I have a golden offer to make that you can't possibly refuse. The sooner we talk it over, the better."

"An offer of what?"

"You'll see. All I'll tell you is that happy days are here again, the skies are clear nor drear again—"

"Make it a late lunch," said Mike. "We'll be there."

He reported this to Amy, and she looked doubtful. "He's manipulating again," she said.

"Naturally. But he did apologize."

"I can imagine how," Amy said wisely. "Still, I'm glad he did. You know, I wonder about it sometimes. I mean about having just one pair of close friends in the whole world."

"According to the statistics, darling," Mike said, "that's way ahead of the average. And it keeps us even with Abe and Audie."

He was, however, braced for the offer he couldn't refuse, so

221

when it came out during the bagels and lox orgy it didn't provide too much of a shock.

"There's this program the city's instituted," Abe said. "All-day kindergarten in the public schools. You must have gotten wind of it even up there in Durie country."

"So?" said Mike.

"So there's this very big wheel in our ed. department, Dick Santana, who's been tapped by the city to help get the program rolling. Yesterday at a faculty thing, he mentioned to me that they've now got a multitude of kids, a paucity of teachers. So I told him all about you two, and he lit up like a Christmas tree."

"All?" Mike said. "Including the blacklisting?"

"All. And as far as he's concerned — considering that I'm personally vouching for an available kindergarten teacher and an instructor with ten years experience — we forget about the blacklisting. Fourteen thousand to start, and kids of an age where there's no dealing in pot and pills. Your big problem'll be getting them into their snowsuits when the weather turns cold. And the only question is when I can arrange your meeting with Santana. Well?"

"And what do I know about teaching at that level?" Mike asked.

"Mike, these are wide-eyed innocents. To kids this age, teacher is God. You'll enjoy the experience."

So here it is, Mike thought, but why the discomfort in him? He looked at Amy and knew from her frown that she was sharing the discomfort.

She said, "It's much less than we're making now, Abe, even without our perks. You know that."

"Darling" — Abe was all the kindly old uncle — "fourteen thousand times two still adds up to a reasonable income."

Amy's jaw hardened. Somehow this wasn't the same old Amy, Mike thought. She had taken his opinion for granted without asking it, and she had the ball and was going to run it straight through the line. She said to Abe, "Not all that reasonable. Not after you deduct rent, food, insurance, and use of car from it. Which we're not doing now in our present employment."

"That music again?" Abe said. When he flushed, Mike saw, that shiny bald pate actually glowed crimson. "Look, darling, I know all about your wonderful five-year plan for piling up the bucks. What you don't know is how long those five years can be and what they can do to you along the way."

"Oh, and exactly what can they do?"

Audrey stood up and asked brightly, "Anybody mind if I go into the kitchen and count the silver?" And in unison Amy and Abe said, "Yes."

Abe promptly amended this to, "I'd like you to stay right here and back me up in this. You agreed with me about it last night, didn't you?"

"Did I?" said Audrey. "I don't remember getting a word in during that harangue, dear. One way or the other."

"Either way," said Abe, "I want you to stay here and apply your usual good sense to this."

"Oh, boy," said Audrey, but she sat down.

"Now," Abe said to Amy, "you did ask what five years of self-elected membership in the servant class could do to you?"

"Yes."

"And you understand that what I have to say is out of a deep and abiding affection for my dearest friends?"

"Of course," said Amy. "And I'm not the one who's angry, Abe. You are."

"Not angry, darling. Worried. Because you two are already—last time we were together, this time—showing signs of what's happening to you. Talking servant talk from the servant's point of view. Mild complaints about the impositions on you, some amusement at the vagaries of the masters, a deep concern about the well-being of Margaret Durie, who, granting that her infirmity is pitiable, cannot only buy anything in the world she may desire for her comforting, but, if you ever step on her little toe, would gladly take off your head just the way you told us she did that poor little canary of hers."

"Hell and damnation," Amy said in outrage. "Abe, that is such a distorted way of seeing it—"

"Not one bit. You are in the forest with your nose pressed up against a tree. I am outside the forest getting the objective view." Abe turned to Audrey. "Would you agree with that much at least?"

"I don't know," Audrey said. "What I seem to be hearing from your corner is that old Bronx socialist blood percolating."

"No, dear. Because I am in no way suggesting that the Duries be stripped of their wealth and sent to the guillotine."

Audrey patted his head. "How kind you are."

"Just practical," Abe said. "I'm of an age to know that the proletariat who'd be handed the wealth would blow it immediately on gaudy foolishness. Matter of fact, the Duries don't come off too badly as among the richest of the parasitical rich. Kind of an anachronism really. Stuffy, inbred, ingrown people, respectable enough in manners and morals. However—"

"Ah, yes," said Audrey, "here comes the however."

"However," said Abe, "they can be an unhealthy influence on certain ingenuous folks who serve them. To the Duries there is Us and Them. Us in here behind the drawbridge, Them out there. The trouble is that some ingenuous souls who serve them may develop the notion that they too are Us, not Them. And why not? It's a very sweet life they feel they're part of, with that hypnotic aura of wealth and power emanating from every quarter. Given just a few crumbs from the table—"

"Abe," said Amy, "you don't really believe that."

"You've changed, darling. The clothes, the hair, the manner, the walk, the talk. Without realizing it maybe, you are on your way to becoming a pseudo-Durie. You weren't too comfortable about it to start with, but you are now, aren't you?"

"So what?" Audrey interposed. "I think the way she comes on now is just great. Matter of fact," she said to Amy, "if you ever want to try selling top of the line at the boutique—"

"No," Amy said, "I don't think Abe would approve. Your kind of customer might corrupt me."

"Darling," Abe said worriedly, "if I've hurt your feelings—"

"But what about me?" Mike asked him. "You haven't hurt mine yet. How about it? Any profound changes you've noticed?"

"Well—" said Abe.

Audrey picked up her empty plate and brought it down hard on the table, shattering it into several large fragments. "Thank you, one and all," she said in the dead silence that followed. She smiled at each in turn. "It's open stock, so don't let it worry you. And now my husband is putting away his soapbox. Then we will go out and walk and talk and look around before winter sets in to prevent it. And after a drink or two we will go to the SoHo South and see *The Cherry Orchard* they're putting on there. An un-tampered-with version we hear is pretty good."

Abe's expression, Mike noted, became one of somebody now viewing impending delights. Never mind music, he thought, Chekhov had the power to soothe that savage breast.

"The sound of the axe in the woods," Abe said dreamily. "Jesus." He leaned forward and pointed at Mike. "That's a thought for your book. The Chekhovian view of your situation. If you consider it in that light —"

Audrey reached over, picked up her husband's plate, and held it high. "Abe, dear," she said.

In fact, it had been pretty good Chekhov, Amy and Mike acknowledged to each other back in the staff hall near midnight. "And," said Mike, "I figured out why he can even imagine our situation as Chekhovian."

"Why?"

"It's his Russian heritage. All Russians live their lives playing roles out of Chekhov." He plucked the schedule slips from the board and glanced at his. "Crap." He held out the slip to her. "Five A.M. Golightly at *R*. Marketing."

Amy confirmed this. "But that's awful. You'll have to set the clock for about four."

"Dawn patrol, Wilson calls it. Anyhow, I'm still down for the usual nine-thirty Craig and Walter drive to the office, so I sup-pose marketing'll be done before then. Want some coffee and cake for a nightcap?"

"No. We go right to bed. You won't get much sleep as it is."

He had left the McEye information folder and the house in-ventory on the bed where he had been scouring through them. He was about to remove them when he thought better of it. He sat down on the edge of the bed and opened the inventory to the place he had marked with a scrap of paper. "Look at this," he said.

"Now?"

"Yes. It's been in back of my mind all evening. It won't take long." He drew her down beside him. "This inventory goes by rooms. And it seems to be comprehensive down to the last penholder. Now these pages here cover that first-floor dining room—"

Amy looked. "Mike, there must be a dozen pages of it."

"At least. But the artworks are listed together on these two pages. Now see if you don't find something strange right here."

Amy scanned the pages. "No, I don't."

"Here," Mike said, pointing. *"Portrait of Miss Margaret Durie.* You saw that picture yourself. Ma'am's gift to her father, she told you. And it's been there a long, long time."

"Yes, but I still don't—"

"No attribution," Mike said. "No artist's name. And every other painting listed here has an attribution. Including all of Margaret Durie's watercolors. But not this portrait of her."

"Oh, that. But she explained that he didn't believe in signing a painting except in back. I'm sure I told you about it."

"You did, and it's all down in my notes. But Ma'am's are only signed in back, too, from what she said, and her name's next to them in the inventory. An inventory like this is a business document. It's supposed to be complete. Yet no one can tell from it who painted that picture. Don't you consider that strange?"

"A little," Amy said. "Yes. But what set you off on this?"

"My notes. Names galore there. Everybody's name—family and staff. But neither Ma'am nor anyone else here has ever mentioned the name of the art instructor who was so important to her. Occupied this apartment, gave her lessons, painted her portrait—no name. Why not?"

"I don't know," said Amy. "But of course the name could be right on the back of that painting."

"Suppose it isn't?"

"Michael, dear, you may have come across a typo in the inventory. And if you expect to get even three hours sleep—"

"Hell, that's right," Mike said glumly. "The dawn patrol."

"Predawn patrol," Amy corrected.

Still, she was the one who, after lights were out, abruptly sat up in bed and switched hers on again. "Mike, do you believe what Abe said about my changing?"

"Baby, you know how Abe dramatizes."

"Yes, but Audie seemed to go along with him on it. Now I want to know. Have I changed the way he said I have?"

"Look, Abe is used to a sweet, shy Amy in blue jeans and sneakers and with hair that looked like it could stand a little combing. Sort of an overgrown kid, full of quiet charm, always a bit deferential, letting him control the conversation. But not anymore. Now it's the eye-fetching dress and queenly hairdo and a readiness to talk freely about strange adventures down the Durie rabbit hole. And most troublesome to him, I think, is the way you now go head to head with him. Suddenly the overgrown kid, the daughter he would have wanted—at least I hope he hasn't been nursing Lolita fantasies—anyhow, suddenly that kid is now an elegant young lady. With a will of her own."

"Elegant," said Amy.

"That's the word for it. Matter of fact, that's what Audie was telling you when she made that remark about your selling at the boutique."

"Do you see it that way?"

"Yep. I'll admit it wasn't exactly what I bargained for when I picked up this pathetic creature peddling flowers in Covent Garden, but I like it. I find it alluring."

"I don't know," Amy said. "Now I feel somehow self-conscious about it. I can just hear myself talking in that terribly genteel way like the McEye."

"No chance. Remember you were genteel to start with. Any more questions before I have to get up and go to market?"

"I'm sorry, but yes, just one. What Abe said about our way of thinking now—I mean, reflecting the Durie attitude—"

"Forget it," Mike said. "No matter how Abe feels about it, for that attitude you need at least three billion dollars."

* * *

227

"**C**OME in," called Ma'am, and Amy pushed open the door and trundled in the breakfast cart.

She pulled up short on the edge of that white expanse of carpet. Ma'am was seated in her usual chair, but close by sat Jocelyn Durie in dressing gown, a formidable figure, a hand making sweeping gestures at the still-open door. A loud signal even if silent, Amy thought. Begone, Lloyd.

Before she could move one way or the other, Ma'am, as if she had read all the nuances here, said sharply, "My breakfast, Lloyd," and that settled it.

"Good-morning, ma'am," Amy said. "Good morning, Mrs. Durie," and wheeled the cart up to the table between them, exactly between, as the McEye had once expressed it, the rock and the hard place.

Jocelyn Durie said heatedly to Ma'am, "We'll continue this later, Margaret. After all, you do have some influence on the child."

"A delusion," Ma'am said. "And she is not a child. Do look closely at her sometime."

"She will always be my child, Margaret."

"She is her own woman now. But I recognize that dreary cliché. So give Craig a message from me, Jocelyn. There are those who are concerned for someone, and there are those who are concerned about someone."

"I fail to see your point. And the concern right now, with those disgusting British tabloids taking notice —"

"Enough, Jocelyn. *Cela suffit.* Lloyd, will you show Mrs. Durie out? And attend to my breakfast?"

Jocelyn Durie stood up. In the process, Amy took note, she seemed to take an iron control of herself and then to go all over sensitivity and understanding. She said gently to Ma'am, "What I will tell Craig is how well you're looking, Margaret. And" — there was no suggestion of irony in the voice — "how spirited you are. That is a joy to all of us."

"Dear Jocelyn," said Ma'am in honeyed tones.

At the door, Jocelyn Durie paused briefly. "Mrs. McEye," she

228

told Amy in an undertone, "has given me very good report of you."

"Kind of her," whispered Amy, and waited until the visitor was on her way down the corridor before closing the door.

Indeed, Ma'am was in high good spirits, relishing not only her coffee but the brioche as well. When Amy opened the *Times* to the obituaries it was dismissed with a fluttering of the fingers.

"Don't bother, Lloyd." The fingers brushed over the packet of mail. "Nothing significant here, it seems. We'll put it aside. What you'll do now is phone Mrs. McEye and tell her that I want the car at eleven. For her information, a visit to the Upshur Institute, lunch out, perhaps a pleasant drive."

And that, thought Amy, really does in Mike, poor darling. Up at four for the marketing, on the go since, and no doubt looking forward to a little nap betweentimes to get his eyes uncrossed.

"For your own information, Lloyd," Ma'am said, "when we leave the Institute we'll stop first at the bank so you'll be in a position to settle all arrangements with Miss Lowry at the gallery. You'll leave me at the Plaza and take whatever time you need for that. You and Miss Lowry are on amicable terms?"

"Yes, I believe so."

"Because from the information I've been given, she seems to be up in arms against the world. Did you find that the case?"

"Well, she does have a somewhat challenging manner."

"Except"—Ma'am held up a forefinger in reproof—"in regard to her devoted grandmother. You did assure me of that, didn't you?"

"Yes, ma'am."

"As for the rest, one can hardly blame her for being on the defensive against a hostile world." Ma'am resumed that straight-backed position in her chair. "You've met my niece Gwendolyn, Lloyd?"

"Yes, I have."

"Do you feel she's unworldly?"

Closer to unearthly, Amy thought. She said, "Well, I only met her very briefly."

"I'm aware of that. Now make that call to Mrs. McEye."

At eleven o'clock, when they got into the car, Amy observed with sympathy that her husband did look tired — after all, he had been up doing since four in the morning — and that his livery did not look quite as natty as it should; good thing the McEye wasn't on hand to take notice of it. And, traveling crosstown, she became aware that he was in a distinctly remote mood, a sign that he could be writing up a storm in his mind.

He pulled up, as instructed, before a weatherworn, old-style elevator apartment building on West Eightieth Street, and Ma'am, emerging from the car, rested her hand on Amy's wrist and maintained it there all the way to the door of a third-floor apartment. Disdaining the doorbell, Ma'am tested the location of the door with the head of her stick, then rapped on it smartly. There was a long silence, then the sound of a succession of bolts being thrown.

"Good God," Ma'am said, "the woman's got herself locked in like the prisoner of Chillon."

She rapped again, this time an impatient tattoo, and the door was suddenly thrown open. The woman holding it wide was pleasant-faced, middle-aged, very round-eyed, and appeared to be in a state of mild panic. Somehow, Amy thought, she bore a distinct resemblance to Alice's White Queen.

The woman said in a flurry, "I'm so sorry, Miss Durie. I was with Mr. Upshur in the bedroom, and he's not well, and this door —"

Ma'am peremptorily cut her short: "Yes, of course. I won't be long, Mrs. Upshur." She kept the hand lightly on Amy's wrist as they entered a large room, sparsely furnished, as much office as living room, Amy saw, what with that rolltop desk and those filing cabinets and the typewriter and printing outfit on the table. "All I require, Mrs. Upshur, is a check from our book. The next in order."

"Yes, Miss Durie. One check." Mrs. Upshur scurried off toward the filing cabinets, stopped suddenly, gave Amy an embarrassed shrug, then changed course to the desk. She searched through a couple of drawers before coming up with a checkbook. "Right here, Miss Durie."

"And the balance in the book is correct?" Ma'am sounded as if she doubted this. "It includes the most recent deposit and with-drawal?"

"Yes. I made sure of that. But if you—"

"Sit down, Lloyd." The stick pointed at the desk. "Now a pen, Mrs. Upshur."

Amy waited to seat herself until Mrs. Upshur, her panic in-tensifying, scrabbled through other drawers to produce a pen. No surprise in store, Amy thought. A check for six thousand dollars made out to cash. So it was, Ma'am, leaning over her, the hand guiding hers—actually riding on hers—through the motions. It works either way, Amy thought with a touch of re-sentment. My hand on hers, hers on mine, she's making sure there are no mistakes, accidental or otherwise.

Ma'am tucked the folded check into her purse. "That's all, Mrs. Upshur. Now you can lock yourself in again."

"Yes. And, Miss Durie, I do want you to know how grateful I am for everything. And Mr. Upshur would want you to know—"

"Good day, Mrs. Upshur," said Ma'am, and said nothing more until the elevator was on its way down. Then she turned her face up to Amy's. "How would you describe her, Lloyd? A bit too eager to please?"

"Well, ma'am, isn't it better to err in that direction?"

"Is it? Wouldn't you doubt the trustworthiness of someone like that?"

"Someone else, ma'am, but not Mrs. Upshur. Watching her, I couldn't help thinking—"

"Yes?"

"—well, how much she resembles the White Queen in *Alice*."

Ma'am smiled. "Featherheaded, but without duplicity?"

"I suppose you could put it that way."

"So I can," said Ma'am.

No surprises either at the bank a few blocks away. The same eager and affable Mr. Fontaine attended to the cashing of the check, though this time it was Amy who walked out the door with the money—six thousand in five-hundred-dollar notes—in her pocketbook. Which, she thought, made for a very pleasant sensation indeed, no matter how temporary.

With Ma'am released to the Plaza's doorman, she slid into the front seat of the car beside Mike. "Tired, troubled, or writing in the mind?" she asked.

"All three," Mike said.

"Why? Golightly give you a hard time?"

"Not the way I thought. It was the damndest thing. We did the Fulton Fish Market first, then the wholesale meat market district on the West Side, then a couple of specialty grocers. And he kept falling asleep every time he'd sit down in the car, and not quite remembering where he was, and losing his shopping list—"

"Stoned?"

"No way," Mike said. "Just on the edge of senility, seems to me. I have a feeling the only time he functions halfway right is in the kitchen. Out of memory. Yet here he is. All right, Mrs. Mac said Domestique can't come up with a competent butler, I won't argue that. But a competent chef?"

"Well," Amy pointed out, "we already know they don't like to retire faithful old servants."

"And that," Mike said, "is where it always gets interesting. Why don't they? Just judging by Wilson, they certainly retire them in style. It's not like turning them out into the street, is it?"

"Far from," said Amy.

"That is what I keep thinking. Anyhow, when I brought the wagon back to the garage, there was Wilson already with the best part of a six-pack in him. We're real buddies now, since I don't object to his cleaning out the cars and polishing them up."

"Tom Sawyer and the fence," Amy remarked.

"Well, I doubt there's ever been much in his life besides those cars. And it keeps him out of Levine's office, which Levine appreciates. So when he started on the wagon—he gave me a whole lecture about what a disaster fish and meat scraps could be—I worked him around to the subject of Golightly. Considering the shape he's in, isn't he overdue for retirement? Doesn't he want it? It's Wilson's response I've got on the mind now."

"Yes?"

"He said Golightly gets real hot if anybody even mentions retirement to him, so he figured the family was just hoping the old coot would drop dead one of these days. And that, as far as they were concerned, would take care of that much."

"That much?" Amy said, puzzled. "Of what?"

"Wait. I've got it down here." Mike dug the notebook out of his pocket and flipped it open. "Now listen. When I naturally asked Wilson what he meant he said, 'Hell, Golightly was right there with me and Borglund when she went down those stairs, wasn't he? He's the one McEye told to carry her to her room.'"

"Mr. McEye, the butler," Amy said.

"Right. And get this. When I said, 'Well, what's that have to do with Golightly being retired whether he likes it or not?' Wilson put his finger along his nose — you know, deep secret stuff to share with your buddy — and he said, 'Mike boy, use your head. Golightly's got a mean streak in him. Cut him loose, and he could talk his head off just to get even.'"

"Confusion seems to be rife," Amy said. "Talk about what? The accident? That's no secret."

"I put that to Wilson and it shut him up like a clam. He even looked a little scared, though he was so boozy it was hard to tell if he was faking it or he felt it."

"He felt it," Amy said decisively. "He was close to telling something he wasn't supposed to."

"But what? That because those three characters were in the house when Ma'am took her fall the family's afraid to retire them? Did it only out of dire necessity in Wilson's case? After all, Ma'am's right here herself to tell anything that might be told."

"There's more to it than that. That fall, I mean."

"Such as?"

"I don't know," Amy said defensively. "But why did Amy Robsart just pop into my head?"

"Amy Robsart? Out of *Kenilworth?*"

"Out of the history books, too. Remember? Her husband thought he might be able to marry Queen Elizabeth but he was stuck with poor Amy, his wife. And suddenly down goes Amy a whole flight of stairs and breaks her neck. You must remember."

"Ah, yes," Mike said. "You mean, did she fall or was she pushed? That Tudor crowd could play rough, couldn't it? But what we have on the present agenda, dear, are not Tudors but Duries, a whole different kettle of cold fish. Not inclined to the melodramatic passage. Nor would the three faithful servitors here be likely to push the boss's daughter down a flight of stairs for any reason. Not unless they wanted to get themselves sat in the electric chair as soon as it could be arranged."

"They weren't necessarily the only ones in the house then," Amy said.

"Well, we've been told the rest of the family was at their Maine island then. Which leaves us with Margaret Durie, age eighteen, tripping lightly down those stairs, catching a heel in that iron-work, and landing headlong all on her own. Want my opinion on the Tudor situation? That's what happened to Amy Robsart, too, most likely."

"You haven't counted that artist," Amy said. "The one whose studio was in our apartment then. The one who did her portrait and gave her lessons."

"Why count him in? There's been no hint from anyone that he was around that day."

"He could have been. And you'd better get the car moving. Ma'am said I had what time I needed, but it didn't mean forever."

Mike got the car moving. "You sound testy," he remarked. "Look, just because I'm being logical about this—"

"That stairway she fell down," Amy said, "was between the third and second floors. Third floor was all staff except for that studio. So my logic says she was on the third floor to visit the studio. He could have been right in it at the time. That was about when the portrait was being painted, wasn't it?"

Mike sighed. "Talk about conjecture piled on conjecture."

"What's the painter's name?" Amy asked shortly.

"His name? Baby, you know we already worked out he seems to be nameless as far as the family—"

"That's what I'm getting at. No signature on that painting. No name in that inventory. Never mentioned in the house by name. Yet this had to be a painter of stature, didn't it? That is quite some portrait."

"I wouldn't know, dear. The ground floor is forbidden territory to servants in my category."

"Oh, Mike."

"Sorry. That was dirty pool, wasn't it?"

234

"No, it wasn't. Mike, I'm sure Abe can still get us those teaching jobs. If that's what you want for us, I'm ready."

"And walk out just when you're also ready to help Ma'am consummate her triumph as closet feminist?"

"That's one thing I'd like to walk out on. I'm concerned about her, I feel close to her, but I can't see this elaborate scenario she's made of it, not when she's involved me in it this deep. You too, for that matter."

"Easy does it, baby. Let's overlook the dirty pool." Mike drew her against him and when in response she crowded hard against his shoulder he said, "Hey, there's only room for one behind this wheel."

"I can be a real pain sometimes, can't I?" she said without changing position.

"Well," Mike said, "dear old Miss Margaret with the best of intentions — *viva* woman's lib — has you playing Mata Hari, and you're just not the Mata Hari type. And there's the atmosphere we live in. Get little hints of happenings that you can't ask about or clear up. You have to be pretty thick in the head not to get edgy about it now and then."

"It doesn't seem to bother you that way," Amy said. "With all those notes you're taking and then sitting at the typewriter with them all hours, I think you like it."

"Half of me. The writer half that finds it interesting. But the other half — no. That's the half that has to function in it. And worry about your functioning in it. Anyhow, what we're getting worked up about happened more than fifty years ago. Ancient history. Irrelevant and immaterial. And there's a fair chance Wilson is full of wind — sure as hell he's full of beer — whatever he says."

"Perhaps," Amy said. She drew away so that he could use both hands on the wheel in the tangle of Fifth Avenue traffic. "But there's something Ma'am said only this morning that's troublesome. It didn't mean too much when she said it, but now it does."

"Do tell."

"I wish I could feel that lighthearted about it. You know those payments she made to someone at the Plaza?"

"At least one."

"Even so. We still don't know who got that money, but from what she said I now have an idea about it. She was talking about Kim Lowry and she said exactly this: 'From the information I've been given about her—'"

"Yes?"

"That's it. That's what's significant. Listen," Amy said, then recited very slowly: "'From the information I've been given about her—' You see? Not from what she heard or gleaned from reviews, but from what was given to her. And it's not likely anybody just happened to discuss Kim Lowry with her. It means she assigned someone to get her information about Kim Lowry and someone did. A slip of the tongue? It could be. But there it is."

"Mrs. Upshur," Mike said. "What's she like anyhow?"

"Very pleasant. Thoroughly intimidated by Ma'am. Profuse in her gratitude. Not very bright really. Put it all together, she's not one to go snooping around like a private detective or whatever."

"Maybe not," Mike acknowledged. "But going a step further, I'd say her braille messages did contain delicate information of some kind. You told me Ma'am gets rid of them at once, didn't you?"

"Yes. Scissors them to shreds. And I'm not saying Mrs. Upshur isn't being used. Or that the Institute isn't a front for handling all that cash without the family knowing. And I agree that, yes, those braille messages did contain delicate information. But, Michael dear, Mrs. Upshur was sure as hell not at the Plaza those times, not when she has a convenient apartment to use for any hanky-panky. Nor was it anybody from the gallery. It was somebody else."

"All right, who else?"

"The one," Amy said, "who dug up that information that Mrs. Upshur then passed along in braille. The one who met Ma'am at the Plaza to collect payment in cash for the information."

"You are seriously talking private detective?" Mike asked.

"Well, doesn't that make sense?"

"I suppose," Mike said doubtfully. "But, hey, all this rig-

236

marole just to keep the family from finding out she's giving a grant-in-aid to an aspiring young painter?"

Amy nodded broadly. "A scandalous young painter, and *scandalous* is a word Ma'am seems to dote on. And that stuff in the gallery is very raw stuff, Mike. I can see dear Jocelyn taking one look and going off like a bomb. Besides, there's the tie-in with the gay movement, more scandal in the making. Suppose Kim Lowry or Jason Cook learned the identity of their Santa Claus? You think they wouldn't tell the whole world about it to get all that gaudy publicity? Put yourself in their place."

"Well, in their place," Mike admitted, "I'd be very tempted and damn the consequences. So it's possible Ma'am is having her cake and eating it too. Santa Claus to them sordid types, and laughing all the way. But face the facts, darling, it's all fun and games. Nothing to get emotional about."

"Just the same I have to keep telling outrageous lies to the McEye about what Ma'am is doing on these little drives. It does foul up the atmosphere."

"You think Mrs. Mac suspects something?"

"Nothing. She smiles all over when I report. Evidently, Ma'am was such a holy terror all those bad years that these little excursions are the best possible news for the family. Proof she's now living a nice normal rich-lady life, I suppose."

"Comfort yourself with that thought, baby," Mike advised. "By the way, were you named after Amy Robsart? What with your dad possibly a Walter Scott and *Kenilworth* fan—"

"He was," Amy said, "but I was named after my grandmother. His mother."

"At least that's what he wanted you to believe," said Mike, "the old romantic."

* * *

K IM Lowry wasn't in the gallery, but the bearded, turnip-shaped Jason Cook was, along with a few others. The females were vaguely familiar to Amy from her previous visit, and they all seemed to be focused on a middle-aged male who, nicely done up in full middle-management regalia, including vest, necktie, and attaché case, was examining the works on display with the somber expression of an aficionado weighing artistic values. He had to be aware of the almost baleful concentration on him, Amy was sure.

"A looker," Jason Cook confided to her sotto voce. "Gets sweaty hands from what they read as porno. It's a type. They are not reading Kim's statement nohow."

"Possibly," said Amy. "But where's Kim? She's supposed to be here, isn't she?"

"Usually, during open time. But she's stuck home playing nurse to granny. Old lady's just out of the hospital after the flu — a real close call — and Kim's the one to make her follow doctor's orders. But I can take the money and receipt it. You did bring it?" He seemed doubtful about this.

"Yes. But I'm instructed to give it to Kim. Is there any way you can let her know I'm here?"

"Well" — Jason Cook managed to sound both relieved and put upon — "if it comes to that, you can go there. It's not that far away, West Twentieth near Ninth. If you want me to get you a cab —"

"No, it's not necessary. Look, you understand that I must follow instructions."

He seemed somewhat mollified by this. "Oh, yeah. And don't get me wrong, Mrs. Lloyd. I want you to know — whoever your Madame X is — how much I appreciate your business. Three works? Cash payment? I mean, this not only provides heavy supportiveness for Kim, but it practically puts the gallery on its feet. Or shouldn't I be letting you in on that?"

"No reason why not," Amy assured him. "And all the credit goes to Madame X. Now I think —"

Jason Cook gave her a meaningful look and motioned with his

head toward the rear of the gallery. "A couple of minutes in private? Don't worry, Kim'll be at home when you get there. I'll write down the address for you. Just a couple of minutes. It could be important."

He led her to the storeroom-kitchen and closed its door as much as it could be closed, which was about halfway. He wrote the address on a scrap of paper and handed it to her. Then he stood looking up at her, obviously trying to line up the right words in the right order.

"Well?" said Amy.

"All right," said Jason Cook, "what went a little bit wrong is when you told Kim on the phone that the buyer wanted her to keep the paintings she bought."

"They're still being paid for," Amy pointed out.

"Yeah, but Kim's not sure now about selling under these conditions. She feels the way someone helps you make your statement is to buy your work and put it up for the world to see. This way it comes off as some kind of handout. She has a lot of pride, Kim."

Amy's heart sank. "If you'd explain to her—"

"I put in half of last night explaining to her. But the way Adela leans on her—"

"Who?"

"Adela. Her grandmother. She told you about her, didn't she?"

"Yes."

"Well, Adela got it into her head that what you proposed is a pat on the head for the artist and sort of a put-down of the art. That is what you are going to run into over there, so if you know about it in advance, all the better." Jason Cook's voice rose in outrage. "I want to tell you that I feel I'm getting the finger here. I've got my financial neck on the block like Captain John Smith, then along comes Pocahontas to save the day, and next thing she's being chased away by my client. And her flakey grandmother. This is not only ridiculous, it's a real downer. And you do want to buy those works, don't you?"

"Definitely."

239

"So if we close the deal on the spot—you and I personally—I would take my chances that Kim—"

"I'm sorry," Amy said from the heart. The temptation was great, but go report this back to Ma'am. What were those precise instructions? *Ingratiate yourself with her.* And yet, so it seemed, without daring to confide to Kim Lowry—and her grandmother, for God's sake—that in this case the buyer was blind, that the works couldn't mean anything to her, that the deal was, as Mike had neatly put it, a grant-in-aid. Hell and damnation, Amy thought.

"What would I say to them?" she asked.

Jason Cook brightened. "I already thought of that. Suppose you just said that the buyer doesn't have a place right now suitable for displaying the works. They're very large, a problem for the average premises. So it's just that Kim is made trustee for them for a while. That could be the case, couldn't it?"

Amy regretfully shook her head. "Not really."

"So you and I know that, but Kim and Adela don't have to. Look, all you have to do is be convincing about it."

"I'm not sure I can be."

"Believe me," Jason Cook said with feeling, "you can be. The way you come on, Mrs. Lloyd, you could sell me a piece of the Brooklyn Bridge. Take my word for it. And all you really have to do is concentrate on Adela. She likes to know she's in charge. And since the buyer is female, well, she's open to argument. If it was male, I'd bet the other way. Just keep in mind that as far as male is concerned Adela knows they're garbage. I'm the exception, and it took me a lot of sweat to get her around that far. Of course, being gay helped. Even if she's psycho on the subject, she realizes I'm a long way from the men in her life."

"I gather," said Amy, "that whoever they are, they let her down badly."

"Were," said Jason Cook. "Not are. Her husband walked out on her when she started to lose her looks, and it seems she had kind of a total passion for him. Then her daughter—Kim's mother—married a hard case who one day took all their money and headed out of town. Never seen again. And Kim's mother, who also had that kind of total passion, drank herself to death.

240

So that made Adela grandma and grandpa *and* mama and papa to Kim. She just laid all that passion on her, along with—well, maybe justified misanthropy. You see?"

"Vividly," said Amy.

"I know what you mean. Actually, I don't think it's healthy for either of them. I mean, that interdependence where if one sneezes, the other starts hyperventilating. After all, the old lady's over seventy now and in bad shape so odds are she'll pass on in a little while, and then what happens to Kim? She'll be stripped of all defenses."

"She's no child herself," Amy pointed out. "She'll knit new defenses. She has talent and a career to concentrate on."

"If she doesn't keep fouling it up, the way she's ready to do with this deal. Anyhow, now you know what you'll be running into over there. I'm counting on you to be persuasive. I'm really grateful, Mrs. Lloyd, that you come on so well-balanced about it."

"Well," Amy said, "I'm as much agent for the buyer as you are for the seller, so I have a stake in it, too."

"Then we're in the same boat, halfway up the creek together." As Amy started to open the door, Jason Cook held up a hand. "One more minute, Mrs. Lloyd? It's something I have to find out. I know I probably shouldn't lay this on you, but it's been on my mind so much I can't help it. Even Kim doesn't know about it."

"About what?"

"Well, last month when I put out the press release about the gallery opening and Kim's show I had someone drop in here for a private interview. Young, but not that young, very enthusiastic about Kim's work. Said he did free-lance articles on contract for a lot of national magazines, and he thought Kim would be a hot subject. He wanted to do a really strong profile of her but without her knowing it, see? No chance of turning it into promotion that way, so he said. So I talked very freely about her, and then it turned out that friends of hers had also been put through the same routine."

Amy felt her stomach turn over. "Nothing wrong with that," she said without conviction.

"No," said Jason Cook, "but I have enough connections with magazine people to find out if any such article was contracted for or even talked about where it mattered, and there wasn't. No interest from any direction. You see?"

"If the man provided credentials—"

"Yeah, but credentials never came up. That's my fault. I remember I had one little flicker of an idea about it, but then I told myself this could turn him off, and we were doing fine as it was. Right now, matter of fact, I'm worried about turning you off with all this. But I have to take the chance." Jason Cook was obviously steeling himself for the payoff. "So is there any possibility, Mrs. Lloyd, that you or your client were having Kim checked out? Having her character investigated or whatever? You're not angry, are you, about me asking?"

"No. Surprised, I'd say."

"So you and your client had nothing to do with it," said Jason Cook.

Amy took refuge in the oldest gambit of all. "Why would we have?"

"That's right," Jason Cook said eagerly. "On the other hand, why would anybody else? But there it was. Maybe there is a profile being worked up."

"That would be the way to look at it," said Amy.

S HE climbed into the car and closed the door with a bang.

"Something's gone wrong," Mike said wisely.

Amy thrust Jason Cook's scrap of paper at him. "Kim Lowry's there with her dear grandma now. That Jason wanted to take the money, but I prefer to give it to her. The sooner the better. If I can."

"Meanwhile," Mike said, "the boss has been quite a time on her own. Maybe a phone call to her at the Plaza —"

"If she doesn't like it," Amy said, "she can lump it."

"Something has gone very wrong. Let's have it."

"All right," Amy said, and let him have it in detail. She concluded bitterly, "So she did hire a snoop to do a job on Kim. She had Mrs. Upshur hire him, and after he delivered the goods she paid him off herself at the Plaza. Any argument?"

"Nope."

"Which means," said Amy, "she's been making thorough damn fools of us."

"So it seems," Mike agreed. "But look at the plus side. She comes out happy in her little triumph, and Kim comes out the real winner. Along with woman's lib and feminist art and whatever." He put his arm around her and she stiffened against it. "Do you mind," he said, "if I offer you a bitter truth to chew on?"

"I'm not so sure."

"I'll take the chance anyhow. It isn't Ma'am's gamesmanship that throws you, it's hurt pride. You felt she was taking you step by step into her full confidence, and now you've learned better."

Amy weighed this. Early in the marriage, she knew, it would have been enough to start a slambang argument, let the chips fall where they will. But they had learned — she first — that where blind emotion took over, logic went out the window and things were said that took an awful lot of unsaying. Eventually it became standard procedure for both of them to stop, look, and listen at the emotional crossroads at the first warning of the bell there.

She said at last, "Not altogether hurt pride. There's that justified sense of betrayal, too."

"Her loss," Mike said. "Not yours."

"Perhaps. I just wish I didn't pity her so much. That's what complicates it."

"Baby, you must know by now that she doesn't want anybody's pity."

"Then suppose," Amy said, "I controlled mine long enough to confront her with all this. What do you think would happen?"

Mike shrugged. "Worse comes to worst, Abe does have those school jobs up his sleeve."

"I don't trust Abe's motives," Amy said shortly.

"Hey now, let's not go over the brink. He's been the best friend anyone could have in time of need."

"It didn't cost him that much. And I'm not being ungrateful. But all that generosity was an ego trip for him. Kept us in our place. I'm a little tired of that."

"And a lot cynical, I take it."

"Yes," Amy said. "It could be time I developed some cynicism about our elders and betters. For that matter, so could Kim when it comes to her precious grandmother. Her own elder and better who seems to be running her life for her."

"Are you sure," Mike asked, "that in your immediate mood you want to go over there and deal with those two? Sounds to me like you're ready to blow the deal just for the fun of it."

"No chance," Amy said. "I do what I'm paid to do."

Mike turned the key in the ignition. "Is there balm in Gilead?" he asked the windshield.

"Twenty percent Christmas bonus," Amy reminded him.

"Ah, yes," he said. "Definitely there is balm in Gilead."

He let her out of the car down the block, well past the Lowry address. "Just in case they have a street view and decide to peek through the window after you say good-bye," he told her. "Also—"

"No more alsos," Amy said.

She went her way down the block quaking inwardly, trusting that this was concealed from him by a shoulders-back, hard-striding gait, Ma'am herself at her most formidable. It was a rather pleasant street—Saint Peter's Church, Clement Moore's *'Twas the Night Before Christmas* church its landmark—where a fair number of ancient buildings had been reclaimed by the new money coming into Chelsea. The Lowry address, however, turned out to be one of those bypassed by the new money. A four-story brick building, the brickwork grimy, the window frames cracked and peeling, the tiny foyer funereally lit by the dimmest possible bulb and reeking of stale urine. She had to peer closely at the row of four bells embedded in the wall to make out the handwritten cards above them. *A. Taliaferro-K. Lowry* marked the fourth bell, underneath which was clumsily penciled in *4 flor.*

Amy rang the bell, a buzzer allowed her to push open the interior door, and she found herself in a scruffy hallway where, instead of that reek of urine there was—a small improvement, she allowed—the choking smell of age-old dust emanating from threadbare carpeting.

Kim Lowry hailed her from high above with a "Who is it?" and Amy called, "Amy Lloyd. Jason said to come over here."

"Surprise, surprise," said Kim, indicating the opposite by her tone. "Top floor. All the way up."

She was waiting at the head of the staircase toward the rear of the apartment when her caller arrived. "Home," she said. "Such as it is. Well, come in."

The apartment apparently occupied the entire floor, its rooms, almost as dimly lit as the downstairs foyer, were high-ceilinged and wood-paneled; it might have been a find, Amy saw, especially with what appeared to be working fireplaces in a couple of the rooms, if it hadn't been as decayed-looking as the building itself. All the furniture in sight seemed to be Salvation Army rejects. And, as in that cluttered workroom-kitchen in Jason Cook's gallery, painted canvases, unframed, were everywhere in sight, hung on the walls high and low and leaning against them. In this light however, it was hard to even make out their subjects, much less judge their quality.

Kim led the way through this to the front room overlooking the street and lit at least by daylight. Here, added to the clutter, were an unmade bed in one corner and a pair of dilapidated overstuffed armchairs that once might have been part of a worthwhile set. One chair was piled high with magazines and newspapers. The other, facing the flickering screen of a small black-and-white television set, was occupied by a stout woman in housedress, heavy turtleneck sweater, and slippers. The sweater, Amy saw with fascination, had the effect of offering a view of the head much like the view of John the Baptist's on a platter. Additionally lit by erratic flashes from the TV set were bright, dark eyes, a small but not unattractive parrot beak of a nose, and a well-shaped mouth lipsticked as heavily as Ma'am's. Most fascinating was the wig of inky-black ringlets like a bowl clamped down on the head just above the ears.

Yet, Amy suspected, despite the grotesque touches, this, like Ma'am, had been a very pretty girl in her day, though where Ma'am's features had simply become more handsomely defined in her old age, this woman's gave the impression of now being embedded in dough.

"My grandmother," said Kim as she switched off the television. The woman reared back in outrage, and Kim said, "Mind your manners, Adela. This is Mrs. Lloyd. You know about her."

Adela coughed a deep croupy cough. She pulled a couple of tissues from a box on the small table at her side, spat phlegm into them, dropped them into an open-mouthed paper bag on the floor. "You get a good look at this building?" she demanded of Amy. "Ever see such a disgusting mess? When I owned it it was kept up right." She turned to her granddaughter: "Is that the truth?"

"Sure," Kim said, "but why not save it for the landlord? Meanwhile, how about your cough medicine? You're overdue."

"Forget it, darling. It tastes poisonous and the cough's loosened up anyhow. You heard it yourself. But I could use a glass of wine. And bring the bottle this time."

Kim looked at Amy. "Glass of wine?"

"No, thanks." Amy made a show of studying her watch. "What I would like to do—"

Kim disregarded the show. She affectionately pressed a hand against her grandmother's cheek. "She's just come out of a bad case of flu," she told Amy. "She's tough, but not as tough as she thinks. I'll be back in a minute."

She was, with half a water glass of wine in her hand and, Amy observed, no bottle to accompany it. Adela took down the wine in a couple of hard swallows, placed the glass on the table, and patted her lips with a tissue. She turned her attention back to Amy. "Mrs. Lloyd," she said, as if testing the sound of it. "Married? Or divorced?"

"Married."

"Happily married, like they say in the storybooks?"

Amy found her hackles rising. "Like they say in the storybooks, yes."

"So you want to believe. Do you know where your husband is right now?"

"Yes, I do."

"And do you know what's really on his mind right now? And what he could be feeling up?"

Amy said to Kim, "You know, I'm here to make payment for one of your paintings. And to arrange further payment for — "

"If you don't like my manners, Mrs. Lloyd," said Adela, "you can just walk out. Nobody's keeping you."

Hell and damnation, Amy thought, at least Kim Lowry, beneficiary of this charity, could help here. Instead, she seemed amused by this baiting. She said to Amy, "I told you she's tough. And she does have her suspicions about this deal."

"What suspicions?"

"I'll tell you what, Mrs. Lloyd," Adela said. She studied Amy through narrowed eyes from the glossy coiffure down to the trim shoes. "I think your husband put you up to buying some original Lowrys because he gets from them what he don't get from you. Right there in the crotch. I think he's a voyeur — you know what that is, don't you? — and you're going along with him in this, because so far he pays your bills, don't he? In style. To keep up that happy marriage of yours, you pimp for him this way. Convert great art into porno ticklers. Want to tell me different?"

"Not especially. What I'm trying to understand — It is Mrs. Taliaferro?"

"That's right." Adela brought up another load of phlegm and disposed of it directly into the paper bag. "My married name. A souvenir from my husband. Kim inherited the only worthwhile thing he had to leave. Talent. He had talent. That I'll never deny. Along with a talent for convincing anything in a skirt to lay down and spread her legs for him. Kim's father had that kind of talent, too. But you said you were trying to understand something. Understand what?"

"Well," said Amy, "Kim told me you were the sustaining force in her life. The inspiration for her career, the one who was always there to help her along in it."

247

Adela looked up at her granddaughter towering above her. "You said that about me, darling?"

Kim smiled broadly. "Don't lay that act on me, Adela. You know I always say it whenever anybody pushes the button."

Amy raised her voice. "And what I'm trying to understand, Mrs. Taliaferro, is why you're now trying to damage that career."

"Me?"

"Oh, yes. I was sent by a woman sympathetic to everything Kim stands for to buy three of her paintings. Half of those in the show. That's a great boost to any career. And if that woman walked in here and made herself known to you — which for good reason she cannot — you'd see how foolish your suspicions are. You and your daughter both had worthless husbands? That's too bad. But I don't see why Kim must pay for that now by turning away a buyer any other artist would be glad to find."

Adela Taliaferro glowered. "Who handed you that line? That useless lump Jason?"

"No," Amy said, "I don't need anyone to instruct me in the obvious." Kim, she saw, was no longer taking this in with a little smile like a spectator watching a couple of tennis players slug it out. She was frowning now.

"Obvious, is it?" her grandmother said. She held out the empty glass, and when Kim finally shook her head no, she banged the glass down hard on the table. "What's obvious, lady, is that you're dealing with a talented artist like some kind of sideshow. What do you mean, Kim will pick out the three paintings? Do they all look the same to you? And then she'll keep possession of them for the time being. What's that mean? That the buyer — whoever you're covering up for — can come around after hours and get a look at them in private when he's in the mood? Or she's in the mood? Those paintings make a statement to the whole world. They're not peepshow displays."

"No, they're not. But as agent for the buyer — without fee" — Amy came down on that hard — "I found all the paintings equally powerful. In that case, I leave it to the artist to make the selection. Her judgment has to be better than mine. As for Kim's keeping them for the time being, the buyer does not have space right now to hang them properly. And having them on display in the gallery even after the showing is closed only helps Kim. Especially when they're marked sold."

Adela looked at her granddaughter. "You heard all that?"

"Uh-huh."

Do you believe for one second that I'd ever do anything to hurt you?"

"No chance," said Kim.

Adela reached out and took her hand. "Then you do what you want about this, darling. I don't understand what's going on, I don't like the smell of it, but you do what you want."

"Eighteen thousand dollars," Kim said to her apologetically.

Amy seized the moment. She took the envelope from her handbag. "Six thousand here," she said. "The rest as arranged." Charity for the undeserving, she thought. She felt as exhausted as if she had just run up those three flights of stairs.

Kim rested the envelope on the palm of her upturned hand, "Van Gogh never had it this good," she told her grandmother.

"As for the receipt," Amy said, "I suppose you can make it out to my name."

Without meaning to, she instantly knew she had given Adela a small triumph. The old woman's mouth twisted in a half smile. "What a fat surprise," she said caustically.

At the head of the staircase Kim said, "You see? She's hung up on an obsession—plenty of reason for it—but it didn't hurt to dent it a little. Next time you're here you might be surprised at how she takes to you."

There are surprises, Amy thought, that one could do without.

* * *

MIKE stood at the open door of the car appreciatively watching his wife and her charge descend the few broad, shallow steps of the hotel to street level. A sort of spotlighted effect there, he saw, and from the response of the throng around them he was not the only one to take notice. The tiny, exquisite old woman in sable, chin high, unseeing eyes fixed straight ahead and her tall, red-haired, serenely poised companion — the favored granddaughter of this aristocratic grandmother? — moved down the center of the stairway eschewing the brass handrails on either side, the old woman's cane briefly searching out each step below, her free hand resting lightly on her companion's extended wrist. Very special people, and as if in recognition of this the crowd coming and going were giving that entire area of the stairway to them.

A lovely descent, Mike thought, the long-ago past briefly made alive again, because after all this was what that portico and stairway had been originally designed for, the making of an exit into a performance for the properly admiring.

The trouble was, he reflected, that the audience — even thought it did seem to be properly admiring — was all wrong nowadays. Considering the Plaza's tariffs, there had to be large amounts of money all around him, whether personal or cor-poration, but too much slob culture was evident around him as well. The open collars — neckties omitted — of otherwise dress shirts, the plethora of faded denims, the club-footed sneakers, the collection of beat-up windbreakers, the nondescript headgear, everything that the well-heeled could do to tarnish the glory of this baroque monument towering over them was being done.

Pass that thought along to Abe Silverstone, a well-heeled par-tisan of the common man, and see the sparks fly. For that mat-ter, even Audie, much of whose boutique's styles could be categorized as rich pauper, would probably side with Abe on this one.

Mike saw his passengers into the car and got behind the wheel. "Straight home, Miss Durie?"

"Straight home," said Ma'am, and as the car pulled away

from the curb she said, plainly directing it at Amy, "That difficulty you were about to describe, Lloyd—it didn't affect the arrangements, did it?"

"No."

"Then it could hardly be of concern. What was it?"

"A matter Jason Cook brought up." His wife's voice, Mike noted, was minus the usual sweetly compliant note in dealing with the boss. "He believes someone hired a private detective to obtain information about Kim Lowry. He asked if you were the one."

"Preposterous," Ma'am said scathingly. "Of course, you told him so."

"Yes."

"And gave the same assurance to Miss Lowry?"

"No. He hasn't mentioned it to her. Afraid she'd be upset by it, I suppose. He seems very protective of her."

"And should be. A talented and hard-beset artist? No reason that she suffer for his irrational suspicions."

"None at all," Amy said pleasantly. "But of course this one is quite rational."

Almost too late Mike realized he was preparing to ram the cab slowing down for the red light ahead. He came down hard on the brake. Ma'am yelped, then said wrathfully, "Lloyd!"

"Sorry, ma'am," he said. Kindergarten teaching, he thought. And apartment hunting. With the old Thompson Street apartment gone forever and Manhattan rents hitting the stratosphere, it would probably save time to start off the search in Queens. Or New Jersey.

"You know, Lloyd," Ma'am said to him, "my niece Camilla complained that you were an overly cautious driver. Try to remember that I prefer this." She returned to Amy. "You were saying that Mr. Cook's suspicions are justifiable. Do you seriously mean in regard to me?"

"Very seriously, Miss Durie. I believe you did arrange for Mrs. Upshur to hire someone to investigate Kim Lowry. Whatever he reported back she put into braille for you as a form of code. You also opened a special bank account for the Institute to secretly do

251

business with him. In the end, you met with him at least twice to pay him in cash and probably get an oral account of his investigation. Then I was made your agent in dealing with Kim Lowry so, at whatever cost, you could maintain anonymity."

"At whatever cost?"

"To my self-respect," Amy said grimly. "And my husband's. I know all this deception was to keep the family from interfering with your plans, but in the process you deliberately deceived us too. It seems to me—"

"Lloyd, do you have any idea of how wildly presumptuous you're being?"

"I don't feel that's the word," Amy said. "When we first met you told me how much you esteemed straight speaking. I'm simply taking that at face value now."

"Are you indeed? I thought I was hiring a confidential secretary. It appears that what I've obtained is a lawyer. A veritable Portia." The tone, Mike realized, was sardonic, not wrathful. "You're a clever girl, Lloyd."

"Thank you. But I am somewhat past being a girl."

"My unintentional error. You are a clever young woman. Now tell me. Have you mentioned any of this to any of the household? Family or staff? Or Mrs. Upshur possibly?"

"No, I haven't."

"But if I were to discharge you on the spot—both of you—for outrageous insolence, you would then—?"

"No, we would not. Believe me, there's never been any possibility of that."

There was a long silence. "You know," Ma'am said at last, "I think I do believe you."

"Thank you."

"So neither of us truly knew the other before this enlightenment, did we? I must admit I find it all very refreshing. But I'm still unclear about one thing. How did you think I'd respond when you confronted me with your deductions? Deny them?"

"I don't know," Amy admitted. "I suppose I was too emotional to even consider that part of it."

"Ah," said Ma'am with satisfaction, "and in that your cleverness failed you. Because, Lloyd, there's a weak link in all my

252

wicked plotting. Mrs. Upshur. Confronted by you she would have tried to lie—after all, I am her Lady Bountiful—but she would have soon given in. No spine at all. So if you and I hadn't reached this most pleasant understanding—if I foolishly attempted to put you off by denial—all you'd need do is extract the truth from her. She did engage a private investigator for me. A most unpleasant fellow in some ways, but highly competent. All this—it hardly needs emphasis—for a most worthy end. Worthy ends, Lloyd, sometimes do require unworthy means. My one regret now is that you were wounded in the process. Yet, I couldn't really know the full measure of your loyalty to me until now, could I?"

"Perhaps not, ma'am. But I've never given you cause to doubt it."

"True. But take into account that I've learned distrustfulness out of bitter experience. The men in my family, Lloyd, never seem to share that experience. Do you know what I mean?"

"Yes, I do. But, ma'am, if you don't mind my asking—"

"Now that we've cleared the air? No, not at all."

"Well then, what could Mr. Craig and Mr. Walter have possibly done about it if you were open in your support of Kim Lowry? The respect you're held in—"

"Respect?" said Ma'am. "The respect that an infant gets from its kindly parents?"

"But I'm sure that isn't the case, ma'am."

"Unfortunately," said Ma'am with finality, "your opinion, Lloyd, has no bearing on the actual case."

So, Mike thought in the silence that followed, a silence unbroken along the few blocks up Madison Avenue and the turn into the street before the house, that settles that. Because reckless Amy, having cleared the air except for this touch of frost, seemed willing to pull up short right here. She must have sensed that the next step—getting into the family's touchy feelings about each other—was altogether out of bounds for the hired help.

As he opened the car door to get out he felt the pressure of the cane on his shoulder.

"Wait," Ma'am said. "Close that door."

He pulled the door shut, then with the certainty that something interesting was coming he angled the rearview mirror downward to get a view of his passengers. Ma'am's face was impassive. Amy was frowning questioningly at her. Ma'am, as if uncannily aware of that frown, turned toward Amy and shook her head. "Nothing to be concerned about, Lloyd. What I have to say is from a sense of obligation to you."

Amy looked uncomfortable. "Really, there's no—"

"Please don't interrupt. I also feel you have a host of questions buzzing through your head right now. And since I'm not being invited to answer them, that you will conjure up false answers. Ordinarily, that wouldn't bother me one whit. However, as things stand between us now, it would. Do you understand?"

"I think I do."

"I'm sure you do. You're not only intelligent, Lloyd, but you have the questioning spirit. That's all to your credit. But it would make me uncomfortable to suspect that any of your time goes to conjecturing about my place in Kim Lowry's life. Why and how I arrived at it. I'll settle that now by providing the answers to your unspoken questions. For my benefit as well as yours."

Which, Mike thought, made him as Mrs. Lloyd's consort about as invisible as he could get. Not quite. In the mirror he saw the cane approaching. He made no move to withdraw from it, and it prodded his shoulder. "It's growing cold in here," Ma'am said testily.

"Yes, ma'am. When the motor's turned off there's the—"

"I am not a mechanic. Just do whatever must be done."

"Yes, ma'am," Mike said. He got the motor running and adjusted the heater. Then he drew out the pencil and notebook and sat with pencil poised.

Ma'am huddled into her coat. "Would you have a cigarette to spare?" she asked. "Either of you?"

"I'm sorry," Amy said. "We gave them up some time ago."

Kindly sharing the rap, Mike thought, since he had been the lone martyr.

"Nothing to be sorry about," Ma'am said, "but they were among my two solaces for fifty years. Fifty-one years. I gave them

254

up as a Christmas gift to myself last year. My other solace was words. Words read to me usually by machine. Literature. Endless doses of literature as an anesthetic. Often the finest of professional performers were employed to make phonograph records of those books for me. My first gift to Mrs. Upshur was almost that entire collection of records. Priceless, I suspect. But as an anesthetic, insufficient.

"For many years" — the voice, Mike observed, was taking on a hard-breathing intensity — "I would now and then wake from a deep sleep knowing that my blindness was only a bad dream. I would call out in panic to whoever was attending me to turn on the light and end the nightmare. I'd hear the click of the switch, but there was never any light. More than once, if that hallucination were strong enough, I would believe the attendant was playing a cruel joke on me, that the light had not really been turned on. I would scream my outrage at this until reality set in. In the literature I listened to I'd now and then encounter such terms as 'a living death' and 'buried alive.' I'd soundlessly cry out to the authors then: 'You fools, you don't really know what this means, but I do!' "

"Oh, no," Amy whispered. "How horrible."

"Don't speak," Ma'am said. "I can stand remote from it now, but you must not speak."

Weaving a spell, Mike thought. Speak, and the horror might seep through it.

"Self-pity," Ma'am said contemptuously. "Half a century of it. And except for one strange turn of luck I could have ended my life in its throes. An unexpected episode suddenly revealed to me that while my eyes were dead my spirit was not. No, not at all. I had simply kept it dormant all those years. And this leads to something only you are privileged to know. I've never revealed it to anyone else — let them all make what foolish speculations they want — and I never will. But I share it with you now, because I believe we've learned a faith in each other that justifies it.

"A year ago it would be, I rediscovered my fully sighted, talented, courageous, youthful self in Kim Lowry. My niece Gwendolyn was reading to me the theatrical news in a Sunday *Times*. A familiar procedure to her and others in the house. Among that

255

literature read to me, plays often gave me the most pleasure, and through newspaper reports I learned what productions might be worth recording for me. Art — the painting I had once practiced — I shut my mind to. That art, after all, cannot be heard, it must be seen."

Mike suddenly realized that he still had notebook and pencil idly in hand. So fascinated by watching the narrator in the mirror, he realized, that he was plumb forgetting to record the narrative. Too bad he didn't have the minirecorder in hand, tuned in to that mesmerizing voice. But who the hell would suspect that the car would become a confessional? Still, one did the best he could. He applied himself to the shorthand as the voice became brisk.

"You've seen my niece Gwendolyn, Lloyd. Is she attractive?"

One thousand, two thousand, three thousand, Mike counted, and then Amy found words. "Well, she has an interesting face."

"Unattractive," said Ma'am, accurately decoding the answer. "Formless. As her thoughts always are. Like Tolstoy she has an excessive love for humanity but finds it impossible to deal comfortably with any human being. But she was always most dutiful when I required someone as a reader. So she read to me that Sunday morning a lengthy essay in the paper about a production of *The Bacchae* that had opened at one of those little theaters in Greenwich Village. An ill-fated production. Do you recall it?"

"No, ma'am."

"Are you familiar with the play?"

In the mirror Mike saw his wife's brow furrow. Euripides, he desperately mouthed at the mirror, those female man-eaters, and then saw Amy shake her head. A body language, he thought, wasted on Ma'am.

"I'm sorry," Amy said. "I know it's a Greek classic, but that's all."

"Hardly enough," Ma'am said in kindly rebuke. "I must find you a sound translation of it. Among the greatest of the classics. Unfortunately, this production was regarded as atrocious, but it did have one point of interest: a scandalous stage setting. A variety of monuments to Priapus, extremely large and realistic, which in later scenes were replaced by just as large and lifelike representations of the female parts. There was no denying the curious talents of the set designer, wrote the critic, but it was a case of the sets devouring the production as surely as the Bacchantes on stage devoured their male victims. Impossible, he wrote, to attend to the lines being spoken while confronted by those images. A typically censorious male reaction. No matter the vaunted sexual freedom of our times, the male still prefers not to see the female as flesh and blood. Don't you agree, Lloyd?"

Amy took her time with this one. "Well," she finally decided, "I'm sure there are exceptions."

Glad to hear it, sweetheart, Mike thought. But it was Margaret Durie who was to wonder about. No, on second thought she wasn't. This was not a child of the Victorian era turning against her creed. By date, she was out of the Jazz Age, or whatever of it had filtered into the Durie household. And as evidence of this, still addicted to that Jazz Age bobbed hair and make-up.

"Oh, exceptions," she said dismissively to Amy. "I grant you the inevitable handful. But beyond that?

"However, what struck me during the reading of that newspaper piece was the overwhelming sympathy I felt for that young artist who was suffering the consequences to her career of being female. At best to be condescended to; at worst to be condemned for the truths she presented the world. The one sustaining force in her life, so she said, was the grandmother who had reared her but unfortunately did not have the means to fend for herself, much less—"

"Her grandmother?" Amy said accusingly. "Then you knew all along— Oh, I'm sorry."

"No, you're right. I did know much more about Kim Lowry and Adela Taliaferro than I revealed to you. But take into account that you and I didn't share this rapport then. I was not disposed to reveal to you more than I absolutely had to. Does that suffice?"

"Yes, of course."

"Much more relevant was my awakening to life that morning. My rebirth. With bitter regret too, for so much of that life

257

wasted. Hating dependence, I had made myself dependent on others in every way. Disastrous, my refusal to go out into the world and find my own way around it. My refusal of the braille method that would have brought the written word directly to me instead of through intermediaries. Oh, yes, a fine and festering life I had created for myself. But there was still time to salvage a bit of it. I knew I had a goal now. I would provide that artist however I could—certainly financially—with the means of holding her own steady course against all odds. My mission alone. I couldn't risk for a moment the interference of family. Its discouragement. Its active resistance. At all costs, not that.

"Thus the steps taken one by one to the goal. I interviewed a dozen instructors of braille before I knew I had found in Mrs. Upshur my necessary instrument. Eventually, I had her searching out through her own clumsy devices all possible information of Kim Lowry wherever published. But when in late summer she brought word that a Jason Cook was opening a new gallery with a showing of Kim Lowry's latest works, I knew that the next steps were beyond Mrs. Upshur's capacity. I had her arrange then for a professional investigator to follow closely whatever was going on with that gallery and the artist. After that—"

"Please," Amy said, "I must ask one question."

"Hardly necessary. I suspect I know the question, my dear, and the answer is yes, I needed someone to help me toward my goal as Mrs. Upshur no longer could. But at least as important, I did need a companion and secretary who'd free me from the stifling presence of those around me. And, of course, a chauffeur was needed to replace one who had become alarmingly incompetent. Indeed, when Mrs. McEye complained about the quality of domestic staff obtainable nowadays I was the one to insist she arrange for the services of a married couple. Ancient wisdom, derived from my father."

And a way, Mike thought with grudging admiration, of killing two birds with one stone, because the new chauffeur was also scheduled to be an accomplice to the plot. Not another Wilson certainly, the gabby kind who reported Miss Durie's itineraries to headquarters. Easy to sympathize with the old lady's frustrations when she learned that the entire well-primed staff serving her

258

was helping record every breath she took.

Amy seemed to share this feeling. "And I do help out Mrs. McEye," she said encouragingly. "Was that her idea, that I serve as her part-time assistant?"

"Hers and mine. She's overburdened, and there's really no one among staff to provide assistance. And—I say this without apology—I was overburdened by Hegnauer's stolid presence too many hours a day. Even spiritually alive now, I must have solitude at times. The division of your services seemed a logical compromise. I can assure you that everyone is most satisfied with the results. Any other questions?"

Amy laughed. "No. And you are being very kind."

"More wise than kind, I suspect. Which brings us back to our *enfant terrible*, our Kim Lowry. A prickly personality, from all reports. Not quite the amicable beneficiary of my offerings I had envisioned at the outset."

"Possibly," said Amy, "because she'd resent being dealt with as a beneficiary in that sense. She wants her work sold on its merits. And her grandmother supports this attitude very strongly. In fact, she was the one who made negotiations difficult. If it weren't that the money was so desperately needed—"

"The grandmother," Ma'am cut in. "How would you describe her?"

Amy pondered this long enough for Mike to catch up on the shorthand. "In a way," she said at last, "schizophrenic. I mean, she plainly adores Kim but is hostile to everyone else. Physically, well, the kind word would be unprepossessing. Of course, she has just come out of the hospital after a very bad—"

In the mirror Mike saw that enlightenment had struck her the same instant it struck him.

"Ma'am, when you had me read you the obituary notices—"

Ma'am smiled. "Ever the inquiring spirit, Lloyd. Yes, I knew when Adela Taliaferro was taken to the hospital in serious condition. And yes, that was the name I was concerned you'd read aloud one of those mornings."

A mistaken concern, Mike thought. If Adela died, her granddaughter might emerge a much more amicable beneficiary of any charity.

259

"Well," said Amy, "she seems pretty much recovered now."

"Good. And she did accept my terms without animus against her granddaughter? The last thing I'd want to do is cause hard feelings between them."

"I don't think there's any chance of that, ma'am. And it's still understood I'm to meet with Kim next week to make the second payment?"

"Next week. You've done very well, Lloyd. Both of you. I am — yes — most truly grateful for that."

Grateful, Mike thought. It didn't come out easily, the long-suffering family probably hadn't heard it in fifty years, but there it was.

A pat on the head for the faithful servitors, Abe would define it.

So what?

H E had no chance to gather with his co-conspirator wife over this confessional stuff until late that night. After fetching the brothers Durie home from the office he had dinner in the staff hall with a few of the help while Amy was holding down the desk in the office. An hour later, with Craig, Jocelyn, and Camilla in the rear seat and Walter, hands clasped on belly, peacefully dozing beside him, he was on the way to the Laura Sandoval estate in Locust Valley, wait and return. From the desultory conversation behind him, he surmised that Camilla had delivered the goods, the Sandoval portfolio was still right where it belonged, under Durie management. The one interesting passage came when Jocelyn remarked that Camilla's designated partner at dinner would be a young man high up in the State Department and rapidly rising higher.

Camilla summed up her reaction to this with admirable brevity. "Washington, D.C.?" she said. "Forgive the language, but dear Laura gives me a stiff pain where I sit."

There were moments, Mike thought in the ear-ringing silence that followed, when Camilla did offer more than mere lusciousness.

Realization that the wait at dear Laura's would likely be a long one was signaled when, after discharging his passengers, he was directed to park on the apron of the estate's multicar garage and found a host of visiting limousines already gathered there. Considering the options then offered — a crap game in the Sandoval chauffeur's quarters above the garage or TV shoot-'em-ups in the garage workshop — he settled for solitude behind the wheel of the car and some reflection on Margaret Durie's confessional. He closed his eyes, the better to reflect, and somewhat after midnight had to be roused from a bone-stiffening sleep by a fellow chauffeur.

It was one-thirty when he tiptoed into his sitting room, a wasted consideration, he found, because a light showed under the bedroom door.

Amy in pajamas was stretched out on the coverlet of the bed surrounded by a host of typed pages that he recognized as his Durie notes. What she had been poring over, however, was an unrecognizable set of pink papers.

"Instructions," she explained. "Big doings tomorrow. I mean today. Starting at noon when you pick up la Principessa di Sgarlati at Kennedy. She is, said the McEye tenderly, a bit flamboyant in her ways but utterly charming."

"Hey, hey. Rich, flamboyant, and charming."

"She is also eight years Miss Margaret's junior, which makes her sixty-two. My advice is to angle for an adoption, not a seduction."

"Will do. And those pink sheets are instructions on what?"

"How to handle a dinner party tomorrow evening at eight for

all the family and a few superguests. Since it's the McEye's day off, I am in complete charge. My first solo, though she was obviously itching to give up the day off and stand over my shoulder. It took some convincing to persuade her otherwise."

"Cool, man," Mike commented admiringly. "Do you really feel that way? No churning of the innards?"

"Nope. I've got four top hands from Domestique Plus for the dining room, and Peters will supervise them. And two more Plussers for the kitchen and Mabry himself to back up Golightly. And O'Dowd and blessed Nugent and I will see to the service from the staff hall end."

"And to open the front door to our guests?"

"The other houseman. Brooks. A sound man, Brooks."

"And the wine? Let us not forget the wine."

"No chance. Walter's already uncorked the bottles he picked out this morning, and they're lined up on the sideboard, breathing. Superior wines," said Amy magisterially, "must be allowed to breath for some time before being served."

"Do tell," Mike said. "Matter of fact, I can hear it now from the dining room. Slow, expensive, vinous breathing. But I must admit I admire your style, Mrs. Lloyd. Facing the fire on one day's notice and not a visible qualm."

"Deliberately. From watching the McEye and being the opposite. She's great on every little detail, but she frets herself sick over them. Communicate that to staff, and that's when accidents can happen. Cool it, and the staff cools it."

"How about a sampler with that on it for her office? Meanwhile, this food talk reminds me that while I did sleep the evening away, I didn't eat. Anything worthwhile in our refrigerator?"

"Everything, and a little more. Take a look."

He did, and found that the everything was a platter of meat sandwiches and a bowl of salad. The little more, to his surprise, was a half carafe of red wine.

"Alcohol?" he said. "In the servants' quarters?"

"Well, I told the McEye we were used to a little wine with our dinner, that neither of us ever — "

"We? Us?"

262

"I felt it sounded better that way. And that neither of us ever overindulged, so it was unreasonable not to trust us in this."

"The language," Mike said. "That's what did it. You just dazzled her into surrender."

"Maybe a little. But mostly," said Amy wisely, "I think it's because when she ducks out of the office to her apartment now and then, she always comes back in a cloud of peppermint. She is tippling in there, and she suspects I know it."

"My lovely blackmailer," Mike said through a mouthful of sandwich. He arranged his dinner on the night table and seated himself on the edge of the bed before it. "More to the point, baby, you really were something during Ma'am's confessional in the car. Let me confide the sweaty truth. I was all ready to start packing when you opened up."

"Perhaps I was, too, but I'm not sure. What I was wondering about — honestly, Mike, what could the family do about it if they did learn what she's up to? What would they do?"

"I don't know. Raise hell in a genteel way, I suppose." He regarded his wife's position, rear-end high as she gathered together the notes. "Which leads me to remark that with the way you look right now — "

"Mike, it's almost two in the morning. You may have slept away the evening, but I didn't."

" — the way you look and with me full of vigor and partly full of wine — "

"Tempting, but by the time you finish eating and undressing and all, I'll be sound asleep."

Mike laid down the remainder of the sandwich and stood up to pull off his jacket. "No you won't," he assured her.

* * *

263

AMY, a phone locked against each ear, pencil in hand and charts before her, mouthed a hell and damnation at the wall.

"In addition," Jocelyn Durie told her on one phone, "the centerpiece is wrong. Absolutely wrong. There were to be no substitutions. Make that plain to the florist at once. I want a proper centerpiece here within the hour."

"Yes, Mrs. Durie."

"—the breakdown, the breakdown," pleaded the accountant on the other phone.

"Yes, I understand," Amy said. "May I put you on hold for just a moment?"

"No, you may not. What you may do—"

"And," said Jocelyn Durie, "the room for Mrs. di Sgarlati's maid was not provided with fresh linen."

"—is dig that third-quarter breakdown of maintenance and repair costs out of your files and get them over here pronto. By messenger."

"Yes, sir, I'll take care of it." Amy shifted to the other phone. "Yes, ma'am, I'll take care of it."

She put down both phones and was flipping through the services index—messenger first, then florist—when the house phone rang.

"Mrs. McEye?" said Camilla Durie.

"Her day off, Miss Durie. This is Mrs. Lloyd."

"Oh, is it? Well, Mrs. Lloyd, in case you haven't noticed, this place is freezing. Let us not be so goddam thrifty that the blood congeals. Do I make myself clear?"

"Yes, Miss Durie. I'll attend to it at once."

"Or sooner," said Camilla in farewell.

To do her justice, Amy thought, getting a grip on her temper, the place while not freezing was mid-autumnal cool. She phoned Borglund in his den down in Xanadu, and he sounded rather pleased to get the complaint.

"I told Mrs. Mac last week," he said. "I told her whenever she wants the heat turned on just send me the extra man for a couple hours. I turn it on any time I get the extra man. She watches the oil bills too close, that one. You got a man for me?"

"I'll get one," said Amy.

"Oh, yah," said Borglund. It was plain from his tone that he'd be waiting for someone not to show up.

Amy scouted through the charts of staff availability. Ridiculous, she thought, not to have a butler bearing half this workload because the McEye would not entertain thoughts of any contender for her high office. Would settle instead for those cartons of cigarettes in her desk drawer and an occasional sip of high octane restorative in her apartment. Work this job singlehanded long enough and it was just a case of which came first, cancer of the lungs or the DT's.

Get stuck with a formal dinner on practically no notice, and it simply speeded up the process. Even the McEye had been taken aback by word of the dinner and had obviously kept her irritation within bounds only because it was the principessa's hitherto unannounced arrival that called for the dinner. She definitely had a soft spot for the principessa. Snob appeal? From the way she savored the title when she pronounced it, oh, yes.

Houseman Brooks, said the chart, was now in the staff hall and available to Borglund. Good. Brooks was not only the more capable of the housemen but had a distinctly cordial regard for Mrs. Lloyd. Amy picked up the house phone, then was struck by inspiration. The blessed Nugent had been filling in for her at the desk when needs be, but always in a state of near panic. It was hard to see Brooks—fiftyish, professionally competent, breathing self-confidence—panicking at anything. A potential ace up the sleeve that the McEye never played, most likely because it was an ace. Perhaps someone who might catch the family's eye as a butler in the making. He had come from service with an eccentric high-society Toronto family, and from the tales he told he did know his way around.

Amy dialed the garage where Mike would be stationed after an earlier than usual return trip from the office with Craig and Walter. When her husband was called to the phone she said, "Mike, darling—"

"Something wrong? You sound all wound up."

"Not really. Well, maybe a little. You know, when you reported you'd delivered the principessa here you didn't tell me she had a maid with her."

"Was I supposed to?"

"It would have been helpful. Anyhow, what I really need for you now is to lend Borglund a hand. Start up the heat here. Right now."

"You mean after all these years he and Swanson can't handle that themselves?"

"Mike, darling—"

"Be there in ten minutes," Mike said. "No, make it five."

"Bless you," Amy said fervently. "And just head straight for Borglund. Don't stop off here. I'm doing fine."

The instant she put down the phone it rang. "Miss Margaret wants that you come here," said Hegnauer.

"Oh, God."

"She says at once, at once," Hegnauer reported.

"Of course. But I must get a replacement first. As soon as I get one I'll be there. Tell her that."

This time when she replaced the phone it didn't ring. And, Amy thought, it might not even ring again for ten seconds. She shifted Mike's name on the chart from *garage* to *Borglund,* then looked at the scrawls on the memo pad.

Breakdown of building's third-quarter maintenance and repair costs. Messenger service. Florist. Maid's room linens. Brooks.

Brooks it would be. Never mind the McEye's designation of Nugent as permanent relief, rules were made to be bent, or so one could only hope. The thought of the easily panicked Nugent on the firing line right now was gruesome. Brooks, at least, always did come on imperturbable, and that was what was needed at this moment, plenty of imperturbable.

She phoned Brooks in the staff hall, ordered him to report to headquarters on the double and to bring one of the junior maids with him. Then she sprinted for the filing cabinet, located the financial reports demanded by that asinine accountant with his scrambled priorities, and thrust it into an envelope addressed to him at the Broad Street office. The call to the messenger service took no time, but the florist in his turn was a hard case.

"I realize there were to be no substitutions, Mrs. Lloyd, but there was certain stock we did not have on hand."

"Look—" Amy said, and heard her voice rising. Emulating the McEye technique she lowered it. "There are other florists in the neighborhood. Call on them for help if you have to. Under any conditions, the centerpiece as specified is to be here within one hour."

"Two hours, if I'm lucky, Mrs. Lloyd. And the price will be more than Mrs. McEye agreed on."

"I am not arguing price. I just want that delivery here within the hour. Or must I call directly on one of those other florists whose help you may be asking?"

"No, no, we'll see to it, Mrs. Lloyd. Perhaps a bit more than an hour, but all will be well I assure you."

It works, Amy thought. Not only was the awesome name Durie magical, but it was clear to that floral gent that this icy-toned female attending to the Durie affairs wasn't bluffing. And if there was a showdown with the penny-pinching McEye about the bill, let Jocelyn Durie be referee.

She looked up and saw Brooks in the doorway, the junior maid Walsh peering wide-eyed behind him. She waved them in and handed Walsh the envelope.

"Are you listening closely, Walsh?"

"Yes, ma'am."

"Good. You're to hold this tight in your hand and wait inside the service entrance door. A messenger will come for it, and you will give it to him. Then you will remain there until a delivery man comes with a floral arrangement. Take it from him and give it to Nugent. Tell her it's to replace the centerpiece in the dining room. Replace it, not add to it. Is that clear?"

"Yes, ma'am."

"And Walsh," said Amy, "I do thank you for being so helpful."

Walsh gaped at her.

"That's it, dear," said Amy. "On your way now."

When Walsh was gone, still gaping, Brooks raised an eyebrow. "You don't mind me saying it, Mrs. Lloyd, you have the touch, if you know what I mean."

"I do. But she is a good kid, and I know just how she feels."

"All in your favor," said Brooks. "Although you have to be careful how far you go in that direction. You wanted me?"

"Yes. As relief here. Just to handle the phone calls. Pull that chair up and I'll show you what it's about."

No sooner was the chair pulled up than the phone rang. "Miss Margaret says now," announced Hegnauer, and it came out like a Wagnerian baritone announcing the *Götterdämmerung*.

"Tell her I'll be there right away," Amy said. The one bright spot in this darkness, she discovered as she explained procedure to Brooks in telegraphic style, was that he came on as quickminded as she had suspected he would. It couldn't have taken longer than two minutes before he said, "No problem at all. Now you go attend to the queen, Mrs. Lloyd, and I'll see to the rest of the deck."

Not only that, Amy thought as she clattered down the iron staircase to the second floor, but he actually seemed to relish the prospect.

She knocked on Ma'am's door, and it was instantly flung open by a red-faced Hegnauer who, breathing outrage, marched off down the corridor, clenched fists held high. Amy closed the door. "I'm sorry about the delay, ma'am," she said to Medusa in her armchair, and waited to be struck to stone.

Stone? "You're all out of breath, Lloyd," Ma'am said sympathetically.

"I'm afraid I am," Amy admitted warily.

"And you sound so tense. Well, you know my infallible treatment for that." Ma'am rose from the chair. "Come here instantly and sit down."

Infallible massage, Amy thought with distaste. Still, anything to maintain this tender mood. She tried to relax under the prodding of those fingers into the base of her neck.

"What I wanted to speak to you about," Ma'am said behind her, "was something not to be discussed over the telephone. Head back now." She reinforced the request by pulling Amy's chin up. The cool fingers rested lightly and unpleasantly on the exposed throat. "Kim Lowry. Her feelings about the situation I've placed her in. Could she be seriously disturbed by my remaining at a distance and unknown? A mysterious presence in one's life, however well intentioned, can be disturbing. Don't you agree, Lloyd?"

Amy found herself even more acutely aware of those fingers on her throat when she spoke. "Yes, ma'am."

"But if I were to make myself known to the girl, could she be trusted to keep this to herself? Not reveal it to another soul? You've come to know her, Lloyd. What would your opinion be?"

Oh, no, Amy thought. "Ma'am," she said, "I don't really feel that I'm the one — "

"Obviously you are the one, Lloyd. Who else could I — ?" Deliverance, Amy thought gratefully, at least temporary deliverance was provided by a sharp rat-tatting on the door. The fingers released her throat. "Oh," said Ma'am in a long drawn breath of what seemed to be recognition.

Amy hastily got to her feet as the door was thrust open. The principessa, she knew at first sight of that figure light-footedly crossing the expanse of carpet. No, better keep the Mrs. di Sgarlati in mind, especially in present company. Almost as small and slight as Ma'am and with those Durie features, she was, Amy thought, an astonishingly well-preserved sixty-two. Part of that, it became evident on her closer approach, was certainly due to a rigorous face job, going by the almost unlined skin and total absence of wattles under the jaw, and part of it would be due to that coiffure of subtly dyed blond ringlets, but the largest part, no question, stemmed from the woman's vivacity.

Bright-eyed and bouncy, she announced herself with a "Margaret, darling," and Amy made way as she moved by to embrace her sister. She stepped back to make a proper appraisal. "And you do look marvelous. Absolutely marvelous." She smiled at Amy. "And this young lady is the secretary who's been so helpful?"

Before Amy could open her mouth Ma'am said, "Yes. Lloyd, there's that accumulation of mail on the desk. Attend to it."

Amy hesitated. Since Mrs. Upshur was no longer sending coded messages, this mail had come to be the lowest-priority obligation on the list, a matter of extracting an occasoinal personal note from the bundle. To waste time on this while Brooks was still new to his office duties . . .

"Ma'am, if you wouldn't mind — "

269

"The mail, Lloyd." The stick pointed. "But first place a chair there for Mrs. di Sgarlati."

Amy placed the small twin armchair into position facing its mate, saw the guest seated in it, then seated herself at the desk across the room. On the other hand, she advised herself, as she unsnapped the rubber band from the packet of mail, there was a sisterly confrontation in the air and this did offer her a front-row seat at it.

"I have something to settle with you, Enid," Ma'am said coldly.

"And I with you, darling," said her sister with all good cheer.

"Your foibles and fancies," Ma'am said. "Arriving out of the blue and requesting a formal dinner the same evening. Is that your Italianate concept of manners?"

"No, darling. Jocelyn's. When I phoned from London yesterday I told her I'd be here for only a couple of days and incidentally mentioned that it would be nice to see some old friends at the table as well as the family. I had no idea she'd then arrange for a full-scale spectacle."

"Knowing her, you should have. And why are you here at all? You weren't expected until the Thanksgiving week."

"What a clear mind you have for dates, darling. As it happens, I was in London on an important mission and, using Gwen's return ticket, I'm here to complete it. But I really do have something to settle with you. I was given the impression by Jocelyn that you were positively thriving and that, contrary to ancient tradition, you'd join us at the table tonight. The first thing I learned when I walked in was that you would not. Now why, darling? What made you change your mind?"

"I did not change my mind, Enid. Jocelyn surmises, God disposes."

"God?" The principessa, Amy saw, looked disapproving. "Darling, there is a tender spirit in God which you—"

"No, Enid, I won't listen to any such nattering. Just get to the point."

"Very well, the point is that from all accounts you are now emotionally unburdened enough to join the company of your brothers and be pleasant to them. After all those bad years, nothing could make us happier."

"Excluding me," said Ma'am in a brittle voice.

"Darling, you're being just plain damn stubborn for the pleasure of it. Whatever strange animus you developed to Craig—well, it's time to put it aside. Or at least explain it to him if you can. Come to some sort of rapprochement that way. There's no reason that—"

"Cela suffit," Ma'am rapped out. "Or for your benefit, Enid, basta. You mentioned an important mission. What mission?"

"Darling, for my sake—"

"What mission?"

The principessa gave up with a sigh. "To have a serious talk with Craig and Jocelyn about what's going on in London."

"Yes?"

"I was suddenly called there from Bologna this past weekend by Gwen's husband, dear boy. I don't have to tell you she's with him there, insisting on a divorce by mutual agreement. He's absolutely distraught and wanted me to serve as intermediary. He feels that she doesn't know her mind at all, but he knows his. I believe he's absolutely infatuated with her."

"With Gwen? I don't believe it."

Amy cocked an ear as the principessa leaned forward and lowered her voice: "I know. I didn't myself at first, but now I do. What I finally extracted from him—"

"Yes? Enid, you know how I detest your conversational theatrics."

As the principessa's head turned her way Amy concentrated on the mail. From the corner of her eye she saw the principessa lean still farther forward to address her sister: "Don't you think, darling, there are some matters that require a bit more privacy than this?"

"Lloyd has my entire confidence, Enid."

"She does? Well then, it seems that on their wedding night he, poor lamb, was as inexperienced as she was. Can you picture what happened? Now she's convinced she was the victim of rape, and he can't persuade her that it was just ignorance on his part and that he desperately wants to make amends any way he can."

"Dear God," Ma'am said. "Craig's choice of suitor. Inevitably the only one of his kind. It's all too ridiculous."

271

"Not altogether. Because he's found that she's saturating herself with tranquillizers and that you, an innocent in your own way, darling, seem to be the one who—"

"Lloyd," Ma'am said sharply, "you may go now."

Regretfully, Amy went. Outside in the corridor she pressed an ear against the door, but not a sound penetrated. Hell and damnation, she thought. On the other hand, it was comforting to know that the door to the Lloyds' apartment was probably just as invulnerable to eavesdropping, no matter how sharp the McEye's finely tuned ear.

She found Brooks making a note on the desk pad, a cigarette dangling from his lip. He looked placid as ever. "All up to date and in order," he assured her. He held up the cigarette. "You don't mind?"

"No." Standing there, she looked over the notes on the pad and the entries in the schedule chart. Indeed, everything did look up to date and in order. "You've been very helpful, Brooks."

"My job, Mrs. Lloyd. You'll also note that I'm off until six, when I vet Mr. Craig for the dinner. Could I be of further help here?"

Amy had the automatic no on the tip of her tongue, then thought better of it. "As a matter of fact, I would like to go down to the dining room and check out the dusting up and seating arrangements."

"Especially the seating arrangements, Mrs. Lloyd. Don't leave that to anyone else or strange things can happen. Meanwhile, I'll just record you here as in the dining room in case you're personally wanted." Brooks held up a finger. "Music," he said. "Listen."

Amy listened and heard a clicking and hissing, the familiar, comfortable, comforting sound of a radiator starting to function.

Blessed Mike. Blessed Borglund. Blessed Brooks. Blessed everybody, with the possible exception of Ma'am and her notion of revealing herself to Kim Lowry. The unpredictable confronting the unpredictable.

Well, sufficient unto the day . . .

O LD age, Mike thought, very old age can be saddest when you try to deny it. Those deep seams in Borglund's face, the bleary eyes, that arthritic hitch and wince when he walked were saddening in a way. But saddest was the small, steady tremor of the gnarled hands, not only in itself, but because Borglund, standing there at the worktable, must have become aware of it and had planted both hands flat on the table, resting his weight on them in an obvious attempt to conceal their trembling. He motioned with his chin at the paraphernalia on the table.

"You know what this is about?" he asked.

Mike looked at the display. One plastic bucket containing a few shiny new radiator valves, one plastic bucket with rags in it, one flashlight, one pair of canvas work gloves.

"Sure," he said. "You just started up the heat and want some radiators here checked for leaks. Where there are any we replace the valves." He had a sudden alarming picture of what he might be getting into. "Say, how many radiators does that mean?"

"All. But the top floor we worry about tomorrow. Swanson does the middle floor now, you do the bottom floor. They use the dining room for a party tonight, so that is first. When the people come for the party you don't show yourself, you're done, wherever you are, and tomorrow you finish. You start right now."

Mike looked down at his custom-made demilivery. "Not in these clothes, Borglund. First I change into something suitable."

"No. There is coveralls on the shelf there. They fit Swanson, they will be plenty big enough for you."

More than plenty, Mike found when he had donned them, all he needed to complete the ensemble was a clown's rubber nose. On the other hand, he told himself, he'd finally get a view of the ground floor. Putting together his studies of the floor plan and Amy's descriptions, he had an idea of what it was like, but, he suspected, reality was likely to exceed expectation.

It did. Walking out of the East Wing staircase foyer on the ground floor he was momentarily stunned by the dimensions of everything around him, the height of that ceiling, the amount of gleaming marble everywhere, pillars, walls, and floors. A scenic ramble to the dining room seemed called for, and, he assured himself, if he did find family behind any of these doors after the required two knocks, at least he had the authority to knock. Besides, sweet thought, Mrs. Mac was nowhere on the premises.

Thus, with never any response to his knock, he surveyed the vast ballroom with its handsomely draped French windows overlooking the street; the East Gallery, a fair-size concert hall with its rows of gilt chairs; the card room — enough room here to run a bridge tournament; and the library, filled floor to ceiling with leatherbound editions that appeared — unlike the books in Craig Durie's sitting room — not to have gotten much wear.

The West Gallery far more than met expectation. Not only did the paintings around its walls look like prime stuff — except for bulk, the statuary didn't compare — but that Sargent portrait of James Hamilton Durie and wife — Amy had provided a vivid description of it — was both a pleasure for the eye and a remarkably telling examination of its male subject. Awesome, Amy had pronounced him, and Mike, viewing the James Hamilton visage, had to acknowledge that this was the word.

When he entered the dining room from the West Gallery he found that here he was not alone. His wife was standing at the long table, its damask cloth already laid, and with furrowed brow was studying a paper in her hand. Without looking up she said, "Right there on the table, Nugent." Then she did look up. "Oh, hell," she said.

"Some greeting."

"I'm sorry, darling. There's supposed to be a floral arrangement. You didn't see Nugent wandering around with one, did you?"

"Nope. Besides, there's a crock of flowers right there on that sideboard in case you haven't noticed. Right next to those hard-breathing wine bottles."

"Wrong flowers." Amy glanced at her watch. "Anyhow, there's time. It's just that time seems to be getting compressed for me."

"Party nerves. And if there is time, why the dark expression?"

"A problem. What are you doing here anyhow? Aren't you

274

supposed to be helping Borglund with the furnace or whatever?"

"This is the whatever. Checking out radiators. What's your problem?"

Amy made a despairing gesture. "Place cards, all diagrammed here by Jocelyn. Somehow she got it into her head that Ma'am would be at the dinner, but she won't. So now it's eleven instead of twelve. And obviously from this diagram it's supposed to be boy-girl-boy-girl. What do I do about that?"

"Try Domestique Plus, of course. It probably provides emergency guests along with everything else."

"I'm serious," Amy hissed fiercely.

"All right, all right, but let's not get morbid." He set his equipment down and surveyed the table. "Where was Ma'am's place?"

"Foot of the table, right there. Craig's at the head."

"Then here goes the Gordian knot." He removed the chair from the foot of the table and planted it againt the wall. *"Voila!"*

"With nobody at the foot of the table?" Amy said.

"Nobody. Just Ma'am's invisible presence. Which mystically maintains the boy-girl circuit. Trust me."

"I don't see what else I can do," Amy said resignedly. "And you'd better get on those radiators before I add a wet floor to my problems. They're behind those grilles. And I have a lot to tell you. I wish I could do it before I forget any of it."

"Then just follow along and keep the voice down," Mike said.

She did, while he removed the wire grille and turned the flashlight on the floor beneath the sizzling radiator looking for damp spots.

"Well," she said, "the principessa dropped in on Ma'am while I was there— What was she like in the car anyhow?"

"Nice. Full of sunshiny prattle about wonderful New York."

"She does seem nice. And from what was said I gather Ma'am's been hostile to Craig for all these years. The principessa was pushing hard for reconciliation and got nowhere."

"Figures." Mike replaced the grille and went to work on the one across the room, Amy hovering over him.

"Then," she said, "there's this thing between Gwen and her

275

husband. She does want a divorce. The reason is that they were both virgins on the wedding night and the experience was traumatic for her."

"Go on," Mike said with disbelief.

"It's true. And he's refusing any polite divorce because he's infatuated with her."

"If so, he's feebleminded. Or is it a case of like seeking like?"

"Could be. But the relevant part is the impression I got that Ma'am's been laying tranquillizers on Gwen. Probably passing along her own supply of whatever Hegnauer hands her."

Mike set the grille back in place. "It would explain much about Gwen," he acknowledged. "And Ma'am. But impression?"

"I was ordered out of the room when the subject came up. Which only made the impression that much stronger."

"Ma'am, the party pooper," Mike said. He stood up and nodded at the life-size portrait of the youthful Margaret Durie, all aglow. "She's changed all right. Gone, gone are the days."

"Well, considering her present age and condition. But she was lovely, wasn't she? And she's still what I want to look like at seventy. Would you say that's a good painting?"

"About technique I'm no expert. But I'd say the artist and subject certainly had a strong feeling for each other. It reminds me of those Renaissance madonnas where the old master and the madonna took time out between poses to commit delicious sins. That's something my art teacher in college once— Unsigned, you said? Except possibly in back?"

"Yes. Hey," Amy said in alarm, "if you try to move that thing—"

"No big deal." The ornate gilded frame, he judged, would be a dead weight, but it was suspended by a single heavy wire from a fixture in the molding and would probably allow easy leverage from the bottom. "I'll pull it away from the wall a little, and you'll get down and crowd in behind it with the flashlight. If it's signed at all, it would most likely be at the bottom."

"Mike, if anyone walks in here—"

"There was a damp spot on the floor, and I'm trying to see if there's any wall leak."

"You mean I am."

276

"Yep. The ever-helpful Mrs. Lloyd."

When he gripped the base of the frame and carefully pulled it forward he found that it was indeed a dead weight and that the leverage came hard. Looking up, he could imagine the tension on the wall fixture. "Move, baby," he ordered, "before the cops break in."

Using a rag from his bucket, Amy dusted the floor under the portrait. Then she sat down, ducked her head and shoulders under the base of the frame, and pressed her back against the wall. The painted canvas, Mike realized, wasn't translucent, but from the reflection of the beam on the polished hardwood of the floor he could track the course of the flashlight.

"Nothing on this side," Amy reported, the light still in motion. "Wait." The light became stationary. She slid down until she was resting on her shoulderblades. "Right here in the middle. Real sloppy. Looks like it was smeared on with a house brush."

"Can you make it out?"

"One letter at a time." Then explosively: "Hell and damnation!"

"Tell me why out here, baby. This thing is heavy."

Amy leggily slid out from under, and Mike gratefully let the frame ride back against the wall. He gave his wife a hand up and saw her expression was that of someone who had just been vouchsafed a glimpse of the burning bush.

"Rembrandt?" he offered.

"Mike, it's Ross Taliaferro!"

"Ah, yes, the immortal Ross Taliaferro. But why that name should make you apoplectic—"

"Taliaferro," Amy said between her teeth. "Taliaferro. Doesn't it mean anything to you?"

Suddenly, unbelievingly, it did. "Taliaferro. Adela Taliaferro. Kim Lowry's grandma."

"Of course. So he would have been her grandpa. And you look pretty apoplectic yourself right now."

"Because I'm not sure whether to laugh or cry. The implications are positively dizzying, baby. The one that stands out sharpest is that our Margaret, for all that touching scene in the car, was still not telling the whole story. Just enough to be captivating. And what a performance."

277

"But still touching," Amy said stoutly. "Because I was right when I told you she must have been coming from the artist's room when she went down those stairs. Ross Taliaferro was the artist, and you yourself just said there could be something between them."

"Hold on, darling. I merely quoted my art teacher about Renaissance artists and their tempting madonnas. And from the way Margaret looks in this portrait—"

"That's right," Amy said. "Tempting. And vulnerable. And alone in the house with him. I'm telling you they had an affair—most likely the one affair in her life—and she's never gotten over it. That's why this whole plot to help Kim, because Kim is his granddaughter. Be honest, Mike. Admit it does make sense this way."

"Theoretically."

"Realistically. Because it also explains why Ma'am is now ready to let Kim know who she is."

"Let Kim know? I don't recall one word during that confessional in the car where—"

"Not then," Amy said impatiently. "Just this afternoon. She was telling me about it when the principessa showed up. Watch it," she said in a lowered voice: "Company." She smiled into the distance. "All right, Nugent, come right in."

Mike turned and saw Nugent bearing what appeared to be a large filigreed silver basin sprouting flowers.

"Ma'am, Walsh gave this to me. She said that you—"

Mike observed that Nugent seemed to be transfixed by the sight of his baggy coveralls. He had a feeling that if Mrs. Lloyd wasn't present, she might have openly snickered.

She placed the centerpiece in position. "Here, ma'am?"

"Yes. And store the other one in the pantry. Then phone Mrs. Jocelyn that the flowers have been attended to. Oh, and tell O'Dowd that Mrs. di Sgarlati's maid needs fresh linens, will you?"

"Yes, ma'am. If you don't mind, would you be coming down to the staff hall soon? They're ready to take out the dinner service."

Amy glanced at her watch. "Oh, Lord, yes." She looked and sounded, Mike thought, the perfect administrator.

In departing, she briefly dropped that role. "Wish me luck," she whispered to him.

"Break a leg," said Mike, and that was the last he saw of her until ten-thirty when she walked into their sitting room where he was at the typewriter fitting together a patchwork of descriptions. From the look of her — dog-tired but blissful — he surmised that his reverse blessing had worked.

"Let me guess," he said. "The dinner went well."

"Beautifully. Divinely. Jocelyn just had me in to hand me the laurels personally. You know, frozen face and all, she can be very pleasant when she turns it on. And that empty place at the table was all right. No problem."

"Or," said Mike, "a problem with only one solution. But now that you've had this triumph, what can you possibly do for an encore?"

"Sleep," Amy said. "Just look into the bedroom in two minutes and see."

SUNDAY noon, at Audrey's behest, they picked up the Silverstones in the wagon and drove across town to the South Sea Seaport restoration, where they spent much of the afternoon eating their way through food stands and doing the tourist bit. After which, they took in the one movie uptown they could all agree on, and then it was back to Thompson Street for a rehash of the movie and the South Street restoration, followed by some dainties from Zabar's that Audrey wanted to try out, and finally a couple of vicious games of Monopoly.

Throughout all this, Amy took notice, Abe was positively angelic, which suggested that Audie must have really landed on him about his company manners. He received the weekly repayment check almost graciously, played the tourist with good humor—discounting one slip where he said, "Quaint. Does every goddam restoration have to be quaint?"—and obviously enjoyed the movie, though he did plenty of nitpicking about it afterward. Not a word about the Lloyds' quaint station in life or about Mike's book. Altogether, Amy decided, a really good day.

"Except," she confided to Mike when they were back home having coffee in the otherwise deserted staff hall, "I was yearning to tell the latest about Gwen and her husband and about the principessa. Audie loves that kind of thing, but I figured she'd rather not have the Duries brought up this time around, so I kept mum. Kind of frustrating really."

"You can lay it on her over the phone," Mike suggested.

"I'd rather not."

"You mean you're getting as paranoid as Ma'am about the phones here being tapped?"

"Hardly. There are just some things to tell where you want to see your audience while you're at it. And now I'm depressed."

"Why?"

"Realizing that Ma'am never sees anyone she talks to. Can't ever watch them respond."

"And," Mike acknowledged, "she is a great little talker. Always plausible, no matter the pitch."

"I wasn't thinking of that. I was thinking that even if she somehow gets to meet Kim Lowry, she won't see her. And she probably wants to, very much."

"You mean," Mike said, "more homage to the late Ross Taliaferro? Luring the girl from her grandma so she can play surrogate grandma? Baby, if she's so intent on keeping the family in the dark about all this, how long could she get away with it under those conditions?"

"I suppose you're right," Amy said.

But, as it turned out, he wasn't. At eight in the morning when she wheeled in Ma'am's breakfast, and Hegnauer had taken her departure, Ma'am made clear how wrong he had been.

"Business matters to attend to today, Lloyd. Mrs. Upshur, the bank, and the payment to Miss Lowry."

"Yes, ma'am." And, ma'am, thought Amy, dear pathetic wily ma'am, what if I told you I know more about Kim Lowry and Adela Taliaferro and the artist in your life than you could possibly imagine? And why, when you revealed so much, couldn't you have revealed it all?

"But there will be more to it than that," Ma'am said. "I've become increasingly troubled about my situation vis-à-vis Miss Lowry. If I were in her shoes, Lloyd, I'd find it a distraction to have any unknown person playing a part in my life. For her sake then, I want you to arrange—and with utmost discretion, mind—a meeting between us. She should be amenable to that, don't you think?"

No total surprise, Amy thought. Because there was a long-range plan operating here. Every move neatly calculated, and here I'm being allowed to see one that was in the making long ago.

She said, "Amenable, yes, ma'am. My concern is with the utmost discretion part of it. Once she knows who you are she might be tempted to publicize it. Certainly it could mean that kind of publicity that any artist—"

"You gave me the impression," Ma'am cut in, "that she seems quite intelligent in her way."

"Yes, she does."

"Then I put my faith in that. You need concern yourself only with the arrangements for the meeting."

"Yes, ma'am. At the Plaza?"

"No. Here."

"Here. In this apartment?"

"Lloyd, what is wrong with you?"

"Nothing, ma'am." Certainly not with me, Amy thought.

"Then you will invite Miss Lowry to be my guest at dinner here. Tomorrow evening. What would be a good time? Eight? Yes, eight. That should be convenient for her, whatever her daytime schedule."

It was getting to be a Durie habit, Amy thought, this one-day's-notice thing. First, Jocelyn's dinner for the now-departed principessa, then this. And even this was nothing compared to the real shocker—having the meeting right here. Sheer bravado?

281

Venomously going one up on the family without their knowing it? Especially the detested Craig? Utmost discretion, hell.

Amy desperately grasped at logic. "There's one thing, ma'am. In case Kim Lowry has other plans for tomorrow evening—"

"Then she must rearrange them. I leave that to your powers of persuasion. Understand that I expect her here for dinner tomorrow evening at eight. To insure that, I want you to accompany her here from wherever she designates. The gallery or her home or any other place. Use the car, of course."

Another mind like the McEye's, Amy thought. Computerlike when it came to all the tiny little details.

"Yes, ma'am," she said. "Of course, since I'll then have to be off premises on a workday and using the car, and since Mrs. McEye is so methodical about staff schedules—"

"I quite understand. Simply inform her that a young woman I've taken an interest in has been invited here by me. For any more than that, she must apply to me directly."

Fat chance of her doing that, Amy thought, and doesn't Margaret Durie know it.

But there were still more of those details. "Now, for the menu," Ma'am said: "tournedos. Will Golightly be on duty tomorrow evening?"

"Yes, he will."

"Then he must be informed that tournedos will be the entrée. Nothing else will do. As for the rest, whatever he feels suitable. That should please him. He does like to be given his head in designing menus, doesn't he?"

He does indeed, Amy thought. His hassles with the McEye over menus were regular entertainments for the staff hall. "Yes, ma'am."

"As for the aperitifs, Lloyd—which would you say Miss Lowry would favor, a dry sherry or the martini?"

"I'm not sure," Amy said, "but I have a feeling it would be the martini."

Something in the way she said it made Ma'am smile. "Martinis it shall be. I want a pitcher of them prepared and waiting here. Then with the entrée, a good claret. And for after dinner, a well-aged cognac. Do you have all that clearly in mind?"

"Yes, I do," said Amy. Also, she thought with some smugness, the information that tournedos were those lovely little round fillets of beef in sauce and that claret was Bordeaux red. Earn while you learn. Just as clearly in mind was the troublesome picture of hostess and guest eventually hitting the ceiling in an alcoholic high. Not so funny when you considered the news Kim Lowry might broadcast to the world out there if stoned enough. Somehow there should be assurance when she left the house that she was solidly in touch with the facts of life about sworn secrecy.

"Meanwhile," said Ma'am, "the car for us this morning at eleven. Now fill Mrs. McEye in on the dinner plans. A surprise for her, I imagine, but perhaps not an unpleasant one."

A shrewd estimate, because the McEye, after her first astonishment, was clearly delighted. "Such good news, Mrs. Lloyd. She's never entertained company in all the years I've been here. The family will be so gratified too. They've been hoping for something like this. And the young lady"—the bulldog face took on a roguish expression—"she was one reason for all those little car rides, wasn't she?"

Oh, dear, Amy thought. "Well, yes, in a way she was."

"A chance meeting at the Plaza, which turned out so well. What a part luck does play in one's life." The pop-eyes surveyed the paper with the dinner instructions noted on it. "No problems here that I can foresee. She didn't ask that you attend to the service at dinner, did she?"

"No, she didn't."

"Well then, with Nugent available—"

"I thought about that, Mrs. McEye. But I'm afraid Nugent's rather awestruck of Miss Margaret. She might be jittery, waiting on her directly. I'd like to recommend Brooks."

"Oh? Well, I know your regard for him, but I don't altogether share it. Too clever for his own good, if you know what I mean."

"Still, he does have great style. And considering the occasion—"

"True. All right then, we'll make it Brooks. And, Mrs. Lloyd, I must say I feel I've been remiss in one regard."

"Yes?"

"Well, I don't think I've really made clear my appreciation for your services. I have a difficult job, the strain is sometimes almost too much, but you've made it much easier. And you are young. I envy you that. The resilience goes out of one with the years."

Amy found this honestly touching. "In that case, Mrs. McEye, why do I find myself always leaning on you?"

It was, going by the McEye's affectionate pat on the arm, the right thing to have said.

NOT until Ma'am was delivered to the care of the hotel's doorman and the car on its way downtown to the gallery could Mike be given the news. Savoring the moment, Amy couldn't resist approaching it roundabout.

"Do you know what I'm supposed to do now?"

"Yep. Payoff number two. Maybe another soothing visit to grandma Adela."

"All that's the least part of it. At the boss's request I'm inviting Kim Lowry to dine with her tomorrow evening. Right there in the apartment."

"No," said Mike.

"Yes."

"Son of a gun. So the curtain's finally down and the houselights up. Let the family do its worst, we libbers will stand shoulder to shoulder against it."

Amy shook her head. "No way. It's still as hush-hush as ever."

"Go on, she can't possibly pull that off. Not with all those eyes and ears around."

"Don't bet on it," Amy warned. "It's Ma'am's idea that the family—through the McEye—will know only as much as she chooses. Matter of fact, it's working out so far. The McEye indicated that the family will be delighted to learn that Miss Margaret is actually having a guest to dinner after all those years."

"But what a guest."

"A nice young lady," Amy said, "whose acquaintance Ma'am made during those Plaza lunches. And I didn't even have to invent that one, thank God. The McEye arrived at it all by herself. Incidentally, you'll meet Kim tomorrow. You and I are escorting her to the house. Also back home afterward, I suppose."

"Where," said Mike, "unless she has inhuman self-control, she will immediately leak the identity of the fairy godmother."

Amy shrugged broadly. "Ma'am's problem."

"Ours too, baby, as co-conspirators. You know, it's not so bad, our pal Abe having those teaching jobs up his sleeve."

"She'd never let them fire us, Mike."

"Maybe not. But she couldn't stop them from making life hell for us, with Mrs. Mac and Jocelyn keeping the coals extra hot. And Camilla's got that mean streak to start with. She'd be the first to suggest that Mrs. Mac can do without you but the kitchen dishwasher can't. See what I mean?"

"Yes. Don't count that twenty percent Christmas bonus until it's hatched. Oh, dear."

"However," Mike said, "if you could cleverly extract from Miss Lowry a refusal to meet her benefactor —"

"And then report this back to Ma'am? Who has her mind made up that there will absolutely be no refusal? Surely you jest."

"What about her newfound tenderness for you?"

"Even so, Michael dear, she is still the Red Queen from *Alice* sitting there on her little white throne."

For that matter, Amy learned, Kim Lowry had some Red Queen in her, too, as well as having, much more than frail little Ma'am, the imposing height to go along with it. All went well at the very start when, in the privacy of the gallery's storeroom-kitchen, Kim received the bulky envelope with a careless "Thanks" and thrust it into her sweater pocket. But with the delivery of the invitation the atmosphere abruptly thickened.

"Dinner?" Kim said. Her smile was somewhere between a smile and a curling of the lip. "A chauffeur? The red carpet? Just like that?"

"Yes."

"And your boss is female? No surprise in store when I get there? If I get there?"

That "if" chilled Amy. "I've already made plain my boss is female. Why would you doubt it?"

"About a very mysterious female? A closet female? Why not? I'm not exactly unfamiliar with the Anaïs Nin shtick."

"What?"

"Anaïs Nin. Is she new to you?"

"No," Amy said, "I've heard of her." No point, she thought, in mentioning that she had flipped through a couple of the books and found then wholly uninviting. "And I still don't know what you're talking about."

"You didn't know she paid the rent now and then by writing porno for hard-up private customers?"

It took a couple of seconds for this to penetrate, but then it did. "Oh, hell," Amy said, "do you seriously believe that all of this—buying those works, this invitation—was just to lure you into painting dirty pictures for my employer?"

"Why not? As Adela put it, weird arrangements can mean weird clients. And porno art for private clients is nothing new in the history of art, in case you didn't know. And dirty, Mrs. Lloyd, is in the eye of the beholder. Like your eyes, when you were looking at my work. You don't like it at all, do you?"

"My job," Amy said, keeping the tone to the cool McEye telephone level, "was to describe your work. Obviously, I did it fairly. As evidence, those paintings were bought and paid for, weren't they?"

"So far, partly paid for. And these cash payments are another weird touch. And the fact that your boss could have walked in and met me like anybody else, not sent a flunky to do it for—definitely her?"

"Definitely," Amy said sweetly. The sustaining thought was of the scene when this tough specimen entered Margaret Durie' presence and met one who could, when so moved, be just as tough. And blind at that, which would make the impact even more of a surprise. If ever there was an impending case of diamond cut diamond, this was it. "If you still doubt me," Amy said even more sweetly, "why not just come see for yourself? You can leave whenever you want to. It's as simple as that."

"Maybe. Eight o'clock?"

"Yes. I'll have the car here at seven-thirty."

"At the house," Kim said, "and all you do is blow the horn a couple of times. I'll be right down. No fancy dress though."

"None required," Amy said.

Walking around the corner to where Mike was parked she decided that, no, despite the urge she would not mention that flunky crack to him. It was just the kind of thing he liked to get down on the record—he had Camilla's venom down, word for word—but in this case, coming from outside the family, it really did wound. And wonderfully well balanced as he was about his position, livery and all, he did have his limits.

He could also be annoyingly perceptive. When she slid into the seat beside him he immediately said, "That smile is false. What went on?"

Amy gave up on the smile. "She'll be waiting at the house at seven-thirty."

"Sworn to secrecy?"

"Ma'am'll have to settle that. As it is, Miss Lowry has gone a little paranoid on this business. From the sound of it, that's Adela's influence. She's got an idea that whoever I represent is most likely a dirty old man who wants her granddaughter as his private pornographer."

Mike cackled. "She's in for a big surprise, isn't she?"

"Yes. Please just let's get to the Plaza and not talk about it now."

"Yes, ma'am," said Mike. "But meanwhile keep an eye on the bright side."

"Bright side?"

"Well, according to that receipt tucked away in your dresser, you are now the owner of three original Kim Lowrys. On a rising market that could mean—"

"Ha, ha," Amy said coldly. "Very funny."

NOR, Amy found, was there any cause for lightness of heart on the trip home from the Plaza. Ma'am, informed that all was attended to, settled back in her seat in one of those faraway moods. Not the dreamily reflective kind, but the kind that suggested exposed nerves right under the surface, where if you dared clear your throat you'd get snapped at.

More of the same the next morning, too, which became a reading morning.

"*Liliom*," ordered Ma'am from her chaise longue. "Bring it here, Lloyd."

Amy drew the bound playscript from the shelf and seated herself in position for a reading. She had a feeling that it was not going to be a good reading, not with the tangle of thoughts chasing each other around in her head.

"Is it familiar to you?" Ma'am asked, her tone suggesting that she pretty damn well knew it wasn't.

"I've heard of it, ma'am. And I did see a replay of *Carousel,* which was made from it."

"By adding sugar water. I saw the original, Lloyd, with Le Gallienne and Joseph Schildkraut. No sugar water there. Well, get on with it."

And even still more of the same when, after an awkward reading, which, thank God, Ma'am seemed deaf to as she reverted to a faraway mood, it came time to report to the McEye for office duty. What with that tangle of thoughts in her head, Amy found, the McEye's euphoria was totally dispiriting. The complete turn-off.

The trouble was that there was no turning her off. Chain-smoking furiously, she kept up a steady stream of good cheer.

"You have no idea, Mrs. Lloyd, how gratifying this is to the family. Especially after that letdown when she refused to attend the dinner, if you know what I mean. Such an encouraging change of disposition now. A young woman, you said?"

"Yes."

"I suppose—" The McEye raised a hand high over her head, palm horizontal. She looked positively coy. "I suppose someone way up there intellectually? If you know what I mean?"

"I suppose."

"And I'm sure I don't have to tell you, Mrs. Lloyd, that Miss Margaret is highly intellectual. Oh, yes, and Golightly himself is being most cooperative about preparing this little dinner in addition to the family's dinner. And Mr. Walter selected the wine and brandy and will also prepare the martinis himself. You know, he actually remarked to me that since Miss Margaret has no disposition to drink she must have certainly invited a thirsty guest. Not that it would do Miss Margaret herself any harm, he said—he does have such a sense of humor—for her to loosen up with a few drinks."

Perhaps not, Amy thought, but that is not the name of this game. What Miss Margaret apparently intended to do was loosen up the guest. There would be no holds barred in this contest for Kim Lowry between fairy godmother and natural grandmother.

The McEye did her looking around bit, as if making sure there were no eavesdroppers in range. "What I wonder, Mrs. Lloyd—in fact, Mr. Walter put the question to me—is whether after the dinner Miss Margaret would, well, mind if he and perhaps Miss Camilla dropped in to share a nightcap with her and her guest. Would you have any clue to that?"

"More than a clue, Mrs. McEye. Miss Margaret made it plain that she would tolerate no visitors at all this evening."

"Oh. But Miss Camilla? Or Mrs. Dorothy? She seems quite fond of Mrs. Dorothy."

"That may be, but her orders were explicit."

It was hard to believe that the McEye could ever look forlorn, but she was close to it now. Amy added comfortingly, "It does seem that Miss Margaret feels very possessive about her guest. I'm sure you understand."

"Oh, yes. Well, I suppose that at another such occasion—"

"One can only hope, Mrs. McEye," Amy said solemnly.

* * *

A S Mike pulled the car up before the building, the bell of St. Peter's down the block struck the half hour.

"The stroke of doom," he said hollowly.

"Thanks," said Amy from the rear seat. "Just hit the horn a couple of times and don't bother to get out."

"If you say so, ma'am. But let's not try that at the Durie end. Just in case someone there is peeking."

"If that's how you feel. But this end is my end."

Mike hit the horn a couple of times and turned to face her squarely. "You are in a mood, aren't you, baby?"

"Yes." Then it slipped out. "My flunky mood. Miss Lowry's descriptive noun." In fact, she found aside from a pang of guilt at having laid this on him, she felt a lot better that it had slipped out. She could never keep any secrets from him. It was somehow reassuring, she thought, to know that she still couldn't.

Mike grimaced. "That artist lady has a sharp tongue it seems."

"And rhinoceros hide."

Mike let it go at that. A long five minutes later, Kim Lowry appeared in the doorway. This rhinoceros, Amy thought, had warned that there'd be no fancy dress forthcoming, but for the occasion—a loss of nerve?—she had switched from the familiar jeans and inscribed T-shirt to something less flagrantly defiant. Grass-green corduroy slacks and an almost matching green corduroy jacket of mannish cut over an open-throated, checkered flannel shirt. Done up like this, Amy saw, she looked even taller, but for that she'd have to be forgiven. This tall for any female was no bed of roses.

Mike seemed intrigued by the approaching figure. "As I live and breathe," he said, "it's not Maid Marian, it's Little John."

"She's just about my height," Amy pointed out.

"Maybe so. But somehow it doesn't look as threatening on you."

Kim leaned over to peer through the window of the car, then pulled the door open, seated herself, and slammed the door shut with an impact that, Amy saw, made Mike visibly wince. He got the car going with what had to be a deliberate, wheel-spinning lunge.

290

Kim righted herself on her seat and looked around at the car's interior. She seemed amused by what she saw. "So far, as promised," she said.

"Yes," said Amy.

"So how about a little briefing on the rest? What's she like? Besides rich."

"Female," said Amy.

"Yeah, I've come around to buying that. And if this chill is because I dumped on you about it yesterday, I'm sorry. Is she into the figure, is that what it is? Or gone hypermodern?"

Amy found that the apology, considering the indifference with which it had been offered, was more irritating than gratifying. "I'll leave any such questions to her," she said. Then it struck her that here was the chance to verify what was—although it seemed such a sure bet—hitherto unverified. It had to be approached with subtlety, however. She softened her tone. "And how is your grandmother? Feeling better?"

"You mean," Kim said skeptically, "let's change the subject?"

"No. I did find her highly impressive."

"Adela? She has her moments. And if going stir-crazy is a sign of improved health, she's improving."

"Good. You know, one thing that impressed me was that for all her bitterness about your grandfather's desertion of her—"

"Where'd you get that?"

"Jason. Jason Cook."

"Of course. His idea of light conversation. So what about my grandfather's desertion of her?"

"Well," said Amy, "for all of that, she still seems to admire him as an artist. I don't think it's easy to be so objective under those conditions. What name did he paint under?"

"Ross Taliaferro. His own. Why not?"

Almost expected, this still delivered a jolt. Verification complete, Amy thought, for better or worse. She said, "Well, if he were that good an artist, the name Ross Taliaferro should be more—"

"Except he wasn't that good. It's just Adela's delusion that he was. Actually, she's in love with those paintings he did of her when he first picked her up as a model. A couple are good, but

291

most of his work was just slick academic. All technique, no heart. Proof of the pudding is, after he ditched Adela he wound up in San Francisco as art director of an ad agency there. No museum retrospectives for grandpa. It's Adela's fond hope that the old bastard died of frustration because of that."

"Sad," said Amy.

"Men," Kim said.

When the car made the turn off Madison and double-parked before the house Mike was quickly around to open the door and then stand at rigid attention with his cap held to his heart. Pure burlesque, Amy knew with some satisfaction, but a signal to her that the guest had not won his favor during the trip. Kim, however, took no notice of this clowning; obviously it was the way things were done in these parts. She stood there getting her bearings as the car pulled away. Delivery and wait at the garage had been the McEye's instructions.

Amy pointed. "That's it."

Kim looked up. "Not a hotel, is it?" She wasn't joking, Amy saw.

"No," Amy said. "Private home."

"Hers? Where she lives?"

Amy savored the moment. "Yes."

Kim scanned the building. Her reaction reminded Amy of that lifetime ago when she and Mike had stood here among their assorted luggage and had tried to comprehend what they were seeing.

"Holy Christ," said Kim. Then her tone changed. "You told me she didn't have room for my paintings. Shit, she's got room here for the Metropolitan Museum collection."

You hear that, ma'am, Amy thought. Oh, what a tangled web we weave when first we practice to deceive? She said, "I'm sure it'll all be explained."

"I can hardly wait," said Kim.

Amy pressed the doorbell and braced herself. By process of elimination — Peters and Brooks not available — it would have to be one of the maids who'd be temporary doorkeeper. If the engaging but homely Nugent, all right. But if it was the curvaceous O'Dowd or one of those ripe little junior maids, all, however demure their outfits — or was it because of those outfits — possibly suggesting a sort of *Playboy* magazine effect to the uninformed and sardonic eye of a Kim Lowry, well, it wasn't hard to anticipate her reaction. And an increasingly hostile Kim . . .

It was Mrs. McEye who opened the door. But surprise at finding her operating on this lowly level was instantly replaced in Amy by the realization of why she was. Really pushing it hard, all right. Getting a close look at the guest. If nothing else, she'd be able to report to the family that the guest was at least as tall as their Mrs. Lloyd. Looking up at Kim, the McEye seemed intrigued by this. For the first time Amy had a vivid picture of how she herself towered over that stumpy little figure.

The McEye also seemed to have elected herself not only doorkeeper but official greeter.

"I'm Mrs. McEye, the housekeeper," she informed Kim too brightly. "I trust the drive here was a pleasant one, Miss — ?"

"Lowry. Kim Lowry. Yes, it was all right."

So there it was, Amy thought. As easily done as that. Add the name to the description of the height. However, what mattered was that this name couldn't mean anything to the family. The name Taliaferro, that one was the payoff. The one deliberately blotted from that inventory book. Kim Lowry? She might as well be nameless.

Mrs. McEye led the way to the family elevator, opened the gate, but there made her farewell. Exercising at least some discretion, Amy thought with relief. It would have taken consummate gall to go along the whole way to the apartment, baiting the guest with leading questions en route.

In the elevator, Kim indicated that she was still trying to comprehend the big picture. "How many people does it take to run this place?"

"Quite a few," Amy said.

"I see. For all such information, ask the lady of the house."

"She would prefer that."

"But suppose," Kim said, "now that I'm right here in her

293

house I asked what her name was? It might come in handy when I say hello. And this kind of mystery mansion act does run thin after a while."

"I know," Amy said. She opened the gate at the second floor and motioned her charge out. "But I'm staff, and staff doesn't make the rules here."

"Doesn't break them either, I have a feeling. Are you allowed to tell me what I'm seeing through those glass walls there? Is that all part of this building?"

"All," Amy said with satisfaction.

"Holy Christ," said Kim.

At the apartment door Amy—with a sinking of the heart she couldn't quite fathom—knocked twice. Brooks opened the door and stood aside in smiling invitation. The round table was set, Amy saw, its Spode and Baccarat all agleam and the two low armchairs drawn up to it. Ma'am was poised on the edge of hers, cane in hand. She looked her absolute best, Amy judged, and even that bright lipstick and the garish circles of rouge on the pale cheeks seemed to go quite naturally with the Jazz Age mannish haircut and, in fact, with the whole decor of the room. Or, Amy wondered, was it a case of getting so used to it that you lost all objectivity?

"Miss Lowry, ma'am," she said.

Ma'am rose and, fingertips barely brushing the edge of the table, moved forward. "Miss Lowry, I am Margaret Durie." She stopped in the center of the room a fair distance away and held out a hand in Amy's direction. "I'm so pleased to meet you."

Kim remained unmoving, staring hard at the sightless eyes. She seemed in shock. Then she turned to Amy. "Blind?" she mouthed soundlessly.

Amy nodded and nudged her forward. She was quick-minded enough, Amy saw, to get her wits together before the silence became unendurable. She carefully took the proffered hand in hers.

"My pleasure," she said awkwardly. "Like, you are my collector, aren't you?"

"Oh, yes. Do you find that any less of a compliment now that you know I'm blind? I trust that as an artist you don't find blind-

294

ness repellent. Though it can be defeating to the artist, can't it? That one little fleck of light added to the iris of the seeing eye on canvas is what brings life to the whole face, isn't it?"

"Well—" said Kim.

"And," Ma'am chirruped, "there's much more to share with each other, too. Now if you don't mind—" She withdrew her hand from Kim's apparently paralyzed grip, moved it lightly up the length of that arm, and rested it on the corduroyed shoulder above her. "Oh, my, you young people today. The older generation literally has to look up to you, doesn't it? Now do sit down on that sofa, and we'll have an aperitif while dinner is being brought up. A martini? I'm afraid there isn't much choice."

"It'll do fine," Kim said, seating herself. In fact, Amy thought, she looked as if she needed at least a couple of really stiff ones—the kind Audie wouldn't let Abe manufacture—to get her back on the rails again.

"Brooks," said Ma'am in the tone one used in addressing staff, and Amy, watching the instantly responsive Brooks move to the white enameled chest of drawers—the most acutely Art Deco piece here with that slender strip of chrome ornamentation running like a bar sinister across its face—observed that the pitcher and two bottles arrayed on the chest made a formidable display, martinis, wine, and cognac enough for quite a party.

"Lloyd," said Ma'am.

"Yes?"

"That will be all. No, wait. Hegnauer's in her room. Tell her she's to leave with you and not return until called for."

"Yes, ma'am."

Hegnauer was sitting up in bed, clothed but with shoes off, watching television in the darkened room. She did not take kindly to her instructions. Amy hastily pulled the door shut as the storm broke.

"Oh, no. No. Now is too much."

"Please," Amy said.

"No. This is my room. Mornings after you come I cannot stay here. Afternoons I must sit inside and watch her. Now is my time in my room. You tell her that."

295

"No, I won't. But I do understand. Tomorrow I'll speak to Mrs. McEye about it."

"Her? You think that one listens?"

"She will when I speak to her. I promise you that."

The storm, Amy saw, was dwindling down to sullen skies. Hegnauer sat up and reached under the bed for her shoes. "Tomorrow," she said grudgingly. "And you don't forget."

As they crossed the sitting room, Amy observed that Ma'am was now sharing the sofa with her company, Kim apparently still in a fog of bewilderment, Ma'am still chirruping away with an almost frenetic vivacity. Brooks opened the door for the departing staff, then gave Amy a wink and motioned with his head over his shoulder. "I wouldn't believe it if I didn't see it," he whispered as he closed the door.

Which, Amy thought, should have been a comfort, but somehow wasn't.

SHE found quite a gathering in the staff hall when she followed Hegnauer into it. Not only O'Dowd and Walsh attending to the dumbwaiter for the family's dinner, but also Swanson and both security men and even Mabry, his evening's stint completed, sharing cake and coffee at the table. And Mrs. McEye. Who, while Amy was filling a cup for herself at the coffee maker, rose and joined her for a private chat. "Everything going well upstairs?" she asked, sotto voce.

"It seems to be."

"I do hope so. Nugent's on her way up now with the cart. I instructed her to leave it at the door and just give Brooks notice that it's there. The tournedos looked positively mouth-watering.

I did have a time with Golightly though. You know how he can be. He suddenly remembered that Miss Margaret dislikes beef, and insisted there must be some mistake," Mrs. McEye looked penetratingly at Amy. "There wasn't, was there?"

"No. That was Miss Margaret's order. No mistake."

"Then I feel reassured. But it is an unusual evening altogether, isn't it? Miss Margaret actually having company, and the family—well, you might say they're celebrating that at their dinner. And the young lady is a bit unusual, isn't she? Miss Lowry. Not quite what one expected."

Amy found the familiar mincing enunciation—especially in this insistent whisper—was affecting her like a fingernail drawn down a blackboard. And this digging for information was just too unsubtle.

Coming on pretty unsubtle herself, she realized, she couldn't help responding with some acid: "I think the one thing certain is that Miss Lowry is what Miss Margaret expected. And approved. Otherwise, there would have been no invitation, would there?"

Mrs. McEye instantly backwatered. "Hardly. Miss Margaret does know her own mind. And of course seeing how tall Miss Lowry is— No offense, Mrs. Lloyd—"

"None, taken," Amy said wearily.

"Well, seeing that, it did strike me that Miss Margaret is—well—drawn to very tall young women. I believe I mentioned to you, didn't I, that one of her strictest requirements for secretary concerned that matter of height."

"My good luck. Yes, you did mention it."

"Her need for a physical presence of substance. So it's hardly unusual after all that she'd find in Miss Lowry a young friend who'd provide that, is it?"

"No, it isn't."

However, Amy thought, it seemed that the McEye, finally aware that her snooping was futile, was giving up on it. The voice took on the official volume. "About the car, Mrs. Lloyd. Did Miss Margaret indicate when she'd want it brought around for Miss Lowry?"

"No, she didn't." The picture of her husband suddenly rose

before Amy: he far away in that garage while she— A passage with Ma'am in the car rose to mind. "But," she said, all innocence, "I have been wondering about Lloyd's waiting in the garage, Mrs. McEye. Sitting there in the car. He could wait here and still have the car around in no time at all, as soon as he's asked to."

"In no time at all? I'm afraid, Mrs. Lloyd—"

"It's cold there these evenings," Amy said, sighting on the Achilles heel. "It means running the motor steadily just to have the heater work. It does seem wasteful."

"Well"—Mrs. McEye was visibly softening—"I'm sure there's a certain wifely concern here as well as a matter of economy, but no harm in that, is there? I was in your position myself at one time, Mrs. Lloyd, if you know what I mean. But one hour will have to do. Of course he'll remain here in the staff hall so there's no time wasted if Miss Margaret calls for the car on short notice."

"One hour it is. Thank you, Mrs. McEye."

"As long as there's no problem forthcoming. I'll be going up to the office now to finish tomorrow's work schedules. I'll phone Lloyd from there. Good-night, Mrs. Lloyd."

As soon as she was gone, Hegnauer moved in for some sotto voce of her own. "You told her?"

"No," Amy said. "She has too much on the mind now. But I will speak to her about you tomorrow. You must take my word for that."

"I know. Yes. And you tell her it is my room. Not just to sleep in at night."

"Tomorrow," Amy said.

She took her coffee to the foot of the table, a fair distance away from the gathering, and when Mike showed up she observed that he certainly had his masculine priorities in order. First a cup of coffee, then a thoughtful selection of the right piece of cake, then some merry banter with the other males present, and finally he deigned to join her. He worked his chair against hers for privacy and leaned close.

"I believe I owe all this to you, Mrs. Lloyd?"

"Yes. And it's nice of you to remember who I am."

"Always. With pleasure. But how'd you spring me? A little grease job on Mrs. Mac?"

"Why not? Some of her damn rules are just too damn insensitive and foolish."

"True," Mike said soothingly. "But to let her think I use the car heater for warmth instead of that radiator in Levine's office—"

"I don't care. I wanted you here with me. Even for an hour."

"And here I am. But keep the voice down, darling. There are interested parties not that far away. Now let's have it. Why the attack of nerves? Did something go wrong with Miss Margaret's private banquet?"

Attack of nerves just about spelled it out, Amy thought. Thank God for small favors, it wasn't Margaret Durie making this diagnosis and getting ready for that infallible treatment of hers, that unwanted shoulder and neck massage. "No," she said, "nothing went wrong. Not that way."

"Then what way?"

"The way it feels. The way she's behaving. Babbling on and on, all sweetness and light. And the way she looks while she's at it. That little fixed smile. It doesn't seem to be her at all. I got the feeling there's somebody else in there, not her."

"Because she's having her own jitters, baby. A whole year's conniving and finally here it is, the magic moment. She has every right to be all wound up. You don't. That may be Mrs. Mac's style—responding to every little vibration from on high—but it should not be yours."

"Well, I can't help it. And I think she's looking to get that girl drunk. But if she wanted her here for a serious talk—"

"That, too. Remember she's gotten detailed reports on Kim, and one of them may have noted that here is a good solid drinker. So as the eager hostess— Hell, come to think of it, I hope this does not wind up with a mess of vomit all over the car. So far I've been spared that."

"Well, that isn't what's on my mind. I don't even know what is, except that it's unnerving." Heedless of the company, Amy slid her arm through his. "But you are a comfort. That's why I want you here. I feel a little better already."

"You know," Mike whispered, "if we could slip upstairs for the rest of the hour—"

"We can't. Aside from really turning off the McEye if we're caught, it would be embarrassing to slip away with everyone looking. This way we probably strike them as rather sweet."

"Now you sound like yourself," said Mike.

"I wish Ma'am did," Amy said.

The trouble was, she knew, that the comfort she was getting was not because those vibrations afflicting her had been tuned out, but because they were being shared. She was also aware of Mike's kindly intent—to get her to stop brooding about this nonsense and about unpredictable tomorrow—when he asked Mabry if he wouldn't rather be back in Jamaica now with New York winter coming on. Which, as usual, because Mabry could sing paeans about the Caribbean and be quite funny at it, got the expected response at length. Then there was some sober talk with Swanson about the plumbing, which apparently wasn't getting some repairs it needed, and then some football talk with Inship and Krebs, the security men, and all in all Mike's allotted hour was up almost before she realized it.

The impending deadline was signaled by Brooks, who came in trundling the service cart, its litter neatly concealed by the tablecloth.

"How's it going up there?" Mike asked him, thus saving Amy the trouble.

"Rewardingly," said Brooks. He stopped the cart by the table, partly drew back the concealing cloth and lifted out a plate. "One steak done to perfection with not a bite out of it."

"Miss Margaret's?" Amy asked.

"And now mine, Mrs. Lloyd. If I put it aside for Golightly he might hit Mrs. Mac over the head with it, and that would be sad on all counts. Cold, it makes the perfect sandwich. Anyone want to share?"

"Don't mind if I do," said Mike.

"Then you fetch the toast and mustard while I carve."

Amy glanced at her watch. "You don't have much time left," she warned Mike.

"I'll wrap up mine and take it along. There's beer there to wash it down."

She resentfully watched him depart for the kitchen. Never mind the loaf of bread, the jug of wine, and thou, she thought. Especially the thou. A steak sandwich, a bottle of beer, and a notebook, that's what he'd settle for.

"Did she eat anything at all?" she asked Brooks.

"Ate nothing, drank nothing." He was holding a stained steak knife and looking at the cart with a frown. Then he folded back its cover all the way and looked closer. "But the young lady did fine for the both of them. Really tucked into the food and libations. Matter of fact, last view I had she looked distinctly under the weather and Miss Margaret was telling her she had an infallible treatment for that. Which I doubt."

Infallible treatment, Amy thought. Infallible treatment. Infallible treatment. She saw that Brooks was now worriedly rummaging through the soiled dishes on the cart.

"What's wrong?" she asked.

"One steak knife short. I don't understand."

"I'll bet it's on the floor up there," O'Dowd said with satisfaction, "just waiting for her to turn an ankle on it."

"Well, thank you," Brooks said. He turned apologetically to Amy. "I'm terribly sorry about this, Mrs. Lloyd, but I'll have to risk intruding on them up there. I'll get it at once."

"No," Amy said. She saw from his startled reaction that it must have come out more violently than intended. "It's all right. I'll do it."

An infallible treatment, she thought. A knife. And a thought that had to be turned upside down to be seen with blinding clarity.

It isn't that she's as tall as I am. It's that I'm as tall as she is.

When she abruptly stood up she found with surprise that her legs were unsteady. She almost went over sideways as she wheeled and headed for the door to Xanadu.

"Mrs. Lloyd!" called Brooks just as the heavy door slammed behind her.

One steak knife, she thought, heart hammering as she hastened through that endless, dimly lit tunnel. As she broke into a run she heard from the distance that door behind her slam again.

301

"Amy!" Mike shouted, the echo resounding ahead of her.

Without turning or slowing her pace, she waved an arm in response. She had no idea what the gesture was intended to mean — don't bother me, come and help, whatever — or how he would interpret it, but that was his business. Her business, irrational or not, couldn't wait.

She raced past the humming boilers, through the door beyond and into the foyer. She took the stairs two at a time, discovering when she reached only the first landing — the ground floor — that she wasn't really in the shape she should have been. Already a little winded, already straining to take the next flight at the same speed.

She flung open the foyer door on the second floor and went down the corridor at a run. She pulled up breathless at Ma'am's door and instantly knocked twice.

No response.

The McEye certainly made an effective instructress, she thought. One could hear that phonily elegant voice laying down the law. If no answer, wait a proper time and knock again. If still no answer, depart and inform her.

To hell with that.

Two more raps on the door, and Amy pushed it open. All that was visible across the room was Ma'am's back as she stood behind Kim's low armchair, and those corduroyed legs stretching out from the chair. But one step forward brought everything into view.

Kim's face was upturned, the nape of the neck resting on the back of the chair. Ma'am had one hand dug into that frizzy mass of dark hair, the other held a knife to that throat. The knife moved once with swift and savage intent, and there was blood. Blood, Amy saw as she croaked out a "No!" and lurched forward, and more blood and more blood. Bright red, it jetted out like a fountain, gushed out, sprayed out. The hand holding the now upraised knife was drenched with it, the green jacket and slacks were dyed with it, that white carpet spattered with it.

And as Amy clutched at the hand holding the knife she found there was still more blood. She felt a sudden sting along her exposed forearm, and as she fell back she unbelievingly saw the line

302

of droplets welling from the arm, the droplets quickly becoming more than a trickle.

Now, she knew, she was going to black out. Didn't want to but couldn't help it, and it would be just as well that way. Just droop forward and droop forward and you'd wind up on that red wetness of carpet without even caring.

But there could be no more hope for this with an arm suddenly tight around your waist. "Just hold on," Mike ordered. He was half lifting her, turning her to face the door. "Just hold on and don't look, damn it."

She let him bear her full weight, and she didn't look. But there was this increasing trickle of warmth down her fingers. "My arm's cut," she managed to say.

"Just hold on and don't look," he said, working off his belt. He looped it around the arm below the elbow and drew it tight. She found this hurt a lot more than the cut.

"Hurts," she said.

"Can't help it, baby." He clamped a hand over her eyes. "Tight shut," he ordered. "Don't look." Then: "Miss Durie, please drop that knife."

A long silence, broken at last by Mike. "Miss Durie, please drop that knife. You're frightening Mrs. Lloyd."

Almost instantly, Amy heard the soft thud on the carpet. With his hand still over her eyes, Mike said, "I have to get to the phone. Can you hang on and make it?"

"Yes. And you can take your hand away. I won't look."

The blackout threat had passed, Amy found, her strength was flowing back, but still with eyes tight shut she clung to him as he dialed. Michael Lloyd, she told herself comfortingly, the one stable element in an insane world. Michael Lloyd. Dear Mike.

"Mrs. McEye?" he said. "It's Lloyd in Miss Margaret's apartment. . . . Yes, something has, so get ready to move fast. There's been a murder, and Mrs. Lloyd is also badly hurt. Call a doctor, then the police. Then tell Mr. Craig. Fast, Mrs. McEye, fast."

Amy heard him clap down the phone. "What was that for god's sake?" she asked. "What did she say?"

Mike's voice was strange. "When I told her where I was calling from she wanted to know if anything had possibly gone wrong here."

SHE knew who she was and where she was and what had happened as soon as she woke. Realized she must have just fallen asleep like this, propped against the pillows in her own bed and wearing her flannel bathrobe with nothing underneath. And that was Mike's hand, she was sure, pressed against her forehead trying to rouse her. She opened her eyes and found that it was. But those red lights chasing each other high up around and around the walls were puzzling.

"Those lights?" she said.

Mike removed the hand from her forehead. "Police cars down below, baby. And TV cars and the rest of the media and some VIP limos. I'm sorry I had to wake you up, but we've got VIP company of our own outside waiting to talk to you. Urgent mission, that's the word."

"More detectives?"

"No, the one who grilled us seems to have taken care of that department. How does the arm feel?"

She touched the cocoon of bandages sheathing her left arm from wrist to elbow. "Not bad. Do you think what I told him made sense to him?"

"Not bad is good," Mike said, "considering there's a dozen stitches under that wrapping. And, yes, what you told him made sense to him. Once he got it straight that you were a victim, not a perpetrator."

"Still, he did come on very polite. I didn't fall asleep in the middle of it, did I?"

"No, he was all finished by then. He told me he's seen that happen before, that falling asleep. Said it was the best thing that could happen to you under the circumstances. But how do you feel aside from the arm? The truth."

Amy weighed this. "I seem to feel like two people right now. There's me, and there's another me watching all this. And as long as they don't get together, I'm all right."

"And if they do get together?"

"I don't know. What time is it anyhow?"

"About midnight," Mike said. "You've only been out for about half an hour, in case you're wondering. You didn't hear the phone ringing?"

"No."

"Abe. There was a flash on the radio about what happened here—even though they got it all wrong—and when Abe and Audie heard the name Margaret Durie they went right up the wall. They thought you might be dead. When I cooled him off he said we're to get over there as soon as possible. They'll be waiting up for us, and the spare room is ours as long as we want."

"Can we leave here just like that?" Amy asked. "I mean, while there's still—"

"Any time, as long as the police can keep in touch. Are you ready to be up and around though?"

"I think so." She swung her legs off the bed and gingerly stood up. She got a good look at Mike's face that way. Poor darling, she thought, thirty-five going on fifty. Which on second thought, suggested to her that she'd be wise not to confront a mirror right now. She tried a couple of steps and reseated herself on the edge of the bed. "A little shaky," she acknowledged, "but all systems go."

"Most of the luggage is in the basement storeroom," Mike said, "but there's that pair of flight bags in the closet. That should do it for the time being."

"I suppose. But didn't you say something about company waiting outside? On an urgent mission?"

"Hell, I almost forgot. It's Dorothy. But that's her urgent mission, not ours. And if you're ready to get going now—"

"I want to see her," Amy said. "I'm curious."

"Well," Mike said, "I'll admit I am too. And she is certainly pent up. You want to slip into something more formal first?"

"No." Amy tugged the robe closer around her. She noticed Mike was wearing ordinary slacks and jacket, not that smeared-up livery. "I hope you told that detective he could keep our clothes he took away."

"Oh, that. Since I got a receipt for them, I guess it's manners to take them back. He informed me—"

"Yes?"

"First tell me if your two selves are together yet?"

Amy saw he meant it. "I don't think so," she said. "Not yet."

"All right then. He kindly informed me that such stains are permanent, and not to waste money trying to have them removed. A penny saved is a penny earned. Now I want you to clear up one question for me, baby. You won't mind?"

"What question?"

"Just before you bolted out of the staff hall you shouted something at Brooks. That puzzler about she's not as tall as you are, you're as tall as she is. What was that about?"

Amy pressed her hand to her head. "Wait a second. I said it out loud? Really said it? Not just thought it?"

"According to Brooks, loud and clear. It shook him up. That's why he yelled for me."

"Mike darling, I didn't know I said it out loud. But oh, God, am I glad he yelled for you. Anyhow, he had it wrong. What happened was, he found her steak knife missing, and I thought: she didn't even need it because she won't eat steak. Then I thought: why would she order tournedos if she won't eat them? It's almost as if she just wanted them for that knife, weird as it seemed."

"Baby, what does this—?"

"Please. It gave me a chill. Somehow I saw Ma'am with that knife. I thought, really a murderous knife. That's when it struck me: it isn't that Kim is as tall as I am. It's that I'm as tall as she is. You see?"

"See what?"

"Mike, listen. Somehow the McEye got to blathering about how tall Kim was and I was. And how dear Miss Margaret must favor tall girls because they'd be physically supportive at least. But of course I knew Ma'am hadn't gone for Kim because of her height. That was just a coincidence. And that's when it dawned on me it wasn't any coincidence. No way. Because Ma'am knew all about Kim first, and one big reason for hiring me afterward was that I was as tall as Kim. Now do you see?"

"You mean—?" Mike said. "Yes. Hell, yes. She's blind. She wanted someone Kim's height to practice on. To know how to position herself when the time came. That's what those phony neck massages were about too. Practice runs. God, that is one

306

terrible woman. To make that girl a victim—"

"You know why, don't you?"

"I'm pretty damn well sure I do now. Sweet vengeance against Adela, because it had to be that Adela pushed her down those stairs. Now let Adela spend the rest of her life in mourning for the one thing she loved. And if that knife had hit the inside of your wrist instead of—"

"Terrible in her wrath," Amy said. "In one instant she forever lost her sight, her lover, her dream of being a great artist. The bottom of the pit, that's where she landed. She must have wished she were dead a thousand times over in those fifty years."

"Better that way, baby. It would have saved one innocent life and one near miss. You don't really feel that tender about her, do you?"

"That's not the word," Amy said. "But if you keep your eyes tight shut when you walk out there to bring in Dorothy—and you understand you have to keep them tight shut the rest of your life—you might know how I do feel."

"Not now. Sometime when I'm in the mood. And when I do fetch in Dorothy, just remember she will not be looking her best."

That was the truth. Thirty going on forty, Amy thought when Dorothy Durie made her entrance, haggard, sallow-complexioned, red-eyed, and with those dark patches like bruises under the eyes. But the husky voice was unchanged. "How are you, Mrs. Lloyd?"

"Fair to middling," said Amy.

"That's something." Dorothy leaned over to touch the bandaged arm. "I'm glad—we're all glad it wasn't worse," she said, and Amy found a reek of whiskey breath filling her nostrils. Unlike the McEye, she thought, family was not required to camouflage that with peppermint. "And of all times to intrude," Dorothy said, "this must be the worst. But it must be done, Mrs. Lloyd. You'll appreciate that when I explain it. Unfortunately, I seem to be the one designated as family representative in this."

"What about Mr. Craig?" Amy asked, and saw Mike look at her curiously as he stood there.

Dorothy shook her head. "Right now, he and my uncle have

their heads together with the police and our lawyers and some psychiatric authorities who've been called in. My Aunt Jocelyn is under sedation. My husband, well, he's now driving Mrs. Mac to New Jersey. She has a home there maintained by her widowed sister. And Mrs. Mac, it seems, is why I'm here."

"She is?" said Amy.

"Oh, yes." Dorothy gestured at the chair against the wall. Mike brought it forward and she seated herself. She lit a cigarette, and then, cigarette poised, looked around the room. "Ashtray?"

Mike solved this problem, Amy observed, by the simple process of dumping her hairpins from the small china bowl on the dresser and handing the bowl to Dorothy. She placed it in her lap.

"As of an hour ago," she said, "Mrs. Mac is on full retirement."

Amy tried to grasp this. "Full retirement? Then she's not coming back?"

"No, she is not."

"That was her own decision?" Mike said, and Dorothy seemed a little puzzled, Amy saw, at hearing a voice from that direction.

"Her hard and fast decision," Dorothy said to Amy. "In fact, everything was done to persuade her otherwise. But she's really not quite as ageless as she'd like one to believe; she's high-strung, she's always taken too much on herself. Tonight—well—she just came apart at the seams. Totally unable to cope. So it was goodbye, here are the keys, I'll be sending for my things. Of course, she did make the idiotic mistake when the police came of leading them upstairs and walking into that room with them. Quite a sight to behold, I imagine, even if you're prepared for it, and she wasn't."

"But Kim Lowry," Amy said, "I mean, the body—it's not there now, is it?"

"Oh, no. Removed to the morgue."

"Has the grandmother been told?"

"The Taliaferro woman? I gather that the police attend to that. By now they probably have. Then there's the business of her making identification. I don't envy the woman. But you do

308

see what I'm getting at, Mrs. Lloyd. It's not only that you're taking over Mrs. Mac's job, but — and I realize the imposition on you — you must attend to it at once. Right now."

"Do I?" said Amy.

"Obviously." From that hint of impatience, Amy thought, Dorothy Durie was not one to bear fools gladly. "Considering your injury, I know you can't go all out, but I'm sure you can handle certain immediate problems more than adequately."

"Right now."

"I'm sorry, but yes. The help is in quite a state — most of them are in the staff hall gabbling all kinds of nonsense — and they want an interface with you about the situation. And I gather that a duty roster for tomorrow hasn't been posted. As it is, we'll have chaos here tomorrow with the press and television vultures closing in. It'll be even worse if the staff isn't given its instructions. And my aunt — that is, Miss Margaret — insists on seeing you. Is making one hell of a fuss about it, in fact. In her condition this kind of emotionalism is the worst kind of thing she can indulge in."

"I see," Amy said. "What is her condition?" She took notice that when Dorothy tamped out the cigarette she looked as if she were trying to drill it right through the bottom of the bowl. A case of rising temper, Amy gauged, not too well controlled.

"In my opinion," Dorothy said, "most interesting. I think you should know, Mrs. Lloyd, since you'll be dealing with her, that she very calmly made a detailed confession to the police. That's not hearsay. I was part of the audience along with my father-in-law and uncle. Since then, she's refused sedation and remained quite calm except during spells when she wants to know when you'll show up. It's painful to her brothers especially that you seem to be the one and only, but I disagree with them. I think it's damn lucky for them there's anyone in the world she has some feeling for."

"Perhaps," Amy said. "But a confession? About what she did? Why she did it?"

"Mrs. Lloyd, I don't feel that this—"

"Look," Mike cut in, and he wasn't being the soul of patience himself, Amy saw. "In a little while it'll all be headline stuff

309

anyhow. I'd say there's a certain obligation due us to at least keep us ahead of the papers."

Dorothy lit a fresh cigarette from the first and drew in a lungful of smoke. She addressed herself to Amy. "She was having an affair with the artist doing her portrait." The voice was emotionless. "That weekend, the family was away in Maine and his wife was supposed to be visiting friends. Adela Taliaferro. However, she suddenly returned to find the couple in bed. Her bed. In the apartment the Taliaferros had been provided with here. This apartment, in fact. She then went berserk, seized a palette knife, and tried to assault, not her husband, but his victim, who ran stark naked and screaming to the staircase to escape her. At the head of the stairs the knife wasn't needed. Just one hard shove was all it took.

"Years later—last autumn—the name Adela Taliaferro was suddenly brought to her notice again. It was—"

"Yes, we're familiar with that part," Amy said.

Dorothy regarded her narrowly, threads of smoke filtering out between her teeth. "You played her game, you know."

"Dutifully," said Amy. "As demanded. But that day it happened—the butler McEye and Borglund and Wilson were the staff on hand here. Did she explain how they managed to cover up everything?"

"No," Dorothy said, "that came from my father-in-law just now, not that it came easy. McEye heard the screaming from his apartment—right next door here—and ran out in time to see it happen. Borglund and Wilson were evidently close by. When they found she was in a coma, McEye took charge at once. My husband's grandfather was head of the family then, a totally domineering man and obsessive about any hint of scandal touching it. James Hamilton Durie. And McEye was utterly devoted to him. He managed to get some clothing on her before he called in the doctor and fabricated a story about an accident. As soon as the family could get home he confided only in James Hamilton. Who, close to his death, confided it only to my father-in-law. A sweet legacy, all right."

"You mean," Amy said, "no one else knew besides Mr. Craig?"

"Not one of us, until he had to come out with it now. Not even

310

my uncle as younger brother. Absolutely grotesque when you think of it. Those three staff people were assured lifetime jobs for their silence, Taliaferro was given that building, which, I understand, Adela Taliaferro still occupies. And she was warned that if she ever spilled the beans she'd be held for attempted murder. And in his turn, my father-in-law, poor soul, kept the faith until the inevitable day—or was it inevitable? Do you have anything to drink here?"

"Wine," Mike said, and Dorothy nodded.

He poured half a glass from the carafe in the refrigerator, and when Dorothy held up a hand, finger and thumb widely extended, he filled the glass. She downed most of it without taking a breath.

"So here we are," she said.

"What happens to Miss Margaret now?" Mike asked, and Amy observed that for the first time Dorothy appeared to take direct notice of him.

"Well," she said, "that's being worked out now among our lawyers and psychiatric people and some police brass and a man from the district attorney's office, and it seems the prevailing winds are favorable. Once certain legalisms are steered around, she'll be placed in the family's charge and be required to undergo therapy. That's about it."

"She's very fortunate," Amy said.

"In a way. But she is seventy years old and blind, Mrs. Lloyd. And does have a long history of what can be labeled psychosis. And doesn't remember anything about the—well, the climactic episode tonight."

"Do you believe she doesn't?" Amy said.

"Do I now?" Dorothy emptied her glass and held it out for a refill. Mike poured the remainder of the carafe into it. She said, "In my opinion—and in the opinion of those parties downstairs investing their good will in this—it would be wise for all of us to believe it devoutly. And now you know as much as I do."

"Thank you," said Amy.

"The best thanks, Mrs. Lloyd, would be your taking over Mrs. Mac's duties immediately."

"Perhaps. But you see, Mr. Lloyd and I were just preparing to move out ourselves."

Dorothy seemed to go into shock. "Move out? Give up your jobs? Now?"

"As soon as we pack a few necessaries."

"No. That's out of the question. Hell, you know, you'd be leaving us in an impossible situation."

Amy displayed the bandaged arm. "Well, my own situation—"

Dorothy instantly brimmed over with sympathy. "I understand that. I appreciate what you've just gone through. But to make any such decision while you're in an emotional state— Look, you must know the job is a very good one."

"An impossible one," said Amy. "At least the way Mrs. McEye structured it. And it would seem to include my serving Miss Margaret as well."

"Mrs. Lloyd, all of this can be worked out."

Amy looked at her husband and saw that he was coming on as imperturbable as Brooks. She said to Dorothy, "If you don't mind, Mrs. Durie, I think Mr. Lloyd and I must talk this over."

"But right now, please."

"Yes. In private." And when Dorothy said, "Of course," and was instantly out of her chair Amy said, "No, we'll go outside. We won't be too long."

It cost Dorothy an effort, she saw, to put on that smile of encouragement. "As long as you make the logical decision," Dorothy said. Then she waved a hand back and forth. "Before you go, would you draw the blinds? Those police car lights are terribly annoying."

* * *

312

MIKE closed the door behind them.

"Well?" he said.

"Well?" said Amy.

"Well, the good news is that the whole book has just written itself in my mind. All I have to do is get it down on paper."

"About Ma'am?"

"And us. A lot about us."

"You just made me very happy. What's the bad news?"

"Baby, I'm afraid I'm not chauffeur material, livery or demilivery. The way things are now, I don't want to tip my cap to these people for their kind favors. And the book is alive now. Even a nine-to-five job putting snowsuits on infants would allow me a schedule for writing I can't count on here."

"So far," Amy said. "But suppose it wasn't chauffeuring anymore? Suppose it was a different job here, from — oh — eight to three? As property manager."

"Property manager?"

"Yes. Since there's no more secrets around here to be hushed up by polite blackmail, Borglund is due for retirement fast. In style, of course. Then Swanson takes over for him, with a new assistant to help out. The property manager uses the upstairs office, supervises his help, handles maintenance and repair contracts. At suitable pay, it's understood."

"And I'm to be property manager," Mike said. "Is that what you were thinking when Dorothy was laying her grief on you?"

"No. It's what I used to think when I was in the office with the McEye, and Borglund wasn't getting things done. The same with Golightly. He goes, and Mabry moves up to chef with a competent cook to back him up."

"You mean," Mike said, "you want to stay on here."

"Only if you do."

"Amy darling, you yourself just told the lady in there that this housekeeper job is impossible."

"The way the McEye has it structured. One thing is her penny-pinching, which is really stupid when you consider the money available. There's no big deal to running the place if you staff it

313

properly. First thing, I'd hire an extra houseman and promote Brooks to butler. He's made to order for that."

"You'd hire? It seems to me I haven't voted yet on staying here."

"All right, whoever. As butler, Brooks would get a desk in the office too, along with that apartment, and be in charge of staff."

"I see. Under the housekeeper's wise supervision?"

"Well," said Amy, "since there can be only one captain on a ship—"

"I know. You learned that firsthand from your father. Even so, you're also being expected to nursemaid Miss Margaret on occasion. And she is a crazy lady. A murderously crazy lady."

"Not murderously," Amy said. "Not anymore. That's over and done with."

"Are you telling me," Mike demanded, "that you're not in the least afraid of her now?"

"Not in the least," Amy said.

She watched him studying her with interest. Finally he said, "If you're wondering what's on my mind, it's that old Quaker tag: 'All the world save thee and me is mad, and sometimes I wonder about thee.' "

"Then you don't want us to stay."

"I didn't say that," Mike protested. "Matter of fact, with the kind of restructuring you have in mind for the place here, well, staying does have its attractions."

"No personal expenses," Amy said, "And now real big paydays. Befitting very essential talents. The kind of talents that come high."

"Oh, yes. But before we count the loot what's the odds on the family approving your household revolution?"

"It's hardly a revolution. And it's not family. Dorothy's the one. It used to be Jocelyn—all self-righteousness—who drove the McEye crazy. But don't you have the feeling now that Dorothy is taking over as First Lady? And she's a lot more approachable than Jocelyn. And not the kind to hand out medals for excessive thrift."

"But her memory?" Mike said. He motioned. "Rest your weary bones on that couch, darling, while I use the typewriter."

"For what?"

"A memorandum of agreement. We put down all your ideas about the restructuring—two copies for the record—and then your friend Dorothy can make our decision for us. If she signs, good. If not, it's her loss. and the family's."

It was evident, Amy saw, that Dorothy was in no mood for any reading of agreements, but read it she did. Then she looked up at Mike. "Property manager?" she said.

"Keeper of the infrastructure, Mrs. Durie."

"I see." She looked from one to the other of them. "You're an interesting team, aren't you? Well, I don't find anything in this badly typed document to object to. My concern is the obvious one. I want this place run smoothly and kept up well, and how you do it is your business. Bearing in mind that the books are audited regularly. Oh, yes, and you will see to my Aunt Margaret right now, Mrs. Lloyd. I suppose I sign both copies. Do you have a pen?"

Mike saw her out. When he returned he looked reproachfully at the empty carafe. "She didn't even leave us a celebration drink."

"Just as well," Amy said. "First help me get dressed. Then while I'm with Ma'am call up Abe and Audie and explain things. Try to get her on the phone. She's a lot more rational about us than he is. Then you have to call the garage and arrange for a standby chauffeur to be assigned here for the next few days. Room and board provided. Then, darling—are you listening, Mike?"

"Listening, looking, and marveling. Go ahead."

"Then get down to the staff hall and cool them off there. Clear up all rumors. I'll be down as soon as I have the job schedules ready. But those rumors can be real morale wreckers. Tomorrow'll be bad enough without that."

"True," Mike agreed. "You realize we're both likely to be in the papers tomorrow? And for a while to come? And on television?"

"Then we will unplug the set and not read the papers."

"Wise of you, baby," Mike said. "Come to think of it, in your new position, do you mind my calling you pet names?"

"Never," said Amy. "In case you don't know it, that's my connection to reality."

IN the second-floor corridor a gathering of solemn-looking men turned to watch her as she passed by. The uniformed policeman near the wide-open door of the apartment gave her a nod as she entered the sitting room. She stopped short there and closed her eyes tight as a qualm seized her.

No, she told herself, you will function.

She opened her eyes and saw blanket-size sheets of black plastic covering the armchair and round table and a wide area of the white carpet. Hell and damnation, she thought, you will continue to function. Very well, as soon as possible that carpet and those pieces of furniture must be replaced by something entirely different. Invite Dorothy Durie to decide how different? No. Right now Dorothy was more in a mood to have her aunt replaced than any furniture.

The bedroom door was also wide open. Ma'am, in negligee, was reclining like Pauline Bonaparte in her chaise longue. Nearby sat a pinch-faced, angular woman in nurse's uniform reading a paperback. A stony Hegnauer in a chair across the room instantly rose when she saw Amy. She was clutching what appeared to be a rolled-up face towel. But before she could speak, keen ears had picked up the pattern of footsteps.

"Lloyd?" Ma'am said plaintively. "You've taken so long. Do come here. I must speak to you."

"In a moment," Amy said.

"I go away now," Hegnauer whispered to her fiercely. "Better I stay in a hotel. Tomorrow I come back for my clothes."

"Lloyd?" said Ma'am.

"In a moment, Miss Durie," said Amy. She shook her head at Hegnauer. "I can only tell you one thing. When you walk out of this house newspaper and television people will chase you everywhere, asking you questions, taking your picture. They won't leave you alone."

"You mean so?"

"You think not? Just look out of that window."

"Oh. Well. Then I wait. But not here with her. I told Mrs. Dorothy I stay with her only until you come, that's all."

316

Hegnauer thrust out the towel. "For you."

"What is it?"

Hegnauer partly unrolled the towel to display Ma'am's letter opener and shears. "Better she don't have them."

"All right, then what you do is take them down to the staff hall and give them to Mr. Lloyd." She slipped an arm across Hegnauer's broad shoulders and gently propelled her toward the door. "Then wait there for me. I'll be down soon."

Privacy halfway assured, she walked over to the nurse. "Your name is—?"

"Henderson. Miss Henderson."

"Miss Henderson, I'd like you to wait outside. Just close the door behind you when you leave."

Miss Henderson didn't move. "Who are you?"

"Mrs. Lloyd, the housekeeper in charge."

Miss Henderson rose to her feet, glowering. "If the doctor tells me one thing, and people walk in and tell me something else—"

"Just close the door behind you," Amy said.

With the click of the latch, she drew Miss Henderson's chair over to the chaise longue and seated herself. "We're alone now, Miss Durie."

The sightless eyes turned toward her. "I'm aware of that, Lloyd."

"Mrs. Lloyd, if you don't mind."

Ma'am nodded understanding. "Of course, now that you've taken Mrs. McEye's place. You have, haven't you?"

"Yes. What did you want to speak to me about?"

The pale lips parted, then compressed. Not for the first time, Amy realized, she was seeing this face without makeup, and it was all the more beautiful for that. But no, she warned herself, you must put aside any such distracting thoughts. You must simply function. If one could manage to function through all this horror and confusion, the horror will fade away in time and order will be restored. Not the same old order but an even better and more sensible one.

Forget that easy escape into the secure, money-tight, self-righteous little nest Abe had prepared. Aside from everything

317

else, he was wrong about this servant thing. Hypocritical, in fact. He liked good restaurants and luxurious hotel vacations and that woman Audie had in every week for the housecleaning, that Puerto Rican whose name he was never clear about. He liked to be waited on, he liked servants. But as Mrs. Bernius of Domestique had shrewdly remarked, there was an ingrained distaste for that word *servant* and that's where Abe's hypocrisy showed. The Duries had servants. Abe and Audie had people waiting on them whom they refused to call servants.

Mrs. Bernius, yes. One must function, and meeting as soon as possible with Mrs. Bernius was an imperative in the staff reorganization. Prepare a chart tonight, and tomorrow show her what was needed. An invaluable ally, all right. The invaluable ally.

"My dear," Ma'am said at last. The small hand groped outward and found Amy's wounded arm. Fingertips traced the bandage, then withdrew. "I never intended to hurt you. I'm so sorry."

"But how do you know you were the one to hurt me, Miss Durie?"

"I was told."

"You don't remember how it happened?"

"I only remember that poor creature saying she felt ill. Beyond that nothing."

"I wonder," said Amy.

"I only know what I was told," Ma'am said tonelessly, and, Amy thought, it had the sound of being well rehearsed. The voice took on warmth. "Believe me, my dear, you are the last one in the world I'd want to hurt in any way."

Lucky me, thought Amy, because if I had been that poor creature . . .

She said, "I'm ready to believe that part of it, Miss Durie. I only wish I could believe the rest of it."

"You will," Ma'am said comfortingly. "And you shall read to me — you read so well — and we'll share music and perhaps those pleasant rides in the car. I look to you for that."

"When it can be arranged."

"I'm sure it will be. Oh, yes, and there's one matter to attend

318

to promptly. The final payment for those paintings will be due, and I don't want to be remiss in that."

"Miss Durie, of all matters to be attended to promptly—"

"No, this is most urgent. I want you to make that payment directly to Adela Taliaferro."

"Directly to her?"

"Yes. You must meet with her. Express my regrets. Then I'll want you to describe to me—"

"Oh, no," Amy said in outrage. "No, not that."

"I don't understand."

"Yes, you do. You've provided that woman with an agony to live with the rest of her life, and now I'm to rub salt in the wound and report back to you how it made her writhe. That's monstrous."

"Monstrous?" Ma'am said in pained bewilderment. "A simple favor?"

"My simple favors, Miss Durie, will extend as far as the reading, the music, and the car rides. And those rides will start at this house and end here, with no stops along the way for any reason."

"My dear, do you mean that I'm to be your prisoner?"

"No. No more than I'm to be your instrument. Understand, Miss Durie, that I now know everything that's gone into the making of this—this—tragedy tonight. Everything. Starting with Ross Taliaferro himself. Every single fact. That's where I want to leave it. There's nothing you can add to it that I ever want to hear. If you take that to heart, we'll get along much better with each other."

"You're angry."

"Among other things," said Amy. "Now I really must leave, Miss Durie. I have a difficult night's work ahead."

"Of course. But you will make time for me tomorrow?"

"Yes," said Amy, "I will. Good-night, Miss Durie. I'll send the nurse right in."

She stood up, and the hand caught hold of her skirt. "One moment more," said Ma'am.

"Miss Durie—"

"One moment more, my dear." The hand held tight. "You

319

see, if you believe that you know all, you're wrong. There is one thing that only I know. It concerns Ross Taliaferro."

Amy found herself transfixed by curiosity and despising herself for it. "What about him?"

"Fifty-two years of darkness," Ma'am whispered. "Fifty-two years and four months and four days from that day to this. And he was never worth it. He was a clumsy lover. Impatient and clumsy. He was never worth it at all."